For one idyllic Nantucket summer, she lived her dream . . . and let herself believe she'd found happiness at last. No more lonely nights. No more shouldering life's problems alone. No more of love's disappointments. And in that carefree, romantic summer of tender passion, she would discover much more . . . and triumph beyond anything she believed possible . . .

NELL

A Novel by

NANCY THAYER

Other Avon Books by
Nancy Thayer

BODIES AND SOULS

NELL

NANCY THAYER

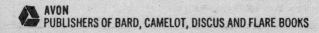

AVON
PUBLISHERS OF BARD, CAMELOT, DISCUS AND FLARE BOOKS

AVON BOOKS
A division of
The Hearst Corporation
1790 Broadway
New York, New York 10019

The William Morrow edition contains the following Library of
Congress Cataloging in Publication Data:

Thayer, Nancy, 1943–
    Nell
    I. Title
PS3570.H3475N4   1985   813'.54   84-29482

First Avon Printing: July 1986

AVON TRADEMARK REG. U. S. PAT. OFF. AND IN
OTHER COUNTRIES, MARCA REGISTRADA, HECHO EN
U. S. A.

Printed in the U. S. A.

K-R 10 9 8 7 6 5 4 3 2 1

To Charley, my husband,
With all my love

One

THIS fine Saturday morning in April, Nell woke up alone. As always. Sunlight flooded through the windows of the bedroom and lay across the floor in such delineated golden rectangles that Nell fancied the day spread out before her like a length of shimmering bright cloth. She yawned and twisted about in her bed, pleased with the luxury of the easy morning, smug, messy-haired, lazy-limbed. Stretching, she knocked a paperback mystery, two cookbooks, a three-ring notebook, a box of stationery, and a pile of catalogues off the bed onto the floor. They all went with a great slither and thump.

For five years now, Nell had used the vacant half of the queen-size bed as a sort of table. It worked well. There was so much space, and things were so handy, at just the right height. Nell loved her bed and was seldom more pleased than when, after an exhausting day, she could crawl into it, plump up the pillows, and rest her body while her mind roamed off in new directions. She made lists, wrote letters, read books. When she was especially tired or anxious, she looked through the glossy, optimistic pages of mail-order catalogues. She was oddly reassured by the knowledge that this was a world in which there were people who spent their lives inventing dog jewelry or writing such copy as "Nouveau is better than not riche at all." She would look at all the pretty dresses and imagine which ones she would buy if she had the money—although where she would ever wear the sweeping white silk with the sequined waist was past the powers of her imagination.

Sometimes she came across a dress or top that she thought the boutique she worked at might sell, and she would clip out the photo and mail it to her boss. At other times the catalogues worked

1

like sleeping pills. The bright and orderly pictures would then seem inanely comforting, like children's building blocks, lulling Nell into such a state of relaxation that she had only enough energy to reach out her arm and switch off the bedside lamp before falling asleep.

Now and then in the middle of the night, her turning might cause a magazine or book or box to go over the edge of the bed and fall to the floor with a thud, but now such sounds no longer awakened her. She had assimilated into her subconscious the harmless nature of such noises, just as she had learned to sleep through the knocking sounds of the dog scratching herself under the bed or the eerie morning cry of her cats singing just outside the window about their springtime catch.

Nell loved being alone in her bed. She loved sleeping there, reading, writing letters there; she *loved* eating there. Almost no pleasure surpassed reading a mystery in bed while eating a giant bowl of salty buttered popcorn or a hot fudge sundae. It was true that her sheets were often less than clean. She had gotten used to sleeping with grits of salt against her skin and thought this was surely no stranger than sleeping in a beach house on sheets speckled with sand.

Her secret desire in life was to own a hospital bed. She often dreamed of the power of it, of pushing a button and having the back of the bed automatically raised or lowered, the section under her knees bent and angled . . . To have a hospital bed and one of those wonderful tables that would swing over her or away to hold her sundae or popcorn and book—well, those seemed real luxuries in life, and ones that, if ever once obtained, could not fade or vanish like other, more social pleasures.

When Nell was divorced, she vowed to herself that she would not disconcert her children with the sight of a man in her bed in the morning. She had kept that vow for five years now, and she was glad. Not only for the children's sake: it seemed to her such a commitment, sleeping all night and waking up to face a new day with someone. Making love was one thing, but waking up in the morning was something completely different, a serious act. She did not want to confuse her children by that—and she did not want to confuse herself.

When her children were smaller, they used to crawl into bed with her at night after a nightmare or a tummyache, or simply when they awakened early and wanted to cuddle. It had been a long while since that had happened. Jeremy was ten now, and didn't want to climb in bed with her anymore—Nell was not sure whether this was because of prepubescent shyness or simple indifference. Hannah, at eight, still had an occasional nightmare, an occasional need for a long warm snuggle, but those too were becoming rare. The children did always come into Nell's bedroom first thing in the morning, though, just to *look* at Nell. Often they tiptoed up—Nell could hear them—and peeked their heads around the corner of her bedroom door.

"Hi, sweeties," Nell would call from her bed. "Come give me a kiss."

"Oh, Mom," they would say, and would wander away.

Nell came to realize that they just wanted to be sure she was there so they could feel free and safe in the world and could get on to more important things. She saw that her body had taken on a sort of utilitarian function in the lives of her children. On arising, Jeremy and Hannah visited her and the toilet, then were able to enter their day. Well, her body always had had a utilitarian function for her children: she had grown them in her body, nursed them, rocked and carried them in her arms until they were too large for her to lift; she had bathed and shampooed them and tended to their injuries. These days they needed only an occasional hug; their need for her body was taking on a necessary distance. Her children were growing up.

She could hear them now, mumbling around in their rooms. Because it was Saturday morning, they didn't have to go to school, and Nell didn't have to go to work, and there was no need to rush. Still, she couldn't stay in bed all day, dreaming like this. She had things to do.

Nell rose, put the dog out, let Medusa in, made coffee, set out an easy Saturday breakfast of milk and doughnuts for her children, put a load of laundry in to wash, glanced at the morning paper, polished Hannah's good shoes because they had been sitting in the fruit bowl on the middle of the kitchen table for two weeks waiting to be polished, talked on the phone to a friend, stared at the doughnuts for five minutes, longing to eat one, forced herself from the kitchen, doughnutless, nagged her children into actually brushing their teeth, braided Hannah's hair, and pulled some cockleburrs off the coat of Medusa, the unappreciative long-haired cat. Her day had begun.

It was time to do her exercises. She hated doing her exercises about as much as she hated anything in the world. But they made an enormous difference in the way she looked and felt. And they provided her with a sense of achievement—afterward, she always felt smug.

They also helped her view the world differently. She managed to force herself to exercise because she knew from past experience that, at a certain point in the middle of her exercises, she would have an adrenaline high. She would put on a rock record—ABBA, Bob Seger, Supertramp—and after ten or fifteen minutes of vigorous movement, she would smile. Bob Seger would be singing his secrets to her, about her. As she felt her limbs grow warm and supple in their moving, so she felt her whole life grow more supple in its meaning—and if this optimism was some kind of lie, she didn't care. She was old enough to know that the *cause* of any pleasure or optimism was not the point. If she felt good, she wanted just to go with that as far as it would take her. Life was too short to live any other way.

Now she lay on her back in her white tights and lavender leotard on the blue living room rug and did scissor kicks to ABBA. Whenever she lay here, she found herself confronted with five gray oval-shaped blotches on the white ceiling. They were her daughter's fingerprints, and as Nell kicked her legs back and forth, she amused herself by wondering just which man it had been who had lifted Hannah above his head so that she could touch the ceiling. It couldn't have been Steve; he was too short. It hadn't been Ben either, though he was certainly tall enough; Ben hadn't been the type to lift Hannah. Hadn't been the type to touch Hannah. Ben, with his trim clipped beard, his careful clothes and body. Ben, whose touch made Nell's blood turn to ice. Yet he was the one man since Marlow whom Nell had seriously considered marrying, and only because he was rich.

She was not proud of herself to remember this; she had not been proud of herself when she had dated Ben. She had met him just a year after her divorce from Marlow, and for a few months she thought that perhaps Ben was the one chance for security left to her in all the world. She had not married him because she had not loved him—although that first year after her divorce she had been too nutty to love any man—but she had not married him in spite of the promise of easeful security he offered.

Of course at times she deeply regretted her decision. At times life overwhelmed her and made her long for the order that Ben had offered.

Just this week, for example: Nell had been racing out the door on Monday morning, and it was the usual Monday morning free-for-all of getting the three of them ready for the day, for the week. Jeremy had wandered out of the house to check his pail, which held some elaborate and inexplicable experiment he had set up involving water and air and leaves, but he had, of course, again forgotten his school books and violin.

Nell had yelled at him in exasperation: "I can't take this any-more, I can't do this anymore, you are ten years old and old enough to assume some responsibility for your life. Get your violin. Get your lunchbox. Jesus, I should make a tape of me nagging you and attach it to your Walkman and turn it on every morning, that would save my voice and my sanity. . . ."

Jeremy had drifted back into the house to collect his things while Nell fumed at the front door, thinking for the thousandth time: Weren't boys of divorced mothers supposed to naturally take on the role of the man of the house, weren't they *supposed* to, hadn't she read somewhere, in lots of magazines, that young boys of divorced mothers *protected* their mothers, became mature at an early age in order to help and shelter their mothers? Some-times it seemed Jeremy couldn't even *remember* his mother, let alone his lunchbox, homework, or violin.

But finally he had gotten everything, and Nell and Hannah and Jeremy came out of the house, and Nell turned to lock the front door, wondering if she should make Jeremy go back in one more time to get his raincoat. The early April sky was ominous. It was going to rain today. And Jeremy was prone to chills and colds and croup and bronchitis. But he had already made it to the car with all his apparatus. . . . Nell decided to forget the raincoat.

She had walked along the long wooden porch and down the wooden steps, suddenly aware for one bright moment of the kind of day it was: it was *spring*. The air wafted against her softly, sweet with the scent of the hyacinths blooming near the house. *This kind of morning*—well, it was so fresh, so gentle, like a lover's first tentative kiss; Nell stood still for a moment, rapt. She did not want to move from this magic moment when she could almost feel what it was like to be a young girl like Hannah again, with the world all sweetly mysterious, with the whole world as tantalizing as spice. Nell took a deep breath. She was thirty-eight, but she could still feel, on a morning like this, that there were amazing possibilities waiting for her in this world.

"Oh *God,*" Hannah said, walking past Nell to the car.

Hannah had heavy blond hair and intensely dark eyes, an unusual combination she had inherited from her father, along with a tendency toward the theatrical. She was always striking poses; Nell was always having to remind Hannah that she was only eight years old. Now her voice was matter-of-fact, world-weary.

"Hannah," Nell said. "I've told you not to use profanity."

"Well, I've got a dead mouse in my umbrella," Hannah said. She tossed the bright green umbrella that said HANNAH in white script away from her onto the lawn with a shrug of contempt and strolled on down the walk to the car.

Nell stood frozen, sick with disgust. "Hannah?" she asked. "Hannah? What do you mean you've got a dead mouse in your umbrella?"

Hannah turned and looked at her mother with slight impatience. "I've got a dead mouse in my umbrella," she said.

Nell picked up the umbrella and looked. A small gray and slightly decayed mouse lay inside the umbrella at the point where all the spokes met, stuck, in its moist and hairy decomposition, to the wire and fabric.

"Oh, God, gross, *yuck!*" Nell said, and flung the umbrella across the yard. "Oh, how *awful,* Hannah, oh, honey, I'm sorry. God, what if you had opened the umbrella and it had fallen out in your hair? Oh, this is disgusting, it makes me sick. Oh, I can't stand it, a dead mouse in your umbrella, I can't take any of this anymore!"

"It's okay, Mom," Hannah said. "It could have been worse. It could have been alive."

"I can't take any of this anymore," Nell said. She stood there on her front lawn in the spring grass, shaking, wishing she could change her life, wishing she could change it so drastically that her daughter would never have a dead mouse in her umbrella again. The house was clean enough—but the umbrella had been hanging on a hook in the basement, and it was the time of year when small creatures began to venture in from the open land near them. Nell knew in the back of her mind that it wasn't a sign that her house was filthy; it was just that the poor mouse had gotten into the umbrella and then been unable to climb up out of the slippery funnel. Still . . .

"We might as well not even have cats," Nell said. "Here we have two cats and we still have a mouse in the house. Where *are* those damn cats? Why don't they do what they're supposed to? No one helps out around here!"

She had felt so alone then. She had felt so defeated. She had felt so keenly the chaos of her life. She had wished right then she had married Ben; she could have married him and not worked and stayed home all day cleaning the basement. If she had married Ben, he would have supported her financially, she could have protected her daughter from this sort of thing. She could have checked the umbrellas for mice if she had married Ben.

But she had not married Ben, and now, as Nell rolled over onto her side to do leg lifts and extensions, she knew that in spite of money and mice, her decision had been the right one. She hadn't loved Ben. She hadn't even particularly liked Ben. She had just been lonely and at the stage in her life when she was so poor and frantic about money that the mere thought of dinner in a good restaurant had made her nearly tremble with desire. Nell wasn't proud of the fact that for three months she had gone out with Ben simply because he took her to nice restaurants and the theater and to concerts she couldn't afford. On the other hand, she wasn't ashamed of herself for going out with him, either. She could have done worse: she had been so scared and wretched then that she could have started drinking or taking drugs or become truly hysterical in front of the children. She hadn't done any of those things. But after Marlow left her, she had lived for a while on the edge of her nerves, mad as a beast, staring out with wild eyes, scavenging what she could, always alert for dangers to her babies. She had had to learn to support herself financially and to be the sole protection for her children at the same time, and so she lived for a while on her animal instincts, moving through life in terror and anger, ready to spit and claw.

Jesus. She hadn't thought about those times, those feelings, for a while. Now she was more financially secure, or at least more relaxed about her financial insecurity.

Nell stopped her exercises and sat up with her legs crossed lotus-style in front of her and lay her hands gently palms up between her thighs. She took deep breaths, rolled her head slowly from side to side. Calming down. Regaining control. Looking for peace.

Nell knew that people liked being around her because she was attractive and because she had a sunny disposition. She also knew what work it had become to remain attractive and sunny. Her optimism and figure were no longer given to her free and easily by the fates: both had become matters of daily philosophical choice and hard daily personal labor. Much of that work had to do with going on in spite of the past. Ignoring the past took up a great deal of her energy. For when she stopped to turn around, she saw her past lying behind her in the most awful confusing scramble, she saw her past in a real snarl of people and fears and dead dreams. If she paid close attention to her past, she wouldn't have the courage to go on into the future.

Oh no, it hadn't been *that* bad. And she had the children: her son, Jeremy, her daughter, Hannah, and her ex-stepdaughter and friend, Clary. She had true friends and memories that would always make her laugh. It was not so bad. It was just that she had supposed as a child—and now that she thought about it, even as an adult—that she would live her life in one true bright line; her life would make a straight kind of sense like a bold beam of sunshine. Instead, her life had taken on no meaning at all; the years, and the sense of those years, had gotten muddled and tangled and broken and even lost. Her past did not illuminate her future with a steady glow. Instead, it sputtered and flickered behind her like a candle that might burn out, leaving her to pitch forward with the next step into total darkness, or like a strobe light, battering her vision of the future with random spatters of glare and blackness.

"I am so *depressed!*" Nell yelled, jumping up from the blue rug, jumping up from her thoughts. She shut off the stereo, stretched one time, then raced up the stairs to her bedroom. She dug through the papers on her desk in the alcove, found her diary, flipped it open to the calendar of the year.

"Thank *God!*" she said aloud. "I'm premenstrual!" She slammed the diary back down and hurried into the bathroom. "It's diuretic time, it's diuretic time," she sang to an old Howdy-Doody tune.

Sometimes she thought the things she loved most in the world were her son, her daughter, her stepdaughter Clary, and her diuretics. They made such a difference in her life. She took one with a full glass of water. Then she went into her bedroom and zipped her old saggy gray sweatshirt robe over her leotard and tights.

Nell loved this robe like she loved her cats and dog, like she loved a bubble bath. This robe was *home*. Hannah reminded Nell at every opportunity that Nell looked like a dying elephant in the robe, but then Hannah had always been critical of her mother. Nell knew in her heart that if Hannah had been able to speak at birth, her first words would have been, the instant she was pulled from between her mother's legs: "Oh gross, Mom, *look* at you. Your hair's all wet and tangled, your stomach's all blubbery, and that hospital gown is really the pits. Couldn't you at least put some lipstick on?" Hannah smothered compassion on every living thing, and even on nonliving things: she could cry for a rock that Jeremy threw in a pond and thus "drowned." But she was a pitiless judge of her mother's looks and seldom could stretch her compassion past her criticism. Still, Nell would wear this robe when she could, when alone in the house cleaning or reading or being sick or paying bills or cooking. It was a comfort, this robe. It just felt right.

But now, before going down to the kitchen, she sighed and unzipped the robe and took it off in order to strip off her leotard and tights—if she left them on, she'd have a hell of a time getting everything down and off when the diuretic made her rush to the bathroom. She dropped the tights and leotard on a pile of clothes that needed to be hung up or folded and stood for a moment, naked, in her bedroom. The mirror on the back of the closet door gave her a full-length reflection of herself, and Nell turned slowly in front of it, scrutinizing her body.

Nell was accustomed to mirrors. She worked around them constantly in the boutique and had learned how to ignore her own image while concentrating on that of a customer. All her life she had practiced poses, acting parts in front of mirrors. They had become her familiars and seemed to speak to her in a sort of ghostly feminine whisper. "Pull those shoulders back! Hold in your stomach!" they would say. The voices of course were her mother's, her dance instructor's, her acting coaches', all echoing in her head. It was her own voice, too—her own judgment, really—that was reflected back at her, but now that her parents were aging and far away, she often felt that a mirror gave as much mothering as she got these days.

Then, too, mirrors reminded her that she was lucky, after all. Directors and friends often said it was her personality that made her so attractive—her intensity, her vivacity—but Nell knew that it was really just that she had been lucky enough to have a body that would always look good in tight jeans. She was tall—five feet eight—and worry had kept her slim, and the early years of dance and the later years of disciplined exercise had kept her limber and taut, so that now as she turned in front of her mirror, she saw that from the back she looked like a smooth young girl. It was on her breasts and belly that time, experience, childbirth, and nursing had made their marks—there the flesh had stretched and now sagged slightly. No amount of exercise would ever bring her small pink-tipped breasts back up to their former plumpness. Never large, her breasts before she'd had the children had at least been firm, even pert. Now—now she had fantasies of having silicone implants, but she knew she could never afford them. And there was a little bowl-like bulge beneath her belly button, a kind of soft round insistency there that would never go away and that, unless Nell exercised diligently, threatened to expand and take over her entire torso. But she looked wonderful in clothes and not repulsive in a bikini, so it was all right, she supposed.

Also, she liked the colors of her body; she had always liked how everything seemed to be of the same tone. Her skin was creamily pale, covered here and there with freckles, which were of the same brownish-red color as her eyes. When she had been younger, she had lightened her hair slightly, so that she was a strawberry blonde, and then her large eyes had seemed darker. But now strands of gray were showing up here and there, and Nell had taken to darkening her hair slightly to a deep reddish-brown, dramatic against her pale skin, more sophisticated than the lighter color. Her hair was thick, slightly wavy, and she kept it long so that she had a variety of ways to wear it—it was a lot, after all, to have long lean thighs and thick rich hair.

When she was younger Nell had worn her hair in odd, extravagant ways: pulled up to the side in a spout of ponytail, or braided when wet so that it frizzed out softly all around her face in the style of a pre-Raphaelite heroine's. But now she had laugh lines around her mouth and eyes and, when she was tired or worried, little bluish pouches under her eyes; she could seldom get away with flamboyant hairstyles now. When working, she wore her hair pulled back in a chignon or she let it fall down and loose, held off her face demurely with a headband or clasp. The rest of the time she just let it go; she brushed it out full so it flew around her head, and she went around that way happily. She liked the scent and swish of her long hair when she turned her head. It gave her a feeling of exuberance. Men liked her long hair, too, the way it would sometimes fall forward over her bare shoulders.

She still had fun with her hair, wearing it in different ways, just as she had fun with makeup. She had the definite, slightly exaggerated features that suited an actress or an opera singer: large eyes, high cheekbones, wide mouth. When she first worked in the boutique, she had used her skill with makeup to create an impressively dramatic face that "went" with her clothes each day. But soon she gave that up, believing the makeup intimidated her customers—and she preferred to use the early morning half hour for extra sleep. Now she wore some blusher and occasionally a touch of eyeliner, mascara, lipstick. When she worked at it, when she was wearing the perfectly right clothes and makeup, she could look like the sort of woman who would fly to Japan or France to attend a fashion show or an auction of antiques.

The gray elephant robe was not that sort of garment. Nell pulled it over her head and immediately was enveloped in a tent of shapeless warmth. She felt comfortable and cozy, but in the mirror she saw a new brown stain down the front of the robe.

"God," she muttered to herself. "What a glamorous creature I am."

She had intended to be a glamorous creature. She even had actually been a glamorous creature. She had been cheerleader and homecoming queen in high school, an actress in college and in her early twenties, then the stunning wife of an important young director. Now she was the not-so-stunning ex-wife of a not-so-important director, and all the acting she did was purely personal. Sometimes she was her only audience.

Now she grabbed all her long reddish hair and stuck it up in a glob on the back of her head with some long barrettes so that it wouldn't get in her way while she was cooking. She was having friends to dinner that night.

"Listen," she said to her reflection in the mirror as she went out of her room. "God gave you your children and your cheekbones. Don't expect any other gifts."

It was about eleven o'clock. Jeremy had biked off to the school for soccer practice and wouldn't be home till afternoon. Hannah was in her room, playing "teacher." This morning she had rounded up the younger children in the neighborhood and brought them up to her room. Before going down to the kitchen, Nell peeked in the door and saw four little children sitting dutifully on the floor while Hannah stood at the other end of her bedroom, holding up a stuffed animal.

"Squirrel," she said. "This is a squirrel."

"Squirel," Hannah wrote on the blackboard.

"Squirel," the four children said.

"Good!" Hannah said with sugar in her voice. "Now, Heather, *you* may hold the stuffed squirrel."

Hannah was wearing the navy blue suit her grandmother had sent her for Easter and a pair of Nell's old black high-heeled sandals. She had smeared pink lipstick over her lips and cheeks and stuck her blond hair back in a severe bun that had several bobby pins dangling down, swinging with every definite nod of Hannah's head. She looked absolutely demented, but the four children at her feet seemed completely at ease and even fascinated, so Nell shut the door without saying a word and went down the stairs to the kitchen.

When Nell had been married to Marlow, they had bought this old, rickety shambles of a Victorian house, intending to restore it over the years to its former solidity, if not grandeur. Marlow had thought the large high-ceilinged rooms would be perfect for theatrical gatherings. Nell had thought all the bedrooms would be perfect for all the babies she would have. When Nell and Marlow had divorced, Nell had gotten the house, along with full custody of the children; she had thought of selling the house immediately—it was so large and falling apart, it needed constant repair.

But at that time the real estate market changed, and she found that in order to buy a smaller house, she would have to pay a much larger mortgage, much more interest on the principal. She had decided to keep the house and for the first two years had been glad to stay there. It had provided a sense of continuity and stability for her two small children, whose lives had been upset by their parents' divorce. And when, in desperation, she had begun a baby-sitting service in her home in order to make survival money and still be with her children, she had been glad of the size of the house.

She had been especially glad on rainy days, when she had nine children under five years of age and two infants to take care of. What had once been a library became the napping room, where the children sprawled on the antique Oriental rug with their sleeping bags and blankets and comforters. The living room had been for quiet play, the kitchen for juice and snacks and lunch, and the dining room, the once-elegant dining room with the intricate parquet floor and the crystal chandelier, had been where little kids rode their tricycles and scooters around the long oak table during blizzards or rainstorms. The landing to the second floor was large enough for the television set, and the children could gather there in a group, sprawling on rug samples Nell had begged from a furniture store, to watch *Captain Kangaroo* or *Sesame Street*.

My God, what a time that had been.

That was four years ago. Nell had been ready to go on that way forever, and would have if the parents of one of the children hadn't intervened. The O'Learys owned one of the best woman's boutiques in Cambridge; they specialized in understated cotton dresses and simple cotton sweaters that cost around two hundred dollars. They had decided to move to Nantucket to open up another shop there, and they asked Nell if she would be interested in running their shop on "the mainland" for them. They would do the major bookkeeping and buying; she would be a saleswoman and manager.

"I don't know a thing about running a store!" Nell had responded.

"But you've got such a long, lean body!" Elizabeth O'Leary had said, studying Nell with her buyer's eye. "You'd look super in our clothes. You'd be the best ad we could get."

"Are you kidding?" Nell cried. "I'd never be able to afford the clothes you sell!"

"Well, honey," Colin O'Leary said, "you won't have to buy them. Just *wear* them—while you're working in the store."

"You don't want to be stuck here all your life with these— these *children*," Elizabeth had said, looking at the horde of jam-smeared midgets who straggled in and out of the kitchen as they talked. The O'Learys' own child, Priscilla, was a lovely little girl of five who wore immaculate and expensive hand-smocked pinafores and Mary Janes with white socks every day. The O'Learys were sending Priscilla to live with her grandparents in Greenwich, Connecticut, so she could go to a good private school. "We can pay you *very well*," Elizabeth had continued.

And they did pay Nell very well, and she had found, after she grew accustomed to the change, that she quite liked dressing up in fabulous designer clothes and working regular hours with human beings who did not spit up on her. Still, she missed the grand chaotic richness of those baby-sitting years.

Not that there wasn't plenty of chaos in her life still. This afternoon Nell was going to clean out her basement or die. The washer and dryer were in the basement, and a playroom for the children was there too, in a corner of the basement where the cement was covered by a torn and faded piece of linoleum. Jeremy's electric train table was in the basement, as were many of Hannah's dress-up clothes and baby dolls. Still, the basement was not Nell's favorite place. In fact, it made her skin crawl. The ceiling was low, with old pipes that crossed just above her head, growing cobwebs and dust jungles in spite of all her efforts to clean. It was not a modern basement, and the floor was cracked here and there and the furnace was monstrous and creepy and there was another room leading off the main room, a room that didn't even have a cement floor, a room with one light bulb in the middle. Nell hadn't gone into that dirt-floored room for years. She pretended it didn't exist. The dark door loomed behind the furnace like the portal to hell. She was always amazed that her children liked playing in the basement. She could scarcely bring herself to stay down long enough to do the laundry.

Just last night, on her way down the stairs with a load of laundry in the willow basket, Nell had noticed in one dark corner of the basement an unusual and foreboding object: a bundle of what— old clothes? a sheet? blood-covered fabric?

"Jesus God!" Nell had shouted, dropping the basket and rushing back up the stairs. "Jeremy! Hannah! Help! Come here! I think we have to call the police!"

Her children had come thumping down the stairs at once. "What's wrong, Mom?" they had asked.

"I think there's a—oh, sweeties, I don't want to scare you, but I think there's something *dead* in our basement."

Jeremy looked at Hannah. Hannah looked at Jeremy.

"Where?" Jeremy asked.

"In the corner across from your playroom. By the door."

"I, um, don't think it's exactly a, um, *dead* thing, Mom," Jeremy said.

"Do you know what it is?" Nell asked, aghast.

They had known what it was. They had heard at school, from an older child, that if you went to a darkened room and put catsup on a mirror, a ghost would appear. The ghost of the house would think the catsup was blood and his spirit would be summoned up. Several nights ago Jeremy and Hannah had sneaked a sixteen-ounce bottle of catsup to the basement and spread the mirror with catsup. And *spread* the mirror with catsup—they had not realized how catsup flowed on a surface that did not absorb. In desperation, trying to clean up the mess, they had grabbed whatever was at hand: Hannah's dress-up clothes, some old baby doll clothes, and a sheet.

"I have told you *never* to take *food* to the basement!" Nell had screamed, freaking out. "Food in the basement will bring rats! God. I've told you *never* to take food to the basement." Her children looked at each other, conspirators' looks, looks that indicated they were now going to have to deal with a madwoman's raving with their superior patience. *"I'm serious about this!* If you leave food in the basement, rats and mice and moles and *God knows what* will come. You aren't taking me seriously. Oh, I just hope you wake up in the night with a rat in bed with you, it would serve you right. No wonder you had a mouse in your umbrella!"

She had marched them down the stairs with a black plastic trash bag and made them clean up the mess while she loomed over them, threatening them with rat bites and disease and finally the definite possibility that they would be orphaned because if she did see a rat in the basement while doing the laundry, she would die on the spot of a heart attack, from terror.

Just cleaning up the mess was lesson enough for the children: the catsup had congealed on the clothes in disgusting sticky splotches that not even they wanted to touch.

"I will never eat catsup again in my life," Hannah had said quietly.

Nell had made them remain in the basement protecting her while she did the laundry.

But this afternoon she would throw open the hatchway door that led up from the basement to the backyard. That would let the warm April air in to freshen the basement—and give any scrambling little live thing the opportunity to scurry up and out while Nell and her children cleaned. She would sleep better tonight; she always slept better after the spring-cleaning of the basement. The children played in it often during the long cold winter days when they were trapped indoors, and over the months things accumulated. Nell knew they would discover lost socks and underpants, books and jewelry, batteries and Lego blocks. She was eager to set to work.

But first she wanted to finish the cassoulet. Nell loved cooking and having people to dinner, but since her divorce, she had learned to serve only those dishes that could be prepared beforehand. Otherwise she would end up in a frustrated snit, feeling like Cinderella, stirring away like an old drudge alone over the stove while far away in the living room her guests laughed and gossiped and she felt outcast at her own party.

Or even worse, she would invite the guests into her kitchen while she finished a dish and, incapable of being sociable and efficient at the same time, ruin the food. There was the night when she was so enthralled with a friend's description of his ex-wife's anger that she had measured tablespoons rather than teaspoons of curry into a sauce: what a party *that* had turned out to be! Everyone had sat around the dining room table with flushed faces and tears in their eyes, blowing their noses into handkerchiefs or, in sheer desperation, the cloth napkins, and finally drinking too much in order to drown the terrible heat of the curry sauce. God, they had gotten drunk and silly. It had turned out after all to be a wonderful time, but the next day they had all had vicious hangovers.

And there had been the time when a friend had confided a sorrow to Nell at the very moment she opened the oven to take out a loaf of bread.

"Oh no, I'm so sorry," Nell had said to her friend, and at the same time had reached her hand in to pull out the rack. But she had forgotten to put an oven mitt on and grabbed the rack with her bare hand.

"Oh *dear,*" Nell had said earnestly, when she had longed to yell, "Oh holy *shit!*" Fortunately, she had been only heating the bread, so the burn was not bad, and she had been able to soothe it with ice water and first-aid cream, and her guest, so overwhelmed with her own problem, had not even noticed. But Nell didn't want to do that again.

So now she did most of the cooking for a party beforehand. And it worked out well, for this allowed her to make huge casseroles and stews, which were not only delicious, but inexpensive. For tonight's party she was making a cassoulet—full of all those wonderful cheap fat white beans. Peasant food. She did like peasant food best. And this dish made her feel so thrifty and prudent, for she could sneak in the leftovers: chunks of roast lamb and roast pork, chicken wings and duck legs, all cooked for other meals and left over and frozen and now appearing from her freezer so that she could turn out this elaborate and time-consuming dish in very little time at all.

Now she stood at the sink peeling a spicy sausage and cutting it into small slices. She brought out her huge white ironstone casserole and layered it with the cooked beans and meat, then poured the thick garlic-flavored bean stock over it all. Now she would bake the casserole slowly, and it would come out crusty, brown, and pungent. She would serve the dish with a crisp green salad, French bread, beer, and fresh fruit for dessert. She licked her lips in anticipation and closed the oven door. She would have only to reheat the cassoulet tonight, after the flavors had mingled together all day. She could concentrate on talking with her friends rather than cooking for them and yet serve them with a delicious meal.

She especially wanted to please the people who were coming tonight, because she liked them all so much. The Andersons were coming: John and Katy. He was a pediatrician; she was an artist taking time out to have babies. She was pregnant now with their first child. They were a beautiful couple, John and Katy; they were a lucky pair, and it made Nell happy just to know they existed, just to know such a golden, happy, busy pair *could* exist in the world. They were proof that good fortune could happen. And they were wonderfully funny and always knew the best jokes.

The Shells would also be coming. Nell had met Ilona through the shop: Nell sold the clothes, and the beautiful, elegant, willowy Ilona bought and wore them. Over time Nell and Ilona had become aware that they had similar taste in clothes and men and music and a similarly offbeat, slightly bizarre sense of humor. They had become good friends.

They had become such good friends, in fact, that at first Nell had been baffled; she could not figure out why a woman as wealthy and sophisticated as Ilona would want to spend her time and friendship on a woman who lived a life as relatively poor and disorderly as Nell's. Then she met, at a party at the Shells', the polite and nearly embalmed social set that was part of Ilona's life, and she met Ilona's husband, Phillip.

Phillip was an insurance executive who was apparently doing his best to live his life out of some handbook on appropriate executive behavior. He was handsome and well dressed, and Nell didn't think he was stupid, but how would she ever know? For Phillip was cold, aloof, secretive, a real tight-ass, a stiff, brittle stick of a man. At one dinner party in which all the people gathered around the table were parents or parents-to-be, the subject had been circumcision—whether or not to circumcise baby boys. Phillip had said, in his I-am-making-a-pronouncement voice: "Circumcision is just another way for doctors to make money. Personally, I've always thought it was a rip-off." And he never did understand why the rest of the table went into waves of groans and laughter.

Well, Nell couldn't have Ilona to her party without Phillip, so he would be coming too, the old bore.

Stellios would not be coming. Stellios was Nell's lover now, but he was younger than Nell and less educated, and he worked for the city road crew. He had told her that he would not feel comfortable with this group. Nell often wondered, on days like this, or nights when she was alone at a party without an escort, what on earth she was doing going with a man like Stellios. He was really not her type. Then she'd spend a night with him and remember quite clearly and intensely just why it was she was going with him.

People knew she was going with Stellios, and they asked about him when they saw her and she always said he was fine, and they moved on to another topic. Some of her friends had met Stellios— Katy Anderson had. Katy had dropped in one evening when Nell and Stellios were drinking beer and watching a football game on TV. Katy had joined them for a while. When she had to leave, Nell had walked Katy to the door, and they had stood in the back hall laughing in whispers like schoolgirls.

"Hubba-hubba," Katy had said. "Boy, do I envy you."

"Well, he is cute," Nell had said. "But, Katy, *I envy you.*"

She did envy Katy Anderson, very much. She envied Katy especially for her husband, who loved her completely and who paid the mortgage and the bills without blinking an eye. More than anything else in the world, Nell wanted for herself the plain old traditional joys: a loving husband, a solvent bank account, a peaceful life.

But she didn't have that, and couldn't. So she went back up the stairs and changed out of her old gray robe and into grubby jeans and an old flannel shirt. She went to the bathroom; her diuretic was working, thank heavens. She had Hannah send the four little kids back to their own homes; she told Hannah to change into jeans. As the little kids went out the front door, Jeremy came in. Nell marshaled Hannah and Jeremy into the kitchen. She would give them lunch, then force them to help her clean the basement. Her desires, she knew, would quickly diminish once they all went down into the damp, dim underworld of their house; she would wish not for a husband or wealth, but only and entirely that they would not find any little furry body, living or dead, mingled with the children's litter.

Nell put a plate with two peanut-butter-and-jelly sandwiches and a banana and a pile of cookies in front of her son. Jeremy had Nell's reddish-brown hair and eyes, her pale freckled skin, and he also had her lean body, which on his ten-year-old frame looked gawky, scrawny, and almost painfully thin. He was all knees and elbows and energy.

"How was soccer, Jeremy?" she asked.

"Fine," Jeremy said. He took a bite of his sandwich, then grinned at his mother. "Hey, Mom," he said. "What's hard and red when you put it in, and it comes out soft and pink and wet?"

"Jeremy!" Nell said, aghast, dropping the butter knife on her foot. "May I remind you," she said sternly, "that your sister is only eight years old?"

Hannah laughed at Nell. "I can guess *that* joke, Mom," she said. "Duh. Bubble gum."

Two

At two-thirty the next morning, Nell was roaming through her house in the dark, barefoot in order not to wake the children, carrying an enormous glass full of water. She had drunk too much alcohol at her dinner party. She had fallen asleep when her guests left just after midnight, but she had tossed and turned and finally awakened with bad dreams. Terrible dreams. Now she was caught in one of the nighttime frenzies she had come to call her Panic Nights, a state of irrational alarm, when she worried desperately about money, her children's mental health, her own lonely life, the fact that she was growing older, the years she had wasted in her twenties . . . everything.

These spells had begun just after her divorce and for a few months were so overpowering that she had developed insomnia as a defense against them. The insomnia had left her exhausted and wired up at the same time, which made the Panic Nights even more gripping. At last she had seen a doctor, who prescribed a tranquilizer for her, and it had helped immensely. She still had a vial of the small yellow tablets in her medicine cabinet, but she used them only as a last resort, only in stages of real desperation.

She would not use one tonight. She knew that now her nervous state was due to having too much alcohol in her system. She was dehydrated. So she wandered around in the dark, going into the kitchen or bathroom for glasses of water, staring out different windows, hoping the gentle moonlight on the lawn would eventually calm her.

Some nights she loved being the only one awake in the house. In the winter she would often sit up in bed as if summoned, instantly lucid and pleased, because the moon was full and shining on the snow and the outside world gleamed magically. Then she would pull her gray robe over her and curl up on the floor, her head on the windowsill, gazing out at the moon-illuminated world that surrounded her house, elated by the mysteriousness of the natural universe, all this lovely silver air that went on and on in spite of her petty life. On some nights in the summer she would creep out at three or four in the morning and sit curled up on the wicker porch swing, smug to be alone and awake, listening for the first bird calls, watching for the first lights of morning to come silently sliding across the horizon and down through the trees onto her lawn. Her children had often found her there in the morning, asleep on the wicker swing, and when she awakened, she would be damp and shivering from the misty morning, but rested and optimistic, as if the night air had provided some kind of mental cure for her.

But this was a night of a different sort, an unpleasant stretch of time she had experienced before, too often: a Panic Night. Tonight when she walked through her house, she looked out the window and saw that the back steps off the kitchen were still broken. Last fall, running up the steps to answer the phone, her left leg had hit the rotting wood just the right way so that the wood gave and her leg plunged through to the thigh. That had been an awful feeling, her leg suddenly trapped in the splintered and shattered damp boards. The steps were old and rotten and dangerous, but it would be expensive to replace them. She didn't think she could afford to have them replaced this year.

And she didn't know what she was going to do about the two dead elms at the back of the property. They were dangerous, too, with their arching dead limbs that crashed to the ground during wind storms. Part of one elm hung over a neighbor's yard, and Nell knew it was her responsibility to have those elms taken down before they fell on the yard in a littered mess or, worse, on an animal or person. But the cost of taking down those elms . . .

What was she going to do? How could she manage it? She couldn't. She would have to sell the house. She couldn't possibly keep up any longer with the outside of her house, not even with the lawn. The first summer she'd been divorced, she had dated Steve, and he had done her lawn work for her—mowed the grass, trimmed the bushes—and had been pleased to do it; he liked doing that sort of thing. Perhaps this year, if she continued seeing Stellios, he would mow her lawn—but she couldn't stay with a man just because he might mow her lawn; that was an awful way to think and she hated herself for the thought. Oh, looking out her windows tonight at the April ground that would soon be overgrown with all that damn *grass*—that did not calm her at all. It made her stomach clench.

When the Panic Nights were especially bad, and this promised to be one of them, Nell would quickly move from worry about the present to the definite philosophical belief that this, her frightening life, was what she deserved, was what she had coming to her, for being such a terrible little vain fool in her youth. She hadn't known a thing then, not a thing. All she had cared about were her clothes and her hair and her fingernails and the length of her eyelashes, all she had attempted was to attract men and be envied because of her looks and acting abilities, all she had wanted had been more of everything for herself, and she had had no compassion, and she had never thought that she could get older. . . .

And now here she was. So much gone, so little left.

Why had she been such a little fool? She wasn't genetically stupid, she had only acted that way.

It was hard not to blame her parents for spoiling her, but after all, really, what had they done but love her and believe in her? She was their only child. She had been beautiful and unusual, with lots of reddish-brown hair and unusual reddish-brown eyes and wide cheekbones, a wide mouth. She had been tall and willowy, lovely. You can do anything, her parents had told her; you can do anything, her high school teachers had told her; you can do anything, they had said to her in college; *you* are one of the special ones, you can be a Broadway star, a Hollywood star, you will be famous, wealthy, successful. You are one of the lucky ones.

She had believed them all. When she graduated from the University of Iowa, she had been ready to take on the world—she had been ready for the world to see her. She had been accepted as an apprentice with a summer theater company that performed at a tourist resort in Maine. She went, prepared to be discovered.

Now she did not know, and she never would know, if she had married Marlow because she loved him or because she had seen all those other beautiful, talented girls and had gotten scared, had run into marriage for the safety of it. Now, leaning against a window, Nell smiled at herself: Ha, she thought, so much for the *safety* of marriage. Well, *then* she had reveled in her little victory:

she had married Marlow St. John and had secretly thought of him as her prize, her trophy, her bouquet of roses at the end of the performance. If she was never to win an award for her acting, she would at least win this award for her life.

Oh God, *had* she loved him? She honestly did not know. She had been so young, dumber than she should have been at twenty-three, and he had been so powerful, so truly enchanting. Even before meeting him, she had thrilled at just his name: Marlow St. John. He had lived up to his name, Marlow had, with his rangy sleek body and his mane of prematurely graying hair and his passionate black eyes. He looked dangerous. He was dangerous. Everyone knew that. It was common knowledge among the women in the acting company: Watch out for Marlow St. John, they said. He's divorced and he charms women and he's had affairs with hundreds. He is irresistible. Nell was half in love with him before she even set eyes on him.

When she did see him, he took her breath away. He was so powerful, so handsome, so *romantic* . . . she stopped longing for parts in the plays he directed and began to long for him. Oh, *had* she loved Marlow then? Or had she only loved the illusion of it all?

She had truly thrilled when he first touched her, backstage, so lightly on the cheek, and later, leaned to kiss her so gently she felt his breath but not his lips. Those late nights after rehearsals, when they met far out at a lonely beach and walked along the water, holding hands, talking, embracing, saying elaborate things to one another: if that had not been love, at least it had been lovely.

What was true? How could the reality be untangled from the vision? She had written a love poem to him. But even as she sat writing it, she was aware of herself doing this romantic deed; she could see herself sitting on a flat rock by the ocean, her cotton skirt rippling up with the sea breeze, her sunstreaked hair falling over her shoulders, her pen poised at her lips as she sat deep in thought. She liked it that others came walking along the beach and, seeing her so intensely involved with her pen and paper and her thoughts, passed on without speaking. She saw herself as a fascinating woman, and she adored Marlow endlessly because he was making her fascinating. He was casting and directing her in the ultimate role.

When they finally did make love, she was terrified. She was so stunned to be in Marlow St. John's arms, so afraid that he would be judging her, so shocked to be really there doing that physical and private act, that she did not feel a thing. She felt nothing. She was so disappointed in herself—how could she feel *nothing;* she was with *Marlow St. John!*—she feigned ecstasy. It was probably the best acting she had done in her life. It certainly convinced Marlow. In a way it even convinced Nell. It was years before she could admit to herself just how much pretense was involved in her lovemaking with Marlow. What if she had been more honest? What if she had been able to say: Marlow, I'm so terrified that I can't feel a thing? Perhaps he would have slowed down, consoled her, soothed her, waited for her to calm down and be there in reality. Marlow was capable of such kindness. But she had not known that then—she had known so little then— and she had lied. So their love affair had gone thundering on like a summer storm of heat lightning, flashing and thundering, leaving the earth untouched. Nell loved the drama of it and did not know until later just how superficial a spectacle it was.

At the end of that summer, she had been aware of several facts of life. She knew now that hundreds of other girls in the country had played the lead in college productions of *Joan of Arc* or *West Side Story.* Scores of other girls were more beautiful than she, or more talented or more ambitious or, finally, just braver. And she, at twenty-three, was already considered "older." She had no of-fers, she had not been singled out. Or rather, she had been singled out, by Marlow St. John, and she had an offer from him, of marriage. She could stay single, go to New York, become a wait-ress, and slug it out on her own against enormous odds, or she could marry Marlow, travel with him, let him cast her in the lead of the plays he directed. Perhaps any woman would have made the choice she made.

Remembering it all, Nell shuddered with revulsion at the woman she had been. Oh surely, she thought, surely she had not been so *practical!* She had been as much in love with Marlow as she could, at that time of her life, have been in love with any man.

Nell thought that if she could have one wish, it would be that she had been given a talent and desire for any other thing in the world than acting. This acting business—well, it had caused her to live her life in such a make-believe land. She couldn't even read her old diaries now, because they made her so mad, they were so full of lies. She had written her diaries to be read not by her, but by the public. She had lied in her most intimate life, hoping to be envied by the millions of women who would read her diaries once she was a famous actress.

The week before she married Marlow, she wrote: "In a week I will marry Marlow St. John. *Marriage.* What an ordinary, common thing to be doing; it does not seem grand enough a ritual to mark a joining such as ours, for ours is no ordinary passion, no pedestrian union, no mediocre love. No, it is a grand passion, a fierce relentless ardor that would burn most mortals, a raging need and devotion for one another that consumes us: how brilliantly we will burn together, illuminating the pale world."

Christ. Nell didn't know whether to laugh or cry when she read entries like that. She knew on the one hand that she had almost believed what she wrote. She knew on the other hand that that week, when she had written that incredibly conceited bunch of junk, she had almost run off with another man. Billy Roe. He was just her age, an actor, a Marlon Brando type, all muscles and grunts and inarticulate hulking desire. He was scarcely bright enough to memorize his lines, but he had that intangible quality called stage presence or charisma or magnetism—or pure sex appeal.

She and Billy had been giving each other looks all summer, and that last week they had ended up one evening in the back of his rusty VW van. They had messed around, kissing, touching. It had been exciting.

"I think we'd be really good together," Billy had said. "I've been thinking that ever since I saw you."

She had been lying on top of him, her long hair falling down in his face. They had had on shorts and T-shirts, and the cotton had felt like nothing at all between them.

"We oughta go to New York together," Billy said. "We oughta go be poor struggling actors together. Then if we starve"—he pulled her hair hard back from her face, and with one swift powerful movement rolled over so that he lay on top of her, had her pinned by the hair, had her caught with the intensity of his look—"at least then we won't be love-starved."

He had kissed her.

Oh God, Nell often thought, if only she had kept still, how different her life would have been. If only she hadn't talked, if only Billy hadn't responded as he had.

"Billy, don't," she said. "Billy, wait a minute. Listen, I'm kind of—well, I've been thinking of marrying Marlow St. John. He's asked me to marry him.''

Immediately Billy had rolled off of her, had sat up, leaned against the metal wall of the van, and stared at Nell as if she had transmogrified before his eyes.

"Marlow St. John!" he said. "Holy shit." He looked Nell up and down carefully, as if searching for something he had up to now not noticed. Nell could almost hear Billy thinking: What's so special about *her* that Marlow St. John would want to marry her? "Jesus, Nell, that's just wonderful," he said. "Christ, Marlow St. John. You must be ecstatic."

"Well," Nell said, sitting up and straightening her wrinkled clothes, "I wouldn't exactly say ecstatic." She had been puzzled and hurt that Billy's passion for her had so quickly disappeared in the face of his awe of Marlow St. John.

"You wouldn't? Are you crazy? He's one of the most important young directors in the United States! He can give you any part he wants. He can choose his plays in order to cast you. Jesus, you women get all the breaks."

"But what about *love?*" Nell had asked. She had been so young, so confused, so easily swayed. She had wanted to believe in *love*, real, true, definite love; she had wanted to believe every single word that the love songs said. If Billy had said to her then that she was right, she shouldn't marry someone unless she loved him, or if Billy had had the sense to try to compete for her, to tell her that *he* loved her, *he* wanted her, that she shouldn't go to Marlow St. John, she just very well might have lain back down in that van and taken Billy into her arms and believed she loved *him*. If he had only leaned toward her again, kissed her then as he had a few moments before, the entire course of her life might have changed.

Instead, Billy had said, "Love? What do you mean, what about love?" He had been nearly screaming, he was so excited. He threw his arms out in such a wide gesture that he hit the sides of the van. "Who couldn't love Marlow St. John? Christ, I could love him, and I'm not even a faggot. Listen, you dummy, he's one fascinating, powerful man. He's going to be a *great* man. If he really wants to marry you, you'd be absolutely crazy not to. God, we're not talking about just anyone here. We're talking about Marlow St. John."

If only she had had a little more courage. If only she had not lived so completely on the opinion of others. It hadn't even occurred to Nell until years later that she didn't have to marry Marlow simply because Billy hadn't dissuaded her. Her opinion of her life had been as good as his; she just hadn't known that. She could have brushed off her clothes, crawled out of the van, and said, "Well, I don't want to marry Marlow, and I don't know why, but I don't, so I won't." The choice had always been hers. But she had been such a coward. That was the fatal and recurring flaw of her life: cowardice. She had been too afraid to face the world alone, too afraid to turn down what everyone else thought was a fabulous chance, too afraid not to take what promised to be the easy and golden road into the future. There it was, all laid out before her: Marlow St. John. She had been too terrified, too insecure, to turn her back on that in order to hack her own road into life.

It didn't bother Nell so very much that she had been married and that that marriage had broken up. But it did matter to her that she did not know just how much of her life had been a lie.

Had she been happy? She didn't really know. Had she ever loved Marlow? She didn't really know. Those last few weeks in Maine she had certainly been high, high on the envy and awe of all those other pretty girls, who suddenly saw Nell as someone different, someone special, because she was going to marry Marlow St. John. After their marriage, they had traveled around the country to universities and local theater companies, where Marlow did stints as guest director, and for Nell it had been more of the same: she had been the woman Marlow St. John had married. That had been her identity. Men had flirted with her, people had praised her acting, women had acted like friends, but Nell would never know whether all that warmth was directed at her or at the wife of Marlow St. John. She had been a stepmother of sorts to Marlow's daughter, Clary, but that relationship had had a schizophrenic vagueness about it: Clary came only in the summers, and because it was legally decreed. Not until Nell's divorce from Marlow was she to discover whether Clary cared for Nell herself—or really, whether she cared for Clary. Nell had moved through her life like a woman always in costume, onstage, doing the best job she could in a prescribed role: wife to Marlow, stepmother to Marlow's child, the chosen companion of a moderately famous, and therefore justifiably egocentric, man.

Then two more events beyond Nell's control had changed her

life: she had accidentally gotten pregnant, and Marlow's star had faded.

Funny, how Marlow had blamed the latter on the former.

When she had studied the past—and she had had plenty of time during the long nights when she was first separated to do just that—Nell finally was able to decide conclusively about one fact in her life with Marlow: she was not responsible for his downfall. He had received lukewarm reviews, bad reviews, cool receptions, long before she got pregnant. She was not responsible that grants did not come through. She really was not responsible that other, younger directors were shooting up like firerockets into the skies of public adoration while Marlow's star slowly fizzled and fell into semi-oblivion. These things happened to artists all the time. It was luck. And maybe it was talent. But she was not accountable for it. It had begun happening long before her first baby started growing in her womb.

It was not her fault. But somehow it had become her fault. Somehow Marlow had convinced himself and her that he had had to take the teaching and directing job in the drama department at the college in Boston because she had gotten pregnant and he had to provide financial stability for his wife and her child. The baby had trapped him, had ruined his career. It was all clear to Marlow, and he had expressed his feelings to Nell with equal clarity. And with anger.

In response, she had acted even more frantically: she had pretended that everything between them was still marvelous and enviable. They *wanted* to live in Arlington in an old rambling shambles of a house—the house had such *potential*. They *wanted* to settle down—all that traveling had been so exhausting. Marlow *wanted* to teach college students, for they were the future of the acting profession and where else could he make such an important impact on the world of drama? She *wanted* to stay home for a while, furnish a nest, have babies, settle down. They *wanted* what they had; they were *happy*.

Oh Lord, Nell thought now, thought often: had any of her life been real?

Nell had gotten pregnant on purpose the second time. She didn't want her son to be an only child. By then Jeremy was two, and she had spent almost three years working hard at making a clever and comfortable life for Marlow and their son. Perhaps she had really convinced herself that Marlow was happy. They gave a lot of parties, and the college plays had received great reviews; she had thought that Marlow had come to terms with his life and was even enjoying it.

So she had been taken by surprise when she told him she was pregnant and he had responded by saying: "You bitch." He had gone berserk with anger. He had thought she was special, that she had understood how special he was, he had thought she would nurture his talent because she was unique, and instead she was just like all the others, a bitch, a sniveling clinging woman who trapped a man with babies and forced him to betray his possibilities for magnificence. *If it were not for her . . .*

Marlow went out that night and drank, and probably slept with someone. It became no secret that he slept around during Nell's burgeoning pregnancy and during the first two years of Hannah's life. He didn't try to hide it. He even tried to flaunt it. He was punishing Nell.

The New Year's Eve when Jeremy was five and Hannah three and Nell thirty-three and Marlow forty-five, Nell and Marlow came home at three-thirty from a party. The baby-sitter had gone to sleep in one of the bedrooms, the children were fine, asleep. Nell slipped into a nightgown—*not* a flannel granny one—remembering the resolutions she had made at midnight: *this* year she would somehow get their marriage back on track. This year she would help Marlow somehow. This year she would manage to get him to love his children. This year she would manage to make him happy again. This year would be different.

"Shall I bring us up a little nightcap?" she asked, smiling. "What?" Marlow asked, looking surprised. He continued to button his blue striped pajamas. "Oh, yeah. That would be nice."

Returning with the brandy and soda in snifters, Nell said, "Marlow, here. Let's drink to this new year. I want it to be different for us."

Marlow studied Nell, gave her the critical searching look that he often gave actors when considering them for a part. "Nell," he said, "there's something I have to tell you. I want to start the new year off differently, too. I want a divorce. I'm in love with Charlotte, and I want to marry her."

Charlotte was Nell's best friend, had been her best friend for the four years they had lived in Arlington. Nell sat down on the bed with a plop that caused her drink to spill over the side of the snifter and onto her lace nightgown.

"You're kidding," she said. "Tell me you're kidding."

"I'm not kidding," Marlow said.

Nell, hurt, struck back. She laughed, shaking her head as she did. "You and your ego, Marlow, really. Ever since I've known you you've been so concerned about being *unique*, and here you are having an affair with my best friend. God, you've just waltzed us right into a perfect *cliché*. My best friend. God. What's happened, are you getting too old to attract the little students?"

Marlow slapped Nell across the mouth. He had never come close to striking her before. It had been years, since she was a child, that she had been struck, and Nell felt an explosion of anger within her at the blow.

"Go on to Charlotte," she said. "*I* don't want you. I've *never* wanted you." She glared at Marlow, defiant, hurt, mad, not caring that he might hit her again, not caring that she did not know if her words were true.

Marlow sat down on the bed next to her then, sat there quietly in a sort of slump. Then he said, "You know, I've always suspected that. And if it's true, Nell, then you and I have led a pretty sad life."

Was it true? Nell didn't know, didn't think she would ever know. Oh, what a thing to say to the man she had been married to for eight years! And if he was right, if that were true, then how sad their life *had* been. In the dark depths of that New Year's morning, they just sat there on their bed side by side for a while, unable to go on from that moment of truth. Their house spread all around them, full of sleeping children, the world spread all around them, and they sat there together, silent in a pool of light from the bedroom ceiling.

Nell looked at Marlow: How could she not love him? He was her husband, the father of her children, a man with a sense of humor, a talented man, a man as good as any, she supposed. She did care for him. She had long ago stopped worshiping him and learned to care for him. But the best she could summon up for him now was the kind of love that made her hope he would be truly happy with Charlotte. Yet she did not say this to him, for she knew it would be an even greater proof of her failure to love him as a wife.

They sat there side by side on the bed, which was spread with a quilt hand-sewn by Marlow's mother, and drank their brandy and sodas and had nothing else to say to each other. Finally they crawled into bed together and lay there, side by side, husband and wife, not touching, never to touch again—they lay there until they fell asleep.

Marlow fell asleep first. Within fifteen minutes he was snoring deeply, his body and mind safely sunk in the depths of sleep. He was not aware of Nell, who lay very still but felt her thoughts scrambling frantically at the heights of her consciousness. *Marlow wanted a divorce.* What did that mean? She could pretty much guess what it would mean in practical terms: the mess and bother of legalities; the anguish of breaking the news to the children and the work of protecting them; boxes packed; change everywhere. Maybe they would have to sell the house. Where would she live? She *could* live anywhere now, in any city, state, country. She was free to go. But she found this sudden freedom confusing. Even if she had not been happy with Marlow, still he had brought order to her life, anchoring her firmly to the ground, giving her something to center her life around. Now she was going to drift free, and she was scared. She hadn't yet figured out what it meant that they had married, and now she would have to figure out what it meant that they were divorcing.

Five years later, here she was wandering around her house at night and she still hadn't figured it all out. She still hadn't decided a thing.

But she had survived. She had managed. She had kept her children safe, healthy, and happy. She had found a job and kept it. She had gotten them this far.

Nell drifted down the stairs of the dark house and carefully opened the front door so that the Indian wedding bells hanging from the nail below the knocker wouldn't chime and wake the children. She slid outside into the night, and as her bare feet touched the cold wood of the porch, she felt a shiver ascend inside her. She walked to the edge of the porch and sat down on the steps. Slowly, her eyes adjusted to the lack of light and she could make out the figures of trees and bushes, street and streetlights. The April air was chill and the porch wood was damp; her gown clung, moist and cool, to her bottom and legs. She would probably catch a cold. But she liked these cold, definite, unambiguous physical sensations. She needed them.

Once, when she was a senior in high school, Nell had driven from Des Moines to Chicago to spend a weekend seeing theater. Laura Morrison, her best friend, another aspiring actress, had

gone with her. They had sped along the highway in Nell's red
Thunderbird, with the white top down and the wind blowing their
hair. They had felt young and lovely and glamorous and adven-
turous, singing with the radio, passing a cigarette or Coke back
and forth between them, waving at other cars. There had not been
such severe speed limits in those days, and Nell had driven very
fast, proud of her driving. As they approached Chicago, Laura
had unfolded a gigantic map.

"Do we want 94 or 294?" she yelled.

"What's the difference?" Nell yelled back.

"I don't know," Laura said, her words carried away on the
wind.

The map rattled and whipped in her hands. It was big and
awkward and flapped like a great colored sail, seemed to fight
like a live bird.

"Hell!" Laura said, and began ripping away at the map. She
tossed complete sections of the map over her shoulder so that the
paper flipped away behind their car. "We don't need this part,
or this," she said. "We've already been there." Finally, she had
nothing in her hands but a small square of paper covered in a
complicated checkerboard of the vicinity immediately around
Chicago. "Now," she said, "I'll be able to make sense of this."

But she had thrown so much of the map away that they couldn't
figure out where they were, not even when Nell finally pulled the
car to the side of the road and studied the jagged remnant seriously. They didn't know anything, couldn't tell anything. They
didn't know if 294 was different from 94 or the same road. They
stared at the flat corn land around them and realized they didn't
even know which towns they had just passed. In the end they had
had to get off the highway eight times in order to find service
stations and ask directions, and that had added two hours to their
trip.

Still, Nell liked that memory. She and Laura had found the
whole trip hilariously funny. And even now Nell liked knowing
that once she had been brave and carefree enough to speed down
a highway while her friend threw pieces of map to the wind.

Then, getting lost had been an adventure.

Now Nell worried that she'd never get on a good clear road to
anywhere, because she wasn't sure where she'd been or where
she was. She was just lost. And it seemed that when she tried to
remember parts of her past, she found that they had been carried

away, out of sight, beyond memory, and she could only remember scenes of her life, scenes sailing past too quickly to catch.

She was thirty-eight, and she had lost so many people.

She had lost Laura very early. Laura had gotten pregnant shortly after that trip and had married her boyfriend. They lived in a tiny apartment, and talented Laura spent her time there taking care of twins, while her young husband worked at a factory in the day and went out drinking with the boys at night. Laura had been every bit as attractive and talented as Nell, both girls knew that. But their situations had changed. Nell was envious of Laura for about fifteen minutes, during Laura's wedding shower, when her friends had given her three sexy beribboned peignoirs and Laura had shown off her diamond engagement ring. But Nell had never been envious of Laura after that, especially not the time she saw her coming out of Sears with two babies squalling in a basket.

When Nell went off to college in Iowa City, she wrote to Laura regularly, but Laura never replied. During Christmas vacation her freshman year, Nell had gone to Laura's house with presents. But Laura had been cold. She had looked so much older, so beaten down, that Nell wanted to cry. Still, Nell had cooed and oohed over the babies and acted as if the minutiae of Laura's life—the blue spotted ashtray on the Salvation Army table, the curtains Laura had sewn for the bathroom window—were marvels. Laura had not been taken in by Nell's effusiveness.

"Nell," she had said when Nell was leaving, "please don't come here again. I know you want to remain friends, but honestly, I just can't bear to see you. I can't stand reading your letters. I can't stand knowing about your life. I need to have friends who are doing what I do, raising babies, making tuna and potato chip casseroles. When I think of what *you*'re doing—well, it sends me into a depression so serious that I sometimes think of killing myself."

"God, you don't mean that, Laura!" Nell had cried.

"I do mean that," Laura had said. She managed a wry smile because at that moment the babies awoke and began to wail. "Oh, don't worry, I won't commit suicide. I won't find the time or the energy to commit suicide. But please, do me a favor and don't write me again. Don't come to see me again. I don't want to know you or anything about you. It's too hard for me to bear."

Nell had complied with her friend's request. She had not seen Laura again.

One time, in their junior year of high school, they had worked on a play about Anastasia, the woman who claimed to be the long-lost surviving daughter of the murdered Czar Nicholas and Czarina Alexandra. They had taken turns being the pleading young amnesiac Anastasia and the skeptical old noblewoman grandmother to whom she appeals. They had played one particular scene over and over again with each other, wishing they were on the Broadway stage so they could thrill the world as much as they thrilled themselves with their passionate acting. At the end of the scene, the grandmother had come to believe that Anastasia was her own, and the two women had embraced, weeping with joy at having found each other. Then, in high school, in their teens, Nell and Laura had believed all that—that life was a process of people discovering each other, that life would be a series of joyful embraces, breathtaking revelations, passionate reunions. They had thought that only through death would people be taken from them.

How little they had known. Nell had written Laura when she was divorced from Marlow: *now* she won't envy me, Nell had thought. But Laura had never replied. She was really gone from Nell's life.

Laura had been Nell's best childhood friend. Charlotte had been Nell's best grown-up friend. During the first few years of Nell's marriage to Marlow, she had had no real friends, only brief and spotty and often competitive relationships with the actors and actresses who passed through the repertory company. It had been her own fault that she had no friends; she knew that. Friendship had not been important to her then. She had been too busy creating and defending the image of her marriage to Marlow; they were so clever and so much in love, the two of them, that they needed no one else. When Marlow began to have professional difficulties, Nell really cut people off, afraid she might slip and reveal just how hard times were for them. She did not want to betray Marlow to anyone. Even when Jeremy and Hannah were born, when Marlow was sleeping around, when things were rotten between them, still Nell pretended. It had been her only defense.

When they settled in Arlington, Nell at last found a friend. Charlotte was an actress on stage and off. She was a student of Marlow's, a beautiful tall girl of twenty-three. Her image was that of a lovely fool, a brilliant, bony, talented nitwit with chopped-off hair who could not be called upon to get the tea kettle from the stove to the cup without a mistake. She took to hanging around Nell every day, openly admiring Nell's maternal competence, marveling at Nell's nurturing abilities, and Nell needed that. She was a mother; she became a mother figure; warm, generous, benign, patient. Dressed in a loose-fitting navy blue corduroy jumper that hid her pregnancy-acquired fat, her hair clumped up in a bun for efficiency, Nell graciously moved through her house and life, doling out homemade cookies to her little children and anyone else who passed through the house. Marlow always did fill the house with actors and actresses and students and general hangers-on, but Charlotte was the guest who transcended all the others. She would sit in the kitchen, idly stirring a cup of herb tea, leaning her cheek in her hand, and watch Nell with admiration and longing all over her face. Nell would be kneading bread or spooning mush into a baby's mouth or chopping vegetables, her hair falling out of the bun and around her face in tendrils as she worked.

"Oh, I'll never have *all this,*" Charlotte would sigh, gesturing with her hands, and Nell would see her grimy kitchen with the handprints on the cupboard doors and the cat and dog hair blowing like tumbleweeds in the corners and the trashbasket overflowing with used Pampers transformed into a warm room wealthy with life. Charlotte looked so skinny and lonely. Nell felt opulent by contrast. She bloomed under Charlotte's admiration. She often dressed for the day thinking of Charlotte, how she would look to Charlotte—Charlotte became more than her best friend. She was Nell's perfect audience.

Charlotte was always being pursued by passionate lovers who were going to commit either murder or suicide because Charlotte had broken off with them. Sometimes Charlotte came to spend the night at Nell's for protection or simply just to get some rest.

"Why is that woman always here?" Marlow would grumble.

Nell would reply, indignant, "She's *your* student, Marlow. And she's my friend. Besides, she's having problems. Mark just won't leave her alone. She needs to get away from him for a while, poor thing."

During the winter that Hannah was one and Jeremy three, Nell spent many nights sitting up in the living room, drinking brandy or Kahlua and cream and talking with Charlotte. Charlotte fascinated her; she was so *honest.*

"I want a *grand passion,*" she said. "Nothing else will do.

None of these simpering little boys I keep running into will do, not at all. You are so lucky, Nell. You have Marlow St. John.''

Nell would listen to Charlotte, enthralled. Charlotte had slept with so many men. She was forever saying, "Of course, he's a dreamy lover, but—" Charlotte would talk in graphic detail about things she had done or felt with various men, and Nell would listen, entranced. She hadn't done or felt half those things with Marlow, but of course she didn't tell Charlotte that.

One evening, though, when Marlow had stormed out of the house in one of his rages and Nell was spent from tending two sick babies, she ended up drinking by the fire and confessing all sorts of things to Charlotte.

"I'm an awful, awful person," Nell had said drunkenly. "I must have something genetically wrong with me. Here I am, married to this wonderful man, and I don't even know if I love him. I know some of the people I love—I love my children. I love my parents. I love some of my friends—I love you, Charlotte. But I don't know exactly what it is I feel for Marlow. I used to worship him, and that's a kind of love. But now it seems the strongest emotion I can dredge up for him is—*concern.*"

"Oh that's so sad, Nell, that's so sad," Charlotte said. "I thought you had everything. I thought you were perfectly happy. I've always wished I had your life."

Well, Charlotte had gotten Nell's life, or at least a great part of it. Marlow had divorced Nell and married Charlotte, and now when Jeremy and Hannah went to visit their father, it was Charlotte who made the hot chocolate and cookies. She was a good stepmother, and Nell, who had once been a stepmother to Marlow's daughter Clary, was a good judge of that. Charlotte loved Marlow, and she was kind, in her vague way, to Marlow's children. Nell wished she could like Charlotte, but she couldn't anymore. She couldn't trust her. She felt more betrayed by Charlotte than she did by Marlow. All those weeks when Charlotte had sat in the kitchen smiling dreamily at Nell, she had been remembering the night before or the day to come, when she would lie in Nell's husband's arms and say, "Darling, I don't see how your genius can survive in such a chaotic place. Nell's so busy nurturing others, she doesn't seem to ever have time for you."

"How could you have done that to me?" Nell had asked Charlotte during their one angry confrontation. "How could you have lied so much to me!"

"I didn't lie to you, Nell," Charlotte said. "I didn't lie to anyone. I envied you your life. But I also really felt sorry for Marlow there. He *is* a genius, and he was getting lost in your household."

"It was not *my* household," Nell said. "It was ours. Marlow's and mine. Marlow's children as much as mine, his litter and mess as much as mine. Just because I was the one who cleaned it all up doesn't mean I was the one who made it."

"Oh, I don't see how you can be so upset," Charlotte had said, running her hand through her ragged hair. "After all, you told me more than once that you didn't really love Marlow. I think you should be a little grateful to me. I've set you free. Now maybe you can go out and find someone you can really love."

Cunning Charlotte. She was not even wrong. She honestly didn't believe she had done anything wrong at all. Arguing with Charlotte, Nell had felt only more and more frustrated. She knew she had been betrayed, but she couldn't logically prove just how. Finally, she had let the matter drop. It was done anyway, there was no going back, no changing things.

Now she and Charlotte were pleasant to each other when making the necessary arrangements for the children to visit Marlow, but other than that they seldom spoke. Nell often thought she missed Charlotte as much as she missed Marlow. Charlotte had certainly admired her more, or pretended to, and it was even possible that Charlotte understood more about Nell, the real Nell, than Marlow ever had. It was a very complicated tangle, their relationship, but in the end, Charlotte was one more person whom Nell had really lost.

When Nell was a little girl, she had been taught a song in her Brownie troop that went: "Make new friends, but keep the old. One is silver and the other gold." It was a pretty song when sung in rounds, and the sentiment was pretty too, but now Nell thought that perhaps the moral was inaccurate, at least for someone Nell's age. She did not think she was the same person she had been ten years ago or six years ago. Having children and getting divorced had taught her self-sufficiency, courage, and compassion; she knew she had those qualities now, and she did not have them when she was younger. Now she knew how to be a good friend, and the friendships she had developed over the past six years were

of great importance in her life. These people might not have
known her ten years ago—if they had met her, they might not
even have liked her ten years ago—but they knew her now, they
knew *her:* Nell St. John. Not Mrs. St. John, the wife of the
director, but Nell. It was a very rich reward, this being known
and liked for herself; it was a real feast. At first her friendships
had been a sort of medicine, a tonic, that helped her get well.
Now these friendships were almost a food. They sustained her
life. She was fit and full in the world because of her friends.

And she hadn't lost Clary. Her relationship with her stepdaughter had lasted in spite of everything. Their friendship had been
like the straw that Rapunzel spun into gold: straw at first, it had
been spun and toughened and twisted and tested by the wheel of
time and had come out gold.

Nell had been twenty-four when she became Clary's stepmother; Clary had been thirteen. She had been a cynical child,
and it had taken Nell a long time to realize that what she thought
was arrogance on Clary's part was really a kind of fierce caution.
Clary looked like her father. She was long-limbed and lanky, with
blond hair and fair skin and dark eyes. But she did not act like
her father. Marlow was impetuous, dramatic, quick, and obvious.
Clary was analytical, still, and slow to action. It drove Marlow
nearly wild that Clary did not want to act onstage. She had even
refused to learn to play an instrument. She did not like to play
tennis. She preferred biking and swimming, solitary sports. She
preferred reading books or watching television to being with people. Marlow couldn't understand her at all, and she irritated him.

Clary came to stay with Nell and Marlow every summer, and
every summer she refused to learn to act. Marlow made Clary a
part of the set crew for whatever play he was directing. Clary
would grudgingly and quietly do exactly what was asked of her.
"Bring the hammer, get some coffee, tell Marlow we need him—"
These were orders she could and would follow. Otherwise she
would just stand around the stage, waiting, watching, chewing
her thumbnail, looking bored. She drove Nell crazy, too; Nell
would have died to have had a director for a father, would have
given up anything to have been around actors and the theater as
a teenager. She couldn't believe that this beautiful young girl
couldn't see how lucky she was, what chances had fallen into her
lap.

The first few years of her marriage, Nell paid small attention to Clary. Nell was still too busy trying to be the most beautiful and talented actress in the world, and then too busy trying to buttress Marlow's falling ego. There was not much room in Nell's narcissistic thoughts for a surly teenager. She cooked Clary's meals, washed Clary's clothes, and did what had to be done, but her life and Clary's revolved around Marlow—around his schedule, his needs, his desires. Nell had no experience as a mother, and so it did not occur to her very often to wonder whether or not Clary was happy. It did not occur to her to ask Clary if there was any other thing in the world she would prefer doing to hanging around the theater where Marlow worked all summer. After Nell became a mother, she realized how few motherly feelings she had had for Clary, how she had not protected her.

Still, she was only eleven years older than Clary, and although she had never done things with Clary out of charity, she had done things with her out of pleasure, and that counted for something. Both Clary and Nell loved horror movies, which Marlow considered trash. Whenever they had a chance that first summer, they would go off together to sit munching popcorn and squeezing each other's arms while vampires or zombies or man-eating wasps terrorized the world. They loved the psychos best. They loved being scared. They loved playing games together, too. Nell was always glad when it was summer and Clary was there to play with, for Marlow was always too intense and busy to settle down to what he considered childish activities. Nell and Clary spent their summers playing Clue, checkers, card games, elaborate games of Monopoly that went on for days. These were frivolous acts, Nell later realized, not the sort of enterprise shared by parent and child. But, Nell also realized, they were the sort of thing shared by friends, and over the years that was what Clary and Nell became.

Clary was in college when Nell's children were born and she worked all summer to make money for college, so Nell and Marlow saw very little of Clary those four years. The summer Clary graduated with a degree in biology, she came up once to visit her father and his family. In spite of the years of friendship between Nell and Clary, that visit had been a disappointment.

It was the last year of Marlow and Nell's marriage, although they did not know that yet, and the air between them was tense with unadmitted anger. Clary could stay only two days, and both those days Hannah and Jeremy, then two and four, were sick with a ghastly intestinal flu. Nell was tired, overweight, and generally miserable. But she was so excited about seeing Clary that she shampooed her hair, put on makeup, and stuffed herself into her best dress. The moment she heard Clary's car pull into the driveway, she grabbed the wailing, sick Hannah from her crib and raced to the top of the stairs.

She stood on the landing a moment, just looking at Clary, who had come in the door and was kissing her father and who looked, all of a sudden, grown-up and devastatingly lovely. Clary had had her thick blond hair cut Dutch-boy style and it swung evenly at her shoulders, making her seem substantial and decisive, a woman who knew what she wanted. The blunt bangs across her forehead accentuated Clary's dark brows and eyes: she turned, and looked up at Nell with a frank, almost stern look. Nell knew at once that Clary had become a person to be reckoned with in the world.

Nell was so glad to see her, this person who was part child of hers, part friend, and she started down the stairs, hoping she looked at least not dowdy in her blue dress.

"Clary!" she called.

And at that moment poor Hannah, who was in Nell's arms, threw up. Thick white vomit erupted from the sick baby's mouth and flowed in a milky waterfall down Nell's dress and, as Nell watched, down one step and the next step and the next. Warm acid-smelling liquid coated Nell's arm and dress. Hannah cried and choked. Nell had to comfort and clean her poor daughter, then turn to the stairs. The thick vomit had soaked the carpet. It was not an easy task cleaning up the mess.

The visit did not much improve from that moment. Clary seemed to Nell to have become elegant, self-sufficient, and haughty. She was impressed with herself for gaining a degree in biology, and she talked endlessly about the experiments she was doing on gypsy moth research at a lab in Connecticut. *She* was doing important work in the world.

Nell scrubbed the carpeted stairs, fixed and served dinner, tended to sick children, and listened to Clary when she had the chance, but as each moment passed, Nell felt more and more hopeless. She thought she must look such a drudge to Clary. She envied Clary's flat stomach, trim hips, smooth skin. She envied Clary her youth, her freedom, her clothes; she envied everything of Clary's. And Clary didn't do anything to make Nell feel better. She scarcely looked at Jeremy and Hannah, and when she did look at them, it was with a sort of scientific scrutiny, as if the babies were bugs or some other kind of slightly bizarre form of life. Nell cried that night when she went to sleep, because she felt old and somehow forlorn.

The next year, when Marlow and Nell were separated and then divorced, Nell didn't know whether to contact Clary or not. Clary was Marlow's daughter, after all, not hers. People tended to choose sides during a divorce, and it was only right that Clary would choose her own father. Blood tells, Nell thought. Besides, Clary had made it pretty clear that she had no interest in Nell or her messy children . . . Nell did not call. That Christmas Nell sent Clary a card and pictures of the children and received a card and a cool message in return. But the summer after that, one long evening when Nell was wandering around picking up the toys that the children she baby-sat had strewn across every possible surface of the house, she began to think of Clary, of the good times they had had together. On impulse, she called Clary and they talked for an hour, spilling out the news of the past year, getting to know each other again. They began to write, to call. Finally, their friendship faced what Nell would always in the back of her mind call the rat test.

The summer that Hannah was four and Jeremy was six, Nell had done a thoroughly modern thing: she had left her children with her ex-husband, their father, and driven down to spend a weekend with her ex-stepdaughter.

By this time, Clary had given up on gypsy moths, or rather the government grant ran out and she had gone to work at a lab at Rutgers. She lived in a small apartment in Piscataway, New Jersey, with a roommate named Sally, who was a waitress at a local bar because she couldn't get a job teaching school. Sally and Clary were both pretty, single, and clever; they had worked their life together into a sort of chic comedy routine. They slopped around in baggy painter's pants and tiny striped cotton shirts, drank countless beers, bopped around their apartment singing Devo songs. Nell sat in their living room drinking beer and just watching, thinking. Here was Clary, who had been eleven when they first met; here was Clary, who had started having periods the first summer she stayed with Marlow and Nell; here was Clary now, a grown woman, a sexual sophisticate, a competent lab technician. Clary and Sally taught Nell to play a game called asshole dice. They drank more beer. Around midnight they decided to smoke some grass, but Nell declined and said she wanted to go to bed. It was not that she cared whether they smoked or not, it was just that whenever she had tried grass she always had anxiety attacks. She didn't need grass anyway, tonight; she was already in a strange enough land. Here she was visiting her ex-stepdaughter, who had been thirteen and was now twenty-four, and she, Nell, didn't feel any older at all. Here she was visiting her ex-stepdaughter, who had spent part of the evening telling Nell about her latest lover's strong and weak points in graphic detail. Here she was visiting her ex-stepdaughter, who told her that she would sleep on the living room sofa so that Nell could have her bedroom.

"The rats won't bother you," Clary said. "They make a little noise at night, but you'll get used to it."

Clary worked with lab rats at Rutgers and had taken two home as pets. Carlos was a white rat with pink eyes, Sophia gray and white with black eyes. They were not large rats, but they were live rats, complete with long buck teeth and very long, skinny, rubbery tails. They lived in a cage at the foot of Clary's bed. They had an exercise wheel and other toys.

Rats were intelligent, Clary said, more intelligent, more affectionate, than gerbils or hamsters. They made great pets. Nell told Clary she didn't want to put her out of her own bedroom; she, Nell, would be delighted to sleep on the living room sofa. But Clary and Sally were planning to stay up till three, watching a horror movie and smoking grass, and there was nothing for Nell to do, once she had made the announcement that she was tired, but to go to bed in Clary's bedroom with the rats rustling and chittering in their cage all night long.

Nell stayed with Clary for two nights. They talked and laughed and drank and went to a movie and ate pizza and Nell was happy. She and Clary had reestablished their connection. Now that they were no longer bound by their association with Marlow, they discovered they were bound by something stronger: they had known each other for a long time, they had gone through changes, and they still liked each other, not as family, but as friends. In spite of the fact that Nell didn't sleep well for two nights—she really couldn't help but fear those rats might get out of the cage—she considered the visit a complete success.

In March of the next year, Nell got a phone call from Clary. Sally was going off to Mexico with a lover, and Clary had to change apartments. She had found a new roommate in a new location, but the landlord did not allow pets of any kind. She wondered if Jeremy and Hannah might like to have her rats.

Nell was speechless. She knew that if she insulted the rats, she would be obliquely insulting Clary: love Clary, love her rats. These were *baby* rats, Clary hastened to add in the long-distance silence caused by Nell's dismay. Sophia and Carlos had lived out their natural lives and gone on to rat heaven; Clary had just gotten these new baby rats three weeks ago. They were so tiny, so cute, and if Jeremy and Hannah played with them every day, they'd become the sweetest pets. . . . Clary wanted to drive up during the weekend with the rats. She'd bring a cage; she'd show Jeremy and Hannah how to care for the rats.

Nell hesitated. She wanted so very much for Marlow's children, Clary and Jeremy and Hannah, to get to know and like one another, and here was the first chance that had presented itself. She did not want to turn Clary down. But *rats* . . . Finally, she told Clary to come ahead and tried to sound enthusiastic as she spoke.

It was a five-hour drive from Piscataway to Arlington. Clary arrived on a Saturday afternoon with the two rats, an old aquarium with wire over the top to make a cage, a sack of pine chips, and a bag of Purina Rat Chow.

Nell sat on Jeremy's bed, smiling, as Jeremy and Hannah, enraptured, let the baby rats run up their arms. Jeremy let his rat go under his shirt and run along his chest and stomach. Nell could see the outline of the little body and the long thin tapering tail through the cotton of her son's shirt. She felt there was something unnatural about watching a rat run over her son's body—she felt a primitive revulsion at the sight—but she bit her tongue. The children were so happy, and Clary was sitting on the floor talking to them, writing out a list of instructions.

The rats were to have fresh water put in their drinking bottle every day. They were to be given dry spaghetti or noodles every day. They needed hard stuff to chew or their front teeth would grow too long and they wouldn't be able to eat. Jeremy and Hannah should never approach the cage and stick their hands in without warning; this would scare the rats. The children should gently tap on the cage and make a little chittering sound before reaching in. The rats would soon learn that this meant a friend was near and would be picking them up. Every now and then the rats could be given a treat, but not too much sugar, which was bad for them. Clary had often made scrambled eggs for her rats; they liked that sort of thing.

Nell had sat on the bed, looking at Clary, marveling. Clary, who was so blond and tall and sleek and lovely, who could have done *anything,* was here before her, seated cross-legged on the floor, writing serious instructions about rat care. How strange people's lives were.

Clary spent the night with them before going back to New Jersey, and it was a successful visit, with much laughter. Jeremy and Hannah kissed Clary good night when they went to bed and again when she left. They looked at Clary with earnest faces as she admonished them to be good to the rats: "Be nice to the rats, and they will be the best pets you've ever had," she said seriously as she bent to kiss them goodbye. Her face was as earnest as theirs. She was such an elegant, regal-looking young woman; she looked like a queen handing over a charge. Nell knew there was nothing for her to do but to survive with the rats, to remind the children to feed them, love them, let them out for exercise, to clean their cage. This was not what she would have chosen to bring these three people together, but it was what had presented itself, and she tried to be grateful for it. The important thing was that now Clary and Jeremy and Hannah were in touch, had a mutual interest.

So she lived with the rats. She made rules. One week Jeremy got the cage and the responsibilities in his room and the next week Hannah got it. She kept an eye on the children's friends and limited the amount of visitors, reminding the children that too many eager little hands might harm or frighten the rats. She vetoed the children's plan to sell tickets to other children to see the rats. She doled out dry sticks of spaghetti to her children so that the rats would not get long teeth, and she told them yes, she thought it was adorable how the little rats sat up in the cage and reached out their skinny little hands to grab for the noodles. When both her children spent the night at friends' houses, she fed the rats herself, although she could not bring herself to let them out for exercise. She tapped on the cage, went "Chee-chee-chee," to the rats, just as Clary had said. She stuck her own hand down into the cage to drop the pellets and the apple slices and the spaghetti. "Here, little rats," she said. "Here's your D-Con."

The rats seemed to thrive. Then one evening Hannah stuck her hand in to pick up her rat and the rat lunged and bit her hand. Hannah ran to Nell, crying. Nell put medicine on the small bite and read Clary's instructions aloud to Hannah: rat bites were cleaner than human bites. These rats were lab rats with no disease, no germs. If by any chance at all one of the rats got scared and bit, they were not to worry, it would be a clean bite. Rat mouths were much cleaner than human mouths. Nell tried to be reassured by Clary's instructions.

But the next day, when Jeremy reached in to pick up his rat, Hannah's rat bit him. Nell put medicine on his wound.

"We've got to go 'Chee-chee-chee' more," she said to her children.

"But I did, Mom, I did!" Jeremy protested.

"Well, do it *more!*" Nell said. "This rat is obviously scared." That evening, however, both children were reluctant to stick their hands in the cage. Nell found an old pair of gardening gloves and put one on. She tapped on the cage, went "Chee-chee-chee," then spoke to the rats in her sweetest, kindest, most soothing voice. When she stuck her hand into the cage to drop the dry noodles, the gray and white rat rose up on its hind legs and, as fast as a snake striking, lunged at Nell's hand and bit. It snatched at her hand with its long scrawny fingers and bit.

"That does it," Nell said, jerking her hand away, shaking with disgust and fear even though the rat had not been able to get through the gardening glove. "This rat is going."

"Mom, we can't kill it," Jeremy said. "That's not fair. Maybe it's just a cowardly rat. Maybe it's just sensitive."

"I don't care what its psychological problems are," Nell said. "We are not keeping this rat any longer. I will not have this rat biting any other person."

Jeremy made a fuss, but Hannah, who had had her feelings hurt because *her* rat bit while Jeremy's didn't, agreed with Nell. They wanted to call Clary to ask her advice, but she had moved apartments without leaving her new number or address, and she was using her new roommate's phone and had told Nell only the roommate's first name.

Finally, Nell carried the cage with the rats in it out to the car and they drove to the country. There, she and the children went through an elaborate procedure, involving sticks and gloved hands, in order to get the bad rat out of the cage without having it bite and still prevent the good rat from running away too. At last the bad rat was out in the countryside. It ran off into the tall grass. Nell drove home, exhausted. This escapade had taken three hours out of their Sunday afternoon. And Hannah was teary, thinking there was something intrinsically wrong with her that made *her* rat bite, and Jeremy was grumpy and worried, saying that now *his* rat would be lonely.

Three nights later, at bedtime, Jeremy called Nell to his room. "Look at my rat," he said.

His rat was huddled in a corner of the cage, shrunken into itself, not responding when Jeremy tapped on the glass. Nell put the gardening glove on and put her hand into the cage. She dropped a fresh slice of apple in. "Chee-chee-chee," she said.

The rat did not respond except to shiver weakly.

"God, Jeremy," Nell said. "I think your rat is sick."

"But it can't be," Jeremy said. "I haven't done anything wrong. I've done everything Clary said!"

"I know, honey. But it's sick. Listen, let's take it down to the kitchen. I can't stand the thought of you going to sleep in a room with a sick rat in it."

They carried the cage downstairs and set it in the middle of the kitchen table. The rat fell over on its side and lay there, limp.

Jeremy started to cry. "I *loved* that rat," he said. "I took the best care of it I could."

At this point Nell got paranoid enough to wonder if this entire rat bit was some bizarre and convoluted stepdaughter's revenge on Clary's part. She tried to soothe Jeremy. She promised him the rat would be better in the morning. Finally, she called a friend of hers who was a vet.

"Marilyn," Nell said, "I've got a problem. Jeremy has a pet rat and it's sick. What can I do? I know it's too late tonight to bring the rat into the clinic, but can you give me any advice?"

Marilyn laughed. "Nell," she said, "people have been trying for thousands of years to find out how to destroy rats. Rats are the best survivors on the planet. That rat will either get well by itself or die." She laughed again. "*You would* have a sick rat."

Nell translated the conversation into a more optimistic and kindly message for Jeremy: "Marilyn said that rats are very hardy creatures and that this rat will undoubtedly be better soon." It didn't entirely convince Jeremy, but it worked well enough to get him to go off to bed.

Just before Nell went to bed, she returned to the kitchen to check the rat. It was shivering, and when Nell came close to the cage, it began to cry out in tiny whimpers. "Eeee-eee-eee," it went, and Nell looked at its limp dreadful body and was overcome with pity and revulsion.

"I'm sorry, rat," she said. "I don't know what to do." She still did not know how to locate Clary. She truly did not know what to do. Finally, she heated some milk and set it, in a small plastic bowl, inside the cage, close to the rat's face.

She arose early the next morning and hurried downstairs, wanting to get to the rat before the children saw it. She was certain it would have died overnight.

But it had not died. It was now stretched out full-length in the cage on its back, its whole body wrenched with convulsions. It shuddered, its skinny legs jerked, and after one quick look, Nell raced to the kitchen sink and splashed cold water on her face, trying not to vomit. Then she went back across the kitchen to the phone on the wall and dialed Marilyn's home number.

"Marilyn," she said. "I'm sorry to call you at home. But this poor rat is having *convulsions*. What can I do? The children will be awake any moment now. Can I bring it into the clinic? Will you please meet me at the clinic and give it a shot to put it to sleep?"

"Nell, don't be silly," Marilyn said. Marilyn lived on a farm; not only was she a vet, but she lived among all sorts of animals. "You don't want to spend the money to have a rat put to sleep. Just reach in and break the poor creature's neck."

"Aaaaargh," Nell said. "Marilyn, I can't do that. I can't. I cannot put my hands around a convulsing rat's neck and break it."

"You'd be surprised," Marilyn said. "It will snap quite easily—"

"Stop it!" Nell yelled. "Marilyn, this is awful! Help me."

"Look," Marilyn said, her voice soothing. "Here's what you can do. And it won't cost you a thing. Do you have a gas oven? Put the rat in the oven, turn the gas on, and gas it to death."

"You've got to be kidding," Nell said. "That's disgusting, Marilyn. I can't believe you're saying this. Do you think I could ever cook a roast in my oven after gassing a rat in it? Jesus. You're weird. Besides, thank heavens, I have an electric oven."

"Nell," Marilyn said. "Remember we are talking about a *rat*. Why don't you just take a hammer and hit it on the head?"

Nell retched. Out of the corner of her eye she could see the rat's scrawny leg spasming. She began to cry. "Marilyn, *please,*" she said. "This is making me sick. But I'm just not capable of doing that to anything, not even a rat. I want it put to sleep peacefully."

Marilyn sighed. "I've got an idea," she said. "Why don't you put it in a paper sack, a lunch bag, for example, and attach it to the muffler of your car with a rubber band. Then run your car for a while and the carbon monoxide is bound to put it to sleep quite nicely."

"You want me to sit in front of my house with a rat in a sack attached to my muffler?" Nell said. "What will the neighbors think? What will the kids think? Marilyn, please meet me at the clinic and give the rat a shot!"

"Well, all right," Marilyn said. "But you know I'll have to charge you. Dr. Hebers is getting very sticky about what I do for friends."

"Charge me a million dollars, but put this poor damn rat out of its misery!" Nell cried.

She got the children up and dressed, carried the cage with the rat in it to the car, and drove it to the vet's. She had secret hopes that the poor animal would die on the way and save her the fee, but she was not to be so lucky. It was still convulsing when she carried it into the animal hospital. Marilyn took the rat—Nell and the children agreed they did not want to keep the cage or watch her give the shot—and went into the back room. Nell drove home in a funk. She got the children off to school, then went to their rooms and stripped the sheets and washed them in hot water. When she got home from work, she spent two hours washing every surface in the children's rooms with hot water and Lysol disinfectant. Still she felt queasy. And she did not know what she would say to Clary about the rats. She didn't want this new, fragile connection between them all to be broken. She was sick at heart.

Three nights later, Clary called.

"Clary!" Nell said. "Give me your new phone number before you say another word. I've been going crazy, unable to reach you."

Clary gave her the number, then said, "How are the rats?"

"Oh, Clary," Nell said. "I have bad news."

"I was afraid of that," Clary said.

"What?" Nell asked, nearly shrieking. *"You were? Why?"* It turned out that all the rats who had been born at a certain time in the lab at Rutgers had been exposed to a virus, and all the baby rats had eventually died of this virus. The rats Clary had given the children had been part of this group.

"I'm so sorry," Clary had said. "I wouldn't have exposed the children to such a sad experience for the world. I didn't know the rats were ill when I brought them up; we only just found out. Believe me, Hannah's rat wouldn't have bitten anyone if it hadn't been sick. Please don't dislike rats just because of this one experience. Listen, do you want me to bring the children new rats?"

Nell had hesitated. Then she said, "Clary, to be honest, I don't want any more rats in the house. I know you like them, and the children loved them, but I just can't. I can't help it. They give me the creeps." She waited for Clary to speak, waited to hear the sound of injury or pique in her voice. She waited to lose Clary.

"Oh well," Clary said calmly. "Lots of people feel that way. Too bad. I think if you spent more time around them, you'd get used to them, and they do make good pets."

"We have two cats and a dog," Nell said. "And the kids barely keep up with feeding them. I think we'd better forget the rats for a while."

"Okay," Clary said. And they went on to talk of other things.

Nell had hung up the phone feeling oddly jubilant. So it was possible to be honest with people she cared for and still not lose them! It was an exciting lesson to learn, and she only wished she'd learned it earlier in life.

The rat test had happened three years ago. Clary and Nell wrote and called each other often now, growing closer and more easy in their friendship with each passing year. There was that much.

Now Nell shivered and hugged herself, remembering all those early years, foolish mistakes, mysterious losses. "Why was I so dumb?" Nell asked, and the sound of her voice breaking the deep silence made gooseflesh break out along her arms.

Well, she thought, she was still dumb, to be sitting out on the porch in the middle of the chilly night. Or—maybe not. Maybe this was, if nothing else, a sign that she had progressed this far, far enough to be outside in the dark. When she was a child, and even in her twenties, when she was married to Marlow, she had been frightened of being alone in the dark. She had seen monsters in the shadows, heard bogeymen rustling in the bushes. In her

twenties, whenever Marlow went off on a trip, she was always
so terrified at being alone in the house in the dark that she could
not sleep. She would sit up all night reading, nervous and alert,
listening for the sounds of rapists, robbers, maniacs; only when
the sun finally shone in the window would she be able to relax
and sleep.

In a way, that fear was a kind of luxury. She could not afford
to be so cowardly once she was the lone adult raising two small
children. She had to be able to sleep all night, because she had
to be awake and alert in the day to take care of the children and
to work to support those children. Of necessity, she had become
brave. She had grown up just that much; if she was not naturally
a brave woman, she was learning to behave like one. That was
worth something.

But it was more than that—more than pretense, more than whis-
tling in the dark. She really did like being out here alone in the
night. The soundless shadows, the dewy air, the inescapable night,
reduced her to an elemental Nell. She had lost so many people.
But she had gained so many people, and it seemed that she still
lived her life through other people, as if always trying for the
prettiest pose in front of an endless mirror. Out here in the night
it did not matter what she looked like or how old she was or
whether she was loved or loving. She just existed, bones and skin
and nerves and senses, hard and substantial against the soft elu-
siveness of night. She was Nell, and by herself she was real.

And cold. She rose, stretched, and pulled her moist nightgown
from the back of her legs and bottom. She knew now that when
she sank into the cozy warmth of her bed, she would fall asleep.
Again she had settled nothing, had reached no conclusion about
the meaning of her life. Who was she? Would she ever be able
to use her acting talent again, or was that part of her life lost to
her forever? Would any man ever really love her? Would she ever
really love any man? Would she have to sell this house? Could
she repair those damn steps by herself? She had not found the
answers to those questions tonight. But the Panic Night feeling
had abated. She was now more tired than scared. She somehow
at least had made enough peace with herself so that she could
sleep. She would rest in the midst of her confusion and loneliness,
like a bird managing to sleep on the most sheltering branch of a
wind-tossed tree.

Three

SUNDAY evening Nell locked herself in her bathroom. She had a date that night, and she wanted one half-hour of uninterrupted solitude in which to get ready. She had settled Hannah and Jeremy in front of the TV with a pizza, milk, and a giant sack of fresh peas in the pod, which the children would crack open and eat like peanuts from a shell. She had asked Jeremy to answer the phone if it rang and threatened them both with death or worse if they got into an argument loud enough to reach her ears. Then she gathered up her paraphernalia and locked herself in the bathroom.

Actually, the lock was a joke. Years ago, when Jeremy was three and Hannah one, Jeremy had managed to lock himself in the bathroom by turning the key in the old-fashioned brass lock. He shut the door, turned the key, took it out, then could not figure how to put it back in.

"Be a brave boy and don't worry," Nell had called to him through the door after fifteen minutes of attempting in vain to instruct him in the art of inserting keys into locks. "I'll call Mr. Milton and ask him to come over and open the door. You just sit down and wait, honey."

Even at three, Jeremy was a resourceful child. "Okay, Mommy," he said cheerfully. "I can play with my bath toys while I'm in here. And if I get hungry, there's lots of candy in here to eat."

Nell's hair had nearly stood on end. "Jeremy! Jeremy, no. You must not eat anything that's in the bathroom."

"But, Mommy, I can see some candy in a bottle—"

"Jeremy!" Nell screamed. *"No!* That is *medicine.* That is *not candy!* Don't eat it or you'll get *very sick!"*

Jeremy was quiet for a while. "Well," he said, "can I drink

51

the pretty red stuff? You gave it to me when I had a cold. You said it made me *well*. I could—''

''*No*, Jeremy,'' Nell said. ''That red stuff is medicine, too. Don't drink it. It only works if you're sick, and you're not sick now, and if you drink it you'll be very sick. Honey, be a nice boy for Mommy and promise you won't eat or drink anything. I'll get Mr. Milton over here right away. And if you promise not to eat or drink anything, I'll—I'll take you out and buy you a *big* ice cream cone.''

Jeremy was silent again. Nell waited, leaning against the locked bathroom door. The silence grew more ominous. Nell knew that Jeremy was in there weighing the power he had now to disobey his mother while she couldn't get her hands on him against the wrath he knew would fall if he did disobey and she finally got through the door.

''Jeremy?'' Nell said, her voice threatening.

''I won't eat anything,'' Jeremy said at last.

And he hadn't. But Nell had been unable to reach the handy-man, and it had been almost two hours before Nell found a friend with a skeleton key who managed to get the door open. By then both Nell and Jeremy were nearly hysterical. Nell had thrown the key in a river, as glad to see it sink as if it were a gun. Then the children had been so little and so connected to her that she could not envision a time when she could lock any door against them. For years she took baths, brushed her teeth, and put on her makeup with them crawling or toddling or rushing in to ask her a question or show her a toad or demand that she arbitrate an argument.

But now they were older and could be left alone, and Nell had put a hook and eye lock on the door herself. It wasn't strong: one good blow and the door would fly open. But it was powerful symbolically. *She* could get in to her children if she had to, but they could not get in to her. They would turn the handle, push, hear their mother yell, ''Go away! I'm taking a bath!'' and then they would actually go away. Of course they could still stand outside the door and call to her. It often seemed they waited until she was locked in the bathroom to ask her questions. She could wander the house for hours, cleaning, vacuuming, dusting, she could sit on the sofa and try to engage them in conversation, and they would get restless and ignore her. But once she had locked herself in the bathroom, they positioned themselves at the door and whined out their questions: ''Mom, where's my hairbrush—

pink barrettes with the hearts—sneakers—boy baby doll?'' The list was endless. Often they were clever at asking questions that needed her to be physically present to answer. "Mom, have I done this math problem right? I can't get it and it's due tomorrow," Jeremy would call. "Mom, is this how you French braid?" Hannah would ask. And often, especially, questions such as, "Mom, do you think I should put a Band-Aid on this cut or just let it bleed?''

The children would turn the handle and push the door so that it opened the one and one half inches the latch allowed. They would stand outside the door and jiggle the handle and sigh until Nell screamed at them. Then they would sulk off with their feelings hurt, only to ignore her when she finally rose from the tub. Nell would sink into the solace of her bath and try to pretend she did not hear the cats scratching and buffeting and mewing at the doors.

The cats disapproved of Nell shutting herself off even more strongly than her children did. If Nell laid out a dress on the bed, then shut herself in to bathe, Medusa, the female cat, would often go sit on the middle of the dress and shed. Nell was sure the cat had the ability to shed at will. She had actually seen Medusa do it to the trouser legs of men the cat didn't like: Medusa would jump on a man's knee, sit there a minute, then yawn and jump off, casually leaving the man's slacks covered with long, fine hairs.

Usually, Nell warned her dates about the cat: "You may not want her on your lap," she'd say. "She sheds terribly." But there had been two or three times when Nell knew exactly what the cat was doing and didn't move to stop her. Those times Nell had disliked the men as instinctively as Medusa had. Then Nell had sat across the coffee table from the man, sipping her drink, talking politely and smiling at Medusa with affection, while Medusa lay on the man's legs, her slanted green eyes narrowed in smug slits as she stared, smiling a cat smile conspiratorially back at Nell, and kneaded the man's trousers, and purred, and shed, and shed.

Nell and Medusa were about as close as creatures of different species could get, but still there were times when Nell wanted to be alone, and this was one of them. Nell had put both Medusa and the gentle male cat, Fred, outside when she fed the children this evening. She was organized for this bath. She needed the time not just to soak and relax and get clean, but also to think. She often did her best thinking in the bathtub. A kind of comforting magic happened to Nell when she bathed. She'd run the water so hot it was almost painful and put in so much bubble bath that when she sank into the water, the white and iridescent foam closed over her from head to toe, a blanket of bubbles. Heat, steam, and silence radiated around Nell's naked body like the rainbows rounding through the bubbles. Nell would lie back, her head propped against the tub's edge, and drift into a state of complete relaxation. And whatever problem she brought into this wet heat with her seemed less significant when she finally rose, dripping and pink-skinned, from the bath.

Now she lay submerged in hot water and wondered whether or not she should stop seeing Stellios, her current lover.

It was strange. It was even humorous, taken the right way, taken, say, with a good friend and a bottle of wine, how Nell had felt, as soon as she was divorced, so optimistic. She had felt: well, *now* I'm ready for *real love!* She had been as hopeful, as naïve, as an infant. There had been a halcyon summer, when Marlow was still paying the bills and she didn't know enough to worry about money yet, when she had lost the weight she'd gained from having the children by being nervous over the divorce—the weight had just fallen away easily, to her amazement—when she looked radiant, better than ever in her life, and felt that way too. She had thought that now she was ready for the real thing. She had thought that now she would do things *right*. She had never thought that now she was set up to get hurt—or to hurt someone else.

One May evening, when the children were visiting their father for the weekend and Nell was in this blessed blissful stupid state, she had gone to the Andersons' for dinner. They sat on the slate patio, Katy and John and Nell, enjoying the warmth of the evening and discussing the great hole in the backyard that was soon to become the Andersons' new swimming pool. A young man in blue jeans and a work shirt and a red cap that said BUDWEISER came around the corner of the house. He was Steve Hansen, the contractor who was putting in the Andersons' pool, and John got up to greet him and talk with him about the progress of the pool.

Nell leaned back in her lawn chair, sipped her gin and tonic, and looked at Steve. It had been years since she had studied a man's body so completely, with such relish. Steve was short, lean, hard-bodied, and tan. He wore a thick silver ID bracelet on his wrist, and the sun glinted off it and off the golden hairs each time he moved his muscular arm. His shirt was damp at the armpits and back with sweat, and his jeans hung low on his hips,

stretched taut over his thighs. He had straight blond hair that hung
shaggily from under his cap. From time to time he glanced over
at Nell: his eyes were a brilliant blue. John Anderson gestured
and talked, leaning with one hand on the back of the lawn chair.
Steve just lounged into his own body, comfortable and sweaty
and strong. He had a tool belt slung low on his hips. Nell couldn't
take her eyes off the man. Katy, watching Nell watch Steve,
finally said in dulcet tones that sounded merely kind to a stranger
but were weighted with meaning to her husband: "John, why
don't you offer Steve a drink?"

So Steve had stayed. He had joined them on the patio and had
been introduced to Nell. They sat with the spring sun warm on
their skin, sat in lawn chairs sipping gin and tonics, idly chatting
till the light began to fade from the sky.

Later, Nell would not remember a word of that conversation,
but she could close her eyes and instantly feel the sun on her skin
and see the slice of lime floating in her glass, that tart green half
moon of fruit trapped in the ice and liquid like a fact caught in
the midst of bewitchment. She had not gotten drunk. She had
only sipped at the drink. Mostly she stared into her glass, because
if she looked at Steve, she felt a flush come up her neck and
cheeks, and if she looked at Katy or John, she broke into a foolish
grin that was usually completely irrelevant to whatever topic of
conversation they were discussing. She just stared at the lime in
her drink and felt wonderful. Felt alive and acutely aware of the
man sitting next to her. She was experiencing the most wonderful
grown-up lust.

Steve was a quiet man. Marlow had always been so dramatic,
theatrical, even grandiose, expressing even the most banal statement with passion; Nell as a young woman had admired him for
that. But then as time went by it seemed that most of the men
Nell knew were this way. Many were actors or were connected
with the theater, and they all had such style, they all prided themselves on their flair. But Steve had an unexamined stillness about
him that fascinated Nell. His answers were simple and direct, and
he had a good, short laugh. He was contained, as if content with
himself and his secrets. As the evening went on, Nell felt a lust
for the man mount inside her until it was nearly intolerable. Each
time she looked at the man she felt an excruciating pleasure seize
her, and soon she could not control her imagination. It rampaged
inside her mind and body: she would glance at Steve and imagine

kissing his tanned neck, kissing down into the collar of his blue shirt, licking his chest—Nell would quickly glance back into her glass. She was agitated yet forced to sit serenely—she was a grown and cultivated woman, after all, not a child, not a savage. But she was very nearly drooling in the presence of this calmly and powerfully sexual man. When he finally rose and left, Nell was trembling, exhausted. She had not experienced such an intensely sexual experience since she'd given birth to her babies and nursed them. She didn't know if she had ever reacted so physically to any man before.

"I wonder if he gives off a *scent* or something," Katy had said as soon as Steve was gone.

"Huh?" Nell said.

"Well, *God,*" Katy went on, "how else can you explain it? He's so sexy. He's like some kind of animal. He makes me just want *to jump* him!"

"It's always nice to know you get on well with the help, Lady Chatterley," John said.

"Oh give me a break," Katy said to her husband. "You're always lusting after Nell's baby-sitters, you have no room to talk. But, seriously," Katy said, turning back to Nell, "what do you think?"

"I think . . . I think he's gorgeous," Nell said. "I think he's just—*uhh.*" She could not think of a word appropriate to that man.

"Well, goody," Katy said, rubbing her hands. "Something to cheer our little Nelly up!"

"Katy, he didn't even notice me," Nell said.

"Nell, *no one* doesn't notice you," Katy said. "He noticed her, didn't he, John?"

John was putting the steaks on the grill. "Uh-uh," he said. "Sure."

"Oh, men," Katy said. "They'll never have the right instincts, no matter how well they learn to cook."

But in fact it was John who set Nell up with Steve. While Nell and Katy were thinking up elaborate plots and ruses—Nell, for example, could never ask Steve over to estimate the cost of putting a pool in her yard, the yard wasn't big enough for a pool and she could never afford it—while Nell and Katy were lewdly laughing over the puns and innuendoes possible in asking a man to dig her yard, while they were trying to be sneaky and creative, John simply said to Steve the next day: "Why don't you ask Nell out? She's divorced and she's nice and I know she'd accept."

Steve called Nell that night and asked her out. Nell accepted, then called Katy, silly with excitement. Katy got excited, too: "God," she said. "A contractor for you, Nell. This is just like *Shoot the Moon!*"

They went out to a movie Friday night, then to a bar. They drank beer and talked. Steve was twenty-five, eight years younger than Nell. He was divorced too, and had a little boy, four. He lived on a small farm west of Boston; he had two horses. He didn't try to sleep with Nell that night, but he did ask her to come riding with him that Sunday. And at the door he kissed her so deftly that Nell's body went warm all over, she went right into an adolescent swoon.

By the time Sunday came, Nell was out of her mind. This was her first date since her divorce, her first man other than Marlow in ten years—if she slept with him, the only man other than Marlow in her life. She was terrified.

She'd been awake most of Saturday night, watching out the window at the sky: she was afraid it would rain Sunday and the ride would be canceled. She was afraid the baby-sitter would get sick. She was afraid her children would come down with a serious illness. She was afraid she'd fall in the bathtub and break her leg. She dreamed of the sexual pleasure of riding horses with Steve and perhaps kissing him in the meadow, then going back to stable the horses—perhaps they would embrace and in their frenzy they'd make love in the barn, on the hay! Nell had never done that. She was so glad to be divorced and free for new experiences—she felt young, she felt young enough to think she could fly.

It did not rain. The sitter came. The children stayed healthy all day. Nell did not break a leg. She wore jeans and sneakers and tied her hair back, but not severely, and drove out to Steve's farm. It was a glorious, warm spring day, a perfect apple blossom day. Steve saddled up a horse named Maud for Nell, and together they rode out into the field. They trotted, cantered, walked; they stopped now and then to admire the view. When they looked at each other, it was very much like kissing, and under the sun, out in the meadow, they smiled at each other, wordlessly making a tacit agreement.

They rode for an hour. As they rode, Nell remained aware of Steve's intense sexuality, but slowly she became aware of something else. She had not been on a horse for a long time, for years, and it took all her strength and concentration to ride and post on Maud and not look like a bouncing fool. When they were finally back at the barn and Nell slid off her horse, she landed on legs made of rubber. Pains shot up her thighs and through her pelvis. She looked at Steve, so near her, so masculine and strong, as he hauled off the saddles, tossed them on their hooks, tended to the horses, his muscles bulging through the cloth of his shirt. She looked at him and wanted him, but knew that if she felt anything between her thighs except warm bath water she would cry out in agony. She almost did cry out in frustration.

"How're you doing?" Steve asked.

"I'm really feeling it," Nell said, rubbing her rear.

"So am I," Steve said, misunderstanding her.

He came over and took Nell in his arms and kissed her for a long time on the mouth. He moved his hands up and down her back, her bottom, her legs, pressed her gently against him. Nell did not know if she was shaking because of the horse ride or the man. She and Steve were almost exactly the same height, so that they matched, all up and down, their legs touching, their pelvises pressed together, and then Nell felt a wonderful oblong of hardness pushing through the fabric of Steve's jeans against her body. She had never slept with any man but Marlow. She began to shake, to quiver. Her legs went weak and would not hold her. Her body became a riot of conflicting sensations because of her desire and because of the pain of her body from the horseback ride. She was all warm and sweet between her legs, but at the same time the muscles in her thighs and back cramped and each slight shift of her legs sent a stabbing pain around her pelvis. She didn't know whether to laugh or cry.

"Steve," she said finally, pulling away from his mouth, "I'm sorry. I have to go. I have to go home."

Steve took her face into his hands. "What?" he asked. "What's wrong? Nell, what's the matter?"

She could not bring herself to tell him the truth. It was too embarrassing. She already felt strange and at a disadvantage, being eight years older than Steve: she didn't want him to think she was physically decrepit, already falling apart. She pulled away from Steve and, walking on legs that sent jabs of pain shooting up into her crotch, she hurried to her car. It took all of her dignity and will power to force her legs into a normal walk: if Steve hadn't been there to see her, she would have wobbled, splay-footed and quaking, across the drive to her car. No, she would not have done that—she would have crawled. By the time she got in the car, tears of pain and embarrassment and frustration were in her eyes.

Steve hurried to the car and leaned down to the window. "Nell!" he said. "I don't understand. Did I upset you? What did I do? I didn't mean to come on so strong—"

It was such a relief to Nell to have her bottom, legs, and back supported by the cushioned seat of the car that she nearly cried out. Her traitorous legs quivered, out of her control, and she hoped Steve didn't see them. She wondered if she would even be able to drive the car. "It's not that," she said. "You didn't come on too strong; I wanted you to come on so strong."

"But—" Steve looked at her, baffled.

"I'll call you," Nell said, and started her car and fled. She had spent that evening and every evening for the next three nights sitting in a warm bath of Epsom salts, taking aspirin, glaring at her wobbly, ridiculous weak legs.

Poor Steve. He had misunderstood it all. Nell never did tell him just why she had left that day, because she couldn't. When they did talk about it, Steve told her that he knew she had been scared by the power of their desire for each other—and how could she tell him it had been not lust but agonized legs that had driven her away? She could not humiliate him or herself with the truth.

And in fact it had not been a bad thing that she had driven off in tears, because it made Steve feel responsible to her, considerate of her; he thought she was emotionally more fragile than she was. Oh, she had been fragile—she had been terrified. She had been so terrified that she would not let him have a light on the first time they went to bed together. They made love in total darkness, because Nell was so afraid that if Steve saw her stretch marks, he would say, "Oh my God!" and get up and leave in disgust. But a strange thing happened to Nell with Steve, one of the strangest things that was ever to happen to her in her life. It was a turning point for her, a milestone.

Because Nell had driven off crying, Steve decided that she was sensitive and virtuous and delicate—and she was, in truth, all those things. She had never slept with a man before Marlow, and she had never been unfaithful to her husband, and in the months since their divorce and the few months before that, she had not made love with any man. So she was in fact sensitive, virtuous, and delicate. But she was also wild with lust. She would have gladly jumped into bed with Steve that Sunday afternoon if it had not been for her ridiculous legs. But Steve did not know this and so he set out to court her, to show her that he did not think of her as just another casual piece of ass. It was a very endearing thing for him to do. On their next date, he took her out to dinner and did not try to do more than kiss her when he brought her home. The date after that, the night they did go to bed with each other, he fixed dinner for her himself in his own house. And by that time this strange thing had happened to Nell: she had come to realize that he was not her intellectual equal, and so she stopped being afraid of his judgment. And that made the most enormous difference in her life.

All of her life Nell had been at the mercy of the judgment of men. Because she was pretty, because she so often "won" in the open and hidden competitions between women, she had assumed that she was one of the lucky ones. It wasn't until after her divorce from Marlow that she realized how crippled she really was, how she could not make a move in her life without considering how she would be judged by men. Of course this was magnified in her youth when she was chosen cheerleader, voted homecoming queen, cast as lead in plays; it was magnified a thousand times when she walked out onto an empty stage before male directors to audition for a part. They actually were judging her. Perhaps she had thought, unconsciously, that marriage to Marlow had put a stop to all that, but in fact it had only had the opposite effect. Marlow had judged her every day of their life together and always found her wanting. He had judged her professionally; he had judged her personally. As she grew older, he casually compared her to younger actresses; as she grew more involved with the business of running a home and family, he found her more and more wanting intellectually. With every year that passed between them, Marlow found more and more to judge Nell by: more to condemn her by. She could act, but not as well as any number of the new students in Marlow's classes. She was attractive, but not nearly as attractive as almost every other woman Marlow saw: look at Nell at thirty-three, how her breasts now sagged from nursing, how her stomach was no longer taut and smooth, how it puckered at the navel! She was a good enough mother, but hear how she yelled at her children, listen to them cry! And she had once been intelligent and well read, but now—well, it was ridiculous really, wasn't it? After all, she found time at night, after the children were in bed, to read mysteries and light novels; why couldn't she read Pirandello, Brecht, Albee, why couldn't she keep up with what was happening in the theater, keep up her mind?

There had been a dinner party during the last year of Nell and Marlow's marriage that Nell would never forget. It had been at the home of the president of the college where Marlow taught. It was a sit-down dinner, complete with silver, crystal, Wedgewood, and placecards. Twelve other people were there, gathered around the long lace-covered table, six other university professors and their wives leaned toward each other in the candlelight, engaging in charming and erudite conversation. Jeremy was four, Hannah two. Jeremy was sick with bronchitis, and Nell had been up for three nights in a row with him. She was too tired to come to this dinner party, but she knew she had a responsibility to Marlow to attend; it was an important party, an honor even to be asked, and she knew she owed it to Marlow to be as lovely and witty and winning as she could. She was seated between a professor of Greek and a professor of architecture. Marlow sat across the table from her, two seats down; from time to time he gave her a smile of approval. She had managed, with the art of makeup, to hide the brown circles beneath her eyes. She had managed, with a loose and flowing gown, to hide the flab around her hips. Now she was doing her best to disguise her exhausted and flabby mind.

"I read in the university paper that you just gave a speech in New York," Nell said to the professor of architecture. She was so pleased with herself for remembering this, for thinking of a topic that would interest and even flatter her companion. "What did you speak on?"

"I was comparing Le Corbusier and Alberti," the professor said.

"Oh," Nell replied. She only vaguely knew who Le Corbusier was and hadn't heard of Alberti at all. "Well," she plunged ahead, bravely, wanting to let the professor talk, "what do they have in common?"

"For one thing," the professor said, "they were both interested in the classics at an early age. For example, they were both interested in Plato when they were young."

"Oh," Nell said. "How strange. Surely you don't mean Play-Doh. Play-Doh wasn't around at that time, was it? You must mean clay."

The professor stared at Nell. "Klee?" he said. "What does Klee have to do with the classicists?"

Nell stared at the professor; the professor stared at Nell. Then Nell burst into a whoop of laughter. "Oh dear," she said. "How embarrassing. You meant Plato, and I thought you said Play-Doh." The professor looked at her, sternly uncomprehending. "Play-Doh," she said. "It's a kind of modeling clay that children work with. . . . Well, you know, I have small children at home and I guess I'm at that period in my life when I think of Play-Doh more easily than Plato." She smiled at the professor, thinking surely he had had little children at one time himself and that she could charm him in this way.

But the professor managed only the grimmest of smiles in return and turned, with ill will and exasperation, to his salad. Nell thought then, and agreed with herself later, that the professor had been a pompous, compassionless, humorless old goat. But her opinion of that man had not saved her from Marlow's judgment. He had overheard the entire exchange and did not find it at all amusing. It seemed to him only another sign of Nell's failing intellectual capabilities.

Much later, years later, Nell told her friends about this episode and they dissolved into tears of helpless laughter, laughter of commiseration, for any mother in the world had gone through at least one similar experience. But that night Marlow was not amused.

"Nell, how *could* you," he said, taking her mistake as a personal insult, just as he took her exhaustion and weight gain as a personal betrayal. He judged her very harshly by the end of the marriage, but that was not the worst of their marriage; the worst was that he had judged her at all, that he had judged her from the very start. There were so many women he could compare her to—his first wife, his other lovers, the women he directed or taught—there were always so many ways in which he could compare her and find her wanting. So it happened in Nell's life that not until she wandered into bed with a contractor from a chance encounter in a friend's backyard, not until she was thirty-three, not until she was so very far into her life!—not until then did she realize what she had been missing sexually all her life. Why, she had been very nearly frigid. She had not acted that way, but she had felt that way, and when she discovered this, she thought, oh, what a little fool I have been.

When Steve took her out to dinner, Nell noticed that he did not know the difference between a Chablis and a Beaujolais. It did not bother her that Steve did not know this; it *did* bother her that she had noticed this, that this piddly fact had registered on her consciousness. The evening was full of just such tiny incidents. Nell hated herself for it, but she could not keep herself from silently remarking on the fact that he did not use the subjunctive, that he knew everything about the Indianapolis 500 and nothing about Broadway. The night he invited her out to his farm for dinner, she was touched by the trouble he had gone to, how he had set the table with placemats and cloth napkins and put flowers in the middle of the table. But she also learned, during the course of the meal, that he thought Jerry Falwell and Clint Eastwood were great men, that he found women's lib amusing, that he thought Burt Reynolds was a great actor, that Kenny Rogers was his favorite singer, and his favorite TV show was *Little House on the Prairie*. He loved Mrs. Ingalls because she was so good and pure and patient. Steve showed Nell around his house. He kept guns. He hunted in the fall and stocked his freezer with venison. He needed a gun on his farm, he told Nell, to shoot any wild animal that intruded. Every now and then a rabid fox or raccoon wandered onto the farm and had to be killed before it got into the pigs' pen. And occasionally a wild dog would come and try to attack the pig. He also killed any stray cats that tried to hang around his farm; he didn't have the money or time to bother feeding them. Also, sometimes the cats got in and killed the chickens or got their eggs.

"*You shoot cats?*" Nell asked, incredulous.

"Just wild ones," Steve said. "Just strays."

Nell knew at that moment that this was not the man for her life. If she had been in college, she would have said something righteous and insulting to Steve: "I don't want to have anything to do with a kitten-killer," she might have said. But she was not in college. At that moment in time she was a thirty-three-year-old woman who had not been to bed with a man in months, a woman who was standing next to a man whose sexuality exuded from him and twined around her and pulled her to him like vines around a tree. A flash of memory rescued her, made the decision for her. When Steve came to pick her up that evening, she had not been ready. He had waited for her in the living room. When she came down the stairs, she had found him sitting on the sofa, with Medusa purring in his lap. Steve had been calmly stroking Medusa; Medusa had been nudging her head into his chest, into his crotch, kneading him with her claws, snuggling into his body. Medusa had not shed on him. Her instincts had been to get close to the man—and Nell's were the same. She decided to forget the stray cats and go with Medusa's instincts and her own.

Still, all those petty facts about Steve—that he shot stray cats, used incorrect grammar, and was less sophisticated and educated than she—all those little pieces of knowledge added up to a great gift for Nell. They added up to freedom. She knew that for once in her life this man could not hurt her; if she could laugh at him or even slightly, secretly, deride him, then he could not hurt her. And so she was not afraid of losing him and she was not afraid of his judgment, and when she finally went to bed with him, she had the most wonderful time she had ever had in her life.

Because Steve thought that she was so delicate and frightened, he took care to be a considerate and gentle lover. He spent a long time lying on his double bed with Nell, caressing her, stroking her, kissing her, lifting her hair up and licking her neck, whispering to her not to be afraid. Nell was shivering all over again, and this time with real desire. When he was finally inside her, there in his dark bedroom where no light shone, not even a candle, so that he could not see her expression or body, could only feel her flesh and responses, then she was able to give way to her desire more completely than ever before in her life.

She had always been so afraid with Marlow, right from the start, that she would do something wrong, that she would look odd or not come quickly enough or not be passionate enough or be too passionate—she didn't have any idea about how to make love. She had always, with Marlow, pretended, until she was incapable of doing anything else.

But as she lay with this strange young man's body moving against her, she became aware of these things: that Steve did not love her and so he could not stop loving her. He had promised her nothing and so he could not betray her. She did not love him and so he had no power in him to damage her. He had not committed himself to her and so she would not have to worry that he would ever leave. If he judged her, it did not matter, for they were in the dark and she could not read his face and she trusted him to be kind enough never to let her know if he held her in any contempt. All this knowledge gave her the courage to say at a certain point in their lovemaking: "Please, if you can, don't stop now." And a little while later to say, "Oh, oh, please, could you not stop again?"

As they lay in bed together afterward, flat on their backs, their hands crossed to lie on one another's bare stomachs, Nell wondered if this meant that she was in love with him. Even though she hadn't done a lot, she had certainly *read* a lot, so she considered herself fairly sophisticated. She knew everyone slept around these days; it didn't mean anything. But at heart she was still a romantic. She still wanted to love the person she had sex with: it was called making love, after all. Also, it was pretty hard to believe that a person could have this kind of ravishing transcendent pleasure with just anyone. And she felt so very *fond* of Steve as she lay there next to him, naked and sweaty and exhausted and triumphant and fulfilled. She felt such affection for him because he had made her so replete. She decided that if she did not already love him, perhaps she was on the way. He seemed to be returning the favor, for when at last he drove her home, he held her to him closely at the door and kissed her hair. He treated her gently, with care.

They saw each other almost constantly for three months. He came over after work and ate dinner with Nell and Hannah and Jeremy. He mowed Nell's lawn on Sundays and did other handyman work around her house. In turn, she fixed him wonderful meals. He climbed thirty feet up into a tree, barehanded, to hang a rope-swing for the children; Nell and the kids stood stunned with awe to watch his strength and courage and agility. When he swung down the rope to the ground and landed with a thunk near Nell, his arms bulging with muscles, his shirt full of his powerful chest, Nell nearly smashed her body into his. But the children were there, so she refrained. That night they made wonderful love together, and Steve went on and on inside Nell until Nell, her hair tangled and damp, her body frenzied, cried out, "Oh God, Steve, I love—" She turned her head to one side and bit her bare arm. "I love this," she finished weakly. She was not sure what she meant. She knew that she thought of Steve when she first awoke in the morning and smiled herself to sleep with memories of his body at night. She knew she really was pretty much obsessed with him. While dressing herself or the children, the slight brush of a soft garment against her bare wrist would make her catch her breath. She would stand there a moment, so caught in the vivid memory of their mutual desire and their sweet obeisance to that desire that everything else seemed a dream. She knew that if she went a day without seeing him, she missed him. This was not what she had ever felt for Marlow. It was closer to the emotions she felt in high school, when she was dating quarterbacks and tennis jocks, although she had never slept with any of those boys.

She had taken to watching *Little House on the Prairie* in the evenings when Steve was there. She had even begun to think it wasn't that bad a show, and she tried to push out of her mind the knowledge that Marlow, in his intellectual scorn, had called the show *Little Shack*. When she and her children and Steve were all snuggled together on the sofa, all those touching bodies, all that responding skin, why then Nell was as happy as she had ever been in her life. She didn't actually watch the television. Covertly, she stared at the hairs on Steve's arms, at the long curve of thigh muscle beneath the cloth of his jeans. She and Steve didn't talk much. But when they did, they were very courteous with each other, even gallant in their conversation. Nell began to think that maybe they were really in love. She even began to wonder if they could have a life together.

On Labor Day Steve asked her to come with him to a picnic some friends of his were having. Nell was delighted. She hadn't yet met any of his friends. For three months they had pretty much kept to themselves. She found a baby-sitter. She went to a secondhand store, the Like-New Shop, and found a loose and silky shirt, which she wore with a pair of jeans and sandals. She dressed casually, thinking that Steve's friends would be casual, and she was right. They were not only casual, they were what her parents would have called uncouth.

The picnic was at the "farm" of one of Steve's friends. It was a thirteen-acre piece of land with a small house and a big shed full of tools such as hydraulic drills and winches. There was plenty of beer in cans in a trash barrel full of ice, and chips were set out in bowls on a picnic table. Nell stood awkwardly looking around at the possessions of the owner—they were all out in sight, spread all over the land: a broken bulldozer, an old pickup truck without wheels, a goat in a pen, a pig in another pen, some spare tires, some motorcycles, some mounds of dirt erupting all over the property, looking like Indian burial mounds without the grass. Everyone seemed to know everyone else. Two groups quickly formed: the men by the beer, the women by the chips.

The men were the sort Nell lusted after briefly when stopped at a service station or for road work. They were truckers, road construction workers, factory laborers. They wore jeans, drank beer, smoked pot, talked sports, laughed loud, and looked good. They looked *very good*. Nell didn't know how they thought, for she was quickly relegated to the group of other ''girl friends''—she was by far the oldest. She stood sipping her beer, leaning against the picnic table, listening to the women talk. She was fascinated, not by what the girls had to say, but by their intense absorption in their topics. Nell knew that she often had clever things to say, but she never tried to dominate the conversation in any group, thinking that monologues were rude and often boring, that it was kind to draw others out. But these girls had no such qualms.

''So I said to him,'' said a skinny brunette who was chewing gum and smoking and flicking her hair and ashes with enviable flair, '' 'I put my money in the tip bowl and I told you already I put all my money in the tip bowl, so what are you trying to do, make me out to be some kind of a liar, huh? I don't go for this kind of insult, you know.' And so he says, 'Cheryl, I'm not trying to say you're a liar. I'm not trying to insult you. I'm just trying to figure out how come the money in the tip bowl don't balance with the checks.' So I says, 'Well, that's not my problem, it's yours, and anyway, I think this is some kind of stupid and unfair system you've got going here anyway, you know, because I don't go for this putting all our tips in the tip bowl and then dividing it up at night. *I* think we ought to be able to keep the tips we get. We earn them.' So he says, 'I know that's how you feel, so that's why I suspected you were probably the one who didn't put all your tips in the tip bowl out of spite.' So I says, 'I don't appreciate this kind of insult at all, you know, I am not a spiteful person.' You know I'm not a spiteful person, don't you, Donna. God, would you call *me* a spiteful person? I am not a spiteful person. I would never do anything dishonest out of spite. By this time I am really getting steamed, you know, I am really getting pissed. So I'm standing there with my arms folded, kind of like this, and looked at him right in the face and thought, okay, Twerp, I'm mad at you, now what are you gonna do? So he says . . .''

Nell stared and listened for a long time, engrossed. There seemed to be no end to such stories, no punch lines, not even a satisfactory solution. But the women continued to listen and respond and talk with a mixture of passionate interest and lazy indifference. No one tried to draw Nell into the conversations.

They smiled at her, though, and when it came time to eat, they handed her a paper plate with a hot dog on it, but they didn't try to get to know her or make her feel at ease. Nell was relieved when the conversation stopped so that the women could watch and scream while the men took turns jumping over mounds of dirt with their dirt bikes and motorcycles.

Again Nell watched, fascinated, but now also a little embarrassed. Here she was, less than an hour from the city of Boston, with its ballets and operas and libraries and museums and theaters, standing with a bunch of young women, watching a sort of impromptu dirt bike rally. The men got on their bikes and at first seemed to spend a lot of time just competing to see who could make the most noise revving up. Then, one by one, they went shooting off into the field. Nell could see that it took great strength and a certain athletic skill to get those bikes over the dirt mounds—the men had to pick up the bikes, weighted with their own bodies, and somehow heft or launch them over the mounds. They would go flying up and over the mounds and land with a huge thud on the ground on the other side, then spin away in a turn with a great deal of screeching of wheels. While they were waiting for another turn at the mounds, the men drove their bikes back and forth in front of the women at a terrifying speed, leaning with their bodies so that the bikes tilted at alarming angles to the ground, screaming around in unnecessary hairpin turns, hoisting their machines back and forth over the ground as if they were wrestling with monsters. The men, Steve included, had such determined expressions on their faces; they looked so serious about all this. Nell decided finally that they were all engaged in some unadmitted fantasy: they thought they were on *Chips* or *The Dukes of Hazzard*. It did seem as if everyone at this picnic was somehow engaged in a bizarre sexual ritual involving the newest technology and the oldest ceremonies: men showing off their power in front of adoring women. Finally, Nell was only embarrassed and sad for everyone there. The only consolation she could find was in knowing that no one else could tell how she felt—and if they did know how she felt, they would only, in turn, feel sorry for her. They would think that she was the strange one. These people were so assured, so confident in their actions.

But when Steve finally shut off his bike and got off, slightly swaggering, to walk over to Nell and take his beer from her—she had been holding his can of Pabst for him like some medieval admirer holding a jouster's colors—Nell felt a cold wash of knowledge rush down the inside of her torso, chilling her blood, stilling every sexual response she had felt toward this man. She could not feel sexually desirous of a man she was embarrassed for. The minor mistakes he had made in grammar or sophistication did not really matter; they had only freed her from his judgment. But this bike-jumping business, well, it changed things for Nell. It ruined things. She thought Steve looked so silly jumping a bike over a pile of dirt—why not go around it? And the men took it all so seriously—they might have impressed Hannah and Jeremy, perhaps, and they certainly impressed the other women at the picnic, but they did not impress Nell. She only wondered how on earth she had gotten to such a place.

"You know what I've been doing to strengthen my thigh muscles?"

It was Steve talking. He had taken the beer from Nell, slapped her bottom with hard affection, then gone back to the other men. But Nell was within hearing distance, and she went alert at this question of Steve's; she hoped he wouldn't say that making love to her had strengthened his legs.

"I go out to my dad's farm and ride his cows," Steve said. "Both my horses are too easy; I can't get any challenge out of them. I just climb on the cows bareback with a rope around their necks and hang on . . . those mothers really move."

Nell stared at Steve as he walked off talking to the other men. She saw that he was still the same man she had lusted after: he was still tanned and tough and powerful and handsome and hard. He was all those sexy things. But Nell's mouth twitched and she took a drink of beer in order to stop a grin.

"Hey, Susan," Steve called to a blonde in a halter top and cut-off jeans who was standing near Nell. "Did the McCarthys sell you and Tom that pig?"

"Oh, yeah," Susan answered. "Yeah, and we got a good price. But the bastard wouldn't deliver. We had a hell of a time getting it home on the bike."

Nell couldn't help herself. She didn't know Susan, but she addressed her directly. "You brought a live pig home on a motorcycle?"

"Well, yeah," Susan said. "Tom's pickup broke. We're gonna

feed this pig all spring and summer and butcher it this fall. We had to get it home somehow."

"Well, well, how did you do it?" Nell asked.

"It was hard," Susan admitted. "I couldn't hold on to Tom and hold on to the pig at the same time. Now of course if we had had two pigs, Tom could of put them each in a bag and put one on each end of the handlebar. That would've balanced out nicely. But with just one pig, even a baby pig on a handlebar, well, it throws the balance off, especially around curves. So finally Tom just stuck it inside his jacket. It scratched him like crazy, but we got it home."

"Well," Nell said. She didn't know what to say now. "Well, that's good," she said.

"We're raising chickens now," another woman said, and Nell eased her way out of the group. On the pretense of getting another beer, she walked away slowly and stood by the picnic table with her back to the women. Pigs and motorcycles, she thought; well, there had probably been stranger combinations. These were young people she was with, young people starting their lives in the best way they knew how. Nell did not feel superior to them, but she did feel different. And uncomfortable.

She sipped her beer and looked at the group of men who were now leaning against their trucks, drinking beer, talking, passing around a joint. Every one of the men was as handsome, in one way or another, as Steve. They were all hard, masculine, muscular, tough, sexy young men, full of health and laughter. Perhaps they weren't all as kind as Steve, but she imagined that almost any of those young men would be as good in bed as he was. They were young studs. They were not like the men in movies, the road crew men and contractors who secretly read Camus or had degrees in English literature but did manual labor for philosophical reasons. They were honest-to-goodness working class men who loved their beer, their motorcycles, their farms, and who aspired not to travel to Europe but to Indianapolis to see stock car racing. They didn't read books, attend concerts, see plays, and they wouldn't be impressed by anyone who did. These were Steve's friends, and this was his real world. Nell knew that if she continued seeing him, she would have to see more and more of this world. The two of them couldn't stay in bed all the time.

After the picnic, they rode back to Nell's house on Steve's motorcycle. She had ridden with him twice before, feeling both terrified and amused about it. Jeremy and Hannah had been wild with jealousy to watch their mother go off on the back of a bike, and Steve had given each child short rides up and down the block while Nell held her breath with fear. She couldn't understand what it was about motorcycles that attracted men so. Was it that they liked having all that power between their legs? Didn't they already have enough? Nell rode with her arms wrapped tightly around Steve's waist and her eyes squeezed closed. It made her ill to see the road and houses fly by so fast and to know there was nothing but air between her body and the hard cement or glaring metal of a car. She knew that when she was in her twenties, she would have loved this, would have found it romantic, but now as her hair and shirt fluttered back from the wind, she could only think of the scene in the movie *Isadora* when Isadora Duncan threw her long scarf over her shoulder as she sat in a low convertible and the wind suddenly whipped it behind her into the spokes of the tire and broke her neck.

She was tired when she got home. She felt much older than she had when she started for the picnic. Well, she thought to herself, people have affairs like this all the time: older women, younger men. She had read about it, seen movies about it; she could do it too, couldn't she?

She couldn't.

She couldn't shake from her mind the image of Steve and his friends hauling their motorbikes over the dirt mounds. He came in the house with her and talked to the children and hung around in the kitchen while Nell fixed Hannah and Jeremy dinner, but now everything Steve did irritated her. The children were tired because their baby-sitter had been a young one who loved to play outdoor running games with them. It was eight o'clock, late for their dinner. They were tired, they were cranky. Nell stood at the sink, slicing fresh tomatoes to go with the cheese sandwiches she was grilling for them.

"Go wash your hands," she said to them over her shoulder.

"Ah, Mom," Jeremy wailed. "My hands are clean enough."

"Do what your mother tells you and don't talk back," Steve said, and flicked his finger hard against Jeremy's head, just above his ear.

Jeremy whipped around in his chair to glare at Steve, startled. Then, before Nell could do anything, he jumped up from his chair and left the kitchen. Hannah sat, stunned, staring at Nell and Steve.

"Hannah," Nell said evenly. "Please go wash your hands now."

Hannah quietly got up from the table and left the room.

Nell turned to Steve. "Don't you ever lay a hand on either one of my children again," she said, her voice murderously low.

"Hell, Nell," Steve said. "I scarcely touched him. I didn't hurt him. He's gotta learn to mind his mother."

"It's no business of yours what he has to learn," Nell said. "He is *my* son, and *I* will discipline him and you have no right to touch him. Don't you ever do anything like that again."

"Well, Jesus, how come you're getting so hot under the collar?" Steve said, backing away from her, looking exasperated and hurt.

The children came slinking back into the room then and silently sat down at the table to eat.

"Look, Steve," Nell said. "I'm awfully tired. Why don't you go home. We can talk later."

Steve paused, stared at Nell, his face full of confusion. She knew she was hurting him, surprising him with her sudden lack of warmth, and she regretted it.

"All right," he said. "I'll call you." He started to move toward the door, then stopped and turned to Jeremy. "Jeremy," he said. "I'm sorry I snapped you in the head. Your mom told me never to touch you like that again. I was only trying to remind you to mind your mom. But I'm sorry if I hurt you or hurt your feelings. Okay?"

Jeremy took on the sort of shifty-eyed look he always got when confronted by adults with a touchy situation. "Okay," he said.

"I'll call you," Steve said to Nell, and went out the door.

"Fine," Nell said, but did not have the energy to say it loudly enough to be sure he heard.

She sat down at the table, where her children were eating their sandwiches in silence, and she leaned her elbows on the table and put her head in her hands. Steve had so many of the wrong instincts—and so many of the right ones. If only he hadn't apologized to Jeremy, how clear-cut things would be for her.

"I'm sorry Steve hit you, Jeremy," she said. "I told him not to do it again, and I'm sure he won't."

"It's okay, Mom," Jeremy said. "He didn't hurt me."

"Don't look so sad, Mommy," Hannah said.

"Yeah," Jeremy said. "We *like* Steve."

Nell stared at Hannah. Oh shit, she thought, they like Steve. But she said, "You're two good kids."

She put the children to bed, then took a long, soaking hot bath.

The silence and heat relaxed her, and soon she was chuckling to herself over the events of the day, thinking how Katy would laugh when she described the picnic and the pigs and the motorbike contests to her.

As she was getting out of the bathtub, just reaching for a towel, there was a knock at the door. She hurriedly dried, slipped into her robe, and went down the stairs. Her long hair was wet at the ends from the bath and clung to her shoulders and back; she could feel it through the robe. She was too tired to care much who could be knocking. It was Steve.

"I'm sorry if I got you out of the bath," he said, leaning on the doorframe. "I just felt so bad when I left earlier, I thought I'd come back and talk with you about it."

"Oh, Steve, that's nice of you," Nell said. "I'm sorry I was so grumpy. Come on in. Do you want some coffee?"

They went into the kitchen. There was a moment when Nell, at the stove in only her robe, barefoot, wet-headed, heating the singing kettle for instant coffee, turned and saw Steve seated at the kitchen table, idly looking at the evening's newspaper, and she felt at home. This was a familiar and comforting way to be: a man and a woman, intimate in the kitchen of the house. And Steve had not changed. He was sexy and he was kind. She was relaxed. She wanted to go to bed with him.

"Nell, I'm sorry I made you mad by hitting Jeremy," Steve said. "But then when I got home, I started thinking about it. Started thinking you and I better talk about it. You know, your kids could use a man around now and then. And you know, well, we've been going together for three months now, and—" he stopped.

"And what?" Nell said. She had fixed the mugs of coffee for herself and Steve and now she brought them to the table, moving slowly, almost dreamily, in a sort of warm trance of sexuality. She was so lazy-minded from her bath. She felt her clean soft skin under her comfortable robe. She saw Steve's strong body there, solid on the chair. Soon they would be in bed together. In a few minutes she would be lying naked with his body against hers. She was not really listening to his words.

"And I think we should talk about a few things," Steve went on. "I'm beginning to be pretty serious about you, you know. I don't have much to offer you, but—"

"Jesus!" Nell said. She tripped over the leg of a chair and spilled hot coffee down her robe. "That's *hot!* Ouch. Damnit! Steve, here, take your coffee. I've got to go change out of this robe."

She set both mugs on the table, her mug still sloshing over with brown liquid, and she fled from the kitchen, up the stairs. She quickly changed into jeans and a sweatshirt, and the entire time she was thinking: "Oh no, now what am I going to do?" It sounded very much as though Steve were on the way to proposing marriage, or at least some serious arrangement, and she knew she wasn't ready for that.

Now, years later, that evening with Steve was one of the evenings of her life that Nell tried to forget. Or rather she tried to forget the details and tried to hang on to the moral, which was: for God's sake, be careful! Steve had thought he was in love with her. He had thought she was in love with him. Had thought he would make a good father to her children. Had thought they might someday get married.

Nell had explained to him as kindly as she could that it was just too soon for her. She had been divorced such a short time. She liked Steve, and she loved being in bed with him, but she wasn't sure, in all honesty, if she was in love with him. She thought it was too soon, too early, for her to really fall in love.

"Well, I don't know how you can carry on in bed like that unless you love me," Steve said.

"I don't either," Nell said. "But come on, give me a break. After all, we both carried on that first night together, and we weren't either of us in love with the other one then."

"Oh yeah?" Steve said. "That's what you know."

They had fought. Nell had cried. To their mutual and awful dismay, Steve had cried. Not much, but enough to make him go red in the face with chagrin. Finally, they agreed not to see each other anymore.

"I really thought I was in love with you," Steve said. "I really thought you were in love with me. I can't see you anymore knowing you just think this is all some kind of half-assed temporary thing."

He had left angrily, and for good. Nell had cried some more. She had sat in the kitchen and held Steve's mug in her hands and put her mouth where she imagined his lips had been and cried.

But in her heart of hearts she knew she was a traitor, for in among the hot muddle of emotions was a pure clean breeze of relief. She had gone on too long not introducing him to her friends, afraid he would embarrass her or feel inferior. She had gone on too long sitting through *Little House on the Prairie* shows with him when she would have preferred to read a book. She had gone on too long using him, as she had heard men use dumb blondes. At the Labor Day picnic, she had tried, and failed, to meet one of his friends with whom she could feel at ease. She had grown hot and impatient and bored and scornful at that picnic, watching the men on their motorbikes. She could never have a long-term relationship with Steve; she could never marry him.

But how horrible it was that she had hurt him. How incredibly insensitive she had been not to see that he thought he was falling in love with her. She thought all those young men just slept around casually with anyone, without ever taking it seriously. It had not given her any kind of pleasure or satisfaction at all to see Steve in tears. It had been as painful for her as seeing one of her children humiliated; it had been a wretched, excruciating moment. She thought of Steve going home alone to his farm, lying by himself in his double bed with the venetian blinds pulled shut against the night and his muddy boots dropped in the middle of the floor. She thought of how foolishly men handled their misery, hiding it in the dark, away from the eyes of others—that was what Steve would do, she was certain. He would not seek solace from his friends. He had already been hurt enough by exposing his emotions to her. She thought of how his face crumpled when she said she agreed that it would be better if they didn't see each other again, and at the memory of his face like that, Nell's heart crumpled inside her, a waste-paper heart, a useless heart, crushed in the fist of circumstance.

She had never meant to hurt that proud man. But she *had* hurt him, and she had done it as unwittingly as any fool. She was not a heartless bitch, but she might as well have been; the result was the same. She sat in the kitchen until three in the morning and disliked herself every minute of that time.

And that was her first time around.

Just months after her divorce from Marlow, she had met and enjoyed and hurt and lost Steve. Wow, Nell had thought, how does all of this happen? Who's in charge here? she wondered, and supposed that where love was concerned, no one was.

That fall she dated no one. Men asked her out, but she was too wary. She didn't want to hurt them; she didn't want to get hurt herself. And she was busy with her baby-sitting, too tired at night to simulate intelligence and charm. She just got her own children to bed and got in bed herself with a good book.

That fall turned into winter and the bills came in and Nell began to worry about money. She began to dream of money. She dreamed literal dreams about figures and dollars and columns of numbers. She dreamed convoluted, disguised money dreams, terrible dreams in which she sold the children she baby-sat to robotlike men who came knocking at her door for money, wild nightmarish dreams of walking black windy city streets with Jeremy at one hand and Hannah at the other, all of them crying with hunger, and she could see Jeremy's toes sticking through his sneakers and Hannah's elbows sticking through holes in her sweater. Nell would awake from these dreams sweating and panicked, her heart pounding an urgent drum-call in her chest: Fire, Help, Emergency, SOS, DANGER. She was tired all that fall and winter, and frightened. Jeremy got pneumonia. Marlow was in Europe, a guest professor at the Sorbonne; he was on half salary at the college and could keep up with the legally decreed child support payments but could give her no more. He was too far away to help, even to take the children for one night so she could have a rest. He was in many ways a great distance from her plight and the children's. She was really alone.

Every morning that winter she would wake at six, dress, start the coffee, and begin to receive the babies and little children who were dropped off to her. As the weeks passed, Nell began to take on a maternal role in the lives of the parents as well as the children. They would come in, drop off their babies and the litter of bottles or potty chairs or Pampers, and complain. The best ones complained of tests they had to take for degrees, jobs they had to do, bosses who were mean. The worst ones complained of exhaustion from organizing charity luncheons and even the terror of a husband discovering a love affair. Nell listened to them all with good will and gave them sympathy and a cup of coffee and sent them on their way, then dealt with their children. More and more children began to come. More and more money was added up in her notebook. Finally, Nell could breathe a little more easily about the bills, although it was always a struggle and she was never far from panic. It was only late that spring, when the O'Learys lured her to work in the boutique, that she had any real sense of financial security. Along with the sharp, biting anxiety about money, a deeper, more thrumming fear set itself up inside her. Was this it? Was this how her life was to be? She was thirty-four! She was unloved, and she seldom left her house except to go to the grocery store or the library or the druggist. She did not have the life she deserved, the life she had planned. She was lost and could see no hope of change.

Women would come to her house to drop off their children for the day, women with violet boots made in a leather so buttery Nell wanted to bite them. Women with clever, stylized coats, women with fur coats. Women who took their big diamond engagement and thick gold marriage rings off and slipped them inside their purses, casually, as they went out Nell's door. Women who left their babies to go have facials and manicures and pedicures and lovers. Nell wore her navy blue corduroy jumper and a variety of old turtlenecks. The children didn't care what she looked like, and someone was always peeing down her front anyway. Nell watched all those women leave her house and looked at herself and her life with a growing dismay. She did not have enough money to go out to lunch with friends or to the movies. All her money went toward paying the oil and electric bills, toward food, toward clothes for her children. She began to keep sterner accounts of the time she baby-sat. She had charged people by the half hour; now she charged them for each additional fifteen minutes, and even five minutes counted toward an additional fifteen. People were so cavalier about her time. They knew she liked the children and that she wasn't going anywhere else anyway, so they were sometimes hours late picking up their children. But they paid their bills without complaining.

It was in February that Nell met Ben. Careful Ben. He was such a reserved man, such a really icy character, that Nell was certain she could never hurt *his* feelings. He was recently divorced and seemed to simply want the company of a reasonably pleasant woman. He took her to movies, concerts, ballets, plays— he took her out to dinner, and she did almost love him just for that. It seemed she had never known such joy as that of being seated in a quiet, candle-lit restaurant with a good wine set before her in a goblet and fat shrimp in ice in front of her and a thick sirloin steak on the way. When Ben took her to bed, she lay there licking her teeth and remembering, bite by bite, the food they had eaten earlier in the day. Ben was an uninspired lover and, after the first few times, almost an uninterested one. He just sort of climbed on Nell and came and got off again and never paid much attention to how she might feel about it all. Nell didn't know what to give Ben in exchange for the pleasures he gave her. Sex didn't seem sufficient; he didn't seem to enjoy being in bed with her nearly as much as she enjoyed eating the dinners he took her to. She tried harder each time she was with him to be animated and charming, to compliment and entertain him; if she couldn't make him happy, she thought at least she could keep him from being bored. But she never thought about Ben when she was not with him. She never longed to see him. She never said one word of endearment to him or pretended that their embraces moved her very much.

So she was startled when, after only three months of dating Ben asked her to marry him. She was so startled she almost laughed in his face. She didn't, of course, laugh in his face, but she did refuse his offer of marriage; she did tell him that she did not love him. And it seemed to her when she looked into his eyes that night, when she looked through the thick lens of his glasses into his eyes, that she could see something glittering there, like the change of light at the end of a long hall when an opened door is pulled shut. She saw that she had hurt Ben. It was a comfort to her to know that at least he was a man incapable of being deeply hurt. After that night, he went off on a cruise in the Caribbean and they didn't see each other again.

That was the second time around.

After that, Nell became even more careful about going out with men, about sleeping with men. One year she dated no one at all. Then she became lonely, so lonely that she thought she would pay money, take money from her children, to have some man just put his arms around her. And she did a forbidden thing, a thing she thought she would never do: she slept with another woman's husband. Mark had a reputation for sleeping around, as did his wife. Nell checked this all out in advance. He was the type of man who got his kicks from sleeping around, and there never was any question of love or marriage between him and Nell. That was a great relief to Nell. She almost felt like someone who met him once a week for a game of squash or tennis, so unemotional was their contact with each other. But he got bored with Nell after a while and moved on to sleeping with someone new.

During the five years after her divorce, she fell in love too, once or twice, for a week or two or a month or two, or thought she did. She was hurt, she was left, she tried not to think about those times. The only consolation was in their brevity.

She would have gotten bitter after a while if she had not had so many other friends who were going through the same sort of thing: falling in love with the wrong man, trying to trust and being forsaken, over and over again. One drunken night she and a friend who had recently been left by men decided that their lives were really nothing more than a cosmic comedy act for bored gods. The Boob Sisters Fall in Love . . . And Fall in Love . . . And Fall in Love . . . And Fall in Love . . . Laughter saved them, friendship saved them, and Nell was at the point in her life when she believed in little else save laughter and the friendship of women. She began to regard people like John and Katy Anderson, people with happy marriages, as mortals who had been blessed with miracles, part of the miracle being that they didn't know how miraculous their lives were.

For the past three and a half months, Nell had been dating Stellios Xouris, the man who had provided for Nell the experience she had been secretly expecting all her life.

It had been early January, a Saturday—Nell's day off and her one chance to do a week's worth of errands. It had snowed and melted and frozen over already; the air was cold and gray and the streets a sheet of treacherous, slush-covered ice. Nell had a cold. She was wearing jeans, boots, a grungy old sweatshirt under a grungy old sweater, her parka, and a wool cap. There was no man in her life. One of the cats had thrown up odiously on the hall rug, which was wool and too heavy for her washing machine. Nell begrudged the expense of having the rug cleaned; she hated having to lug it to the cleaners; she wanted someone else to take care of this particularly repellent task. She was wearing no makeup, but her slight fever had made her eyes bright and her cheeks rosy, and as she passed the hall mirror on the way to the car, she regretted the absence of some man to notice and admire the flare and glow of her hair and face, her hot prettiness on this cold, drab day. She yelled to her children that they must keep cleaning their rooms, that she'd be right back, and set off in her car for the dry cleaners on Mass. Ave.

Something had broken: a gas line, or a water line, or something. Half a block on either side of the dry cleaners was torn up, and three men were cursing and mucking about at the edge of the sidewalk, throwing broken cement around. The entrance to the dry cleaners was an obstacle course of slick ice and jagged chunks of pavement. Nell had parked her car two blocks away, grabbing the first available spot she saw. She had lugged the heavy rug this far—now, suddenly, the impossibility of negotiating it over the broken curbing hit her like a tragedy. She thought she would die right then and there—a stupid, mediocre death brought on by one too many inconveniences in her life.

As she stood at the edge of the work area, trying to decide whether to try to negotiate her way through the cement, shovels, pipes, and picks or to just drop the rug and leave it there forever, one of the workmen looked at her. He stood up and walked over to where she was standing.

"You want to go to the cleaners?" he asked, his speech heavily accented.

Nell looked at him. Automatically but unemotionally, she noted that the worker was tall, slim, dark, and handsome.

"Yes," she replied, glaring. She felt anger flare up inside her because he was young and strong and good-looking, the type who'd throw cement around, build up his muscles, then impress some pretty young woman at a bar tonight and have only pity or disdain for a poor exhausted working mother like Nell.

"Wait!" he exclaimed. "You must wait!"

While she stood, startled (was he an inmate loose from an asylum, out on a work permit, perhaps?), the man began to build a path for her, a bridge of cement blocks over the slush and dirt.

"Here." He gestured at last. "For you. You must not trip and fall. And I will carry your package for you."

"Oh no," Nell said, more alarmed than anything else. What about his foreman, she wondered, wouldn't he be angry that his worker left the job?

"Please," the young man said, extending his hand. "I *must. You* are a *princess.*"

Well, Nell thought, *at last. Someone's finally noticed.* She smiled at the man, surprised, pleased, delighted—and not for one minute doubting his seriousness.

During her childhood she had had a favorite fantasy: somehow it would be discovered that her kind, ordinary school-teacher parents had adopted her and that she was actually the child of the grand monarch of some lovely foreign country. When she rode in the back seat of her parents' Ford station wagon, she had pressed her face against the window, hoping that someone on the street or in another car would see her and cry out, "Stop! That's *my* daughter!" She would be rescued and restored to her proper parents and rightful place as a *princess*. It was a purely irrational fantasy, filled with detailed images of the glittering, beribboned gowns and bejeweled tiaras she would wear as princess—but lacking the explanations of why she had been taken from her parents in the first place, how she had come to live in the unprincesslike locale of Des Moines, Iowa, or exactly where her new realm was located on the map—all that was vague, a blur of circumstances that didn't interest her much.

As she grew older, though, the fantasy changed, became more rational, more focused. She was not *born* a princess—that was a stupid dream. No. She would *become* a princess. She would meet and marry a prince. Grace Kelly had done it, after all. It truly happened in the real world.

But it didn't happen to Nell. Realism finally prevailed, and by her late teens she had traded the princess fantasy for the actress dream. Still, those old yearnings never really went away. Nell knew there weren't many women alive who, nurtured on Cinderella stories in the crib, didn't secretly envy and identify with Lady Di, even in their wise maturity.

Stellios's words were magic, the ultimate seduction. *He* could see past the jeans and smelly rug to the truth: Nell was a princess.

"Thank you so much," she had said, letting him take the rug from her. "It is heavy," she added, flashing a dazzling smile, "although it probably won't seem so to you."

He followed her into the cleaners. The owner took a blessedly long time to appear after the bell on the shop door announced their arrival, so Nell and Stellios became friends and exchanged telephone numbers.

Stellios courted Nell with diligence and flourish. He brought her blossoming flowers in the dead of winter, bottles of sweet wine, records recorded by men with smoldering dark eyes singing sentimental ballads. He continued to treat Nell with courtesy even after he realized she was not, in spite of her education and large house, wealthy. And Nell continued to see him even after he confessed to her that his dream was to marry a wealthy American woman. She had no doubt that he'd succeed. He was handsome, gentle, quick-witted. She wished him well.

Stellios had been born in Greece and had grown up there, yet in many ways he reminded Nell of Steve, the young and very

American man Nell had dated just after her divorce. Like Steve, Stellios was a manual laborer, a young, hard, strong, sexy, uneducated, rather simple man. Nell was beginning to think that perhaps this was the sort of man she was destined to meet for the rest of her life. She met so many of these types, young muscular jocks who coached Jeremy's baseball team or painted her friends' houses. She wasn't sure what to do about this—wasn't sure she wanted to do *anything* about this. This sort of man provided for Nell the temporary pleasure of companionship without that dreadful specter of Serious Intention lurking in the background. She never had to think whether she would give up some part of her freedom in order to make the relationship last—she knew it wouldn't last from the start. So she was relieved rather than threatened to know that there could be nothing permanent between her and Stellios.

Back in Greece, Stellios had been engaged to a young woman who suddenly ran off with another man; rather than commit suicide or murder—for Stellios was passionate and sincere in his actions and emotions—he had fled to America. Now he lived with one of his mother's aunts, surrounded by loving and watchful relatives. Nell had been to dinner at the Xourises several times and the assemblage of cousins and Greek friends had been pleasant to her, easily affectionate. But they had made it quite clear that Nell was not the right woman for Stellios—she was several years older than he, and divorced, with children—! She was, in their eyes, a kind of tramp, whose body would provide for Stellios a smooth and pleasurable final passage from his native country to the new one. The men at the Xouris house touched Nell. They hugged her when she arrived or left, patted her bottom or arm, and complimented her effusively. They told her she carried herself like a queen. The women stood in the background, judging Nell with their eyes.

So Nell had thought she was safe enough with Stellios. They provided pleasant company for each other, with no chance of involvement, no chance of pain. They really were good for each other, for a while. Nell helped Stellios improve his language and his manners without embarrassing him; she taught him useful things like how to light and use a charcoal grill and how to dance without clapping his arms above his head or waving them in the air. In turn, Stellios was a charming escort who complimented Nell intelligently, noticing the things she wanted a man to notice—a new dress, a new way of wearing her hair, her slender ankles. He was sensitive to her moods and rubbed her back when she was in her period. She had been perfectly content to enjoy his company and was prepared to watch him move on, when the time came, with no regrets at all. There wasn't a doubt in her mind that every day while he worked for the city road crew, digging here and there on the streets of Cambridge, he said to each promising woman he saw: "Please. Let me carry that for you. You are a princess." It was only a matter of time, Nell knew, until a man as handsome as Stellios met another woman who knew in her heart that she was a princess and would let Stellios become her prince.

But recently Stellios had been acting strangely—serious. He was acting as if he were in love with Nell. He was beginning to bring her roses, ice cream sundaes, dreadful (he didn't know they were dreadful; he liked the TV ads) perfumes. He was playing up to the children more and more, playing ball with them, even going up to kiss them good night at bedtime. And he was looking at Nell with a different expression on his face. He had even mentioned living in the house: "If I lived here, I'd tear out the fireplace and put in a wood stove. They're more efficient." Nell knew what he was up to; he was trying to believe he was in love with her. And she did not want him to be in love with her. They had so little in common except good will toward each other. He loved sports, was baffled by drama and music; he loved to go to amusement parks and ride the roller coaster—oh, they really had nothing in common, except, perhaps, loneliness. She knew Stellios better than he knew himself. She knew he wanted to believe he loved Nell so that the pain of his fiancée leaving him would be lessened. She had thought they would help each other, that she would, simply by being his lover and friend, help him in his desolation. But now she saw that it would be no help and perhaps even more harm if she continued the affair with him.

But she didn't want to end the affair, either; he was the only man she was seeing these days, the only man on the horizon. In the past five years she had learned very well to do most things alone: she could manage the house, hold down a job, keep two children healthy and happy, take sustenance from her friends, and live a pretty pleasant life. But in spite of all her intelligence, in spite of all her love of books and drama and movies and friends, she still took the most pleasure from an intimate association with a man. It was not just the sex, although that was of course a great part of it. It was all the other things: she liked the sound of men's voices, the male presence they exuded, like a scent of sage or bayberry, around her house. She liked the way they always surprised her with the way they thought; so different from the way she and her friends thought. She thought of woman as having fiction minds and men as having non-fiction minds, and she liked having men around in the same sort of way that she liked looking at *Time* magazine or the evening news. She might not agree with everything that was said, but it opened up her world to know such viewpoints were there.

It would be the kindest thing to do to break things off with Stellios before he got more involved, more liable to hurt. But the summer was coming, the lovely season when laziness and sensuality spread through her limbs like a lazy stream through a meadow. The evenings would be long; she did not want to sit on her porch and sip strawberry daiquiris alone every night. The summer was coming, when men took off their flannel shirts and sweaters and went around in cut-off jeans and T-shirts, when she could see the hair, the sweat, the muscles of their arms and legs and backs. . . . The summer was the worst time to be alone. She knew that. She had spent summers alone, lying in bed at night, drinking iced tea and reading a mystery and trying to ignore the soft summer breeze that blew gently in her window and played across her skin. She did not want to hurt Stellios, but she did not want to be alone in the summer. It seemed to her that as the years had passed she had compromised greatly with life, she had learned to ask for less and less and less. Now she did not even ask for love or the security of marriage, now she only asked for—for what? For a little more pleasure in her life.

She did not know what to do. She did not understand why nothing in her life would be uncomplicated. She worked so hard; why could nothing come or stay easy? She lay in her bath a long time, waiting for the heat to soothe her, waiting for some answer to come. She lay there until all the bubbles evaporated into the air and the water cooled to lukewarm and she was left looking down through transparent water at her foolish fleshy body, which never could seem to learn not to ask for more.

Four

SUNDAY night Stellios insisted on taking Nell to a restaurant she knew he couldn't really afford. When she tried to convince him she would prefer pizza or Italian food, he was offended, and she saw that it would hurt his ego more than his pocketbook for her to refuse to let him give her this treat. At the restaurant he gazed at her with great affection and constantly held her hand, so that it was difficult to eat. She silently vowed to have a discussion with him, to tell him that they should stop seeing each other, that they were getting too serious for their own good. She intended to do this. She wanted to wait until they left the restaurant—she didn't think it would be fair to dump something like that on him in the middle of a wonderful meal.

But the ride in the car to the apartment in his aunt's house was too brief for them to have an emotionally involving discussion. So she went into the apartment with him and turned to face him, her face stern. "Stellios," she began, and he took her in his arms and kissed her. Her good resolutions faded. She went to bed with him. He had a beautiful body. And she knew she was making him happy—it seemed the right thing to do.

After they had finished making love, Nell lay in his arms, feeling all flushed and drowsy, completely relaxed, her good intentions forgotten, until she heard Stellios whisper in her ear, "You mean so much to me." Then she felt a chill pass straight through her and she went all tense and miserable. She did not want to mean so much to him. And now she knew that each time she was with him she would be encouraging him to let her mean more. But she could not bring herself to speak of breaking off— not then, when they were lying so close together. She only hugged him and made a noncommittal "umm" sound into his chest.

Finally, he drove her home. She did not sleep well. She got up in the middle of the night and took a shower, as if cleansing or baptising herself, as if she would be a new, calmer, better person after the ritual. She still did not sleep well.

She was plagued by old superstitions, old patterns of guilt and fear. She had certain mental habits that were as ingrained as her ways of walking and holding a fork, and one of these was left over from her childhood: she believed that any bad news that befell her was somehow the result of some previous bad deed she had done, and so guilt was always with her, foreshadowing even the beginning of any selfish act. She could not go out to dinner with a friend or to bed with a man or even read an enjoyable novel if her children were on a car trip with Marlow, until she knew they had all arrived at their destination safely. Now, even with children as old as eight and ten, she could not leave the house for an evening at a concert, no matter how expensive the tickets, if the children were sick. She knew her superstitions were irrational, illogical, and often inconsistent, but she couldn't shake them any more than she could change the color of her eyes. There resided within her some primitive belief that even the tiniest of sins on her part would bring about certain and disproportionate disaster.

So it did not surprise her on Monday, when after making marvelous love with Stellios on Sunday, that all sorts of strange things fell from the sky in the nature of changes and sorrows. Monday morning Jeremy awoke feverish and vomiting.

She knew a flu was going around. After the first round of vomiting, Jeremy's stomach seemed to settle down and he was able to keep down some ginger ale. She got Hannah dressed and off to school and settled Jeremy in front of the TV. He still wore his pajamas, and she brought down his pillow and favorite blanket. She pushed a low table near the sofa and put on it a glass of ginger ale and a large bowl, in case he had to throw up again. By the time she had to leave to open the boutique, his fever had dropped. She brought the phone in and plugged it into the jack in the TV room wall; he could easily call her if he felt sick again. She had left him before, and he had been fine. He would spend the day sleeping, watching TV, feeling sick, waiting for her to come home, slightly pleased at missing school. She would spend the day worrying about him, trying to be pleasant to customers, phoning him and wishing she could stay home and tend him the way her mother had tended her when she was ill.

When she got to the boutique, she found Elizabeth O'Leary already there.

"I didn't know you were in town," Nell said, hoping Elizabeth wouldn't notice that she had come in just a few minutes late.

"Oh, I just buzzed in," Elizabeth said, making a graceful silly gesture with her hand. Her rings flashed. "Listen, Nell, let's leave Arlene here to take care of things. It's always slow in the morning. Let's go have coffee. I want to talk to you."

Now Nell nearly threw up. If she lost this job—she would die if she lost this job. There was no reason for her to be fired, but Nell could think of no other reason for Elizabeth to want to talk. And she was being so obsequious, holding the door open for Nell, complimenting Nell on the way she looked, when Nell knew that Elizabeth's clever eye could guess precisely the price of Nell's clothes and at just which unfashionable department store she had bought them.

"Listen, darling," Elizabeth said when they were seated across from each other at Helen's Coffee Shop. "Order anything you want. You look like you could use a good breakfast."

"I'm not hungry," Nell said. "I've already had enough breakfast. If I eat any more, Elizabeth, I won't fit into your beautiful clothes."

"Well, then." Elizabeth smiled, and ordered two Swiss almond coffees for them. She turned back to Nell. "Listen, darling," she said again. "You know we think you've done a divine job at the boutique here."

Nell felt an icicle plunge into her chest. If any statement ever sounded like the preamble to a dismissal, this one did.

"So we're going to ask you a *huge* favor," Elizabeth went on. "The Nantucket shop is open now after being closed for the winter. And we're planning to open a new shop in New York this fall. That means we have to be down there all summer—God, the *worst* possible time to be there, we'll die of the heat—setting up the shop, ordering, getting things ready. One thing we've learned is that we just can't trust the design and set-up of a store to anyone else. It's the same old thing: if you want something done right, you have to do it yourself. Anyway, dear, what I'm getting at is this: Colin and I want you to go to Nantucket for the summer and manage the shop there."

Nell, stunned past words, looked at Elizabeth.

"Have you ever been to Nantucket?" Elizabeth asked. "No? You'll *love* it there. It's *divine*. We've just loved being there. But we can't find anyone who's as good-looking and sensible and reliable as you are to take over for us. People like to drift there. We need someone who will not skip out on us in the middle of the season. The summer season in Nantucket is very, very big.''

"But," Nell began, "I can't just go there. Where would I live?"

"Oh, don't worry about that. We'll give you our house to live in—and we'll give it to you rent-free, of course. Why, in a way it's as if we're offering you a holiday, Nell. You can walk on the beach and in the moors, eat at fabulous restaurants, meet gorgeous people . . . people *kill* to live in Nantucket for the summer. You'll have our little house, and you can make your own hours; we know you'll need at least three part-time girls there."

"But you see," Nell said, "the children—"

"Well, the children spend a lot of their summer with their father, don't they? That was *my* understanding."

"Yes," Nell said. "Yes, they do spend a lot of the summer with Marlow. But not all of it. I don't know what his plans are. And really, I wouldn't want to be away from the kids for the entire summer—"

"That's crazy," Elizabeth said. "Here you have a chance for a yummy vacation, no little whiners to slow you down, and you aren't happy. Anyone else would jump at the chance."

"Well, I'm sorry," Nell said, bristling. "But Hannah and Jeremy aren't little whiners in the first place, and in the second place, I enjoy having them in my life. Most of the time."

Elizabeth was quiet awhile. "Well," she conceded, "I don't see any reason why they couldn't stay in the house too. There are four bedrooms. As long as they were—well, you know how messy children can be."

"Look," Nell said. "I know you're trying to do me a favor, Elizabeth, but the idea of going away from my home for the summer just doesn't appeal to me."

"I suppose you're talking about men," Elizabeth said. "Listen darling, I don't know who you're seeing now, but you'll find more gorgeous men in one square yard on Nantucket than in the whole town of Arlington."

"I'm *not* talking about men," Nell said. "I'm talking about—everything. I work hard to keep my life organized, Elizabeth. I work hard to keep my life centered. And my house and my friends and my bedroom and my routines are all very important to my sanity."

"We'll give you a substantial raise in salary and a summer bonus," Elizabeth said.

Nell looked at Elizabeth, shocked. Elizabeth must have thought that she, Nell, was negotiating for something, Nell realized with surprise. And all Nell was doing was telling the truth.

"Look," Elizabeth went on, repeating herself. "The truth is that you really are doing a fabulous job, Nell, and there's no one we can find anywhere who can do all you do—who can look so good and be so honest and reliable and sensible. We really need you. And believe me, you *will* love Nantucket. It's beautiful. Everything about it is beautiful. Just ask *anyone*. I wouldn't send you to the moon, you know."

They drank their sweet coffee; they talked more, but Nell knew at that point that she really had no choice. She could run the store in Nantucket, or she could lose her job. Elizabeth had a beautiful smile but a heart of lead. And she had made up her mind; there was no argument Nell could make that Elizabeth couldn't counter. Fortunately for Nell, Elizabeth countered a lot of Nell's objections—who would take care of the house and animals while she was gone, how would she manage child care while she worked—with offers of more money. Visions of solvency began to dance in Nell's head.

Still, Nell was more rattled and worried than pleased when she and Elizabeth finally left the coffee shop. The women parted ways. Elizabeth walked down to her white Mercedes convertible, and Nell walked back to the boutique. She would have to talk to Marlow right away, to see what he and Charlotte had planned for the summer, to see how long they could take the children. She would have to find some responsible person to live in the house and watch the animals for the summer. She would have to line up baby-sitters for the brief trips Elizabeth wanted Nell to make over to Nantucket in May in order for Nell to get to know the shop. Well, if nothing else, she supposed this would make it easier to break things off with Stellios. Out of sight, out of mind, and so on, she thought. She wondered how Jeremy was; she would phone him as soon as she got in the store.

But when she got to the boutique, she found the salesgirl, Arlene, standing bewildered in a pile of their most expensive clothes. No customers seemed to be in the store, only young, glossy-faced Arlene, standing there at the back by the dressing rooms. When she saw Nell, she made a gesture with her hands and an expression with her face that indicated complete helpless confusion. Then a scarlet silk jacket came flying out of one of the dressing rooms, landed against Arlene, and slipped to the floor.

"That one, too," a voice said.

Nell recognized the voice at once; it was Ilona Shell. Nell stalked to the back and pulled open the thick dressing room curtain.

"Ilona," she said. "What on earth are you doing?"

"I'm getting ready for the summer!" Ilona said. "I'm getting ready for the summer of my life!"

The dressing room was spacious and marvelously lit, with mirrors angled on two walls so that the customer could see the back view as well as the front. The third wall was papered in Laura Ashley paper and studded with heavy brass hooks. There was a white wrought-iron chair in the corner and a white wrought-iron table to hold the customer's purse, shopping bags, and so on. The rooms could be beautiful—one would wish for a house so lovely—but this dressing room had become a disaster area. Clothes were everywhere, so many outfits hanging from the hooks that they were nearly bending under the weight. Some of Elizabeth O'Leary's most expensive orders were scattered on the floor at Ilona's feet, orange silks mixed with wheat-colored cotton mixed with black linen. Ilona stood in the middle of it all in her sapphire-blue underwear—stood swaying in the middle of it all, red-eyed.

"Jesus Christ," Nell whispered. She stepped into the room and sniffed. "Ilona, are you *drunk?*" For the second time that morning, Nell almost retched. She could no more drink alcohol in the morning than wake up and take a ride on a roller coaster.

Ilona laughed. "Here I am," she said, waving at Nell through a mirror. "That's me, in Three-D; drunk, divorced, and delighted."

"Divorced?" Nell said. "Ilona, what are you talking about? You're not divorced."

"Not yet, but I'm gonna be! I'm leaving the old prick!"

"Ilona," Nell said, "you're stepping on the clothes. You're going to tear that skirt if you don't watch out."

"Fuck the skirt—I'll pay for the skirt, I'm buying all this shit. Just give me a bill, you know I always pay my bills, Nell. Jesus, what kind of friend are *you* worrying about your fucking little clothes. That's all anybody cares about—clothes."

"Ilona—" Nell edged her way around the dressing room, began to pick up the scattered garments.

"I want those clothes!" Ilona yelled. "I'm buying all those clothes! I mean it!"

"Good, fine," Nell said. "Now calm down."

"You think I'm crazy, don't you," Ilona said. "Well, let me tell you something—you know what you and I have in common? All you can do in your life is *sell* clothes, and all I can do in my life is *wear* them."

"Ilona," Nell said. "Come on . . ."

"Come on?" Ilona asked. "Where? Where are we going, Nell? Tell me, so I'll know what to wear."

Nell handed an armful of clothes to Arlene, who was standing, fascinated, just outside the dressing room. "Charge these to Mrs. Shell, Arlene, and box them, please. And the other clothes she's given you." She pulled the dressing room curtain closed again. She turned to Ilona. "Ilona," she said. "Stop. Stop right now."

Ilona collapsed in Nell's arms, which made Nell feel rather silly, since Ilona in high heels stood a good five inches taller than she and, with all her blond hair, seemed even taller. But she felt so sorry for Ilona, who was now sobbing onto her shoulder, saying, "I want to die, Nell. I just want to die. I want to die."

"Well, you aren't going to," Nell said. "I won't let you." She staggered slightly. Ilona was a slender woman, thin to the point of emaciation, but she had dropped her entire drunken weight on Nell's shoulders, and Nell's knees were buckling. "Look," she said and gently shoved Ilona into the wrought-iron chair. "Sit down. Blow your nose. Get dressed. I'll send Arlene for some coffee, and we can talk in the office."

But no sooner had Arlene returned with the coffee than the UPS man arrived with some orders and some customers came in. Nell got Ilona into the office, gave her the coffee, asked her to wait. When she got back to the office about fifteen minutes later, she found Ilona passed out, her head resting in the middle of the papers on the desk. Nell didn't mind. That made it possible for her to call Jeremy. He was fine and hadn't thrown up again. Nell got some of the dresses unwrapped, priced, and hung up, and Ilona's dressing room cleaned up before lunch hour. Then she went down the street for coffee and yogurt, went back to the office, and woke Ilona up.

"Christ," Ilona said, raising her head off the desk. "My head feels like a pumpkin."

"Looks like it too," Nell said. "Here, drink this. And here

are some aspirin. Do you want to talk, or would you rather just go home?'' Nell sat down in a chair across from Ilona.

"Home," Ilona said. "Hah. No, I do not want to just go home. I guess I want to talk. I'm sorry to dump all this on you, Nell, but do you realize you're the only person in the world I can have a fit at? Everyone else I know, from Phillip and his relatives and his friends on, is so—*recessed.*''

"I think you mean repressed," Nell said.

Ilona considered. "No. I think I mean recessed. I mean that anything and everything that is of the slightest real importance to them is hidden away in a little drawer in their minds, shut off in a cranny behind a maze behind locked doors and steel walls.''

"Ueuegh," Nell said sympathetically.

"And I'm so *tired* of trying to get through," Ilona said. "Do you know something, Nell? I love Phillip. Now I know that will come as some surprise to you, because I know what you think of him—no, don't try to tell me otherwise, I can see your beady critical mind picking away at him every time he enters the room. Phillip is a pompous prig, I know that. Don't you think I know that? After nineteen years of marriage? I know that. But I love him anyway. And I *want* him so much.''

"But, Ilona, you have him," Nell said.

"No I don't," Ilona said. "No I don't, not at all. Never have, never will. My mistake in wasting this much time trying. Twenty years." Ilona hung her head, was quiet for a few moments. When she lifted her head, her eyes were full of tears. "Nell," she said, "I'm sorry about the scene here. Really. It's just that I'm so frantic. I have an appointment with a lawyer this afternoon, and I'm going to go through with it, I'm going to get a divorce. I'm a beautiful woman—people tell me I'm a beautiful woman—and I'm not as dumb as I look, and there's got to be more for me to do in life than give dinner parties for Phillip and wear clothes.''

"Your children—" Nell began.

"My children are both in prep school, and Lindsey starts college next year. Aaron goes to Europe this summer. They don't need me anymore, not in the old way.''

"Have you tried to talk to Phillip about all this?''

"Nell, I have tried to talk to him for so long that it's pathetic. I've tried to talk to him about it for years. I've done everything but send him a mimeographed letter every month. It's always the same: I nag him to give me more of himself and he looks puzzled and says coolly, 'But I don't understand.' "

"Well now, Ilona," Nell said. "I don't know Phillip very well, but he does seem to be a more—recessed—person than you."

"Psychologically, he's absolutely anal," Ilona said.

"All right. That's a given, then. And you are, well, the opposite extreme. Passionate, demanding, impatient."

"That's the way you know me, Nell. But you've seen me in my house at my parties. You have to admit I can be pretty cool. I can be as aloof as anyone. I can be controlled. I can wait. I'm not a maniac."

"Yes, that's true," Nell agreed. "I know."

"Nell," Ilona said. "I fell in love with Phillip the moment I saw him. I became obsessed with him. I spent two years doing nothing but manipulating him into marrying me. You never saw anyone as cool as I was then—you're an actress, you would have appreciated the performance! Then I spent nineteen years with this man, loving him, touching him, talking to him, being there for him—Nell, do you know what I do? Do you *know* what I do? When he goes out of town for a few days, I keep his dirty underwear by my pillow and I smell it. Look at me! I'm a beautiful, wealthy woman and I sneak around my own house holding Phillip's soiled underwear to my face, breathing in its fragrance as if it were life. *That's* how I feel about Phillip. And yes, he did marry me, but he has never once given me a fraction of the passion I've given him. My psychiatrist says that some people just don't know how. Some people just can't. Phillip is one of those people. Oh God, for so long I thought it was *me*. I went through hell thinking Phillip told other people his secrets, lost control sexually with some other woman, went just slightly berserk with another woman, that it was *me* he couldn't love. But thank God Dr. Kletterman helped me get that straight. Phillip is a person without passion. Jesus, he's practically without *blood*. And I can't go on with him any longer. I finally told him I was going to divorce him—and he didn't even fight it. He said, 'If that's what you want.' IF THAT'S WHAT YOU WANT! I could knife him to death. I could easily just knife him to *death!* I would love to dig a knife into his bony chest and see if there really is a heart in there."

"Ilona," Nell began.

"His father died," Ilona said. "We went to the funeral. Phillip did not cry. He was the perfect host later, making elegant dry martinis. His mother died. He did not cry. He did not shed a tear. If *I* died, he would not cry. If his children died, he would not cry. He has no tears in him. He's all dried up. He was born dried up. I thought that over the years, if I loved and caressed and nurtured him, I'd—I'd change him a little bit. But no. No. Nell, I even bought leather underwear, leather boots. I mean, it's the same with our sex; he's *recessed*. Sex only made him retreat even further into his shell; he couldn't even get it up. He likes his sex twice a week, after we've showered! Now you *know* he's crazy. You know he's a little crazy. And I'm more than a little crazy if I put up with it anymore! I've got to get out while I've got some energy and sanity left. And I *am* going to do it. I am determined to do it. It's just that—I'm so scared. Nell. Please. Help me.''

"Oh, honey," Nell said. "I'll try to help you. But look, right now I have to get back to work. And you have to get cleaned up and get ready for your lawyer's appointment. Come over to the house tonight and we'll have a celebratory meal and drink champagne to your new life. Okay?''

"Okay," Ilona said. "Great. Nell—thanks.''

Ilona tidied herself up, gathered up her packages, and left the store. Nell finished off her afternoon, working with the efficiency of a robot. She was tired. She was also a little cranky. She cared for Ilona, but in her heart of hearts, she also resented her a little. Ilona had so much—beauty, a husband who loved her the best he could, in his own stodgy, reliable and faithful way, and more money than anyone would ever need. And here Ilona was, throwing herself into Nell's care, asking Nell to help her. Nell kept looking at her reflection in the mirror, wondering what it was about her that made people come to her as to some wise old nurse. Elizabeth's words earlier that morning: Nell was so *reliable*.

Good old helpful reliable wise old Nell. Nurse Nell. Nanny Nell. Nerd Nell.

Nell hoped Ilona would have the sense to bring the champagne. She didn't feel like cooking dinner for Ilona. Since Jeremy was sick, she would have preferred to feed him clear soup, saltines, and ginger ale, and Hannah would have the same, or feel ill-treated. Nell would have preferred to drink a beer, fix any old sandwich, and get into bed with a book and a bowl of popcorn after this day. She thought of calling Ilona, of postponing the dinner; she had a good excuse with Jeremy home sick. Why did she always think she had to fix a dinner for a sad friend?

But then she thought of Ilona's tears, Ilona's face. And she remembered a woman she had known only briefly in Vancouver.

Marlow had been teaching in Boston then, but he had a summer job as guest professor at the university in Vancouver. It was a beautiful place to spend the summer, and Marlow got to direct three plays of his choice. It should have been a marvelous summer, but Hannah was newborn and Jeremy was just two. The university in Vancouver had found them a rental house in Capilano for the two months. It was a fine house, but isolated, and Marlow had to go off with the car every day. So it was the same old story familiar to many women: the mother stuck at home in a strange place all day with two babies. Nell knew it was for only eight weeks; still, she was miserable. Vancouver was so beautiful; she could *feel* it spreading all around her in its beauty, and she was imprisoned in the little rental house with babies and bottles and diapers and rash. Of course the children got sick. Of course Jeremy fell, just fell off a rock and cut his leg open. Of course it rained a lot. Nell thought she would have died, would have been one of those mothers who kill their children and then themselves, leaving a note saying: *life isn't worth living.* But the next door neighbor, a woman named Jackie Grant, saved her. She drove Nell and Jeremy to a doctor when Jeremy cut his leg. She invited Nell over for lazy, sloppy meals with her own family on the nights—and there were so many of them—when Marlow worked late. When she could manage it, for Jackie had three children of her own, she drove Nell and all their children out to parks for afternoon outings. When the time came for them to go back to Boston, Jackie watched Nell's children all day so Nell could pack and clean the rental house.

"You have been so kind," Nell said finally to Jackie that afternoon before she left. She had felt her throat swollen with emotion as she spoke. "You have probably literally saved my life. I don't understand it. You have given me so much, and there is no way in the world I can ever repay you. I probably won't ever see you again."

"Listen: my husband is with an insurance company," Jackie said, smiling. "We've made eleven moves in nine years. I had three children in those nine years. And *I* would have died if strangers hadn't helped me.

"Once we were in Windsor, a town in the middle of Canada, across the river from Detroit. We were very poor. I had just had my third child, and my life was nothing but food and milk and diapers. I had just moved into the neighborhood—corporations move you at their convenience, not yours. I gave birth to my third child in a town where I knew no one. We were living in a rental apartment. I just stayed in that apartment and took care of my children and sobbed all day every day.

"Then one day, when my baby was about a month old, someone knocked on the door. It was a woman I had seen only briefly, a woman who lived in the apartment across the hall. She worked. She was always on her way to work in some wonderful dress with matching shoes. I couldn't imagine what she wanted. She said she wondered if I might like to take a day off. She would come watch the children for me for the day. I could go off and wander, or use her apartment to sleep or read—whatever.

"Well, I thought she was mad. I was afraid she'd kidnap the children or something. But the offer—I couldn't refuse it. So I let her baby-sit for me. I went out and walked all over Windsor, along the river, looking over at the city of Detroit, gaining perspective, thinking of how things could and would change with time and distance. I hadn't had time to think like that for years. I couldn't have had a better day if God had personally visited me.

"When I got home, I asked her how I could possibly repay her. She said she was moving to Ottawa in a week. We probably wouldn't see each other again. I was so puzzled, I really did think she was mad. I looked around the apartment: she had managed to clean it a bit. The children were happy. I said, 'I don't understand.'

"She said, 'I'm an executive, but not a rich one. I've had to move a lot with my firm. Along the way perfect strangers have been helpful to me in ways I could never repay. Of course I've been helpful to you. I wish I could be more helpful. I've heard you crying. I'm sorry I'm leaving. At least I gave you today. And of course you can't repay me. But you can pass it along. Someday you can do a kindness for a stranger who won't be able to repay you. It's like a chain letter, you see. It will eventually get back to me in the end.'

"So, Nell, that's what I'm doing. I'm repaying that woman executive. I'm passing some kindness along. And your turn will come to do the same someday."

Now Nell thought: Ilona was no stranger, but still Nell knew she should pass some kindness along. So she sighed, shut up the boutique, and headed for her car, thinking, all right, Jackie, okay. I'll make some kind of dinner for Ilona tonight.

Still, in her heart she knew her charity was grudging. Perhaps it would be easier to help a poor stranger than a wealthy friend. When she got home, after checking Jeremy and hugging Hannah and paying the paper boy and feeding the cats and dog and doing a thousand other chores, she checked her refrigerator and nearly collapsed in front if it, crying. She had milk, eggs, juice, lettuce, cheese, but no meat. What could she cook? She had fed Ilona only Saturday night, for Christ's sake! Did she have to feed her again so soon? The hell with it, she thought, Jeremy *was* sick, Nell had not had much sleep, she was tired, she had worked all day—they would send out for pizza.

As soon as she had this heretical thought, the phone rang.

"Nell? It's Ilona. Listen, I can't come for dinner tonight. I'm going *out* to dinner with a *man.* One of the partners in my lawyer's firm is taking me to the Coq d'Or."

"Well," Nell said, monumentally relieved enough to tease. "If you'd rather go out to dinner with some dull old fogey than spend the evening—"

"Oh, Nell," Ilona cut in, all seriousness and intensity. "You know I'd rather be with you. You saved my life today. But I met Bob Jackson in the office today, and he *is* dull, but he's handsome and Phillip doesn't know he's dull and it won't hurt him a bit to know I'm going out with other men. It might be the keg of dynamite I've been waiting for all my life."

Oh, Ilona, Nell thought. Oh God, don't we women ever give up? Don't we ever stop trying to manipulate men with our foolish games?

" . . . and if that doesn't work, which I'm not stupid enough to think it will, actually, well then, Bob Jackson is a nice man. I think we'll have a lovely evening together. And this will get the word out that I am available."

Nell and Ilona talked some more, then Nell hung up, relieved but somehow depressed by their conversation. She cheered herself up by making a cheese and tomato sandwich she grilled slowly, to a crisp, in lots of butter. She spent the evening with the children. Jeremy was over his flu in that miraculous way children have of getting well; he was bright-eyed and wild with energy from sitting around the house all day.

"Can't I just go outside and ride my bike a little, Mom?" he pleaded. "I'm really all well."

I live in a world of endless decisions, Nell thought. She said no, then relented. The April light was too tempting. Jeremy was well. While he rode off, Nell went out and sat on the wicker swing, and after a few moments Hannah joined her. Hannah chatted happily about her day at school, her friends, the subtraction she was learning, and Nell listened— sort of—and gently pushed her foot against the wooden porch floor so that the old swing moved ever so slowly back and forth. I will not tell these children about Nantucket yet, she thought. Not until I have made arrangements for the summer with Marlow. She would call Marlow and discuss it with him when the children were in bed. *Nantucket.* She had not had a free moment in her day to think about Nantucket, to let the thought in all its possibilities roll across her mind. She was too tired to think in any acute and sensible manner about it. She could only sit there on the swing, slowly tilting back and forth, listening to her daughter's light and lilting voice, watching the April light shimmer gold to silver to gray. She could only let the thought of a summer in Nantucket lap at the edge of her consciousness as she imagined the ocean must be out there calmly lapping, this gentle evening, on that island's sandy shores.

It was late when she finally got the children into bed. She showered, fixed herself a cup of herb tea, and crawled into bed with her nightgown and robe on. For a few moments she simply sat, relaxing, without a thought in her head. She had her bedroom windows opened a bit, but the temperature was dropping and she didn't want the furnace to click on, so she reluctantly got out of bed and shut them. When she turned back to her bed, she found that Medusa had confiscated the spot at the end of the bed, where Nell's feet went. The cat sat there, calm as a Buddha, innocent as a lamb, regally indicating with her slanted cat eyes that Nell was a vulgar intruder, but Medusa would share the bed anyway.

"*My* bed, Medusa," Nell said. She was in no mood to humor the cat. She stuck her feet under the covers and kicked them back and forth so that Medusa rolled over sideways. Medusa would get her back. The cat would sneak up in the night and take this space and Nell would end up curled in a ball or slanted across the bed with her feet sticking out in the cold. This didn't really make Nell mad; it just seemed part of the normal scheme of things.

One of the great reliefs to everyone in the family after Marlow's and Nell's divorce was that the animals were allowed to sleep in bed with whomever they deigned to choose. Marlow never had been able to bear this. Nell could see his point. If you hadn't been raised that way, it did feel a little odd to go in at night to check a sleeping three-year-old and to see a German shepherd bigger than the child curled up next to the boy, the dog's head hogging the pillow. And Marlow had objected to the animal's hair on the sheets. But Nell knew that was only because Marlow was too dim to notice the animal hair that lay in wisps across every other surface in the house.

Nell did not believe that animals were human beings. She did not tell her friends about their clevernesses; in fact she never spoke about her animals at all to her friends. She felt a loyalty to the animals: they were necessarily mute about *her*, even if they were judgmental. She didn't knit little coats for the dog or buy rhinestone collars for the cats. She didn't believe in treating them as if they were people. But she did believe in living with them. They brought such comfort. They were so amazingly beautiful. They were always ready to give themselves over with complete sensual abandon to being petted and stroked. They taught the children the lesson of the necessity of kindness to smaller, weaker creatures. But mostly they were just there: warm breath, furry lives, acute intelligence, carriers of optimism and faith, for while they seemed never wholly convinced of man's wisdom, they still, with the trust of their lives, gave him the benefit of the doubt.

Having made her point to Medusa, Nell sighed, sipped her tea, and reluctantly turned to the phone. She had to start making summer plans with Marlow. She dialed his number, and Charlotte answered: Marlow was out at rehearsal. Of course, Nell thought but did not say, he always was. She told Charlotte about Nantucket.

"Do you have any idea what Marlow's summer plans will be?" Nell asked. "I mean, will he teach summer school here or direct here or will you be going off on the road?"

"I really have no idea," Charlotte said. "You know how it is, Nell."

"Well," Nell said, "please have Marlow call me tomorrow. You and Marlow can have the children for as long or as short as you want them this summer. It's just that I need to start making arrangements."

"Ummn," Charlotte said. "Okay. I'll have him call you."

Nell hung up, unsatisfied. Charlotte, bony Charlotte, who had once been her best friend. Now she was not Nell's enemy, but she wasn't going to give Nell an inch. Oh well, so what, Nell thought. She was too tired to think about another thing. She hung over the side of her bed, searching through the pile of books and magazines that still lay spilled on the floor, and dug out her delicious paperback mystery. She settled back into her pillows. Medusa crept closer, finally curled up on top of Nell's ankles. Nell didn't mind. The warmth was sweet.

The phone rang. It was Clary. Clary in tears.

"Nell! I've lost my job! Can you help me?" Clary wailed. "The grant at Rutgers ran out and it won't be renewed and I don't have a job after the middle of May. I don't know what to do!"

Not all days are like this, Nell reminded herself. Whole weeks could go by when her friends and relatives went without crises. This was just turning out to be a peculiar day, the sort of day that made her want to start reading her astrological charts. Jupiter must be on the descent or something. Nell wished she'd fixed herself a brandy instead of herb tea. The tea was cold now anyway, and cold, it tasted like nothing more than stale water. She set it on the bedside table and concentrated on Clary's words.

Ever since the rat test, Nell and Clary had kept in touch. For four years they had written each other, called when they could afford it or were excited or desperate, sent each other silly greeting cards. Clary had come to visit them all once a year, tying that visit in with one to her father. Nell had gone down to Rutgers one weekend a year ago, leaving the children with Marlow. She and Clary were close; they could discuss everything now: children, lovers, money, life, sex, friendship. Sometimes when Nell was blue, she phoned Clary and Clary played the role of the older and wiser one; she cheered Nell up. But now Nell was definitely being called upon to act the part of the old wise one. Clary was in a fix.

"Have you thought of talking to Marlow about this?" Nell asked. "Maybe he can help you find a position in one of the labs or colleges around Boston."

"I called him," Clary said. "And he said he'd try to help. But of course he and Charlotte are going to be gone all summer. Summer stock in Illinois. Always summer stock. He said if I can hang on till fall, he can help me then."

"When did you talk to Marlow?" Nell asked.

"This afternoon," Clary said. "Or this evening, I guess, whatever, around six. Why?"

"And he told you that he and Charlotte were going to be in the Midwest all summer?"

"Yeah," Clary said. "Why?"

"Oh, it's nothing," Nell said, thinking, thanks a lot, Charlotte. "Go on, Clary."

"Well, it's just that I don't know what to do," Clary said. "I want to get out of here, and as a matter of fact I'm tired of working with rats. I'd like to try my hand at something new. But on the other hand, Jesus, Nell, do you realize I'm almost *thirty years old?*" Horror vibrated from Clary's voice.

"Clary, you are twenty-seven," Nell said.

"Still," Clary went on. "I'm getting awfully old to have my life in such a mess. I'm not married. I'm not engaged. I'm in love, but with the wrong person. Now I don't even have a job. Not only do I not have a profession, I don't even have a job."

"Well, have you talked to your mother?"

"Oh yeah, you know Mom. She's great. She said, 'Oh come on out to Denver, honey. Live with us, we'll get you back on your feet.' But I don't want to go out there. I want to stay here in the East. All my friends are here, and besides, I like it here. And I can't keep going home to Mom every time the bottom falls out of my life. I promised myself the last time I wouldn't run home to Mother again, I've got to grow up sometime."

When Marlow had asked Nell to marry him so many years ago, he had said, "There are some things you should know about me. I'm not wealthy. I have an artistic temperament. I don't think I'm easy to live with. I'm divorced, and for the next nine years I'll have to pay child support to my ex-wife. I have a daughter, Clarissa, who's twelve years old. She stays with me in the summer."

Clarissa, Nell had thought, what a pretty old-fashioned name, and she remembered Richardson's epistolary novel, and she envisioned Clarissa St. John: a frail girl, slim and wan, with hair tied back in ribbons, a quiet, shadowy child who would drift around in white, reading novels, writing poetry. Nell could deal with that. Clarissa, Nell had thought, sounds like the type of child who dies a romantic and early death.

When Nell finally met Clary, Clary was wearing orange polka-dot bell-bottom trousers and an orange-striped pullover shirt. Her blond hair hung lank to her shoulders in some androgynous hippie non-cut, and she stood, at thirteen, as tall as Nell, meeting Nell's gaze eye for eye, evenly. She was extremely thin, and long-boned and gawky; she could have been mistaken easily for a boy. Her mouth was clamped shut in a hateful clench that suggested that not even laughing gas would make her smile; Nell did not understand until later that Clary was only trying to hide her dreadful braces. Nell smiled and tried to be friendly to Clary; Clary only stood there, staring at her with a face full of warning. She was thirteen years old, Clary, with an adolescent's hormonal sullenness and the instinctive distrust of a child of divorce. She had just flown from Denver, where she lived with her newly remarried mother, to Bangor, Maine, where she knew no one, to spend two months with her father and his new wife. She was contemptuous of every single thing in the world. Nell thought Clary was one of the most terrifying things she had ever seen in her life.

There seemed to be no way to win this person over either, and Nell was certainly adept at charm. Nell had put a bouquet of wild flowers in a water glass in Clary's room in the little house the theater had rented for them for the summer. Clary's first deed in the house was to bring the flowers into the kitchen. "I have hay fever," she explained curtly. Clary's second act was to unpack the portable record player she had brought. She shut the door of her bedroom, turned the stereo to its highest possible volume, and stayed in her room all afternoon, listening to David Cassidy and the Monkees. That was what she did most of the time she was in the house. When Marlow requested that she join him at his rehearsals, she did; when he asked her to go anywhere with him, she would, but not gladly.

Nell made a few halfhearted attempts to be chummy. She was only twenty-four, she didn't know about kids.

"Want to help dry the dishes, Clary?" she asked the first night, envisioning them sharing the work, chatting away, getting to know each other.

"Huh-uh," Clary said, and left the room.

Well, Nell had thought, now what? Do I demand that she help with the dishes? Marlow had already left the house for rehearsal. She let the matter drop.

They were on the road then, living in a rented house in Maine. Nell had no friends there, although if she wanted, she could always socialize with the theater company. And those people might be fickle, dramatic, foolish, or vain, but at least they *talked;* they believed that part of human life involved interacting with other human beings. Nell let Clary go her own way. She did not try to woo her anymore—she did not *want* to woo her—she felt no responsibility for her, and after a few days began to feel a deep resentment toward her. Always slipping back into her room, her face sullen, to listen to her insipid music. Little *churl,* Nell thought.

Poor Clary. One morning after she had been with them for three weeks, with perhaps thirty-two words passed between her and Nell, she came into the kitchen, where Nell was finishing her coffee. Marlow had gone for the morning. Nell had a list of errands to run for him. She thought she'd ask Clary if she wanted to join her—it couldn't be that much fun staying in the bedroom all day—but the past few times when Clary did join her, it had been like having a robot along.

"The ocean's beautiful, isn't it, Clary?" she would ask.

"Um," Clary would answer, noncommittal even about the ocean.

You don't like the ocean? Let me find you a nice filthy slum, you creep, Nell would think. She was always silently retorting to Clary in her mind; it saved her sanity. She knew that she was the adult and Clary the child, Marlow's child, so she had the responsibility of courtesy. But it was hard work.

"Good morning. Want some breakfast?" Nell asked that morning when Clary entered the kitchen. It was not a warm greeting, but it was the best she could do given that icy stare.

Then she looked at Clary, who seemed to have passed from icy to bloodless. Her lips were white. Her dark eyes were wide and tremulous around the edges, as if she were straining to keep back tears. She looked mummified standing in the kitchen doorway, erect, tense, wrapped rigidly in her white skin as if in a binding. She seemed to be holding herself together with her skin and her own thirteen-year-old will power. God, Nell thought, what has she seen? Did she hear me and Marlow making love? Is she going to kill me? Is she going to kill herself? Is something dead in the house that I haven't seen? Is she insane?

"Clary . . ." she began. "What's wrong?"

Clary stood white and frozen in the doorway. She raised her lovely judgmental head and glared down at the seated Nell. "I need—" she began, then stopped. "I've started having my period," she said, her voice excessively casual. "Do you have—I just used some toilet paper, wadded up . . ."

That's why she's walking that way, Nell thought, weak with relief.

"Oh Lord, I thought you'd seen a ghost," Nell laughed. "I

thought you *were* a ghost! Come on into the bathroom.'' Then, seeing that Clary still remained rigid, she knew in a flash what was going on, and it made her brave enough to be intrusive. ''Is this your first period?''

Clary nodded. Nell got up and led her to the bathroom and dug out the necessary equipment for Clary from a shelf.

''Do you know how to use all this stuff? Do you know all that's happening? Do you want me to explain anything?''

''No,'' Clary said. ''It's okay. Mom told me everything. And school. And my friends have all started. They all started long ago.'' Her face began to crack. ''I thought I was never going to start,'' she said. ''I'm *thirteen* years old. I thought . . .''

Clary could not go on, but Nell knew what Clary thought. Clary thought she was either ill or doomed. She thought that she out of all women on the earth was deformed, did not have all the necessary sexual apparatus functioning within her. Boys were lucky. They could look right down at any time and see proof of their masculinity. But women had so much hidden away from sight; it wasn't fair. Nell remembered how it was to be a teenager, when your own body was such a frustrating mystery: would you start your period, ever? Would you be ''regular,'' or would you live life in a series of surprises and embarrassments? Would you ever have breasts, or would they always be this size? Everything was so far beyond any pitiful control you might try to exert. Things just popped out, or not: pimples, pubic hair, breasts, blood. And it all seemed so weighted with significance, seemed to *mean* so much.

Nell walked over to Clary. She put her arms around her and hugged her. Clary stood rigid, her arms at her side, not breathing. Still Nell held her. Like it or not, kid, you get this, Nell thought, hugging Clary. She stroked Clary's blond hair one time, gently, then released her.

''Well,'' she said. ''Welcome to the real world. Look, here's all the stuff. Why don't you call your mom when you're fixed up; she might like to know. You might feel better after talking to her. And then I'll tell you about when I started!''

Clary did not smile, did not say thanks, but slowly, color was returning to her face. Nell left her alone in the bathroom. After a while, Clary came out, called her mother, who wasn't home, then sat down at the kitchen table across from Nell.

''Do you feel okay?'' Nell asked. ''Any cramps?''

"No. I'm fine," Clary said.

Nell set some juice and toast in front of her. "I fixed you a nice piece of liver while you were in the bathroom," she said, then, seeing Clary's horrified face, hurried on, "That's a joke, Clary. I won't ever fix you liver. But you do need to start taking vitamin pills with iron now, you know. You can take mine. And I use Midol for cramps. If you feel bad, let me know and I'll share my medicine box with you. Having your period can make you feel really bad sometimes. Or maybe you'll be one of the lucky ones."

Clary didn't respond. She drank her juice, ate her toast, did not speak. But there was a new look in her eyes now; one layer of defense the thickness of a fish scale had fallen away from her face, and even that much made a difference. She's not really such a bad kid, Nell thought. I wouldn't want to be thirteen again.

"Let me tell you about *my* first time," Nell said. "This was in Iowa. In the summer. We went to a little farm town, Solon, to visit some relative's relatives. Old people. I can't remember why, maybe it was a funeral. At any rate, I was there with my parents, staying in some old relative's big old house, and there were some other people there too. I was twelve. The only other kid there was a girl who was sixteen. Carol. She was *so cool*. She was so experienced. Sophisticated. She wore a bra; I didn't. She had a charm bracelet; I didn't. She had a picture of her boyfriend in a gold locket around her neck. I didn't have a locket, a picture, or a boyfriend. She kept perfume in the refrigerator to spray on her wrists or the back of her neck—she would lift her long ponytail up and it seemed the most exquisite thing anyone could ever do. My hair was chopped off in a sort of pageboy, God, I looked like a little Sir Lancelot. Boys came by in their cars to pick her up and take her off for Cokes, and my relatives made Carol take me with her! Oh God, it was agony. I knew she hated me.

" 'Now, Carol,' the old farts would say, 'don't be rude. Nell doesn't have anything to do. You children should stick together.'

"Carol would stand there, just looking at me. I knew she thought I was a *worm*. I kept saying I didn't want to go, I wanted to read, I wanted to hang around the house, but they pushed me off on Carol. It was just shit. We'd drive around that town, Carol and the two boys in the front seat and twelve-year-old me in the back. Can you imagine how I felt? I wanted to die. The three of them would sit up there, smoking, laughing, making jokes I couldn't understand. And I would just sit back there wishing I could die.

"Well, one night when we got back from driving around with these boys, *as I was getting out of the car,* I felt this wetness on my thighs and underpants. I couldn't get into the house fast enough. It seemed I could hear them all giggling in the car behind me. It was dark, and surely no one was looking at me anyway, but still I felt—like I had a phosphorescent, glow-in-the-dark bottom. Carol stayed outside, flirting with the boys. I went on in, went right to the bathroom, pulled down my shorts and pants— oh God, I can still see the awful sight. Blood on my pants.

"Now here's the worst part: when Carol had deigned to talk to me, she had of course asked me if I had started having periods yet, and I had of course said of course I had. I was desperate to appear grown-up. I had been so blasé when I answered her. I said, of course I've started. She said, oh, isn't it a *drag.* I said, yes, thank heavens I had just finished my period last week before coming.

"So there I was, stuck. I knew from life-science class that your period comes only once a month, not every week. I didn't have anything to wear, and my pride wouldn't let me ask Carol for anything, and my mother was asleep. I couldn't think what to do. So do you know what I did? I just decided *I wouldn't have my period.* I sat there in that old bathroom—I can still see the floor, I stared at it forever, it was covered in little white octagonal tiles lined in black, those octagons repeated themselves endlessly—I sat there and thought, well, damnit, I just won't start yet. This isn't a good time to start having my period. I don't want it now. And that's all there is to it. So I pulled up my pants and brushed my teeth and put on my nightgown and went to bed. And when I got into bed, I didn't lie there thinking, oh gee, I've started my period. I just forgot it. I thought about what a bitch Carol was. I fantasized about those boys driving by and asking Carol to sit in the back and asking me to sit up front. I daydreamed about that till I fell asleep, and I really forgot about my period.

"Well, when I woke up the next morning, you can imagine what my nightgown and the sheets were like. I sat up in bed, looked down, and wanted to scream: I looked like a disaster victim. Blood everywhere."

"Oh, gross," Clary said.

"Yeah, it was gross," Nell replied. She laughed. She went still. "It was also scary. I sat there in bed looking down at those awful stains on the sheets and my nightgown and the gob of stuff all over the bed, the horrid mess of it all, and realized what had happened to me and that there wasn't a thing I could do about it. My body was doing it without my permission. It was like—it was as if I had awakened speaking Chinese, unable to say another word in English. It was that strange, that radical a change."

"Hadn't your mom told you about periods?" Clary asked.

"Oh yeah, of course," Nell said. "And thank heavens she was there then. Finally I got up, pulling the sheets off the bed and wrapping them all around along with me, and waddled over to the door and called her. Thank God she was upstairs and heard me. She came in and helped me clean up the mess and fix myself up, and she didn't tell anyone anything. But then I spent the next two days until we left in fear that something would show or someone would say something and Carol would know I had only just started my period. I never did see Carol again. I wonder where she is now. The little bitch." Nell sat in silence for a minute. "Well, look," she went on, "do you want me to tell Marlow? Do you want to tell him?"

"Why tell him? You think he'll give me a banquet?" Clary said, and she grinned, so that her braces flashed briefly.

Nell was stunned. She looked at Clary, looked away, so that Clary could not see just how astounded she was. Those words of Clary's, so cynical, so bitter, so *realistic*, mixed with her tone of voice and smile, which indicated good humor and sympathetic understanding, seemed to be characteristics of a child far older than thirteen. *She has some idea of just what kind of man her father is,* Nell thought in surprise, and in further surprise she knew that Clary was okay about it. She could handle it.

"I mean," Clary went on, "I don't think this will exactly be a magic moment in his life."

"No," Nell conceded. "Still . . . he's a man, and they don't know . . ."

"Wait till I'm back in Denver to tell him. He's only going to take it as some kind of inconvenience to him if you tell him while I'm here. He'll think, oh hell, now Clary will probably have cramps when I need her to carry props."

Nell was quiet. If she agreed with Clary, she felt she would be in some vague way betraying Marlow, but to disagree would be to lie. How does she know her father so well, she wondered, then realized that Clary had known Marlow for thirteen years; Nell had known Marlow for only a little over one year. Nell could not remember having had such acute insight into her own father's personality in her teenage years.

"Okay," Nell said. "I'll wait to tell him. I think you're right. When he's directing, everything that happens in the universe somehow directly ties into his play. We won't bother him with this now. But I feel we ought to do *something*, Clary. I think we ought to, oh, not exactly celebrate, but do something to make an occasion of this day. I mean, you have started having your period. You're not a child anymore. I remember, after I started my period, when we got back to Des Moines, my mother took me out to a store and bought me my first pair of high-heel shoes. White high heels. And a bra. Even though I didn't need one. And a hat for church." Nell saw the horror springing into Clary's eyes. She laughed. "Oh God, don't worry," she said. "I promise I won't take you out and buy you a pair of white high heels. Or a bra. Or a hat. But I do think we ought to do *something*. God, what would be appropriate for these days? I suppose I should take you to an X-rated movie, something like that."

Clary's face brightened. "I wouldn't care about an X-rated movie, Nell, but it would be neat to see a movie."

Nell grinned. "It would be neat to see a movie, wouldn't it," she admitted. The town they were living in on the Maine coast was certainly quaint and picturesque, and for that reason tourists flocked to it and to the celebrated summer theater. But there was no movie house. Marlow was delighted about this, of course—it meant no competition for his plays. But Nell found it a drag. "Look," she said, inspired. "Let's drive to Bangor tonight. If we go in early enough, we can see two movies, an early and a late. How would that be?"

And Clary smiled again.

They went to the movies that night. They laughed and talked in the car on the long drive to and from Bangor. But the next day Clary spent most of the time in her room, listening to records. She never did offer to help Nell with a single chore. They didn't immediately begin to share intimacies. But they were on their way to becoming friends. There were times during the years of their relationship when Nell simply wanted to kill Clary, and knew that Clary felt the same way about her. But there were also times—for example, at a restaurant with a theater company, when some particularly vain actor was holding forth—when Clary and Nell would glance at each other and quickly look away, conspirators in judgment, and times, especially in the past few years, when they would both fall all over the sofa in a mutual laughing fit over some joke or episode, and times when they could say in writing or over the phone, "I love you." Some friendships happen as effortlessly as a natural act, like the seed of a tree lodging in the earth, the deed is at once instant and complete, containing the future in the moment. Unless there is some disaster, that seed will grow and flourish with each year, with roots as deep and powerful as all natural forces. Other friendships do not have that ease, but take the kind of painstaking nurturing that a parent gives a sickly child; it is as if nature is not willing this friendship and so the human has to fight for it against all sorts of setbacks and odds. That was the sort of friendship Nell and Clary had. Now here they were, ex-stepdaughter, ex-stepmother, and their friendship often seemed to Nell as exotic a thing as a Hawaiian orchid in a New England greenhouse: but then it was that beautiful and valuable, too.

Now Nell lay in her bed in Arlington, Massachusetts, and spoke to Clary in Piscataway, New Jersey, and Nell thought how odd it was to be so close like this while so far away physically. Sometimes when on long-distance phone calls, Nell would hold the receiver of the phone away from her ear so that she could look at the little round holes in the earpiece. She could never *see* the voice, yet it was *there,* real, powerful, instantly recognizable as the voice of the specific person, capable of arousing any number of emotions in the listener. From this incredible plastic instrument in Nell's hand came Clary's voice now, filled with all of Clary's present needs, with the resonance of all the years and the history of their friendship.

Nell was awfully glad the development of the world had not been up to her. She did not have sufficient imagination for the world. She could never have invented the telephone. She could still scarcely conceive of the telephone. She read with pleasure and wonder about Sally Ride, that appropriately named first American woman astronaut, and she was so glad to know that here was a woman who was expanding the work of women. She was so glad that Sally Ride existed in the world, for she, Nell, would never have been able to do what that woman did. It was not that Nell was not brave or intelligent enough. It was just that she was so limited in her desires. And Nell's desires did not have anything to do with space or machinery or invention or money or numbers or chemicals or power or corporations. Nell's desires all had to do with people. She had started off her life as an actress, wanting to entertain people, wanting to *be* other people. She could never get enough of people. In time she had realized that her desires also had to do with *tending* people: God, what a dreadfully embarrassing thing to know about herself in this day and age. But it was true. She loved tending to people, especially to their bodies: more than that, she needed to. She missed rubbing sweet-smelling talc into a chubby baby's body. Now she knew that was a thing she had needed to do in her life. She could still remember rocking her children in her arms when they were babies, rocking them in the middle of some dark night, humming to them softly, feeling their moist warm baby's breath, the breath of life, on her arm or breast, rocking, holding the real and delicious life against her and thinking: who is getting more pleasure from this rocking, the baby or me?

Only last summer at a pond she had been shocked to realize how happy it made her to say to nine-year-old Jeremy: "Come over here, let me put some lotion on your back or you'll get a worse sunburn than you already have."

"Oh, *Mom,*" he had said, exasperated.

But she had taken her time rubbing lotion into his shoulders and down his long bony back, down his arms. She did not get to touch him so much anymore; he did not need physical tending. He did need more verbal supervision, though: that was the hard thing. More and more, her interaction with her children was becoming verbal rather than physical. Unfair, unfair. The pleasure was hers for such a short period of time—and so much of that time she had been too tired or just too shortsighted to appreciate it. Her children were slowly removing themselves from her, and the physical nurturing was the first part to go. Often before, Nell had wondered why her friends had been so accommodating to their teenage children, why they had been so almost servile. How her friends had rushed about, making special foods for their teenagers, doing the teenagers' laundry when the kids were certainly old enough to do it themselves, even making their beds. . . . Now Nell knew why. She would do it too. She would smooth the sheets on her children's beds, she would bake them brownies, cakes, pizzas, she would wash and fold and iron and sew their clothes as those clothes grew bigger in size: in this way she could touch them, even though once removed.

She had never physically tended Clary. There had never quite been that guardian-child connection between them. Yet the commitment Nell felt toward Clary was stronger than those she felt to most of her friends. It was not any old niggling sense of duty. It was a more vigorous, definite, immediate response, as she might turn and run toward any child who cried or fell from a bike. Something of the maternal was in Nell's reaction—but Nell was glad for that, trusted that. And there was more of the friend in her reply to Clary's call for help; there was even, Nell thought, a particle of wisdom, for Nell knew that Clary did not at this point in her life need to be simply taken care of again. Clary did not want to be taken as a child, a child who has goofed up again and has to come home in defeat. Clary had to earn her way. Well, that was not just philosophically true, it was financially true; none of her relatives was rich.

Nell was pleased to offer what seemed to be an excellent solution. She told Clary about the job and the house she would have in Nantucket that summer. She told Clary she would be welcome to come live with her and that Clary could either look for a summer job on Nantucket or Nell would try to see if Elizabeth O'Leary would hire her at the boutique. That would carry Clary through to the fall, when she could try getting a job in the Boston area, with Marlow's help.

Clary was delirious. "*Nantucket!* Oh wow, oh wow, Nell! I've always wanted to spend a summer on Nantucket. Oh, heaven!"

They talked some more, making arrangements, and finally hung up. Nell looked at her watch; it was almost midnight. She slid out of bed and went into Jeremy's room to check him. He was sleeping peacefully, his forehead cool. He really was over the flu and would be able to go to school the next day. She slipped into Hannah's room for a moment and stood there, just watching her little girl sleep: what peace. Hannah had always been able to fall asleep easily, sometimes right in the middle of a sentence.

Well, Nell was not going to fall asleep easily, not tonight. She was tired, but she was wired up. Too many things had happened, she had too much to consider. She roamed through the darkened house down to the kitchen, turned on the light, and began to heat a cup of milk. She had heard that warm milk had different properties from cold milk, could actually induce sleep. And sometimes this had worked for her. So she stood over her stove, stirring the milk, waiting for it to get warm.

As a girl, Nell had never been able to decide which life she wanted to have. She had *known* she was going to be an actress, and a famous one—that much was given, she thought. She would never give that up. But then her visions split into two extremes. On the one hand she dreamed of being a wonderful earth-mother woman, competent, caring, full of deep and healing laughter, making the theater company she worked with and her own husband and children into a giant family revolving around her. She saw herself settled somewhere near New York—so she could easily go in to perform—living in a vast rambling house, with ponies in barns and ducks on a pond, with a husband who adored her absolutely, and with endless, countless children. Eight children, *ten* children. Always pregnant, smug, and the house buzzing with life, all those children, all their friends; she would be a marvel of womanhood, an actress and mother par excellence.

Or: she would be an actress, but not a mother. Not a wife. She would be too wild, too impetuous, and far too much sought after to settle down to just one man. In her second dream life, she saw herself as a willful, romantic siren, always fleeing from lovers on trains while wearing fur muffs, kissing one man goodbye in London and being met at the airport in Paris by another, being courted with jewels, mansions, and flowers by endless, countless hopelessly adoring men. She would never marry, though she might have a child or two—never knowing just which lover was the father.

As a child, there had been many days when Nell had been sincerely worried about which life she would choose to lead.

How her dreams had changed.

Now the life she would choose if she could would be much more modest: she wanted John and Katy Anderson's life. She wanted a secure marriage, real love, and good will and humor and caring shared with a man; she wanted to look back on memories with a man, to plan for the future with a man. She had stopped caring so much about the acting; she realized that not much joy was to be found in a string of lovers, and her two children made her life absolutely bulge at the seams, unlike the phantom children of her dreams, who drifted by without problems. She didn't care about jewels, flowers, furs, or mansions; but she thought it would be nice to have a little peaceful love.

She had been trying for a few years to make a bargain with

God. Or fate. Look, she would say, I know I'm lucky. I know I'm full while others on this planet starve, I know I'm healthy while others lie ill, I know I'm spoiled and often think I'm deprived. But here's a deal: I still want more: I want to live with a man I love. I don't think that's asking too much. I think that's a fair request. Let me have that, and as soon as I get my kids raised, I'll turn whatever talents and energies I have to doing some good work in the world. How about it? What do you think? Okay?

Of course there had been no answer from God, or fate—unless the answer was in the negative, which Nell did not want to believe. But though she did not want to be cynical, she was having trouble being optimistic. She was having such trouble believing that her life made any sense. Everything was so random, chaotic, disorganized. She was an intelligent person, but she could not seem to get her life in control.

And now she was faced with this summer, this Nantucket summer. She would not be in her house—what would she do, just let the grass grow, let the place look deserted and be broken into? Who would take care of her animals? How would Medusa and Fred and Wolf fare without her for three months? Would Marlow and Charlotte take the children? She didn't want them gone from her for three full months, but what would she do with them on the island while she worked? She could ask Clary to baby-sit—no, she couldn't. Wouldn't ever do that. That would be stupid. Oh, it was so *irritating,* this Nantucket thing. She felt like a derailed train. A car sidetracked on a detour. What a waste of time it would be, three months away from her home, away from her real life; she wouldn't be able to get on with things. She felt like some poor damn little *ant,* some little black female ant, carrying her children and her house and her animals and her dreams on her back like a piece of food, some plodding old ant creeping along, trying to get over to some shelter that she could just barely see, and here Elizabeth O'Leary had come, like fate with a broom, knocking her sideways off the path. She would have to struggle to right herself and gather her life together and get back on the road.

Nell stuck a finger in the pan. The milk was warm. She poured it in a cup, looking down at the white liquid, and sighed. She could feel the Panic Night feeling coming on again. Warm milk was good for normal sleeplessness, but it did nothing against the Panic Nights. Nell got some brandy and poured a great slug of it into the milk and added a touch of sugar. Now she had a deadly drink that was sure to give her a headache in the morning but would be a great help toward sleep tonight. She desperately needed sleep, needed to stop thinking for a while.

She went back up the stairs and settled into her bed, knocking Medusa sideways. She picked up the paperback mystery once more and stared at it while she drank her milk and brandy. But the words swam before her eyes, and she could only think: Nantucket. Clary. Ilona. Stellios. Hannah. Jeremy. Marlow. Charlotte. What a bizarre mixture, what a *glop* her life had become. At the front of the mystery was the detailed drawing of a family tree and Nell sat staring at it, admiring the clean lines, the definite arrowing and connecting and conjoining of the lives and histories. Those people's lives were lived as cleanly as roads laid out on the earth. They knew where they came from, and they had a sense of destination, and they knew with whom they were traveling. Their lives made sense.

Nell let the paperback fall to the floor. It filled her with envy. Even this paperback *mystery*, this fiction, filled her with envy. She finished off her drink in one great swallow, then clicked off the light and slid down into the bed. She felt slightly dizzy from drinking so much so soon, but was glad for the dizziness; she knew now she would soon fall asleep. She lay on her side, looking out her window at the sky, and as her eyes adjusted to the light, she saw more and more stars come twinkling into view. The night sky was speckled with them like a great egg. All those random dots that made no pattern. That was what her life was like, Nell thought, musing, and Medusa at this moment came creeping back over to settle in a warm ball on Nell's hip. Nell was lonely, frightened, and confused. She felt that she was wandering through the vast space of her life like a child struggling through a complicated dot-to-dot puzzle; she could not find the clue; she could not find the meaning. She was roving through her life when she longed to be settled. There was no map for her to follow, there were no instructions, she was lost. Nell lay staring at the stars that had been thrown out in the universe in a pattern as mysterious and fluky as the pattern of her life, until the stars blurred before her eyes and she slept.

Five

Nantucket island lies twenty-five miles off the coast of New England, just south of the most southeastern mainland point of Massachusetts. It's shaped like a fat quarter-moon lying on its side, with two tips pointing back to the continent. It is approximately fifty square miles in area, and its year-round population is about seven thousand. Its summer population is somewhere between forty and fifty thousand. Its first era of prosperity began with the capture of the first whale in 1668, and its second era of prosperity began sometime in the twentieth century, with its capture of rich tourists.

Because it is an island, there are only two ways to get to Nantucket: by boat or by plane. Either way necessitates an element of trust in the traveler.

Nell first went to Nantucket by plane. It was May, and the weather was fine and the O'Learys were paying her way so that she could fly over for the weekend to get acquainted with the town and the boutique. But Nell began the trip disgruntled. It had taken the patience of a saint and the tactics of a four-star general to organize her household so that she could make the trip. She had had to wheedle a neighborhood child into caring for the animals the days she would be gone, pack up weekend clothes for Hannah and Jeremy, and make certain that Jeremy didn't forget his homework, and pack weekend clothes for herself, and leave the Cambridge boutique early in order to drive the children to Newton to leave them with Marlow and Charlotte, and drive back home, lock the car, take a bus to the Park Square bus station in Boston, change, take the subway to the airport. Finally, at six in the evening, she was on her way to Nantucket.

The O'Learys had made it clear that they were doing her a favor by buying her airplane ticket, so Nell kept quiet about the fact that one of the things she hated most in the world was flying. During any week before she had to board a plane, she had nightmares about plane crashes, and she was stiff with terror for the entire flight. Optimistic statistics were no help to her; her fear was not rational. it did not help her to know that her fear was not rational. She did not like to fly. She was not even sure yet that she believed it was possible to fly; she couldn't understand it, and every time she boarded a plane, she did so believing that the insane leap of faith required here was the same that operated for mystics who believed they could walk through fire without being burned.

Still, Nell knew that this kind of attitude was useless on her part. Her friends said to her, "Oh, *Nantucket,* you get to go to Nantucket, how *lucky* you are." As Nell entered the airport, she said to herself: Look, Nell, you've got a weekend free of children, knowing they are safe with their father. You've got on pretty clothes, and you're on your way to a vacation spot that people kill to visit. The plane ride will be short and safe. Don't be such a drag. It's all in your attitude. Enjoy.

There was a bar at the PBA gate at Logan Airport, and while Nell waited for her flight to be called, she bought herself a Bloody Mary, which was served in a plastic cup. Just the idea of this— of being a woman alone in an airport at six o'clock in the evening, wearing a turquoise silk wrap dress and drinking a Bloody Mary— made Nell feel adult and even slightly wicked and glamorous (which just goes to show, Nell thought, how pathetically tame my life really is). But the act of buying the drink helped. The alcohol helped too.

Nell strolled up and down the waiting area, looking out the great high walls of windows at departing and arriving planes, and felt the alcohol ever so slightly curb the bite of anxiety within her. A handsome man in jeans and loafers and a blue cotton shirt bought a drink and smiled at Nell, was looking at Nell each time she looked over at him. This made her feel even more brave. She stopped thinking of plane crashes and thought of plane adventures. Fifty years ago people used to have romantic encounters on ocean voyages; now they had them on airplanes, Nell thought. Forty-five minutes wasn't much time for an encounter, she mused, but then, just as planes moved faster these days, so did people. By the time her flight was called, she was feeling almost devil-may-care.

The plane was a Cessna 402. It held nine people. It was smaller than most station wagon cars; narrower than Nell's car. There was no bathroom, no steward, no curtain or door shutting off the front windshield and the pilot and co-pilot's seat and equipment from view, no way to look into the middle of the plane, as Nell did in larger planes, to pretend she was in a movie theater full of people instead of in a metal mechanical can. Two rows of seats ran side by side, with a window at each seat. There was only one door, and it was necessary to duck to get through it. Nell buckled herself into her seat and felt the anxiety in her stomach begin to slither up past the power of the calming alcohol.

Four other passengers got on. The handsome man in jeans was among them, but a little old man of perhaps eighty came before him and took the seat next to Nell. A chubby kid with rosy cheeks, wearing black slacks and a white shirt with black and gold epaulets got on and sat down at the front of the plane. How cute, Nell thought, the pilot must be teaching him how to fly. Someone behind her shut the door. The apple-cheeked boy put the headphones on his head and began playing with the controls. Oh my God, Nell thought, *that child is the pilot!* Nell couldn't help herself; she leaned over to the little old man seated next to her.

"How old do you have to be to get a pilot's license?" she whispered.

"I don't know," the old man replied. "I think you can get one if you're old enough to have a driver's license. But I'm not sure."

I think I want off this plane, Nell thought, by now shot through with adrenaline and fear. But it was too late. The boy had gotten the plane off the ground. Nell could only sit, staring out the window at the propellers that spun like deranged pinwheels at the front of the wings of the plane. Well, she thought, at least they would all be the first to know if something went wrong.

The plane flew south, low, the shoreline of Massachusetts and the Atlantic Ocean passing beneath them in a curving harmony of green and tan land, blue and green sea. Nell had never flown this low to the earth before; all her other trips had been on commercial planes that immediately zoomed way above the clouds. But now she could look down on fields and forests and highways and houses and the ocean, with its occasional dot of white ship or black boat. She could not, in fact, *not* look down unless she closed her eyes, which she was afraid to do because the motion of the plane was making her slightly dizzy. The plane was small enough so that Nell could feel the buffeting of the wind. Some-

times the wind came as a blow she could feel at the side, sometimes the plane simply dropped a few inches in the air. Nell kept
looking at the solid earth, hoping it would make her feel secure.

Then the solid earth disappeared. Or rather the plane disappeared,
into a cloud. Nell thought the plane rose, and at last they were
suddenly above a cloud, with blue all around them and white down
below them. She checked her watch; the plane was due to land soon.
She hoped she would get a view of Nantucket from the air.

"Fog again," the old man next to her said aloud to no one in
particular.

"Yup," said a woman from behind Nell. "Wouldn't you know."

The plane began to descend into the cloud. It continued to go
down in fog. The apple-faced boy at the controls was muttering
into his headphone. All Nell could see out of any window was
the grayish-white blur of fog.

"Won't be able to land in this weather," said the old man next
to her.

Still the plane plummeted into the vaporous gray. I've had a
good life and the children will be okay with Marlow, Nell thought.
Then, as she watched, the fog disappeared from the front of the
plane and immediately there in its place was the runway and the
boy was landing the plane on it. They touched, bounced lightly,
slowed.

It seemed everyone in the plane sighed at once.

"That was an unbelievable landing," said the old woman behind Nell. "I'm surprised you could get us in."

The young pilot took off his headphones, turned to his passengers, and grinned. "The airport's officially closed now," he said,
pleased. "They closed it as we were landing. Fog," he added,
as if anyone needed the explanation.

Nell stared at the boy, weak with gratitude and admiration.
Now there was someone with confidence, she thought. She admired him and envied him for his ability to trust not only the
mechanics of the universe but his plane, the ground controller
and, most of all, his own abilities. She wanted to thank him
somehow—but then she always felt enormously grateful to pilots
who had landed their planes safely, and she knew better than to
make a scene. People didn't thank pilots, it just wasn't done. So
she rose and squeezed herself out of the plane and onto the ground.

The Nantucket airport was small, a cluster of gray and white
buildings all by themselves beside a field of tarmac. Elizabeth

O'Leary was waiting for her in the PBA building. She offered Nell her cheek.

"Hello, darling," Elizabeth said. "I'm surprised you could make it in." Before Nell could reply, she went on, "Oh dear, you're too dressed up. You'll die in high heels here. The streets are cobblestone, the sidewalks are crooked and broken brick. You're bound to break either the heel of your shoe or your ankle. Your dress is all right, but just barely. You don't have quite the right look. But you'll get it. Do you have any other luggage besides that bag? Good. Come on. Let's go to the boutique."

It took only five mintues to drive in from the airport to the main street of Nantucket, which was called, appropriately enough, Main Street. This part of Main Street was straight, wide, and cobbled, bordered with charming shops. Nell could tell immediately, from the ride through the town and down the Main Street, just how tasteful this place was. The streets were wonderfully winding and narrow, and the houses were mostly gray-shingled saltboxes with an occasional red brick Federal or white Greek Revival mansion here and there. Flowers and trees flourished everywhere, and even the small hills seemed to be dotted tastefully through the town, providing now and then a gentle rise and dip in the landscape. The golden dome and white spires of the local steeples rose gracefully above the town. Shining tidy boats bobbed in the harbor, while a few larger yachts lay still on the ocean, smug in their grand size. The people strolling Main Street seemed to have walked straight out of Ralph Lauren or L. L. Bean advertisements: they wore cotton sweaters tossed loosely over their shoulders and khaki slacks and loafers without socks, and even though it was May, they were tanned. Ah, Nell thought, how very New England this place is, how quintessentially Episcopalian. She knew that Nantucket would have little trade with ambiguity: everything here was clean, crisp, and clear. You knew at once if you belonged here or not.

The O'Learys' shop was just off Main Street, on the corner of Main and Orange, tucked behind the savings bank. It was a small shop with a discreet little sign that said simply, ELIZABETH'S. The building had at one time been a small cottage and was now made over, for the O'Learys' purposes, into a long, narrow boutique downstairs, with office and storage space on the second floor. They had decorated it much like the Cambridge boutique, with plain sanded wooden floors, plain white walls with dresses hanging, angled, like clever decorations, and dressing rooms at the back, papered in Laura Ashley and furnished in brass and wrought iron.

Nell and Elizabeth spent two hours in the store, going over the inventory and the books, discussing the other saleswoman who would be working in the store during the month of May, looking at the clothes. The O'Learys were selling a type of clothing slightly different from that in their Cambridge shop, though it all had Elizabeth's trademark: expensive casualness. Nell's favorite dress was one made of white cotton. It was wide and sort of permanently wrinkled and looked on the hanger like nothing so much as an old sheet, but it was cut so beautifully that anyone who put it on would look elegant immediately, and it would hide a multitude of physical flaws. There were blue-and-white-striped shirts, pink-and-white-striped sweaters, green-and-white-striped dresses, sweaters in cotton oatmeal and cream, in thick chocolaty wool.

"The clothes are delicious this year," Nell murmured, and thought to herself how working with these clothes would satisfy so much within her, even her sense of taste. She felt calm and optimistic in this airy store, where so much was pleasing to the eye and the touch. This kind of luxury had a lulling effect for Nell.

When Elizabeth decided they'd done enough, Nell went through the store with her, locking up. But when they stepped outside, Nell did not go to Elizabeth's small Mercedes right away. She walked a few steps down the street to the corner. She turned, looked, and there was Main Street spread out in front of her with its brick sidewalks and cobblestone street. It was twilight now, and the air was cool but mild. The street glowed gently from shop lights and lamplight. The tall old elms that lined the street shone a soft green where the light fell on the leaves, then rose up out of the light and into the darkness of the night in a leafy gray, so that it looked as though the trees were made of mist. This town had an other-worldly beauty and Nell felt as though she were in Europe, on a side street in an English village, or perhaps not in another place, but in a different time: this could almost be the nineteenth century. Things moved at a different pace here; she could feel that. The air was different here, and why shouldn't it be, for this was an island, and no matter how many new people walked here or how many modern contraptions were placed here, still the land itself was an island, surrounded by water, separate from the rest of the world, and Nell could sense how the elements of this island continued to rise from the earth, from the sidewalks, from the old red brick of the buildings so that the air was and always would be just that much different.

Nell was entranced. She could have stood at the corner staring at the beautiful street forever if Elizabeth hadn't honked her horn several times. "For heaven's sake, Nell," she snapped when Nell got in the car. "What's the matter with you? Aren't you hungry?"

"It's just so beautiful," Nell offered in her defense. "I could look at it forever."

"Yes, well, it will look a lot more beautiful to me when the tourists get here and it's raining and they stroll into my shop to pass the time and spend their money," Elizabeth said, deftly slipping the car into third gear and taking a corner.

Nell looked out the window as Elizabeth drove, trying to establish where they were in connection with the shop, but there were too many twists and turns. Some of the roads were so narrow, scarcely wider than one car. They drove very close past houses with heavy wooden doors with brass knockers, white picket fences, ivy-covered arched trellises leading into arbors. Again Nell had that sensation of being in another time, another land.

The O'Learys' house seemed wonderful to Nell too, although Elizabeth called it the cottage and seemed impatient with Nell's exclamations of pleasure. Elizabeth hurried Nell through the house, showing her the various rooms ("You'll sleep in the guest room tonight, but of course in June we'll be gone and you can have the master bedroom for yourself."), flicking on lights, calling down to Colin ("Fix me a martini, we'll be right down!"). The front part of the house stood squat and four-square, four small rooms up and down, with new bathrooms making rectangular intrusions into two of the rooms. It had not been an old cottage or an especially pretty one, but the O'Learys had spiffed it up with their special flair. All the rooms were carpeted ("because the floorboards were nothing to look at, unfortunately") in a thick nubby golden brown, so that it was like walking through a field of ripe wheat. The walls were all white, and the oak woodwork was natural and pale. The furniture was new, low, modern. There wasn't much of it. This gave the small rooms a feeling of airiness. A narrow hall led past the front two rooms into the small square kitchen, and the back kitchen door had been removed and widened so that the addition to the house beckoned: it was one great open room with a cathedral ceiling and windows all the way around. The wheat carpet was here, and the walls had been paneled in a wood of similar texture and color. It was like walking into a pot of honey. The furniture was teak, glass, tubular aluminum, and somehow these hard and shiny materials had been made to curve and soften, or perhaps it was the effect of the plump cushions on the sofa and the depth of the carpet beneath it all, but the room seemed new, clean, clever, and yet still comfortable, inviting repose.

"It's a marvelous house," Nell said when she sat down with her hosts in the living room.

"It has no architectural integrity," Colin replied.

"There's no view," Elizabeth added. "No view of the water, no view of the moors, and the rooms are far too small."

So Nell said nothing else, not wanting to expose her ignorance, but she was eager to finish drinks and dinner so she could go back and just sit in the small bright guest room. Dinner and drinks went on and on, however, and the talk was mostly business, about clothes and the people Nell should meet and take care to please; the evening was as much work for Nell as pleasure. She didn't get back to her room until almost midnight. It was too dark for her to see anything from her window, and she knew that she'd have an entire summer to enjoy the house, so she just climbed into bed and fell asleep. It might have been the effect of the sea breeze that came in the window Nell had opened or, more likely, the effect of all the wine she had had with dinner and the Bloody Mary earlier, but she had no trouble falling asleep in the strange house and she did not waken all night long. She slept a perfect and restful sleep.

She awoke because the room was full of sun. She felt instantly awake and marvelously rested, as if she had slept deeply for days. She stretched and listened, and heard only silence in the house. "Shit," she said softly, thinking that she must have overslept and that Elizabeth and Colin had gone off to the boutique without her. Elizabeth would be in a snit. Nell sat up in bed, ready to fly into action, and grabbed her watch off the bedside table. It was five forty-five.

She went to the window and leaned on the sill, looking out. The street lay below her, vivid and bright in the morning. Gray-shingled cottages were scattered at random in a rather merry muddle of trees, shrubs, flowers, and grassy yards. Nell knew that once she was on ground level the street would take on an appropriate regularity; she would see how the picket fences and great hedges divided properties into their official lots. It was very green outside and the sky was purely blue. The fog of the previous day had gone.

Nell looked at her watch again. Surely no one would stir in the house for an hour or so, and the shop didn't open until ten. . . . She quickly dressed in jeans, a cotton shirt, a wool sweater, and sneakers, then grabbed up her old windbreaker and tied it around her waist in case it was chillier out than it looked. She went to the trouble of brushing her teeth, but couldn't be bothered to put on any makeup, and why should she bother? she thought, she didn't know anyone here and she doubted that she'd run into anyone at this time of the morning. At any rate, she was going to go walk by the ocean, and she knew that ocean walkers always left each other alone.

She felt rather gay and childish, sneaking down the stairs and out of the house, and upon shutting the cottage door behind her, she felt a strange sensation in her chest, as if her soul were a kernel of corn that had just popped. She was alone! She was free! She was by herself, on her own, to do whatever she wanted for the next few hours.

She began to walk down the street in what she hoped was the direction of the ocean. The O'Learys had said their cottage was only six blocks from the Jetties Beach, so she knew she couldn't go too far wrong no matter which way she went. She didn't quite run, but she walked very fast, exhilarated by the cool morning air, and each time the cushiony rubber soles of her sneakers hit the solid pavement beneath her feet, she felt a great satisfaction run right up her legs and through her body. How much time she had spent in her life *not* walking! Usually she wore dress shoes, in the boutique, or boots in the winter, or anything other than sneakers—she wore these only when cleaning the basement or garage. They had been work shoes, but now they were play shoes and she was delighted. She could tell after a block or two that sneakers were right for Nantucket, because the sidewalks were so cracked and broken, bulging up from the roots of trees, or simply old. It didn't matter. The sidewalks seemed right. Everything seemed right. Here she was alone, without her children, without her bosses, without any man to please or desire, without even her dog and cats—she was just walking down the street in the very early morning, and no one else was in sight. She couldn't remember when she had ever done this before in her life. She turned a corner and saw a sign pointing to Jetties Beach.

It was a longer walk than the O'Learys had indicated, for although the cottage was close to the water, it was not close to any public way to the water. Nell walked for blocks, past streets of cottages, large houses, summer houses, summer mansions, until she came to the street that led down to the sandy beach. She ran down that street, pleased with each step that she could see more and more of the blue. No cars were parked at the end of the road, and the concession stand was closed. The beach was quiet. Nell walked about two hundred yards down the stretch of sand until at last she touched the water. Then she sat for a while at its edge, just looking out at the expanse of blue. This was the harbor side, the Nantucket Sound side, the safe side, and the waves that came in gently were breaking into a flat washing. It was shallow for a great way out, or seemed to be. Nell decided not to test the water today. It would be too cold. She rose and began to walk down the beach slowly, kicking aside seaweed aimlessly, stooping to pick up an interesting shell, tucking ones she liked into her pocket, tossing the others into the water when she had finished studying them. She wasn't really even thinking, she was just walking along.

After a while she saw another person on the beach, a very tall slender person, walking toward her. As the figure drew nearer, Nell saw that it was a man, wearing khaki trousers, old docksiders, a heavy long pullover sweater. He was very tall and lean and dark-haired, and he had a sort of huddled look about him, as if he were trying to withdraw into himself. His shoulders were hunched and his hands were in his pockets and he stooped a bit, as if he were the sort of man who had gained all his height as a young boy and never did learn how to handle it.

When she and the man were just a few feet from each other, they both nodded. Serious, short, silent nods, acknowledging each other's presence but not intruding. They passed each other by.

Nell walked on. The sun was rising higher, and all the water danced, and she wanted to look everywhere at once. Although she couldn't see the mainland, she knew she was facing it, that if she could see far enough, the easy shores of Hyannis would be in view. But the expanse gave her the illusion that she could see forever until the world curved around until she could see herself from the back, a lone woman on the shore. She walked. She found an especially hideous skate's egg case, a long black swollen thing with four creepy antennae sticking out, and she put it in her pocket to take home to Jeremy.

As she bent to pick it up, she noticed that the man she had passed was no longer walking away from her. He was moving toward her. He was perhaps fifty yards away and moving toward her very fast and deliberately.

Nell froze. She tried to act casual, as if she were frozen casually, on purpose. She worked hard at putting the egg case in her jean pocket. No doubt about it, the man was coming toward her. He was very tall, very thin. Anthony Perkins, Nell thought: *Psycho*.

She looked up and down the beach. No other human being was nearby. There wasn't even a dog. Some seagulls were flopping about, but of what help could they be? They only added to her fears with their awful chilling cries. Nell turned away from the man and began walking down the beach a little faster than she had before. She was suddenly cold in spite of the beaming sun. She looked up at the houses that loomed on the hills above the beach—they were too far away, set too far back, and most of the houses seemed empty, with uncurtained windows revealing no signs of life,

Oh my God, Nell thought, I'm going to be killed. Stop it, she told herself, don't be ridiculous. You're not in the city, you're in Nantucket. But why had he changed his course, why was he coming back this way, and why was he walking so much faster?

She stopped on the pretense of inspecting another shell and looked sideways as she bent over and saw that he was gaining on her. He was almost running.

Then he called out to her. She couldn't hear well over the thump of the waves, but it seemed he yelled, "Wait!"

Nell didn't know what to do. She couldn't outrun him. If she screamed, no one would hear. He was so tall and intense a figure but it was broad daylight, a beautiful May morning! So she turned, heart pounding, toward the man and stood watching him as he came up to her.

"I think this is yours," he said, and held out to her her sodden old windbreaker.

"Oh," Nell said, chagrined. She took it from him and held it out from her so that it could drip away from her clothes. "It must have fallen off when I was looking for shells,'' she said. ''Thank you so much.''

''Not at all,'' he said. '' 'Bye.'' Then he turned and plodded steadily back down the beach away from her.

Nell stood and watched him go. She wondered if he could feel her eyes on his back. She wondered if he had felt her fear, her impulse to run. The man really did resemble Anthony Perkins, which would have been all to the good if the movie *Psycho* had never been made, but Nell had been terrified of showers and tall lean men ever since she had seen that film. She wondered if the tall man was aware of this resemblance. She thought he had to be. Maybe that was why he looked so hunched and—lonely. He had a kind face, though, an intelligent face. God, she thought, I wonder what he thought of me. And she put her hand up to her hair, which the sea wind had blown into a thicket of tangles, and remembered that she had no makeup on at all. Oh well, she thought, who cares, I'll never see him again.

She walked on down the beach until she saw, up past the sand dunes and eel grass, steps leading up and up the hill. She climbed the steps and was rewarded with a panorama of the beach and the water. Then she walked along the streets, finding her way through the winding and slanting roads back to the O'Learys' cottage. Some streets were broad and spacious, with large gray-shingled cottages set on well-kept lawns and adorned with carved and painted wooden quarterboards announcing the cottages' names: Blue Harbor, Sans Souci, Little Spouter, Paradise. The closer she got to town, the smaller the streets got, until, near the O'Learys', she once again walked down streets so narrow they could hold only one car at a time. Untrimmed branches of rose or yew brushed her arm as she passed. Here the lawns were smaller but the houses more stately, set closer to the road. Nell could see through the windows of these houses the glitter of crystal chandeliers, the sweep of ornately bannistered staircases, and large gilt-framed oil paintings of ships and seascapes. All the yards were small and neat. Ivy grew up the sides of houses and over picket fences, and daffodils and tulips abounded. Occasionally, Nell saw a metal hitching post in front of an especially old house. Green and yellow wooden weathervanes, shaped like ducks, with wings that flapped in the wind, stood on posts in some yards, but that seemed to be as frivolous as one got around here.

Nell thought of her own yard, which now in the spring was

adorned with bikes, trikes, roller skates, hula hoops, balls, and other more or less predictable outdoor stuff, and also with oddly shaped pieces of furniture the children had dredged out of the basement to build a fort, old plastic bowls and cheap spoons (the children had been playing house, or perhaps Jeremy had been doing another experiment) and, on closer inspection, a multitude of miscellaneous little plastic items that had sunk into the grass—old straws, pink wands used for blowing bubbles, popped balloons, a doll's bracelet. Every time Nell looked out the kitchen window, she could see a yellow knit baby dress that Hannah had worn when she was six months old and that was now hanging from a shrub. Two or three weeks ago Hannah had dressed Fred the cat in baby clothes and wheeled him around the yard in her baby carriage. Fred was as good-tempered and obliging a cat as Medusa was bitchy; Fred was the sort of cat who drooled when petted. He quite liked wearing baby clothes and being wrapped and cuddled and pushed about in a carriage. But a neighborhood dog had come through the yard one afternoon, sending Fred out of the carriage, past the shrubs, and up a tree in a flash. Nell had had the foresight to insist that Hannah not put the baby clothes on Fred tightly, and so as Fred scrambled through the shrub and up the tree, his yellow baby dress had been torn off by a protruding twig. Now it hung there like a limp flag. Once or twice in the past few days when Nell went by the window she stopped quickly and looked, thinking she had spotted a rare bird, a goldfinch perhaps. Then she would realize that it was just the baby dress. She meant to make the children get the dress, just as she meant to make them clean up the yard. But it was spring, and there was so much to do, and the children were so glad to play outside, and she was so glad to have them outside so she could get organized for the summer. . . . Thinking of the children, she walked past the O'Learys' house without realizing it and had to retrace her steps.

It was almost nine o'clock when she reentered the house. Elizabeth and Colin were having coffee in the dining room and going over accounts. Nell joined them for coffee and a croissant, then went back upstairs to shower and dress. She would work by herself in the boutique all day, helping customers and unpacking merchandise. She dressed in her own skirt and shirt, but when they got to the boutique, Elizabeth told her to wear one of the summer dresses they were selling. It was gray and pink striped, with a blouson top that came to the hips and then flared out in huge pleats. The stripes were horizontal. The dress cost around two hundred dollars and would make the wrong person look like an elephant. As Nell stood in the dressing room, looking at the pink-and-gray stripes going around and around her body, she thought of Jeremy's most recent joke: What is green and red and green and red and green and red? A frog in a blender.

God, Nell thought, what a thing to think. She clipped huge pink plastic earrings in her ears and brushed her hair again so that it flew out all over, and came out of the dressing room to open up the store.

Elizabeth hung around until she was sure Nell knew what to do, then left for the day. She had told Nell that it wouldn't be very busy. May was when the season began, but things were still pretty slow. Nell spent the morning arranging jewelry and accessories in a glass case, stopping now and then when someone drifted into the store and back out again. Elizabeth had said she might not be back to relieve her for lunch, and when she wasn't back by one-thirty, Nell closed the store and went upstairs. A small refrigerator was in the back of the office, and she found some new cherry yogurt and a plastic spoon. She spent thirty minutes sitting at the desk eating and reading a paperback novel she had brought with her. Then she put on fresh lipstick and opened the store again.

About three in the afternoon, Nell saw a tall thin man pause in front of the shop, study the clothes in the window, walk away, come back, stand around. At last the man sort of bumbled in the door. He looked helpless, completely lost; he looked just as Nell would have looked in a store that sold computers. He doesn't look like Anthony Perkins, Nell thought; much more like Abe Lincoln. Without the beard. His clothes were all right; his clothes were actually quite nice—khaki pants, a blue cotton button-down shirt with the sleeves rolled up, old loafers without socks—and he had lots of thick brown hair. He looked modern enough. But he carried himself with an air of such bewilderment, such preoccupation, as if he had to work a bit to bring himself down to this plane of reality.

"May I help you?" Nell said, standing up from behind the glass case, where she'd been fanning out a display of scarves.

"Oh," the man said. He looked at Nell. He blinked. She could not tell if he recognized her from their morning encounter at the beach or not. "Yes," he said. "I'd like to buy something for my daughter. For her birthday."

"Oh good," Nell said. "How nice. How old is she?" The man was probably in his forties; the daughter could be any age.

"Sixteen."

"Sweet sixteen," Nell said. She came out from behind the counter and walked toward the dresses. "What size does she wear?" Nell asked. "What's her favorite color?"

"I don't know," the man said, and his face took on an even more gentle cast of melancholy so that he did resemble Abe Lincoln quite a bit. When he spoke he didn't seem uncomfortable or apologetic, merely resigned. "I haven't seen her for a while," he said.

"Oh," Nell said. God, she thought. "Oh well. I'm sorry." Then she bit her lip, thinking she might have said the wrong thing, an intrusive thing.

"I am too," Abe said.

Nell gave her head a little shake as if to clear it of inappropriate thoughts. She was thinking, Does this mean he's divorced? Lives alone? She forced her mind to the task at hand. She looked around the store, thinking. "Well," she said. "Let's see." She walked over to a pile of bulky cotton pullovers that had been hand-knit in Mexico and were shipped to the O'Learys at a ridiculously low price. "How about this sweater?" Nell said. "If you get a small, it will probably fit, and these sweaters are supposed to be baggy. I mean, that's the style. Loose-fitting, even sort of sloppy. That's the look. She could wear it over anything, and this cream color goes with everything. She could wear it by itself if it's hot and over a turtleneck when it's cold." She held it up for Abe Lincoln to look at.

"How much is it?" he asked.

"Sixty-five dollars," Nell said. "It's a good buy, really."

The man stood looking at Nell and the sweater, considering. Then he said, "Why did you show me that?"

"What?" Nell said, startled. "Excuse me?"

The man slowly moved one long arm out into the air, indicating with a slight turn all the clothes in the store around him. "Why didn't you suggest any of these? Why not *this?*" And he stalked over to a dress on display, a marvelous dress of crimson and melon silk.

"Well," Nell said, puzzled, slightly defensive. "Well, that dress is over three hundred dollars. Not that I'm implying you don't want to spend that on your daughter," she hastened to add. "But teenagers don't usually need such expensive clothes . . . and then the style of that dress is so sophisticated. It's too dramatic. Too what we call architected. I don't think a teenager would like it. But of course if you want to look at dresses . . ."

"No," the man said. "No. Thank you. I like the sweater. I was just wondering why you didn't push something more expensive."

"Push?" Nell said. She felt herself flush. "I don't—I'm not in the habit of *pushing* things here," she said. She stood staring at the man, the cotton sweater still in her hands. The customer is always right, don't offend the customer, some of these customers are jerks, but humor them . . . all of Elizabeth and Colin's admonitions rang in Nell's mind. But in spite of herself, she spoke, keeping her voice even. "That was actually a nasty thing to say to me."

"Was it?" Abe Lincoln said. He shook his head. "I'm sorry. I apologize."

"Well," Nell said, now even more nonplussed. "Well. Well, do you want the sweater?"

"Yes," Abe said. "Please. And could you gift-wrap it?"

Nell wrote up the sale. He gave her cash; she did not learn his name. She carefully took the price tag off the sweater, wrapped it in fuchsia tissue, then boxed it in the gray and fuchsia gift-box that said ELIZABETH's. As she worked, she felt the man's eyes on her. When she handed him the box, she met his eyes and said what she had been trained to say to customers, "Here you are. Thank you so much. Please come in again." But her voice was cool.

Abe Lincoln looked at her for a long moment. "I really meant that as a compliment, you see," he said. "I mean so many people try to encourage you to buy the most expensive thing, whether it's suitable or not. I always feel rather helpless when I go into a women's clothing store. I don't know a thing about any of it and so it's easy for a salesperson to take advantage of my great stupidity, and I guess that makes me cranky. But I meant to give you a compliment. You showed me something that you thought my daughter really would like."

Jesus, Nell thought, what rock did you crawl out from under? Listen, Abe, go back to your farm, she thought. Can he be for real? she thought. He made her slightly uneasy, because he seemed so unbelievably honest and helpless. Honest Abe, she thought. At the same time she became aware that he was a man not completely without charm. In fact as she looked at his face, she was reminded of the dogs she had loved most in her life, dogs with the same kind brown eyes and slightly puzzled expression. Those dogs had consistently shown loyalty, an easy if bewildered compassion, and a mute physical generosity. They were the big lanky dogs who had ridden next to her in the car, walked close to her on the street, lain at her feet when she read, and sometimes curled up next to her in bed. She thought this man had the same sort of loping, unstudied appeal.

"Well," Nell said at last. "I'm glad you weren't insulting me. And I do hope your daughter likes her sweater. I really do think she will."

"Thank you," the man said. He left the shop but came back a few minutes later. He stood in the doorway. "I'll probably see you tomorrow morning," he said, and went away.

Nell stood, just staring. Could he possibly have meant that he'd see her again on the beach, that he was looking forward to seeing her again on the beach? Surely not, she thought. But *maybe*, she thought, and grinned.

The rest of the day was uneventful. Some New York tourists came in and bought a lot of stuff but left the dressing rooms in a shambles. Nell rehung everything, straightened up, and realized she was tired when the shop closed at five.

She locked the shop and walked back to the cottage, hoping the walk would refresh her, and it did, but the drink she had with the O'Learys made her sleepy again. Tonight the O'Learys were short-tempered and absorbed in some new legal problem that had arisen with the lease on the New York store, and dinner conversation that night was given over to business. Elizabeth and Colin had cooked the meal of Cornish game hens and rice and fresh vegetables, and Nell insisted on doing the dishes and cleaning up the kitchen.

It was a clever little kitchen, full of the newest appliances, all of which worked, and the can opener was not thick with gunk like the one Nell had on her wall at home, and the knives were sharp and the pots and pans not blackened by use. It would be fun to cook elegant meals here sometime for someone, Nell thought as she worked. She thought of her lover, Stellios. He liked things the children liked—tacos, pizza, cheeseburgers—and for a moment she stood in the kitchen dreaming of a man who might like a soufflé or even, simply, a steak. The children didn't like steaks—they thought they were "too chewy." Which actually was fine with Nell, because she couldn't afford steak anyway.

After she finished the dishes, she sat down with the O'Learys and politely drank a Drambuie with them, but she felt her eyes closing in spite of herself and at ten she managed to excuse herself to go upstairs to bed.

"You can sleep late tomorrow," Elizabeth said. "The shop's closed. Of course we'll have to go in to unpack and price the rest of the merchandise, but we don't have to be there early. We'll have a lovely lazy morning."

"Wonderful," Nell called back.

But when she got to her room, she decided not to pull down the shades. She stood in the middle of the room, making a deal with herself: she would *not* set the alarm, but she would also *not* pull down the shades. So if she woke up early, well then, she would just wake up early and go down for a walk on the beach. And if she slept late, well then, she'd sleep late and love it, for she never got the chance to really sleep late on Sundays, not with the children around.

Sunday morning she woke up at five forty-five. She sat up in bed, grinned, and thought to herself: why not? She felt rather silly as she dressed and—this time—combed her hair and put enough makeup on her eyes to make them look as if they were open. But she was glad to feel silly this way.

Today there was more than a sea breeze, there was a real wind, so that it felt much cooler than the bright sun indicated. Nell strode down the street, hoping the exercise would warm her. The branches of the trees, now opening with their spring-green leaves, looked very pretty dancing in the wind, but Nell thought they would have looked much better if she were seeing them from inside a house while sipping a cup of hot coffee.

What am I doing? she thought, zipping up her old windbreaker and turning up the collar. What do I think I'm up to? But she kept on going. She was warm by the time she got to the water, and she was rewarded by the sight. Today it was as deeply blue as a bluejay's wing, with white caps frothing to the beach. Gulls flew overhead screaming at each other, dipping down into the water, setting back off into the air again. I'll have to bring bread-crumbs sometime, Nell thought, watching one gull pick in the sand. I'll have to have the children bring breadcrumbs; they'll like the gulls.

She looked to her right, toward the harbor side of the beach, and saw an old couple slowly coming through the sand, stopping to pick up shells. She looked to her left and saw the lone lean figure of Abe/Anthony far down the beach, walking her way. She didn't know what to do. Should she walk toward him? Maybe that would be too forward. Too eager. Should she walk away? Then he might think she didn't want to talk to him. She didn't know what to do, so she sat down in the sand and wrapped her arms around her legs and tried to lose herself in studying the ocean.

After a while the older couple came even with her. "Good morning," they said.

"Good morning," Nell replied, smiling.

The old couple toddled on past in the sand, and Nell turned to watch them and saw that Abe/Anthony was nearly to her. He walked with his head shoved forward a bit, as if he were leading his body, and he had the stilted and very stiff gait of a long-legged, soon-to-be-extinct bird. He seemed at once very serious and very silly—gawky. Nell was aware of her unkind thoughts and chastised herself: what do you think he'll think of *you?* she asked herself. She knew her nose would be pinched and red from the cold.

"Good morning," she said when he had drawn near her.

"Good morning," he replied. "Is this space reserved?" He indicated with his hands the space of sand next to her.

She smiled. "No."

"May I join you?" he asked.

"Of course," she said, still smiling.

He settled himself down next to her and then just sat there a while companionably, looking out at the water.

"I'm Nell St. John," Nell said finally, smiling at him again. The sun was in her eyes and she had to squint to see him.

"I'm Andy Martindale," the man said, and held his hand out to her.

Andy—Abe/Anthony, Nell thought, I wasn't that far off! She felt her smile broaden. She shook his hand. "Do you live here on Nantucket?"

"Yeah," he said. "I do. I'm what they call a year-round summer person. That means I've lived here for nine years but I wasn't born here and my family wasn't born here so I'm not a native. I came here every summer as a child and I have lived here full-time for nine years and this is my only residence, but I'm still considered a year-round summer person, and I guess I always will be. Not a *real* Nantucketer, you know."

Nell grinned. "Well," she said. "I'm a *real* newcomer. I mean this is my first time on the island. I'll be in here this summer, though. I guess that makes me a summer person."

"Where do you live?" he asked.

"In Arlington," Nell said. "I live in Arlington and work in a boutique in Cambridge. The O'Learys—Colin and Elizabeth, you might know them—own both the boutiques. They want me to run the Nantucket one this summer. That's why I'm here."

"Why do you work in that boutique?" Andy asked.

Nell was startled. "Why? Well, because I need to support myself," she said.

"Yeah. But why a boutique? Do you like it?"

He was almost peering at her as he asked this question, and Nell felt a bit like a scientific specimen. What kind of person asks that sort of question? she thought. But he did not seem flippant. She considered. "Yes," she said at last. "I like it very much. I like clothes. I love clothes. I like fabric and color, and I like people. It's really quite wonderful to see someone transformed by a good dress."

"Yes, but it's not very important work, do you think? Not really a challenge?"

You're a real charmer, Nell thought, but in spite of herself she laughed. "Listen," she said. "The last thing in the world I need is a challenge. I've had challenges all my life, I've got enough challenges just getting through the day." She stopped, grew serious, looked at him. Okay, buddy, I can be as intense as you, she thought. "And you're wrong if you think it's not important. It's very important. Well." She stopped, thinking it out. "Perhaps not *very* important. Not as important, say, as doing research on cancer, that sort of thing. But maybe as important as flying to the moon. I mean clothes in general and the moon in general. Beautiful clothes aren't necessities, but then neither is going to the moon."

Andy stared at her. "That point is debatable," he said. "Well, but is this it for you? Your goal in life? To sell expensive clothes in a boutique?"

"How come you're so rude?" Nell asked. She glared at him, finally angered by his boorishness, and the wind whipped her hair in her eyes and made her wince.

"Oh God," Andy said. "Was I being rude? I'm sorry." He stared back out at the ocean as if reconsidering.

Nell sat next to him and glared out at the ocean. You may be attractive, she thought—and he was, he was very attractive sitting next to her there with his very long legs and his doggy face. He had hazel eyes and dark brown lashes and lines around his eyes that crinkled when he smiled or squinted. His face had that craggy bony homeliness that fell just short of great handsomeness. You are attractive, Nell thought, but I think you're too rough at the edges for me.

"Listen," he said, turning to her quickly. Nell thought he was going to say: here's what I mean to say. Instead, he said, "Let's go have a cup of coffee."

Nell paused. "Well, where? I mean, it's early for a coffee shop to be open. . . ."

"No, no," Andy said. "My house is just up there." He pointed to a huge gray Victorian on a cliff.

Well, Nell thought, I don't think he's going to murder me. He'll just insult me to death.

"Okay," she said, and they rose and began walking along the beach to the steps that climbed the long hill. They didn't speak as they walked. It was necessary to walk single file up the narrow steps. Then Nell had to work to keep up with him, he had such a long stride.

His house was mammoth, fabulous, and echoing. It was a sprawling Victorian with porches and bay windows and gables and peaks and views of the water, and most of the rooms were completely or partially empty. As Andy fixed the coffee in the kitchen, Nell looked through the downstairs and saw rooms with beautifully sanded floors and ornately carved marble-manteled fireplaces. And no furniture.

"Did you just move in?" Nell asked, coming back to the kitchen.

"Oh no," Andy said. "I've lived here nine years."

The theme music from *Twilight Zone* began to play in Nell's head. She looked around the kitchen. This room, at least, was normal. There was a refrigerator, which was in fact a deluxe snazzy affair with an appliance in the door that gave ice water and ice cubes. There was a wonderful gas oven, a Jennair range top for grilling, and a microwave oven. Every conceivable appliance lined the clean countertops, and a long silky-looking walnut table was placed next to the window so that one could sit at the table and look out at the ocean. The room was not decorated; the walls were off-white and there were no curtains, but it did look lived in.

Andy was fiddling with the Mr. Coffee machine. "I prefer the rooms upstairs," he said at last. "They give a better view." He poured cups of coffee into thick pottery mugs. "Sit down," he said, motioning to the table by the window, and Nell sat, and so did he, on antique walnut chairs softened with quilted cushions. They sat for a moment in comfortable silence. "I live here alone," he said after sipping his coffee. "So I guess I don't need as many rooms as a family. I keep all my stuff upstairs. I guess it does look queer to a stranger. But I wanted a house with a view of the ocean, an old house, and this was all I could find."

"What do you do?" Nell asked.

"Huh?" Andy said. "Well," he said, and leaned back in his chair and thought about it for a moment. "I don't really know," he said finally.

"You don't really know what you do?" Nell asked, incredulous.

"Now wait a minute," he said. "I'm trying to explain. Well, I used to invent things. And then I stopped." He turned to her and nodded, seemingly satisfied with his explanation.

"You used to invent things?" Nell asked. "What sort of things?"

"Terrible things," Andy said. "Really terrible things. That's why I stopped. I'd rather not talk about it."

"Well now, you can't just stop there," Nell said. "I mean you've got to be a little clearer. Did you invent bombs? Special poisons? That kind of terrible things?"

Andy laughed. "No, oh no," he said. "Nothing like that at all. Look at the sailboat." He pointed out to the water, where a boat with a rainbow-striped sail was skipping along the waves.

"I think you're trying to change the subject," Nell said.

"I am," Andy said. "They've got a great day for sailing."

"Thanks for the coffee," Nell said, and rose and zipped up her windbreaker.

"What?" he asked. He had been leaning back in his chair so that it rested on its two back legs—one of Jeremy's favorite and most irritating tricks (Nell was always afraid he'd fall over and break his head open)—and now he brought his legs and the chair back down with a thud. "You haven't finished your coffee."

"I know," Nell said. "But I'd better go anyway." She started across the kitchen.

"You're going to leave just because I won't tell you what I invented, aren't you?" he asked.

Nell stood in the doorway leading to the back door and porch they had come in. "Yes," she said. "That's right." She stared at him. He stared back. Neither of them spoke. Nell turned and went out the door.

"Ashtrays for mobile homes!" he called after her. "Toilets for private jets!"

Nell stopped on the top step. Andy came to the door and stood, pressing his face against the screen. She turned and looked at him.

"See?" he said. "See what I mean by terrible? I designed gadgets for private luxury vehicles. There's a lot of money in it. You'd be surprised. And I love technology; love figuring out little problems. But after a while I thought I just couldn't go on in life designing toilets. So I moved here. Now I'm designing a software package for home computers. And writing a book about twentieth-century technology. But both projects are just in the embryo stage. Nothing to show anybody yet." He shrugged, then looked at her in appeal. He was a very appealing man.

"I guess I'll finish my coffee," Nell said.

She went back into the echoing Victorian house and sat with him for the rest of the morning, talking and drinking coffee and eating toast with rose hip jelly. He continued to talk in starts and lurches, as if conversation was for him a rusty contraption that hadn't had much recent use. Now and then he made her smile. Now and then she made him laugh, and she saw that he had the most endearing smile. He had beautiful, evenly spaced white teeth. As the morning went on, it grew warm in the kitchen and he pulled his sweater up over his head and rolled up the sleeves of his button-down shirt and Nell noticed that he had thick black hair on his arms and even on the back of his hands and the knuckles of each of his long fingers. He didn't say much more about himself. Nell found out that he was divorced, that he had one daughter who was in prep school, that his ex-wife lived in New York City, that he liked mysteries, Alfred Hitchcock movies, jazz, Scotch, solitude. Mostly Nell talked about herself, because he asked so many questions. Finally Nell said she had better go, that her hosts, who were also her bosses, would be expecting her. They had work to do even though it was a Sunday.

"Look," he said, when she rose to go the second time. "Can you have dinner with me tonight?"

"Oh, I'd like to," Nell said, "but my plane leaves for Boston at seven."

"Oh," he said. "Well then, let's just eat early. We could eat at five and then I'd drive you to the airport."

"Oh," Nell said, and her heart flipped a bit at his persistence. She was pleased. "But are any restaurants open that early?"

"Well, I thought we'd eat here," he said. "I don't much like eating in restaurants. And I'm a good cook."

Nell smiled. "All right, then," she said. "That would be nice. I'll have Elizabeth drop me off here around five and we can eat and then you can drive me to the airport. If you're sure you don't mind . . ."

"No, no," he said. "I wouldn't mind driving you to the airport at all. It would be a mild price to pay for the pleasure of your company," he said, then grinned at himself, as if surprised at his courtliness.

Nell grinned back. A current of attraction that was as definite and enticing as a cat's purr ran between the two of them. "See you then," she said, and left.

Nell looked at her watch as she walked. It was ten-fifteen. How had it gotten so late, she wondered. Amazing. She hoped the O'Learys wouldn't be upset at her absence; she hadn't thought to leave them a note. When she got to the house, she found them rushing around downstairs, fully dressed and in a snit, but not at her.

"I forgot there's a gallery opening in New York this afternoon that it's essential we go to," Elizabeth said. "I really need a secretary," she muttered, glaring at Colin. "Three shops in three different places; it's just too much to keep track of. We've got to go, we've got to catch a plane. Look, Nell, you finish the un-packing today and be sure the store's locked tonight. And the house. All right. You know, it would be an enormous help if you could just come on over now and run the store for us. I hate leaving it in the hands of that girl." Elizabeth stared at Nell.

Nell stared back at her employer. "I really can't come before June, Elizabeth," she said. "I've got to stay in Arlington until the kids get out of school. I'm sorry."

Elizabeth continued to stare at Nell, her face set. Then she sighed. "Well," she said, "I suppose nothing disastrous will happen while Mindy's in charge, and the really busy season won't begin till you get here. Still. Look, why don't you plan to come back over in two more weeks. We'll have more stock to price and arrange, and I don't know if I'll be able to get here then. All right? We'll take care of the plane ticket again, of course. All right. Now here's the key to the house and here's the key to the shop. You know where everything is, and what needs to be done. You can get yourself to the airport okay, just call a taxi. We've got to run. You are a jewel." Elizabeth kissed the air near Nell's cheek, grabbed up her Gucci bag, and flew out the door.

Her husband followed close after her. "We're counting on you, you know, Nell," he said. "Be sure to lock up."

After the O'Learys were gone, Nell stood, a bit stunned, still in the entrance hall in her jeans and sneakers. She watched the O'Learys ride off in the taxi, and then everything was silent. She sighed. She stretched. She walked through the house, studying each room more carefully now that she was alone. It was not a beautiful house, she thought, but it was uncluttered and bright. And she would have it for three months! It really was going to be fun.

She went upstairs, showered, put on a fresh shirt with her jeans, and walked to the boutique. She worked hard. She had orders to unpack and price and hang, invoices to check, boring paperwork to do in addition to the pleasurable tasks of fiddling with the lovely clothes. But Nell was conscientious. She was happy. She found a radio and turned on a rock station and worked steadily all morning and most of the afternoon. When she finished, she surveyed her work with satisfaction. Mindy, who would run the store for the next two weeks, would have little to do other than just sell the clothes and smile at the customers.

Nell shut and locked the shop around four and walked back to the O'Learys' house to pack and get ready for her dinner date with Andy. She took her time putting on makeup. She wanted to do it so artfully that it would seem she was wearing no makeup at all. Her hand shook a bit as she applied the mascara. Andy was the first attractive, intelligent, grown-up man to interest her in a long time, in years. She wanted everything to go right—this mattered to her. It seemed that this could be the beginning of . . . She could not find the courage to articulate anything more than that awful word, *relationship*. Well, this could be the beginning of, if nothing else, an interesting relationship. What bland words,

what a jaded expression, when here she was, as confused and
hopeful about the possibilities of this evening and this man as if
she were a teenager. She knew she wanted to kiss him. She had
wanted to kiss him that morning. She had wanted to reach across
to touch the black hair that ran down his arms to his hands. She
was intensely attracted to him—but what should she do? What
would he do? They scarcely knew each other. She was grateful
that she had to catch a plane back to Boston. That would prevent
her from having to make too many decisions.

Then, as she stood, freshly made up and perfumed in her bra
and pants, she faced another problem. She had come in a dress
with high heels, and she had brought jeans and shirts and sneakers. Now she had to walk to his house, which was a good thirty-
minute walk. She wanted to wear her dress; it was a becoming
dress, simple and alluring. But she'd never survive if she tried to
walk all those blocks in her high heels. If the cobblestone streets
and brick sidewalks didn't get her, the cracks and bumps in the
cement sidewalks would. But she didn't want to put on her jeans
again. She stood for a moment, miffed at the O'Learys, at their
thoughtlessness in not leaving her their car. Then she realized
how ridiculous that thought was and decided to call a taxi. But
she had very little cash in her purse, and she had no idea how
much a taxi would cost here—everything seemed to cost twice as
much here as in Boston.

Finally she put on her elegant cotton dress and her sneakers.
She packed everything else in her canvas suitcase and put her
high heels on top. She locked the O'Learys' cottage and walked
to Andy's. When she was two blocks away from his house she
stopped, leaned up against a picket fence, and changed shoes.
Then she went on.

She was glad she had worn the dress. Andy had shaved and
put on gray flannels and a white cotton shirt. And he had gone to
a lot of trouble with the dinner. She was pleased and surprised
and also a little horrified at how delicious and exquisitely prepared
everything was. They sat in the kitchen again, but the dishes were
thin china and the flatware was heavy silver. Andy had chosen a
different wine for each course. First he served a homemade vegetable soup. The liquid was clear and the vegetables almost crisp,
so that each bite scintillated against her tongue. While Nell
watched, he prepared escalopes de veau à la chasseur. It didn't
take long, but it was an elaborate undertaking requiring, Nell

would have thought, great concentration. But as Andy worked, doing mysterious things with wine and shallots and mushrooms, deftly mixing butter with cornstarch and stirring it in a shining copper-bottomed pan, he continued to chat with ease. Nell was impressed. She would never have tried such a feat in front of another person, especially not for a first dinner. She hated making clever sauces. She always scorched them or used too much thickening or not enough. And she certainly couldn't have *talked* while fixing such an elaborate and delicate dish.

Andy arranged the meat on a platter in a geometric design with the shallots and mushrooms and poured the sauce over it all. He brought it to the table, set it down, then took hot French bread and a casserole of green beans and almonds from the oven. Nell looked at the platter before her and was almost more astounded than hungry. She thought she would have felt rather silly arranging mushroom caps and shallots just so like that, serving up something that more closely resembled a work of art than a plate of food.

"I don't know whether to eat this or photograph it," Nell said, smiling.

"I like to cook," Andy said. "Food tastes better to me if it's well prepared and served. We are human beings, after all, not animals, and eating should be a pleasure, not just a necessity."

Jesus, Nell thought, how can he be so serious about this? She thought eating was *always* a pleasure, even if it was a junk food hamburger served in a cardboard box. Often nothing was more pleasurable than standing over the stove at the end of a meal, scraping the crisp, oil-soaked crusts of meat from the bottom of the skillet and eating them while the cats and dog stood glaring at her with greed, or scooping hardened homemade fudge from the sides of the pan, or surreptitiously spooning uncooked cookie dough into her mouth when the children weren't around to see.

"I'll never be able to have you to dinner," she said as he served her. "I'm already completely intimidated. Honestly," she said, smiling.

"Well, don't be," Andy said, looking gruff.

They ate for a few minutes in silence.

"This is delicious," Nell said. "This is unbelievable." She grinned. "Awesome," she said. "Totally." Seeing the expression on his face, she added, "That's what the kids say when something's good beyond description."

Andy was silent for a while, still looking gruff and rather worried. Then he looked at Nell, leaned his elbows on the table, and said, ''Well, you see, if you live alone and eat alone, if you aren't careful, you can eat all your meals in just about five minutes. Then your stomach might be full, but you don't have that satisfied feeling of having had something. I mean, the times before and after eating are different. Eating is a sort of time-out, and it makes each part of the day different. But if it only takes five minutes to eat, then the whole day just sort of stretches out, all the same. I'm not making very much sense, am I?''

Nell studied Andy a moment and wondered to herself how she would cook if she lived all alone and didn't have to work. She doubted very much that she'd start cooking escalopes de veau à la chasseur for herself. More probably, she'd lie around all day reading and eating candy bars and chili from cans. But it touched her that Andy did this, and it touched her that he told her about it. It made him seem endearing and a little vulnerable.

''You are a strange man,'' she said, smiling. ''But a great cook.'' They smiled at each other for a long moment, then went back to eating.

After a while Andy said, ''Well, how do you cook? What do you cook?''

Nell laughed. ''It depends,'' she said. ''I've told you I have children eight and ten and that I work in a boutique—well, somedays I'm too tired to cook at all. Then we order pizza, or eat frozen TV dinners—don't look so disgusted, some of them are quite good—or just sandwiches. I'm really pretty limited by the children, actually, because they like so few things. Hamburgers. Tacos. Pizza. Chicken. Baloney. Hot dogs. Don't look so alarmed! You must have liked all that stuff when you were a kid.''

Andy shook his head. ''It's a long time since I was a kid,'' he said. ''It's been a long time since I've had a hot dog, for that matter. I can't remember when I last had one.''

''Well, now, I know what I'll serve you when you come to my place,'' Nell said. ''Nice juicy grilled hot dogs on a bun with mustard and relish and tons of chopped onions.'' Nell laughed. ''I'm afraid I sort of equate the deliciousness of food with the amount that drips on my hands when I eat it.''

This made him laugh, and Nell was pleased. They talked more about food, and he asked her about her children. He removed her dinner plate and set a green salad in front of her. When they had finished that, he put a board with various cheeses and fruits on the table. He placed grape scissors and a heavy ornate fruit knife next to the board. He served her aromatic coffee in a china cup. Nell watched Andy as he moved around the kitchen, handling all his delicate dishes with an unconscious awkward gentleness. He was beginning to seem more and more to Nell like some exotic and slightly melancholy creature caught in a strange world. He had the elegance and bewilderedness of, say, a giraffe who had through some sort of spell been constrained to wear the clothes and live the life of a man.

"I can't stay much longer," Nell said. "My plane leaves at seven. I hate to eat and run, but . . ."

"When will you be back?" Andy asked.

"In two weeks," Nell said. "For the weekend again."

"Will you have dinner with me in two weeks, then?"

"Of course." Nell smiled. "And I'll be able to have you to dinner, too. The O'Learys won't be here. They have to stay in New York. I'll have their house then, and for the entire summer." She smiled at him and he smiled back and they sat like that awhile until Nell felt embarrassed and warm all over. "I'd better call a taxi," she said, shaking herself a little and looking away.

"No, no, I'll drive you to the airport," he said.

Nell rose and walked through the house to the front hall, where she had left her bag. Andy followed, taking the keys from his trouser pockets as he walked.

"Here, let me," he said, taking the bag from her. There was an awkward moment as he tried to take the bag too quickly from her shoulder while her arm was still caught in it so that their arms were caught together. Nell was too shaken by the touch of his arm against hers to have the sense to smile, and then, thank heavens, he put his other arm around her and drew her to him and kissed her. They stood kissing in the hall with her suitcase hanging from both their arms.

When they finally stopped kissing, Andy drew back a bit and studied Nell's face. "You're wonderful," he said.

"Oh," Nell said. "Oh my. Well, you are too."

"I wish you could stay," he said. "It's been a long time since I've wanted anything like I want you to stay right now."

"I wish I could stay too," Nell said, and her voice cracked a bit. She was having trouble talking. She was having trouble breathing. She wanted to press herself back up against him and wrap herself around him and get lost in his kiss again, but instead she pulled back. "I really do have to go. I'm sorry."

They got to the airport on time, and he kissed her again, and she boarded the plane and it lifted off the ground. This time it didn't occur to Nell to worry about plane crashes.

Six

On June fourth, at three-thirty in the afternoon, Nell drove her old and very heavily loaded Toyota up a ramp, off the mainland of Massachusetts, and into the bowels of the giant ferry that would take her to her summer in Nantucket. She parked where instructed, just inches away from a station wagon in front of her, and saw a yellow Jeep convertible come looming up behind her. Next to her a golden retriever sat calmly in the driver's seat of a Volvo, looking as if he himself had just parked the car. All around her car doors were slamming as people left their cars to go to the upper decks for lunch or to watch the ferry take off or simply to sit in a more comfortable spot. But Nell sat rooted in the seat of her car as if glued there. She was having trouble getting her breath. She did not think it had to do with the fumes from other cars and trucks on the ferry. She knew she was close to hyperventilating from fear and joy and anxiety and hope

If her children had been with her, they would have been clamoring at her by now to move. She could almost hear them: "Mo-*om*. Come o-*on!*" they would whine, full of impatience. But they were not here now, forcing her to act normal. It was not normal that they were not here. That was one of the reasons she was hyperventilating.

Hannah and Jeremy were in a car with Charlotte and Marlow, somewhere in the United States, on their way across the continent to Chicago, where Marlow would direct summer theater and Charlotte would reluctantly play stepmother to Nell's children. The children would not be wearing seat belts on this cross-country trip. Marlow was rabid on the subject of seat belts; he almost equated them with a communist plot to hinder Americans in their expression of personal freedom. No restraints in his car! Nell nearly got sick thinking about it. It was very hard to give the children over to Marlow, to give over the responsibility of their lives and health and welfare to the wildman who was their father. She had done it physically just this morning, when she kissed them goodbye as they got into Marlow's car. But she was having a hard time doing it symbolically. It was as if by sitting in her car, thinking of them, she could keep them safe, but by going up on deck and beginning the summer, she was somehow consigning them to the careless whims of fate. Oh God, she missed her children so. She wished she hadn't let them go. But Marlow had wanted them with him, and they had wanted to go, and legally it was right, and she would have them back with her on Nantucket for the month of August. . . . Still. It was almost intolerable for her to be without them for such a long time.

The world seemed a very odd place to her today. It seemed so odd that it wouldn't have surprised her if the golden retriever in the car next to her had lit up a cigarette and started reading a newspaper. The world seemed topsy-turvy. There her children were, zooming across the earth in a car with Marlow and Charlotte, who had dyed her short spiky hair orange and had taken to wearing silver glitter stars at the outer corner of her eyes even in the day—Nell thought that Charlotte was having this fit of punk because she was going to be thirty this summer—and here Nell was, on her way to three months in Nantucket, where she would live with her ex-stepdaughter, who would be arriving the next day.

Nell wondered if her children would ever have the sort of relationship with Charlotte that Nell had with Clary. Certainly Hannah and Jeremy liked Charlotte well enough. It didn't bother *them* that she didn't remind them to brush their teeth or eat their vegetables. Last summer the children had spent a month with Marlow and Charlotte. When they returned to Nell, their hair felt like wire. They had not washed it for the entire month. No one had told them to. On the other hand, Charlotte was not mean to them, and apparently, when she fixed food for Marlow, she fed the children too, and that was important. Charlotte was undemanding and occasionally amusing. She let them watch television as much as they wanted and wear dirty socks to bed if they wished, and now and then when she was bored, she would play a game of cards or Monopoly with them. She was really more like another child, Marlow's favorite child, with Hannah and Jeremy, than she was a stepmother. Oh, it was fine, they would be *fine*.

Stellios would be fine, too. Nell had put off seeing him for almost three weeks, afraid that when she told him she was involved with someone else, he would be hurt. But when they were finally seated across a tiny table from each other at a cozy Greek restaurant, he confided that he, too, had met someone else. An American girl of Greek ancestry, a young student. His family thought she was a very fine woman. Nell wished Stellios well, and he wished her well, and they toasted each other's future luck and love with red wine over a plate of stuffed grape leaves. And so that part of Nell's life ended, more pleasantly than she had thought it would.

Nell felt a thump and shudder pass through the long boat as it pulled away from the dock and began its trip across the water. The ship's motion was actually very slight and pleasant. She knew that she should be on deck, because today was a beautiful day, bright and clear and warm. But still she sat in the relative gloom of the car deck, huddled in the safety of her car. She did not want to be exposed to the beauty of the voyage. She especially did not want to watch the ferry pull away from shore. It would move her too much. She was afraid of beauty, afraid of change, afraid of leaving the security of her known life for this Nantucket summer. She was afraid for herself, because she thought it very likely that she was falling in love.

Falling in love: an apt phrase, Nell thought, for she did feel like Alice in Wonderland, falling down the rabbit's hole, with the entire world whirling and revolving around her with no place ever to catch hold. This was really more frightening than fun, she thought. This was not just infatuation or lust or the silly smug pleasure of being admired by some good-looking man. No. She was afraid this was it, the Real Thing, the dreaded falling in love.

After Nell returned from her first trip to Nantucket, Andy had called her almost every other night, and when she flew over for the second time in May, he met her at the airport. Nell worked at Elizabeth's—worked hard, worked well, flying about with a giddy manic energy that let her accomplish twice as much as usual. When she wasn't working at Elizabeth's that weekend, she was with Andy.

Friday and Saturday evenings when she closed the boutique, he drove her around the island, showing her the different beaches and moors, which shimmered under the clear sunlight, full of the promise of spring. He knew a lot about Nantucket and told her what he knew in the same earnest, slightly amazed way that Hannah and Jeremy told Nell about all the discoveries they were making about the world. He stood on a large flat rock at the Jetties Beach and said, "You know, when I was a boy, this *very* rock was surrounded by water. *Surrounded.* Now the water doesn't touch it even when the tide comes in. Think of how the sea is endlessly, silently, constantly depositing sand. How it builds up. Such *persistence.*"

With his hands jammed into the windbreaker pockets and his head and shoulders hunched forward, Andy perched on the rock, pondering the ways of the natural world. Nell stood away from him, admiring him because he loved what could not love him back. It seemed the quality of a superior man. She was not particularly impressed that the ocean deposited sand on the beach—she was much more impressed with the storky length of Andy's legs—but she liked him for his thoughts.

Friday he took her out to dinner, and Saturday he cooked another gourmet meal for her at his home. Both times he continued to regale her with Nantucket tales. She liked the ones about the wives of sea captains who, missing their husbands so desperately, turned to the use of laudanum. She liked hearing stories of passion and desire on this island. More often than not, however, Andy would wander off from such tales onto his pet topic, the environment. Sometimes Nell was interested, sometimes bored— and once they got into an argument.

They had been in his kitchen. It was dark, they were seated at his long table, and he had just served Nell Nantucket scallops sautéed in wine. She was eating them slowly, savoring the delicate sweet white flesh.

"You know," Andy said, "you must *never* buy chunk light tuna in cans."

Nell grinned at him; she couldn't help it. He spoke so very seriously. "Why not?" she asked. "God, Andy, we live on tuna at our house."

"I know. It's not the tuna. Tuna's good for you, and there's enough of the fish so that it's not endangered. No, it's the dolphins. They swim along just over the tuna, you see, and the fishermen who catch the tuna do it in such a way that they also bring up the dolphins, which are then killed and thrown back into the sea. Useless deaths of intelligent creatures. Horrible. Fortunately, there's been a national organization formed to lobby and

protest, to try to stop the companies from using that method to
catch the tuna. They have other ways.''

"But would the other ways be more expensive?'' Nell asked.

"That doesn't matter,'' Andy said.

"Oh, but it does,'' Nell replied. "I mean, Andy, I think dolphins are nice, they're cute, the pictures I've seen of them, I
mean. They seem endearing enough. But I also find eating an
endearing thing. I mean, tuna is something that I can afford to
feed my children, and it's nutritious and non-fattening. I'd hate
it if the price went up. It would really make a major difference
in my life.''

"Oh, I don't think so,'' Andy said.

"But it's true!'' Nell protested. "Andy, it's true. You're living
alone, but believe me, if you've got two children to support . . .
and it's not just me. There are lots of families who would be hurt
if the price of tuna went up.''

"There have to be some things more important than money— ''
Andy began.

"That's easy to say if you've got plenty of it,'' Nell interrupted.

"—and man's the only creature on earth who puts acquisition
first in his set of values.''

"Man's the only creature on earth that *has* a set of values,''
Nell said. She was so upset, she stopped eating her scallops and
took a big drink of wine. "Do you think the sharks, or whatever
it is that eats dolphins, something out there in the ocean must, do
you think they feel any guilt about it? No, they just go up and
take a bite out of whatever neighboring fish looks tasty to them
at the moment. Human beings at least don't do that.''

"No, what we do is worse,'' Andy replied. He, too, had
stopped eating and was leaning forward now, speaking quietly
but determinedly. "We kill what we can't eat, as in the case of
the dolphins and the tuna. We kill and waste. We litter the seas
of the world with unnecessary death.''

"Perhaps. But not on purpose. It's accidental, it's a consequence of necessary actions. Man has always had to plot to eat,
and we can't foresee everything.''

"Man is evil,'' Andy said. "Wasting lives is evil, wasting the
world, using it up greedily, is evil. It's not just the dolphins,
Nell. Everywhere you look you'll find man wasting the natural
world. Just look at Nantucket sometime. Drive out into the moors
and see how that fragile landscape is being trashed up, its natural

beauty becoming ruined forever. People build houses and drive
their cars and Jeeps and mopeds on the beautiful moors. They
scar the land; they waste it forever. It's terrible what man does
to nature.''

"Yes, Andy, I think you're partly right, but what is the world
for? Isn't it for men to use and love and enjoy?" Nell asked.

Andy leaned back in his chair, pondering Nell's question. He
ate a scallop as he thought, and as Nell watched, a strange, worried expression came across his face.

"What's wrong?" Nell asked, slightly alarmed.

"We've let the scallops get cold," Andy replied, his voice
funereal.

Nell burst out laughing. She let Andy take her plate and quickly
reheat her scallops in a pan of wine. They finished their meal
before resuming their discussion; after dinner, over coffee and
brandy, they argued again. Andy was on the side of nature. Nell
championed the needs of people. Their argument grew heated,
but Nell didn't mind this difference of opinion. Rather, she was
secretly euphoric—*at last* she was having an affair with a well-
read, thoughtful, intelligent man. And he actually treated Nell as
an *equal* in their discussion, which Marlow had never done. She
found their argument more romantic than a dozen red roses, more
seductive than poetry and champagne.

And they were very good in bed together. They were so very
good in bed together, and it was so intense for Nell that she was
afraid. It was as if in their making love together, Andy had somehow opened a Pandora's box within Nell and out had come all
sorts of violent and imperious emotions that Nell had never known
she possessed: addictive lust, irrational jealousy, desperate ap-
petites. Every emotion in her had been switched to high. When
she was with Andy that weekend, it had been heaven to feel this
way, with the sex and the simple pleasure of his presence filling
her with joy. But when she went back to Arlington for three
weeks and was without him, she missed him terribly, more than
she should have. It really was *uncomfortable*, being in love this
way.

Nell sat in her car feeling as wild as a junkie craving a fix, and
almost as ashamed. How could she let herself get into such a
state? She hardly knew Andy Martindale; how could she let herself feel that the meaning of her entire life revolved around his
presence? She felt as if she'd been strapped in a spaceship and

was just now taking off for the moon. You're only going to Nantucket, she told herself. You'll be fine, she muttered to herself: *Nell, you'll be fine.*

The dog in the car next to her whined. She looked at it. It was looking at her. Perhaps she had been talking aloud. Perhaps her presence was worrying the dog. Poor dog, she thought. Poor me. She undid her seat belt and got out of the car, locked it, and went to the upper deck of the ferry to buy herself a sandwich and a beer.

The ferry was packed with vacationers, and every one of them looked calm and happy. College and high school boys sprawled shirtless across chairs, trying to get an early tan. Here and there boys and girls sat in shorts, looking out at the ocean, heads bobbing in rhythm to the beat coming from the Walkman plugged into their ears. Everywhere people sat smiling, talking with each other, their faces turned up to the sun.

Nell took her turkey sandwich and beer and sat down in one of the orange chairs on the deck of the bow. She could swallow the beer, but she was having trouble with the sandwich. This had happened since she first met Andy, this problem with swallowing solid foods. When she was with him, she could do it, but when she was not with him, her body went into a kind of shock, a sort of paralysis, as if in its extreme need to sort out the emotions that had hit her like a hurricane, it was incapable of dealing with anything else, as if it did not want one more piece of anything put into it. She had lost almost ten pounds in the past three weeks. This was fine—she looked great in her bikini now—but she didn't want to lose any more weight. And she didn't want to make herself sick. She swallowed some beer to make her mouth wet and took a small bite of food. Perhaps, she thought, if she could think of something else, something other than the children or Andy and this summer she was facing . . .

"That's a nice dog you have there," someone said from behind her.

Nell turned slightly and looked. A nice elderly man in whale pants and a patchwork cap was sitting down next to a young man who had a huge black and white husky dog at his feet.

"Yes, she is nice, isn't she," the man said. "Her name is Guinevere. I'm taking her to Nantucket for the week to teach her to swim."

"Really," the old man said. "Well, what do you know about

that? That's interesting. That's something. Now, she's a husky, isn't she? She's not a natural swimming dog, is she?''

"No, she's not a natural swimmer," the man said. "In fact she's afraid of the water. I've had her for five years now and I've never been able to get her in the water. So this year I just decided this is it. This is the time. So I'm taking time off from work, and I'm going to teach her to swim. I've got it all planned.''

"Well now, maybe she doesn't *want* to swim," the old man said. "Some dogs don't.''

"No, no, Guinevere wants to swim. I know. Whenever I go in, she always sits there looking at me with this pleading expression. She's just about *saying*, 'Henry, why won't you teach me to swim?' I know she wants to learn. So I've got this plan. I've got ten days. I'll keep her on a leash. The first day I'll just take her walking in the surf, right at the edge. She'll just get her feet wet. The next day we'll go walking a little further in. And so on and on. I expect about the sixth day I'll have her swimming.''

"Well, Henry, I think that's real nice," the old man said.

Well, Henry, I think you're crazier than I am, Nell thought, but it gave her great comfort to sit there listening to Henry talk about Guinevere. Guinevere was clever; she could fetch and pull sleds. She was loyal, she was brilliant. Henry thought if they lived on the West Coast she would probably be in the movies. But he was glad they didn't live on the West Coast, because he didn't think Guinevere would like that kind of lifestyle.

Henry talked about Guinevere until Nell couldn't stand to listen to any more. She got up and walked around the ferry, only slightly calmer from her beer. Maybe *I* need a dog named Guinevere, she thought, maybe then I'd be more serene. She had left her own dog and cats with the college student she had hired to take care of the house while she was gone; Elizabeth and Colin didn't want animals in their house. Nell thought she would miss the animals, especially Medusa, but she didn't think their presence would help her that much in this situation. At least they hadn't made her any calmer in the past few days. Medusa's gorgeous arrogance and Fred's amiable stupidity did not for one second relieve Nell of her burden of infatuation.

A lot of people were in love on this ferry. In fact everyone on the ferry seemed in love except Henry, and he had his dog. There were young couples in love all over the boat, and especially there were the families. Nell strolled past these families casually, but she felt her soul looking in at them like a starving child watching through the window of a restaurant. Dads and moms and children clumped together everywhere, at tables, down below on benches, up at decks by the railings. Short lean kids leaned against tall lean mothers, who leaned in turn against tall lean fathers, in tableaux of family perfection. Or sometimes the kids ran off and back to ask their parents for money, and the parents handed it to them, then went back to reading companionably together, side by side.

Nell watched one family who sat inside at a table eating. There were four in the family, and they were all very handsome and healthy looking, all wearing white shorts and running shoes and pastel cotton shirts. Nell couldn't hear what the children said, but she saw the mother smile and nod and reach over with a napkin to wipe the little boy's mouth. The children pushed back their chairs and ran off. The mother turned and looked at her husband. They smiled at each other. He ran his hand across her shoulder and up and down her neck as they talked, stroking her lightly. She inclined toward him. Imagine, Nell thought, just imagine: Imagine loving the father of your children! She thought these people must be the luckiest people on earth.

Long ago Nell had stopped attending church or scout meetings or any other meeting where she had to be confronted with the sight of happy, perfect families. It just hurt too much, made her go home feeling too lonely, too aware of her own plight. On the other hand, she had never wanted to join any group of single parents; she couldn't imagine how organizing in such a group would ease her individual situation. She was happy enough most days, or at least not suicidal, but now, watching this affectionate husband and wife . . . she turned away. She went downstairs and into the stern lounge and sat down in a chair by a window. She sat staring out at the sea.

One day a few weeks ago Stellios had picked Nell up at work to take her out to dinner, and Elizabeth had met him. The next day, Elizabeth had casually remarked, "My, he's gorgeous, Nell, but he's younger than you are, isn't he? And not quite your—social equal? I mean, I'm not trying to interfere, and I certainly don't disapprove, in a way I suppose I'm jealous. But why is it that you prefer these young hunks?"

"I don't *prefer* them, Elizabeth," Nell had said. "Somehow that's just the only type I ever meet. Don't you know I'd be thrilled to meet a single doctor or lawyer or accountant, even a vet!'' She had been miffed.

But now Nell thought that perhaps it was a little more than that. Long before her divorce from Marlow, but during a time of unhappiness with him, Nell had begun to have a suspicion that by now had hardened into a simple conviction. She believed that there were two kinds of women in the world: those who were loved well by a man and those who weren't.

There wasn't anything a woman could actually do to gain entrance into that special category of women who were loved by men. It didn't help if you were beautiful or good or persistent or kind or patient or anything at all. It didn't hurt to be ugly or dumb or mean or shrewish or flighty. It was all completely a matter of luck. Some women were loved well and truly by men and some women weren't.

It seemed to Nell as the years went by that she might as well face the fact that she had been placed by fate into the latter category, and there she would stay. It did not mean that she wasn't lucky in other ways. It did not mean that she wasn't attractive or clever or good; it didn't mean anything at all except that she would be alone all her life. She didn't feel unique in this; she had plenty of friends in the same category. These friends, however, never seemed to admit this truth to themselves, or maybe they just weren't aware of it. They went optimistically plunging on into affair after affair, coming out again each time more bitterly disappointed. The men, the problems, the reasons for the breakups were never the same. The variety was endless. But it always made Nell so sad when one of her friends was shattered at the loss of a hopeful love. Her friends seemed to her like beautiful birds who could not see the pane of glass that separated them from the other side and so continually flew into the glass and were bruised and smashed and defeated.

Some people were lucky at cards. Some people were lucky at horses. Some people were lucky at love. And some people weren't. The older Nell got, the more she believed that this kind of luck was unshakable; the person got luck in love the same way she got blue eyes or long legs. And just as a short person would be a fool to continually compete at the pole vault, so it was, Nell thought, just as foolish for a woman to hope continually for love after learning from a few trials just how far short she fell of her goal. Why make the effort, why take the beating, why endure the grief of failure? Much better, far better, Nell thought, to accept and enjoy and never get tricked by hope.

It was much easier to live out this philosophy if you dated only young hunks, men who were pleasurable but who could never cause any false expectations about living a life together. Part of her truly wished she had never met Andy Martindale. She was afraid that he would prove to be more or less like some drug for her, like heroin—addictive, providing great pleasure, but bad for her health and her sanity. But all of her friends advised her to stop worrying about the future, about the long-term conse-quences. Don't be so pessimistic, they said. Good grief, don't give up love and happiness because it may not *last*. What lasts? Live for the day, they said. Cheer up, Nell, they said, the world might come to an end tomorrow and you would have wasted today worrying. Seize the day, they said. Nell was going to give it a try.

Nell had in her suitcase a black satin nightgown trimmed with black lace. Ilona had given it to her after dropping in unan-nounced one Sunday morning and catching Nell in her elephant robe. Nell had thanked Ilona, but she had serious doubts about the gown. It had a matching jacket of black lace that cascaded and drifted from the silk bow at the neck to just below her wrists and waist. It could be very alluring if a woman were able to saunter gracefully through a room or lie about seductively in just the right position. Nell had little practice in sauntering or lying about, however; it made her feel silly even to think of arranging her body on the bed in a come-hither pose. She thought it much more likely that she would end up wearing this outfit while trying to fix coffee and that the billowing black lace would float with the movement of her arm onto the burner of the stove and catch on fire. But when she had tried to express these thoughts to Ilona, Ilona had exploded.

"For heaven's sakes, Nell, you're a beautiful, sexy woman!" Ilona had yelled. "And from what you've told me of this man, he sounds like the type who would appreciate a little elegance in the bedroom. Look at how he cooks. I'm sure he's not like your young studs, who just want to rip off your clothes and throw you on the bed. Don't you want to look *romantic?*"

Nell had smiled, listening to Ilona. Actually, the few times she had been with Andy, their lovemaking had more or less been paced to ripping and throwing. They hadn't cared about clothes;

they had just wanted them *off*. But she supposed she could see Ilona's point. She knew she would have two months without her children and without the dog and cats, so she didn't have to worry about getting up in the night to clean up someone's vomit. Perhaps she could get away with wearing this luxurious gown. It was likely that Andy would be spending some nights with her while the children were gone—why not try for a little elegance, she decided. She just hoped she didn't end up feeling too self-conscious. Andy was going to meet Nell at the ferry and go with her to the cottage to help her with her bags. Then he was going to take her out to dinner. Then . . . Nell grinned and leaned her head against the window of the ferry. The ocean was peacock blue today, and as the boat cut through the water, capricious sprays of white foam leaped up at the window as if trying to peek in. Sunlight sparkled across the water. A large sailboat slanted by, and all the people on it waved at all the people on the top decks of the ferry. Everything was light and dancing.

Nell could tell by the movements of the other passengers that they were nearing Nantucket. She rose and went up to the deck to watch. The ferry rounded Brant Point and headed steadily for the harbor. The engines hummed firmly in the heart of the boat, and all around on the decks another, lighter, kind of humming passed through the air as people laughed and talked in anticipation, gathered up their belongings, waved to people on shore. It isn't often, Nell thought, that you get to see yourself arriving at a new time and place in life, but now here she was, watching this island and whatever joys or sorrows awaited her for the next three months, come closer, closer. Sunlight sparkled off the water; eager laughter sparkled in the air around her. All these people are happy, Nell thought. She spotted Andy in the crowd on the wharf. He was really there, waiting for her. Her heart thumped.

All right, damnit, Nell thought, I'm scared and I don't trust it, but I don't seem to have much choice right now. I guess I'm going to be happy for a while. She went down to the car deck and in no time at all she was driving down the ramp onto the island of Nantucket.

That night, deep in the night—Nell didn't know what time it was—she was awakened by Andy lightly kissing her face and neck. She had been in a profound sleep, but she was not confused on awakening like this. She was instantly responsive. She wrapped her arms around him and began to kiss him back. He was covering her with kisses, all over her face, down her neck and arms, across her shoulder blades, and down and around her breasts. He nuzzled at her breasts and stomach. It was very dark and she could not see him. She could only feel him, greedily moving in the dark above her, and she finally just lay back and let him be all over her. She reached up and grasped his thick hair in her hands. His desire made him seem both vulnerable and powerful. He was coming at her helplessly, and she received him with the same absolutely natural and thoughtless lust. In the dark bedroom it was much like being in a dark cave; they might have been Indians or bears. When it was over, though, he became very human, tender. He held her in his arms to soothe her.

"Did I hurt you?" he asked, because she was crying and trembling.

"No," Nell said. "Oh no. You didn't hurt me. You just . . . it was just . . ."

She could feel his puzzlement in the dark as she lay in his arms. She knew she could not explain it to him, because he was a man, and the intensity of his having satisfied his lust could never approach the intensity of his need for that satisfaction. Whereas women's bodies just seemed to go haywire with gratitude for such extravagant pleasure.

"It's all right," she whispered. "Really. I'm fine. I'm not sad. I'm happy." Still he held her. "That was very nice," she said, to reassure him, though she felt a quick little snort of laughter pass through her at the extremity of her understatement. Oh, Nell, she thought, you're lost. But she was so exhausted that she fell immediately back into her profound sleep.

Nell woke up again that night. Andy was lying next to her, so close she could feel the rise and fall of his chest in his rhythmic breathing. She could hear his breathing. Her body was all on its own, unconsciously adjusting to his weight in the bed, and she lay tilted away from him slightly so that she did not roll right down onto him.

I'm *sleeping* with a man, Nell thought. *Shit.*

This time she did not fall back to sleep so easily.

* * *

She awoke at eight-fifteen, when her alarm clock went off, to find that she was alone. She rose and looked around. He had left a note on the bed for her.

"Sorry to leave without saying good morning. But I have a habit of rising early and taking long walks, as you know. I did kiss you goodbye—but you were too much asleep to know it, I think. I'll stop in the boutique later. Love, Andy."

Nell slipped into her elephant robe—since he wasn't around—and had her breakfast, then wandered through the O'Learys' bright cottage sipping her morning coffee. She felt wonderfully fit and optimistic. Andy had greeted her with flowers and champagne when she drove off the ferry. He had carried her luggage into the house for her, then carried her right up to the bedroom and made love to her. He had then taken her out to a marvelous restaurant for dinner. He had awakened her in the night to make sweet love to her. He had left her this note; she would see him later. Every time Nell passed a mirror on one of the walls, she caught a glimpse of herself—and she was always smiling, a true goony smile. I wonder what he meant by writing "love" on that note, she thought.

She stared out the window at the summer day and thought, with a thrill passing through her, that this was only the first day—all the days of June and July stretched out in front of her, all those days when she would be free of the responsibility of running a house and caring for children. She was free to work and play in the sun and be loved by a wonderful lover. It was an incredible luxury.

Something about living in the O'Learys' house and being without children made Nell feel both more adult and more childlike. She felt eminently capable and responsible, full of energy and bright ideas, and at the same time she had a delicious feeling of playing house, playing shop. She was dressed and ready to go early, so she walked to work and had to keep from skipping, for the day was brilliant. Everyone she passed looked happy. A woman in running clothes jogged by her, accompanied by a happy black dog carrying a yellow ball in his mouth. A father pedaled by on a bike, pulling a black two-wheeled carriage holding a grinning toddler. Nell walked down Main Street to buy a newspaper at the Hub. She walked on down the street, passing a store with a window full of solar-powered toys. A brass stick figure pedaled furiously on a bike, airplanes dipped and lifted, Ferris wheels spun. She felt like that, felt that she was now effortlessly moving, powered by the sun. She walked farther down the street to the wharf, where the Hy-Line ferries docked, past the great red Nantucket lightship, past the little wooden shops selling frozen yogurt, oil paintings of the sea, and shell jewelry. She stood for a while watching large and small boats slip in and out of the harbor.

Next to her, a child yelled, "Mommy, Mommy! Look at the seagull!" Nell looked where the child was pointing: a gull was soaring on the wind. "I wish I could do that," the child said.

I *am* doing that, Nell thought, and smiled to herself.

She walked back up the street and opened the boutique and set to work. She had never been more efficient, more helpful to the customers. Mindy, the salesgirl who had run the store in May and who would be Nell's assistant for the summer, came in at one to work until nine that night. Mindy had graduated from college the year before. She was a pretty girl, and bright, but talkative. She wasn't sure what she wanted to do with her life, and she wasn't sure which boyfriend she was in love with, but that didn't stop her from discussing her life and loves in great detail. Sometimes her chatter annoyed Nell, but today she just took it in her stride.

"Look, Mindy," Nell said. "I'm going to take my lunch hour at three instead of one today. My—uh, friend Clary is arriving on the three o'clock Hy-Line. I want to meet her and get her settled in my house. She'll be living with me this summer. So I'll be gone for an hour, from three till four."

"Fine," Mindy said, snapping her gum.

At three Nell walked back down Main Street and past the five and dime and the gift stores and restaurants to the Hy-Line dock. The small blue and white ferry approached, its decks so loaded with people in bright clothing that from the distance it looked like a boat full of balloons. Nell felt a shiver of excitement go through the crowd of people waiting at the dock. She would not have been surprised if everyone had cheered when the ferry slipped so perfectly into place and the ramps were let down to connect with shore. It was a real occasion, this ferry-arriving business, Nell thought. She watched lovers and friends and relatives greet and hug each other and it seemed to her she had never dreamed that the regular old world could be so full of daily joy.

Clary came down the ramp. The sight of her filled Nell now, as always, with a medley of emotions. She loved her, as one loves a child she has watched turn into an adult; she loved her as a friend. But she was also struck by her vivid beauty and, unavoidably, by her youth. Clary was so stunning, so firm and flaw-less. She was slim and taut and both sophisticated and nubile at the same time. Just the sight of Clary made Nell feel old, and though she had been feeling almost beautiful, she now felt merely well preserved. Clary's presence made Nell aware of all her wrinkles and sags, all the marks of time. She could not help the momentary twinge of alarm and the thought that perhaps Andy, on seeing Clary, would fall in love with her instead of Nell.

Clary came on down the ramp, unaware of her ex-stepmother's jealousy. She was wearing loose white jeans, a gray T-shirt, and a backpack, and carrying an enormous bulging suitcase.

"Clary!" Nell called. She rushed up to her and gave her a hug. "You're here!"

"Don't look behind me," Clary said, kissing Nell on the cheek. "Whatever you do, don't look behind me. Where's your car? Hurry up. Let's go."

Nell drew back. "What on earth?" she said.

"Ssssh!" Clary said. "I'll explain as soon as we get in the car. Where's your damn car?"

Clary was walking away even as Nell tried to take her bag from her.

"Clary," Nell said, "what's going on? Here, let me help you with your bag."

"I can carry my bag," Clary said through clenched teeth. *"I can carry my bag. Can we just go to your car?"*

"Clary, I didn't drive here," Nell said. "My car's at the house. It's only a short distance. A nice walk. What's wrong?"

Clary stopped short, so quickly that Nell, who had been scurrying along next to her, trying to keep up with her, ran right into her arms. "Jesus, Clary," she said. "Would you please tell me what's the matter with you?"

"Oh, this is hopeless," Clary said. "This is *ridiculous.*"

"Clary!" Nell said.

"You must be Mrs. St. John," someone said.

Nell turned. Throngs of people were passing by, some just off the Hy-Line, some looking at the shops, and out of this crowd came a handsome young man with blond hair and the most beautiful blue eyes in the world. He was wearing jeans and a T-shirt that said I GOT SCROD LAST NIGHT.

"May I call you Nell?" he said. "I'm Bob Walker."

Nell was stunned. She looked at Bob; she looked at Clary. Clary's face had gone into its mask of deep inscrutability that always indicated strong emotion on her part. "Clary?" Nell asked, touching her arm.

"You really are crazy, you know," Clary said. She turned in a flash and was glaring at Bob. The two of them were the same height, and with their blond hair, T-shirts, and jeans, they could have been twins. "You really are crazy," she repeated.

"I know," Bob said. "I'm crazy about you."

"If Nell were my father, you wouldn't be here," Clary said. "If Nell were my mother, you wouldn't *dare* be here."

"Clary," Nell said. "What is going on?" People were beginning to glance at the three of them as they stood there, blocking the flow of walkers. "Do you suppose this could be discussed in private?" Nell asked. "Whatever it is?"

"There's nothing to discuss," Clary said.

"I'm Clary's boyfriend—" Bob said to Nell.

"Was," Clary said.

"—and we're having a little disagreement," Bob continued.

"Well, look," Nell said. "Why don't we all walk to the cottage. I've only got about thirty minutes left in my lunch hour. Then I've got to get back to the boutique. Let me show you where the cottage is, and then you two can finish this—disagreement—in private."

"Thanks a *lot,* Nell," Clary said, glaring. But she picked up her bag. "Okay, let's go."

Nell led the way. Clary followed. Bob followed Clary. Clary walked stiffly, not talking, taking elaborate and extravagant pains not to be touched or bumped by Bob as she walked. After a few minutes of silence, Nell found herself doing what she often did in stressful situations: she babbled. "And this is Robinson's, the five and dime," she said. "It's got everything. If you keep going straight up this street, this is Main Street, and go left at the corner, you'll come to the boutique. But we'll go this way to the cottage . . ."

Clary didn't respond.

"What a beautiful place," Bob said at one point, and Nell agreed. She talked about the beaches, the houses, the stores. She talked about Jeremy and Hannah and Charlotte and Marlow. Clary just stomped along, her face set. The walk took forever. Finally, they reached the cottage.

"This is your room for the summer," Nell said, showing Clary to the back upstairs bedroom.

"It's really nice," Clary muttered. She stood at the window, her back toward Nell and Bob, unapproachable.

"I've got to go back to the boutique," Nell said. "Clary, I'll draw you a map. When you're ready, come down and I'll talk with you about summer jobs. Everyone wants salespeople, waitresses, and so on. You'll be able to find something good, I'm sure. Or you can wait till tonight. I'll be back home a little after six. Uh, Bob, it's been nice meeting you . . . I guess . . ." She laughed, trying to ease the situation. "Will you be staying . . . for a while?"

"Yes," Bob said.

"No," Clary said.

"Oh," Nell said. She waited. Neither Clary nor Bob elaborated.

"Well," Nell said, "I'll see you at least, Clary, later." She left them and walked back to work. It was the only thing she could do.

The store was busy enough to keep Nell from having much time to wonder about just what was going on with Clary and Bob. She was worried, though, for in the past few years Clary had seemed to develop a sense of humor and reasonableness that had been eclipsed this afternoon. Nell was afraid that in spite of Bob's winning smiles there was some serious trouble between the two of them.

When Andy came into the store, Nell said reluctantly, "I'm sorry, Andy, I don't think I can see you tonight. Clary's arrived, but I haven't had a chance to talk to her about anything at all. Her boyfriend followed her over on the ferry and when I left, they were in the middle of a fight over something. I don't know if he's going to stay or not. I don't know what's going to happen. But I think I'd better see how Clary is before I plan anything tonight. I'd better have dinner with her, since it's her first night here. Can I call you?"

"Sure," Andy said, and smiled, but he slouched a bit in disappointment.

"I'm sorry," Nell said. "I'm really sorry." And she was, she was especially sorry for herself.

Mindy took her dinner hour, then came back to run the store until it closed at nine. Nell worked till six, then left and walked back to the cottage. She found Clary there alone, crying.

"Clary," she said. "Oh, *Clary.*"

For Clary was clearly miserable. Her face was puffy and her nose was red. It was obvious that she had been crying for some time. "Come on in the living room and sit down and tell me what's happened," Nell said. "What's been going on? No—wait a minute." She went into the kitchen and got a beer for herself and one for Clary. "Now."

"It's all over," Clary said. "It really is all over now. And I love him so much." She sobbed. She sat on the sofa with her knees drawn up and her arms crossed on her knees and her head buried in her arms. "Goddamnit," she said.

"Well, Clary, surely it's not all over," Nell said. "He must love you, too. I mean, he followed you here. So he must at least *care.* . . ."

"Oh, he *cares,*" Clary said. "He cares. But not enough. Not enough to make a commitment."

"Well, Clary, isn't this the guy you wrote me about last year? Isn't he the one you've been going with for about a year now?"

"Sixteen months," Clary said. "And yes. I've been 'going with' him. What a goddamn stupid adolescent phrase. Going with. I've been *going* with him, but we haven't been *getting* anywhere."

Clary tossed her head and shook out her hair. She blew her nose. She took a sip of beer. Then she inhaled deeply, pulling herself together, and her breath came out in a little shudder, like Jeremy's and Hannah's did when they were heartbroken. Clary and Hannah had the same blond hair and dark eyes; Nell could still easily see the little girl in Clary's lovely face.

"Look, Nell," she said. "I've been going with Bob for sixteen months now. We haven't dated anyone else. We've both been working at the same place, the lab at Rutgers. We're both biologists. He's ahead of me; he's just finished his Ph.D. I'm just a lab assistant. But the point is, we have all these interests in common. So it's not just sex or anything, it's everything. *Everything* is there. We have been so happy together. It has been so wonderful. Now he's just gotten his Ph.D., and last month he got an offer of a full-time job at a lab out in Michigan. He wants me to come with him."

"Why, Clary, that's wonderful. What's wrong with that?" Nell asked.

"He wants me to come with him as his live-in," Clary said. "He doesn't want to get married. Oh, *goddamnit!* It's so embarrassing. I hate it, I hate this situation, I hate myself. I hate it that I had to bring up the idea of marriage. *I* had to be the one to say: do you mean you want to get married? And goddamn him, he said no. He says he's not ready for a commitment like that yet. He says he just got through with the pressure of getting his Ph.D. and he's going to be under a lot of stress trying to get situated in a new job. He doesn't think he could take the additional stress of being married yet. He says he loves me, he wants to be with me, he doesn't want to be with anyone else, and yet he doesn't want to marry me. Jesus Christ, Nell. Don't you think I feel like some kind of dumbbell? Some kind of *nincompoop?* Can you imagine how humiliating it is to be the person to suggest marriage—and get refused?''

"Oh, Clary," Nell said. "Oh God." She was thinking: I thought it had changed for your generation. I thought it would be easier. "How old is Bob?" she asked.

"He's thirty," Clary said. "He was thirty this November. Boy, *that* was something. Talk about a crisis. We nearly broke up for good then. In fact we're still having trouble over that. I don't know if I'll ever get over it."

"What happened?"

"Well, what do you think?" Clary said, tossing her head again. "What would you expect to happen? Here's this good-looking man, working like a maniac to finish his Ph.D. and hold down a full-time lab job, and he turns thirty and decides he's suddenly *old,* like *really old,* that he's been wasting his whole life working, he's in a rut, all his life is just a rat race, he never has any fun . . . he went out and balled every teenager he could find.''

"Oh God, Clary," Nell said. "How awful."

"Yeah, it was awful," Clary went on, not crying now, but very sober. "I had planned this big surprise dinner for him. Six of his best friends. I made a wonderful birthday cake. I made a *fucking birthday cake.* I might as well be my mother, making a cake. Nothin' says lovin' like somethin' from the oven. Jesus Christ, what a sap I am sometimes. So I made this cake, bought these steaks, had presents, champagne, and his friends came over and we were all ready for a big marvelous party. . . . He never showed up at my apartment. It was . . . it was just shit. Finally Rod, he's Bob's best friend, went down to this bar where they hang out a lot. He came back after a while and said some other people had seen Bob in there. He'd left with a girl, a teenager.

God, can you imagine how embarrassed I was in front of his friends? One was his fucking boss at the lab! Everyone went home except Roni, she's a good friend of mine, we just sat and drank the champagne all night. When she left, I drove over to Bob's apartment. It was about four in the morning. I took that gorgeous birthday cake—it really was a gorgeous cake, Nell, you should have seen the mother, three layers, I'll never be able to make anything like it again! I took it and smashed it all over the inside of his car. On the steering wheel, the seats, the windows. I left a note saying, 'Happy Birthday, you rotten creep.' "

Clary stopped talking then. She drank some beer. She sat for a while. Nell didn't rush her.

"Well, he called the next afternoon and said he was sorry and could we talk. But I said no, I didn't want to see him again. So he said all right. That killed me, Nell. That was even worse than knowing he'd gone out and screwed a teenager, his just saying all right like that. Giving up, as if I weren't worth some kind of struggle. I didn't hear from him for about two weeks. Ten days exactly. His friends told me he was going to the bars and taking home some teenybopper every night.

"I wanted to die. I went out with a guy, and then I met another guy at a bar and went home to bed with him, but you know, I never did like doing that too much. I keep thinking of *Looking for Mr. Goodbar*. It always scares me a little. So mostly I just stayed home and cried and was miserable.

"Then all of a sudden one day I came home from work and there was a big box. Inside was a teddy bear, with a note taped to the bow. The note said, 'I am the world's biggest asshole. Please forgive me. I really want to see you. I really need to see you. Love, Bob.' "

Clary stopped awhile and smiled a bit. "Well, I thought about it, but of course I'm so much in love with him, I knew immediately what I would do. But I didn't call him that night. I waited. I was cool. Finally he called me. He came over, and we talked and talked. I didn't go to bed with him again right away. I wanted to, I always want to go to bed with him. But I didn't. I guess I was still confused. Scared. But he really did come after me then. I mean he sent me flowers and called me on the phone and wrote me letters and said all this nice stuff about how he loved me and needed me and he'd never do that again and he had just needed to be crazy and young for once in his life . . ."

"That's pretty crazy and young, all right," Nell said.

Clary looked at Nell and instantly her eyes flashed in defense of Bob. She did not want Nell to criticize this man whom she loved, no matter how he acted. "Well, Nell," she said. "I can kind of understand it. I mean, his family is super poor. He had to work like a maniac all his life. He was a scholarship student at college. He's never had the time or opportunity to play around. He's just worked and worked all his life. I've read psychology books, and I've come to understand—it's hard to be a man. It's hard to know you've got to work all your life and support a family. Even if women are supposed to ·be equal now, the man still feels he's got to be the one, bottom line, who supports his family. That's hard to face.

"So I guess I can understand why he had that fit of playing around. Anyway, we're way past that now. I know he hasn't been with anyone else since last November. It's been *so good* for six months now. It's been perfect. We've been so close.

"Oh, Nell, I can understand why he's scared of marriage. I'm scared of marriage, too. Look at Mom and Dad; they're divorced. God, look at *you;* you're divorced. I know marriage doesn't mean security. It doesn't mean we'll love each other to the grave and beyond. God, marriage doesn't mean much at all. But it does mean something, a little *something.*"

Clary finished her beer. "Well," she said, smiling ruefully at Nell. "What do you think?"

Nell smiled back. "What do I think? I think I'm hungry, for one thing," she said. "And you've got to be hungry, too. And things will look better when you've got some food in your stomach."

"God, Nell you sound just like a mother," Clary said.

"I *am* a mother," Nell said. "Come on. I'll take you out to a nice restaurant tonight. After tonight we're going to have to be frugal and eat beans and boiled newspapers at home, but tonight I'll splurge. After all, it's the beginning of your summer here, Clary, and I really do think you'll have a good time." Nell grinned. "We'll go to the Atlantic Café. That ought to cheer you up."

When they got to the Atlantic Café around eight, they found it already packed with families, couples and, at the bar, an amazing line-up of what Elizabeth succinctly termed "trust-fund scallopers." At least thirty men were gathered around the bar, drinking and talking; they were handsome, rugged men who obviously worked outdoors and liked it. Nell smiled to see them: Stellios would blend right into this crowd. For one brief moment Nell missed Stellios, wished he were there, wished she could lean against his easy body. But she had broken off with him last month, before coming to Nantucket the second time and sleeping with Andy. Oh, how could she be thinking of Stellios! She did not want him. She wanted Andy. It was just that these guys with their jeans and T-shirts and work boots and muscles made her think of him.

As they walked past the bar to a booth in the back, Nell whispered to Clary, "Now you see, this isn't a bad antidote, is it? A lot of handsome men there."

"A lot of men with herpes there, I'd imagine, Nell," Clary said, her voice and look skeptical.

They ordered pig-out food, feel-better food: cheese and jalapeno pepper nachos, chicken fingers, zucchini fingers, beer. As they ate, dipping into the greasy rich food and licking their fingers, they talked some more. Nell told Clary about Andy, but kept it light while she talked. She didn't want to admit to Clary how excited she was about this man, how *hopeful* she had so quickly become. Clary listened with interest and drank. She drank two beers for every one of Nell's.

When all the food had been eaten, Clary leaned back in the booth and sighed. She had cheered up a little, Nell thought. At least she wasn't crying.

"You know what?" Clary said. "You know what I'm going to do? I'm going to get rich. I've got this plan. I'm going to sell rats."

"You're going to sell rats," Nell echoed, thinking: Oh God, she's gotten drunk.

"Yep," Clary said. "I'm going to sell rats. I'm going to market them as the new pet for the modern age."

"Well, Clary," Nell began.

"Now listen to me a minute," Clary said. "I've got it all worked out. I'll tell you why. Rats are special, you want to know why? Not just because they're intelligent and affectionate and cute. It's more than that—guess *what?*"

Nell stared at Clary. She is drunk, Nell thought, and an old slightly maternal wave of concern passed through her. "I can't possibly guess," she said.

"Rats only live for two years," Clary said. "Two years. That's it. So you see they'll be the perfect pet for the modern couple. You fall in love, you move in with someone, you get a pet rat.

Then at the end of two years, when you and your lover break up, you don't have to worry about hassling over who gets to keep the rat. You don't have to worry about rat support or rat visitation or the rat's emotional trauma from the break-up. You don't have to stay together for the sake of the rat. 'Cause the rat dies.''

"Clary," Nell said, "let's go home. Let's go home and get some sleep. Things will look better in the morning."

"Nell," Clary said, and tears were beginning to streak down her face again. "Nell, I'm so miserable. I want to die. I told Bob I never want to see him again. Oh, Nell, why does it have to be so hard between men and women?"

Nell sat there peeling the label off her beer bottle, knowing she should say something wise right now. But what wisdom could she possibly offer on the subject of men and women? She was divorced from Clary's father. She had spent five years of her life being lonely and dating men who were not right. She certainly had never found it easy between men and women. Now that she had met a man who was grown-up enough to take seriously, a man she thought she could honestly love, who could honestly love her back, she was too afraid and just too experienced to even enjoy the luxury of hoping it might last. But then, Nell thought, it wasn't fair to apply her life's experiences to Clary's.

"Clary," she said at last, "you are so young. And you are so beautiful, so wonderful. You really are special. I don't know about Bob; he's certainly handsome and well mannered, but I didn't get to talk to him enough to get a sense of what kind of person he is. All I can say is that if he really loves you, he'll come back for you, even though you've sent him away. Sometimes these fights and separations are necessary. You know," Nell went on, seeing that Clary had at least stopped crying, "I guess I really believe that falling in love can be as natural as having babies. It's the way the world goes on. Now when I was pregnant with Hannah and Jeremy, I had terrible morning sickness. God, I was sick. I was *miserable*. And I remember an old nurse in the doctor's office telling me that that was a good thing: It's a good sign, she said. The worse the morning sickness, the stronger hold the baby is taking in the womb. Maybe that's not a good analogy, but maybe it is. It's natural to have babies, it's natural to fall in love. And maybe you and Bob have to go through this really terrible time so your love can take a good hold. Do you see what I mean? Am I making any sense?"

"No," Clary said, smiling. "I think what you're saying is ridiculous. I think it's the most foolish and untenable analogy I've ever heard. But you make me feel better."

"Look, Clary, I don't know what's going to happen with you and Bob. It may be that he really is too frightened of marriage to marry you even though he loves you with all his heart. That is one definite possibility. Maybe that's the possibility you have to live with. If so, at least you know you're young—"

"I'm *twenty-seven*, Nell."

"—you're *young*, Clary, and you're lovely, and you're bound to meet other men while you're here in Nantucket. I think you could have a wonderful summer here."

Clary didn't look convinced, but she was grateful for Nell's conviction. After they talked some more, they went back to the cottage. Clary went to bed in the room Nell had given her for the summer, and Nell sat in the kitchen and talked to Andy on the phone. She told him about Clary and Bob, hoping in the back of her mind that this might open up an avenue of exploration into Andy's personal life. Andy did not speak much about his married life. Nell knew only that he had been married, that he had a sixteen-year-old daughter who was in prep school in Connecticut and whom he seldom saw, that his wife had not remarried, that she didn't work, but traveled a lot and loved the arts. He had not told Nell whether or not he had loved his wife or loved her still. He had not told her any of the intimate things she was curious about, and this night as they spoke on the phone, he was still reserved. He said only that he was sure Clary and Bob would work it out somehow, but he had nothing to say one way or the other about love or marriage or men and women. He did say that he missed seeing Nell and wished he were with her, and she invited him to dinner to meet Clary the next evening. He said he'd come, but Nell hung up the phone feeling slightly depressed.

Still, the next evening, when he came to dinner, bearing flowers for the table and a bottle of excellent wine, Nell felt a bright, irrepressible light of hope spark right up inside her at the sight of him. When their eyes met, he smiled and she saw how happy she made him. They had one of Nell's easy dinners of lamb stew and corn bread and salad, and Andy was charming to Clary. He complimented her and made her laugh and did not throw her with blunt questions. He asked intelligent questions about her lab work with rats. Occasionally, as the three of them sat at the table, even though the main current of conversation was between Andy and Clary, Andy would make a point to draw Nell in. Nell was pleased. She could tell he was trying to please her, to show just the right amount of interest in her stepdaughter, this beautiful dark-eyed blonde, but not too much.

Later they all sat in the living room drinking coffee and eating fruit. Andy sat on the sofa next to Nell and stretched his long arm across the back so that he could softly stroke her neck just up under her hair. It was a soothing and sensual thing for him to do. Nell felt at peace sitting there with him, being touched by him. Then, when it was almost ten, Andy said to Nell, "Listen, can you come over to my house for a while? I want to show you those photographs."

Nell stared at him. "Photographs?"

Andy grinned at her, looked at her right in the eye. *"You know,"* he said, "those photographs I wanted your opinion on." His grin grew mischievous.

"Oh," Nell said. *"Those* photographs. Sure. Clary, I'm going to be gone for a while, but I'll be back later. Shall I wake you in the morning when I get ready to go off to work?"

"Yeah," Clary said. "I've really got to find a job. I guess I'll unpack and go to bed."

Andy and Nell left the cottage and drove to his house. As soon as they were inside the door, he pulled her against him and began to kiss her. Nell wrapped her arms around his neck. "I thought this was what you had in mind," she said. When he brought her home hours later, she climbed the stairs, took off her clothes, and fell into bed without even brushing her teeth.

Clary found a job in a jewelry store on Main Street. She was to work six days a week, including Sundays, from three in the afternoon until nine at night. That gave her the morning and part of the afternoon to go to the beach and the evenings to go out and party. Before a week had passed, she'd found plenty of people to party with. She became friends with a young woman who worked in a jewelry shop owned by the same person but located on Old South Wharf. Her name was Felicity, and when the shops weren't busy, Clary and Felicity would call each other and chat on the phone. She also got to know Mindy, the rather silly girl who worked with Nell at Elizabeth's, and through Mindy and Felicity, she got to know all sorts of men and women her age.

Nell gradually made friends too; people who knew the O'Learys, or friends of friends in common back in Arlington or Cambridge. Soon the calendar that hung on the kitchen door was scrawled with dates and plans for Clary and Nell: cocktail parties for Nell, tennis dates for Clary. The phone rang a lot. The house was sometimes filled with the sound of Clary and her friends laughing. Sometimes Clary had friends in for dinner; more often they went out. Dishes piled in the sink, dirty clothes piled in the laundry room, but sooner or later it all got done. Through an unspoken agreement, Nell did Clary's whenever she thought about it, and Clary returned the favor.

As the summer deepened, the boutique got busier, and finally Nell hired another girl to work part-time during the day. She was often tired from standing and moving and selling and unpacking and thinking about what needed to be ordered right away. But she always found new energy in the evenings with Andy. It was such a pleasure, she thought, often with a twinge of guilt, to be able to relax and be lazy, selfish after work, instead of having to tend to the myriad needs of the children. She didn't have to fix dinner, help with homework, settle arguments, decide whether to allow bugs to live in a box in the house, worry about whether there was enough fresh fruit and vegetables, or tell anyone to brush his teeth. The evenings were all her own.

Andy had taken over the task of cooking dinners for them—they had tacitly agreed that he was the better cook anyway and had more time for it. The evenings were always so pleasant. Nell would shower and change after work and walk to Andy's—because Clary often needed the car to drive to the Muse or 'Sconset to meet friends—and there they would eat some delicious meal and talk about the events of the day. Sometimes they watched the news on television. Sometimes they walked along the beach together. Sometimes they sat side by side reading. Each night Nell felt more at ease with Andy, sensed how the rightness of this routine firmed and deepened until the pattern of their lives together seemed as smooth and lustrous and becomingly mature as a string of pearls. She began to think they had found a reliable love.

Once a week Nell got a phone call from the children, who were safe and happy in Chicago. The first week in July Nell came down to eat breakfast and found Clary and a young man already in the kitchen, drinking coffee. His name was Sam and he played the guitar and became a regular member of their household. By the middle of July, more nights than not, Sam was sleeping with Clary in the O'Learys house and Nell was sleeping with Andy all night in his house, coming home only to change clothes before going to the boutique. Nell and Sam and Clary became used to passing each other in the hall in robes, or fresh from the bathroom, or bleary-eyed.

Monday nights, which both Clary and Nell had off, they ate together in the cottage, often with Andy and Sam and Mindy and Felicity and their boyfriends joining them. Just as Nell's Arlington refrigerator had been stocked with milk and pudding for Hannah and Jeremy, now her Nantucket refrigerator was stocked with Diet Pepsi and six-packs of beer and gallons of cheap white wine for Nell and Clary and their friends. Monday afternoons and some mornings, Nell and Clary would go to the beach to swim and work on their tans.

The first day that Nell went to the beach with Clary, they went to the Jetties Beach, which was closest. Nell and Clary were just walking along, lugging their beach blankets, a cooler of ice and Tab, their suntan lotion, and paperback books, when Nell found herself brought to a standstill on the hot sand. She was stunned. Spread before her as far as the eye could see was a vision of life so beautiful and gay that it could have been painted only by an impressionist, by Monet or Renoir. The sea stretched out forever in every possible variation of blue, and the blue horizon was dotted above with white clouds, below with white sails. The beach was speckled with dots of color—people in bathing suits, sand toys, beach towels, and everywhere stood the bright multicolored beach umbrellas, opening out like a forest of fanciful pink and yellow trees.

Nell and Clary walked on and found a place near the water. They spread their blankets and oiled their skin and lay in the sun. Nell meant to read, but didn't. She was too drugged by the deep peace that was a natural consequence of the hot sun and generous scenery. The beach was fairly crowded with people, but no one was intrusive and there was more than enough space for everyone to spread out and have a little territory. Nell liked watching the other people on the beach. She enjoyed looking at all the different bodies. There was such an endless variety, and a human being in a bathing suit always seemed to her such a brave and trusting sight, so much bare flesh exposed to the judgment of strangers.

All ages passed by Nell as she lay on her stomach watching,

loving all those bodies: tall, short, thin, fat, bony, bouncy; children with their unabashed bottoms winking like silver half-moons from bathing suits; young girls in bright bikinis that showed off their taut bellies, high breasts. Nell watched a couple who must have been in their seventies going into the water together. They had saggy stomachs and gray hair and wrinkled elbows, but they were sweet together, because they were so obviously in love. The man urged the woman farther into the water; he held her hand. They stood in the water and smiled into each other's eyes. When they came back out to their towels, they knelt next to each other and she dried his back; he dried, gently, her face. Those two have been in love for a long time, Nell thought, smiling. It seemed to her the prettiest sight on the beach.

People bent in front of her, looking for seashells. Children and adults swam and bobbed in the waves, staying close to shore, and farther out some brave woman floated serenely on her back, rocking in the sea's cradle. Kites with many-colored tails flew above the sand dunes, and now and then a plane would pass overhead bringing a new load of summer people to the island. An earnest plodder with plaid trunks and glasses stomped past Nell, obviously on a serious mission of health. A young woman with a Renoir face—full lips, plump cheeks—came out of the water and surprised Nell with her skinny El Greco body. A seagull flew down just behind Nell and tried to steal a bag of cookies from a family who had carelessly left them open on a blanket. If Nell put her head down in her arms, she could close her eyes and think of the night before and she could remember with perfect clarity the words Andy had spoken about her breasts, her eyes, her legs, her hair. She could remember how his hands had felt caressing her almost as vividly as she could now feel the sun beating on her skin. The air smelled of coconut oil and Coppertone and salt. Laughter drifted up and down the beach like the kites that drifted in the blue sky up above.

Nell turned over and lay on her back. She could hear the seagulls chortling. Now and then a gull would fly low over her, and that was slightly alarming, the way its black shadow swooped over her body like an omen. Then Nell would raise her head and see the cheerful red or blue sails of windsurfers and be reassured.

After Nell and Clary had been at the beach about an hour, they noticed that all the people who had been swimming or wading in the ocean were coming out of the water. "Look," Clary said, and Nell and Clary sat up. The lifeguards in their orange trunks and suits were passing up and down the beach, blowing their whistles, motioning for the people to come in. Their gestures were definite. It looked like a scene from *Jaws*.

"Sharks?" Clary asked the people on the blanket next to her.

But no, it was not sharks. A child had been lost, a little boy, and the lifeguards wanted every single person out of the water. As Nell watched, all the people on the beach who had been lying on their blankets just as she had gradually begun to sit up, and then to stand, to cover their eyes and search the water, the horizon. Fear passed through the crowd like a shiver.

"The boy is four years old," someone told Nell and Clary. It could be my child lost out there, Nell thought, and felt chilled. It was very quiet all up and down the long stretch of beach. Then came the murmur and then the swell of news: the little boy had been found. From the people on the blankets and those standing in the sand, from all up and down that whole great long expanse of beach, there came a sort of exhalation of relief, and more than that, a sense of joy, like a balloon being let into the air.

"The child's been found," people said to each other. "The child is okay." They passed the news up and down the beach, and all at once, when the news reached everyone, people began to applaud.

"That's good luck," Clary said to Nell.

Nell smiled at Clary. "Yes," she agreed. "You see, there is such a thing."

That night, which could have been any of many nights that summer, so alike were all those warm and gentle evenings, Nell dressed for a party she was going to with Andy. Her skin was brown from the sun and smooth from lotions. She was radiant with happiness. Nell took a scarlet dress from her closet and thought to herself that now it was as if her life were flying out around her as full and bright and vibrant with color as the skirt of a dancer spins out from a woman in a rapturous turn. She realized that she was happy in her life. She knew she would always remember these days.

Seven

ONE evening in July, Nell walked back to the cottage after work and found Bob Walker sitting on the front steps. He was wearing jeans and a T-shirt that said NINE OUT OF TEN MEN WHO HAVE TRIED CAMELS PREFER WOMEN. His eyes were the sort of crystalline blue that made women feel just helpless in their love.

"Hi," he said, smiling his engaging smile. "I thought I'd stop by and see how Clary is." He was so casual, as if he lived just around the corner or down the street, as if it hadn't taken a major effort to get to this island, this house.

Nell grinned. "She's working," she said. "At the Golden Island on Main Street. She doesn't get off work till nine. You can go on down and see her there—or you're welcome to wait here for her."

Bob followed Nell into the house. "If she's working, she might be too busy to talk, right?"

"Right," Nell said.

"Then if it's all right with you, I'll just hang around here till she gets back."

"That's fine," Nell said. "I'm going out for dinner, but you're welcome to make yourself at home. Watch TV—find something in the refrigerator if you're hungry. There's a lot of food around."

"Great," Bob said. "Thanks a lot. That's awfully nice of you."

Nell went upstairs and got ready to go over to Andy's. She wondered if she should call Clary and warn her. She knew from discussions with Clary that she still loved Bob and that behind all the surface laughter was a well of misery because she missed him, because he was all she wanted in life and she could not have him. Nell decided not to call Clary. Bob's appearance could only mean

175

something good, could only mean, at the least, that he still cared about her too, cared enough to come back to see her even though Clary had said it was over forever. Perhaps Bob was coming to propose! Nell's heart leaped with anticipation. Then she grinned sardonically at herself in the mirror. Jesus, she thought, even now, after all I know, I get a buzz from thinking a man might ask Clary to *marry* him. It must be physical, hereditary, she thought; that second X chromosome that women are born with and men aren't must be the one that fishtails inside us with joy at the thought of marriage, that drives us like salmon upstream, blindly wishing for marriage above all other things.

When she went back downstairs, she couldn't resist saying to Bob, "I'm going now, and I won't be back until later, if at all. And I suppose I should warn you, Bob. Clary might not come back after work—or she might not come back alone."

But Clary had come back alone, as Nell found out the next day. And she had talked with Bob and he had spent the night and they had said they loved each other . . . and then he had left, because after all, they still could not agree and would not change their minds. Bob wanted Clary to move in with him as a lover, and she wanted to go with him as his wife.

Nell sat with Clary awhile that morning. They drank coffee and talked. Clary's face was swollen again from crying.

"It's so humiliating," Clary said. "It's so embarrassing. That I am the one who has to push marriage," she said. "It's so degrading."

"What do your parents think?" Nell asked.

"Oh well, you know Mom," Clary said. "She'll always be old-fashioned. She doesn't think I should *sleep* with a man until I'm married to him. And Dad, well, his advice was, 'Why should a man buy a cow when he can get the milk for free?' "

"God, *gross!*" Nell said. "Marlow said that? To you?"

Clary laughed. "Well, Nell, it may be crude, but it's not wrong. Oh, I don't understand it. Why can't Bob want what I want? All that stuff that marriage means—that we announce to the world that we love each other, that we'll plan our lives together, that we belong to each other . . ." Clary started crying again. After a while she looked up at Nell and asked, "What about you?"

Nell was startled. "Me?" she asked. "You mean what about

me and Andy? Oh, Clary, it's way too soon to even think about that. I've only known him a little over two months."

Of course that was a lie. Already Nell was wondering if there were a chance that she and Andy could have a life together, could have a marriage. They seemed to be so good together; it was such a pleasure to live as they were living, spending as much time together as they could. But Andy hadn't mentioned the future, and Nell hadn't either. She tried not to think of the future. She tried to live for the day.

That night Nell took Clary to see *Flashdance*. Andy didn't want to go, and Clary had told Sam and her friends that she didn't feel well, that she just wanted to go to the movie with Nell and then go home to bed. Nell loved *Flashdance,* and at the end of the movie everyone in the theater cheered and clapped. But as Nell and Clary were walking home to the cottage in the warm July evening, Clary said, "I hate that movie. I really hate it."

"Good grief, Clary, why?" Nell asked.

"It's a lie," Clary said. "It's a schmaltzy lie. It's the 1983 *Sound of Music.* In that movie Julie Andrews was a nun and a governess who ended up getting happily married, getting what she wanted. Now here's Jennifer Beals playing a welder and a dancer who gets to be a ballerina and have that gorgeous man, her boss, be dithering around after her with love. That just doesn't happen in real life. Not even to girls who look like her."

"Oh, Clary, you're as beautiful as that girl in the movie."

"Yes I am!" Clary said, turning on Nell as if Nell had insulted her. "I think I am. But it's not much good to me, is it? Look, I worked as hard and long to get my degree in biology as that girl did to get into ballet school. And what has my degree gotten me? I can't even get a decent job unless I want to go with one of the huge firms in Piscataway and spend my days cleaning out rat cages—a rat janitor. And I'm as pretty and clever and nice as that girl, and I don't see Bob running around after me, trying to make my life easier."

"Well," Nell said, "maybe someone will make *Flashdance Two.* In which the girl realizes after working for four years that there are other women who are better ballerinas than she is and that she'll never be the star, she'll never get the roses. And her boss will end up chasing after another woman and he'll never ask her to marry him, because why should he buy the cow when he's already getting

the milk for free? Would you like that? Would you like it if they
made a movie like that? *Flashdance Meets Real Life?''*

Clary walked along beside Nell in silence for a while. "No,"
she said quietly. "No. I'd hate that movie, too."

Nell worried about Clary. She was afraid she'd sink into a slump.
But when they got back to the cottage, Clary said, "I'm going to
call Sam," and after she called him, she said, "I'm going to go
down to meet him at the Atlantic Café. I'll see you tomorrow."

So Clary was pushing on with her life, Nell thought. Still she
felt melancholy, for Clary and for men and women in general.
She called Andy to say good night, then went to bed alone. She
couldn't fall asleep, although she was tired, although she very
much wanted the oblivion that sleep offered. She missed Andy's
body next to hers in bed, missed his warmth and bulk. And she
thought how it would be very soon, when the children came back
and then in September, when she went back to Arlington. Then
she would be sleeping alone again every night. She was beginning
to sense just what sort of price she would be paying for the rich
pleasures she was reaping this summer. She lay in bed, on her
side, hugging herself with her arms, feeling hollow and melancholy, deep into the night.

Andy was a funny man. She had known him for over two months
now, and in some ways she knew him very well and in some ways
she didn't know him at all. She knew that he liked Dan Rather and
why, and what jazz musicians he liked and why, and what he thought
of Russian/American relations and American foreign policy—she
knew that sort of thing in great detail. She didn't know how much
he had loved his wife or why they had divorced or whether he had
loved other women or whether or not he preferred his solitary life.
Whenever Nell talked about Marlow or her children or the divorce,
Andy would listen for a while, but gradually he would show a kind
of polite impatience—he would get up to fix himself a drink and
remark on an interesting boat or sunset out the window, or he would
remember a note he needed to jot down for his book. He never
returned the favor of confiding the intimate details of his life. He
did not seek out such details from Nell.

She tried, in what she hoped were subtle ways, to draw him out.
"Where did you go to school?" she asked one night after talking about Jeremy's love for science.

"Snotty New England prep school," Andy had replied.

"Oh," Nell said, trying not to be daunted. "Well, where did you go to college?"

"Snotty New England college," he had replied shortly.

"You're pretty snotty yourself," she had said, teasingly, smiling, "if you won't even tell me the name of your college."

"Harvard," he had admitted. Then, with a combination of deft sidestepping and obvious complimentary interest, he had gotten Nell to talk about her college experiences.

Another time, Nell had been telling him about the way Hannah and Jeremy often squabbled. "Did you have brothers or sisters?" she asked.

"No," he had replied, his tone flat, ungenerous.

"Did you want one? Were you lonely? I *always longed* for a brother or sister," Nell said.

"I don't know," Andy replied. "I can't remember. I don't suppose I did. It wouldn't have mattered. I was sent off to school in first grade. I was always at school or camp. I never would have seen a sibling if I'd had one. I seldom saw my parents."

"Why?" Nell asked.

"Well, they were busy," Andy said, calmly stating the fact. "Then they got divorced and my mother moved to New Zealand. We lost touch. When I was old enough, though, I spent a lot of time with my father, going through his factories. He wasn't ready to deal with me until I was old enough to understand concepts like quantum mechanics. He died soon after I reached that stage."

"How awful. I'm so sorry," Nell had said. "You had such a lonely life."

"Don't be sorry," Andy replied, genuinely surprised by her sympathy. "I was happy. I didn't miss people. People aren't everything, you know." He paused, then said, looking right at Nell, "Maybe you should know that someone once told me that I have more meaningful relationships with machines than with people. She thought that as a newborn I must have been imprinted by a computer."

Andy's voice had been full of warning then, Nell thought, and when he tried changing the subject, she let him. At first a romantic fantasy, a throwback to the times when she believed in fairy tales, rose in her, so that she thought, well, it will be *different* for *us*. But as time went on, she could not seem to make it different. Andy obviously wanted things to stay on the surface, in the present. And it was lovely that way, Nell had to admit, but now and then she felt lonely, and more, she felt a sad twinge of foreboding. She was afraid that Andy's unwillingness to entrust her with some knowledge of his past indicated an equal unwillingness to entrust her with a share in his future.

Still, he could charm her. He could please her as no other man ever had. It was easy, it was the easiest thing in the world, to stop worrying about the future when she was with him, with his hand on her arm as he guided her across the street, or when his long, lanky body was stretched out next to hers in bed. He was always courteous and undemanding and understanding. He was a marvelous cook—what a treat it was for her to be presented with gourmet meals, which included artichokes, shrimp, capers, and other items her children made gagging noises over! He loved modern technology and would grow as excited as a little boy when describing the possibilities of computers, robots, satellites. He had a vision of the future that was extravagantly optimistic.

Many evenings Nell would sit with him, sipping a creamy liqueur, gazing out at the water, trying to turn the conversation toward some intimate, personal subject. Andy would be bored, monosyllabic, and even petulant until they had come to a more neutral topic: politics, the weather, Nantucket gossip. Before she knew it, and without her knowing just how it happened, Nell would find herself listening to Andy going on about something scientific—the theory behind space flight, the history of aeronautics—until Nell felt her eyes nearly crossing with boredom. She tried to console herself at such times by believing that he was at least sharing something he considered of great importance with her.

He had not told Nell that he loved her, but he had said, "You are beautiful." And "You are special." And "You mean so much to me." And "God, how wonderful it is when you are around."

On Mondays, Nell's day off from the boutique, Andy would rise early, as was his habit, to walk to the beach. Sometimes Nell would rise with him, but more often than not she would stay in bed, sleeping late. Andy would awaken her after he had had his walk and his coffee. He would take off his clothes and slip into bed with her, his skin cool from the ocean air, his breath smelling like coffee. He would hold Nell in his arms. He would press her up against him, all up and down, until her legs touched his legs and her stomach touched his torso and her face was nuzzled into his chest and his lips were pressing against her forehead. He would hold her like that against him for a long time, and it seemed to Nell at those times that she could feel the need in him. That she could feel how he needed to come back and find her in his bed, to be able to lie down and hold her in his arms, and that when he lay naked against her, holding her against him, he was trying to tell her that he loved her. Sometimes it even seemed to Nell that she knew Andy better than he knew himself, that she was able to admit what he felt—love and need—while he was still capable of articulating these feelings.

"You are so beautiful," he would say over and over again, stroking her hair, running his hand down her back. "You are so beautiful." And Nell would think how she must really look, in the morning with the sun exposing all her wrinkles and stretchmarks and sags, with her hair matted and her eyelids so swollen with sleep that she knew she looked beady-eyed, pig-eyed, and she would think: I am not so beautiful, Andy, or I am beautiful only to you, because you are in love with me. Those mornings in his arms she felt an almost indescribable peacefulness and security.

But those mornings did not last long, and the effect of them evaporated like a sweet perfume in the air by the next day. Nell would go into work at the boutique and a married couple would come in, fussing slightly in their married way about what sort of present to buy their mother or their daughter. The woman would say, "This is like the blouse you bought me last year." The man would say, "Why don't we get this for Annie for Christmas? We'll never find one we like as much." And Nell would look on with yearning, with envy, at this couple who shared a past and a future with such carefree reliability.

As the first of August drew closer, Nell began to dream of her children. Andy had not yet met them; he would be surprised, she thought, at how beautiful they were. She thought about Jeremy, with his boyish bony body that was just now beginning to show signs of manhood—his shoulders were so wide, his chest broadening, although his skin was still as smooth as a baby's. She thought of Hannah's eager laughter, her willingness to share good news or bad, her self-reliance. Hannah was never bored. She could always turn the dullest day into gold. She was a powerhouse of energy, and when she was around, the world seemed brighter. If a friend couldn't come over for the day, Hannah would put on a record, dress up her dolls or Fred the cat, and create her own friends. She would argue, discuss, share, laugh, all with her dolls or an imaginary friend, and she would be just as satisfied, it seemed, by that illusory presence as by the presence of a real person.

From time to time, in spite of all her attempts to the contrary, Nell found herself wondering what it would be like if she and Andy were to marry, if the four of them were to live together as a family. It was a hard thing to imagine. She had gotten used to Andy's idiosyncracies. She knew now how much he liked his privacy and solitude, how impatient he was with small talk, how tactless he often seemed with his blunt questions. He was not a gregarious man, and at first Nell had been delighted by this. She knew she was prone to irrational and extravagant jealousy, knew that if she saw him talking with another single woman—or married woman, for that matter—she would be eaten up inside by her own nasty suspicions. She knew she was most content when she was with him or, if she couldn't be with him, knew he was by himself. But soon she began to wish that he enjoyed people just a little more. She liked parties. When she was invited to cocktail parties or dinner parties, she always asked Andy to join her, and more often than not, he had at least a nodding acquaintance with the hosts and other guests. He would be polite at a party, although from time to time Nell had seen him peering at a person with his forehead wrinkled in a frown and she knew that Andy was thinking: can this person be for real? Why would he choose to spend his life this way? Andy was arrogant; he found almost all of the professions of modern man almost hilariously unnecessary. Sell insurance? Make jewelry? Run a hotel? Write ads? Surely that was no way to live a life.

At one party Nell had been smoldering with jealousy because a lovely woman had approached Andy, swiveling as she walked, and had engaged him immediately in a serious conversation. God, Nell thought, I wonder what *she* does. When she could stand it no longer, Nell had excused herself from her conversation and made her way across the room to Andy's side. She was glad she did, for Andy was, in his own quiet way, lambasting the poor lovely woman for selling real estate on Nantucket. Nell arrived just in time to hear him tell the woman that she was a parasite on society who destroyed the land for her own gain.

Still, Andy could be wonderful if he liked someone. He enjoyed talking to Clary about her work with rats. He listened to her stories about them carefully and asked innumerable questions. He was more lenient in his judgments about Clary and her friends, perhaps because he thought of them still as children, even though they were in their twenties and early thirties. He was able to excuse their silliness because they were young.

What would he think of Jeremy and Hannah? Nell wondered as the first of August approached. At least they were young—he couldn't judge their choice of profession yet. But she wanted him to do more than tolerate them; she hoped he would *like* her children. She hoped he would be charmed by them. She tried to prepare him—and herself—for their presence by talking about them more often as the day of their arrival drew near. She wanted to impress on him just how young they were, how innocent, how much at the mercy of adults they were. She tried to describe the children to him. Many of the things she remembered them saying or doing seemed strange as she repeated them, seemed too cutesy or almost unbelievable.

"One year," she told Andy one evening, "Hannah came home from her first day in first grade. She told me about the different projects and classes she would have at school, and she gave me some forms to fill out. One was permission to go on field trips. One was permission to take a section in sex education. Hannah said, 'Oh, that slip is about sex. We're going to have a bunch of lechers at the school.'

" 'You what?' " I asked.

" 'The teacher said we're going to have some lechers.' "

Nell continued her story, telling Andy how puzzled and slightly worried she had been, how she had finally called another mother before managing to figure out that the word Hannah was trying to say was *lecture*. But she could tell long before she got to the end of the story that Andy had immediately understood what the misunderstood word was and was listening to Nell only out of kindness. Oh dear, Nell had thought, if he thinks they're boring when they're cute, what will he think of them when they're awful?

And she didn't know what to do about the sleeping arrangements. It had been so wonderfully easy and natural with the children gone. Almost every night for two months they had slept together—whether they made love or not, they had slept all night together, either at the cottage or his house. She supposed that now and then when Clary was sleeping in the cottage she could slip off to Andy's for the night, but she didn't especially want to do that. And she didn't know how to tell Andy that she had never slept with a man all night around the children. She was afraid that by broaching this subject she would be pushing their relationship into a seriousness that Andy was not yet ready to discuss.

One morning she talked it over with Clary. They were at the Steps Beach, lying on towels, wet from the ocean, tanning and lazing in the sun.

"Clary," Nell said. "Can we talk?"

"Sure," Clary said, turning over on her stomach and shading her eyes to look at Nell. "What's up?"

"It's about Andy," Nell said. "I don't know what to do. I mean about him sleeping with me."

"It's all right," Clary said, grinning. "You can sleep with him. I won't tell anyone."

"Listen, kid," Nell said. "This is serious. I mean what about Hannah and Jeremy? I've been thinking about it a lot, and I've decided that if I explained it to them, if I said, look, I'm in love with this man and he's in love with me and we like to be with each other and so we will be with each other a lot, including sleeping with each other at night, I think if I explain it like that, it will be okay with them."

Clary thought a while. Then, "Yeah," she said. "I think you're right. I think honesty's the best policy with kids. Besides, you're just telling them what they should know anyway, in case they wake up in the night or something, so they won't be shocked to find a man in your bed. All you have to tell them is that he is sleeping with you. They might think you're doodling once or twice, but they probably assume you mostly don't. Kids never can believe their parents doodle."

Nell laughed. "Doodle," she said. She was quiet. Then she said, "But, Clary, I want the children to know that I don't sleep with a man unless I love him."

"Sounds okay to me."

"But how can I tell the children I love him when I haven't told Andy I love him?"

"Do you love him?" Clary asked.

Nell's heart clenched. "Yes," she said. "I guess I do. I know when I first met him, I was in love with him, infatuated. But it is lasting and it's getting stronger. Deeper. Better. All that stuff. Clary, I really do think I love him."

"Well, that's really nice, Nell," Clary said.

"Yes, well, but he doesn't know," Nell said.

"Why not?"

Nell turned over onto her stomach and put her head on her arms. She looked sideways at Clary and grinned. "I haven't told him because I'm *scared,*" she said. "Besides, he hasn't told me he loves me. He should be the one to say it first."

"Whoopee, Nell, women's lib has sure done a lot for you," Clary said.

"Well, Clary, it's not so easy," Nell pleaded. "It's scary."

"What are you afraid of?"

Nell felt her face go serious. She looked up at Clary steadily. "You know what I'm afraid of," she said. "I'm afraid that he doesn't love me. I'm afraid that I'll tell him I love him and he'll smile and oh, tousle my hair or something and tell me I'm sweet. And I'll just die."

"Well, better now than later," Clary said.

"You're a heartless woman," Nell said.

"Yeah, well," Clary mumbled, and buried her head in her arms. "I'm working on it."

Nell put her head down, too, for a while. Poor Clary, she thought. Clary had broken off with Sam and was seeing another guy now, a handsome young man named Harry. Clary liked Harry, but she was still in love with Bob, and since she had told him to bug off after his second visit, she hadn't heard from him again. It had been almost a month. She was sure that this time it was really over. Clary was dating Harry and other men, she was even sleeping with Harry. But she was certain that she'd never love anyone else in the world as she loved Bob, and she saw her whole life stretching out before her, endlessly worthless. Without Bob in her life, nothing mattered very much.

"Love is just shit, isn't it," Nell muttered after a while.

"It certainly is," Clary agreed.

But that night Nell got her courage up and decided to try to talk seriously with Andy. She spent the entire day in the boutique carrying on imaginary conversations in her mind. She tried to think of the perfect way to phrase all that she wanted to say. She wanted to let Andy know she loved him without seeming to supplicate. But she also wanted him to know that she considered it a serious business, this having him in her bed when her children were around. What she wanted to say to him was that if he considered their relationship a serious one, one that might have some future, then she would gladly be his lover in front of her children. But if he thought of their relationship as temporary . . . She remembered a term Ilona had used once recently, referring to what she intended to do once she was divorced: "sport-fuck." Nell got nearly sick at this thought and could not come up with anything but a fanciful and unrealistic scene in which she haughtily drew herself up and said, "Well, if that's the case, then I never want to see you again," and tearlessly left him standing alone. She knew she would not be tearless in real life if she said she would never see him again.

At his house that night they had a wonderful dinner of bouillabaisse with a chicory salad and hot bread. He had cooked it all himself. They sat over white wine and green grapes and chocolate cookies at the kitchen table, watching the boats sail out on the horizon in the silver evening light. They were content in each other's company. Andy was a kind man, Nell thought: what was she afraid of?

At last she blurted out, "Andy, we need to talk."

Andy looked at her, smiling, his smile slightly amused. "Sure," he said. "Let's talk."

"I mean seriously," Nell said. "I mean—I mean, it's going to be different with the children here. It's not going to be as easy. They'll be in camp all day while I work, but I'll have to be with them at night, and they'll be around all the time and since I won't be with them in the day, I'll have to spend some time with them at night, which means I won't have as much free time to be with you as I have had and besides, I want you to sleep with me, I mean all night at the cottage, while they're there, but I want them to know this is special, at least to me. I've never had a man sleep with me before in front of the children, oh God, I don't mean that like it sounds, I don't mean have sex in front of the children, I mean I've never had a man sleep in my bed with me all night, because of the children, because I want them to know—and I would like you to know, although I guess you already do know—" Nell stopped. Help me out, Andy, she prayed.

Andy waited, looking at her.

"Christ, Andy," Nell said. "Don't you know what I'm trying to say?" She was having trouble breathing. Andy was looking at her with concern and affection but not with any particular gleam of understanding. "Oh shit, Andy, sometimes I think you're really dense!" Nell said. "I love you," she finished, and looked away.

She sat there then, staring out at the ocean and feeling tears come traitorously out to her eyelashes. She made her eyes wider and wider, trying to keep the drops from falling down her cheek so he would not see them. She felt him looking at her. Stupid ass, she thought, why doesn't he say something?

"Well," Andy said after a while, "I guess I love you too, Nell."

"You guess?" Nell asked, glaring at him.

"I know," he said. He reached across and held her face in his hand so that she had to look him in the eye. "Nell," he said. "I love you. I do. And I'll tell your children that, too. Okay?"

"Okay," Nell said. "Wow." Tears ran down her face.

They went upstairs to bed shortly after that, and Nell just gave herself over to the great warm joy of making love with a man whom she loved who had said he loved her. Later, as she lay in his arms, she thought what a pleasure it was going to be to tell Clary that Andy loved her. What a pleasure it would be to tell Ilona. To tell Katy and John Anderson. She knew that in the telling, in the repetition, it would seem more and more true, more and more real. She loved a man who loved her.

The last Monday morning before Hannah and Jeremy arrived, Nell put on her blue leotard and went downstairs to the living room of the cottage to do her exercises. She went mindlessly, cheerfully through the routine, moving to the rhythms of a Bob Seger album. When she was almost finished, she looked up to see Clary standing in the doorway. Clary had on a black leotard that made her look as dark as chocolates and her body as thin as Nell's wrist. Her blond hair was in a long sweeping ponytail.

"Hi," Clary said. "Listen, I want you to try exercising to this record. It's got a super beat."

She crossed the room and put a record by Men Without Hats on the turntable. Immediately, the room was filled with the deep thrumming of a bass guitar and an exuberant counterpoint of clapping. Then came the futuristic notes of a synthesizer and a man singing in a cheeky, dispassionate voice. Nell envisioned robots, dancers in aluminum clothes. But the music was moving. Clary started doing leg kicks and waist bends in time to the song. "Come on," she said, smiling up at Nell over her shoulder. "It's the Safety Dance."

Nell watched Clary a minute more, and then began to dance herself. She was overcome with emotion and turned her back as she moved so that Clary couldn't see her face. She was thinking:

I love you, Clary, not because you are my child, or even because you are such a miraculously pretty sight, but because you are so generous that even in the midst of your unhappiness you wish me happiness, you will me love.

Nell did waist bends and leg kicks. The music was hypnotic and exhilarating; she wanted it to go on and on and she felt she could go on and on, too. Just now, dancing seemed as natural as breathing. It didn't bother her that her waist and hips were wider than Clary's, that she didn't move around the room with the same skinny grace as Clary, that her body wasn't as supple as Clary's. Her body was fine, and she turned and started matching her step to Clary's. She and Clary started kicking and clapping in time to the record. They bounced and puffed. They grinned at each other.

"We can dance if we want to," Clary said. "It's safe to dance."

Tuesday, Nell took the nine-thirty plane to Hyannis and the bus to Logan Airport. She was surprised at how shocking the mainland seemed to her after two months on Nantucket. There was so much clatter in the world, so much noise! So many cars! So many people! So many houses! She felt as disoriented as a stranger from another planet. The bus from Hyannis to Boston was crammed with people, and not with the beautiful tourist types who strolled the Nantucket streets and beaches, but with weary, resigned souls who talked to each other about the heat, or their bunions or their husband's cancer operation. Nell was sobered. She realized she had been living in an unreal world.

It was a shock seeing the children again after two months, too. They were a little taller, a little older-looking than she had remembered: she had expected that. But Hannah's front tooth had come in while she was away, and to Nell's dismay, that tooth had come in crooked. It was headed sideways and back, a nice huge front tooth aiming at Hannah's throat. Jeremy's front teeth, on the other hand, were slightly bucked, and one of the lower teeth seemed on its way to the moon. Christ, Nell thought, they'll both need braces.

The children were euphoric to see Nell again, and for the first few minutes they all indulged in a rapture of hugging and kissing and touching and shouting their news at each other. Nell hurried along through getting their luggage and out the door to a that they would make the six o'clock bus back to Hyannis.

How beautiful these children are, how beautiful, Nell thought. But in the taxi Jeremy got mad at Hannah because she kept interrupting him, and Hannah wailed, "But, Jeremy, I want to tell Mom stuff, too; you're hogging the whole conversation!" And Nell leaned back against the seat and thought to herself that she had forgotten just how demanding even lovable children were. She was surprised to find herself amazingly short-tempered. She wanted to snap: if you can't speak politely, don't speak at all! But she knew they were keyed-up from the trip, and more, that they were probably overloaded with emotion and apprehension. They had just come from two months in a strange place with their father and their eccentric stepmother. Now they were on their way to another strange place with their mom. They were away from their normal routines, from their school, all their friends, even the refuge of their own home and bedrooms and stuffed animals and pets. They needed her patience. They deserved it.

During the two-hour bus ride, she divided them up. For one hour (she timed it exactly to prevent quibbling), she sat next to Jeremy and listened to him talk. For the next hour she sat next to Hannah and listened to her. They had so much to say! And so much of it was boring! Jeremy described in great detail all the roller coaster rides he had gone on at the Great America Theme Park north of Chicago and all the food he had eaten, and then he recounted, scene by scene, *The Return of the Jedi*, which he had seen three times. Nell wished he would stop talking so that she could put her head back and take a nap. She was sleepy from rising early to get ready for the children, and the day of traveling on ferry, bus, taxi, and now bus again was exhausting and boring. The bus fumes made her sick to her stomach. Oh, can't you just look at the scenery, Jeremy, she thought, longing to close her eyes. I'm a monster, she thought. I should be thrilled to hear every word he says. Here my children are, safe and whole and with me. Marlow didn't kill them in a car accident. Charlotte didn't poison them with her cooking or lose them in some Chicago crowd. The plane didn't crash. She tried to show more interest in Jeremy's stories.

On the ferry back, Nell bought the children sandwiches and Cokes and bought herself a sandwich and beer. It was nine-thirty and they were all tired, hungry, and cranky. She was slightly revived by the food and the brisk sea air—and by the adrenaline that started pumping through her blood when she decided the time had come to tell the children about Andy. Jeremy and Hannah were tired now, too, and, after the first excitement of being on a ferry and running over every square inch of the boat, were content to sit quietly inside the lounge area, eating. It was too dark to see much outside except for the lights of an occasional passing boat.

Nell told the children she had some important things to discuss with them. She told them that Clary was living at the cottage and working on Nantucket and that the cottage would be full of her friends. She told them that they must remember that the cottage didn't belong to them and so they must be careful to keep their rooms neat and clean. She told them that she would be working all day during the week and that on those days they would attend a day camp. The counselors, two college girls who exuded more healthy enthusiasm than a breakfast cereal commercial, would bring Jeremy and Hannah home at four-thirty. They were to rest in their rooms or watch TV till Nell got home at six. Some Saturdays they would have to entertain themselves while she supervised the shop. *If* they stayed alone without fighting, occupying themselves nicely, she would pay them fifty cents an hour, and that would add up to be their spending money. She told them about the pleasures of Nantucket.

Then she told them about Andy. She told them how she had met him and about his house and that he would be eating dinner with them a lot and sleeping with her in the cottage, because she loved him.

"What about Stellios?" was Jeremy's first question.

"What?" Nell asked. It was the last thing she thought the children would think of.

"Well, aren't you going to see Stellios anymore?" Jeremy asked.

"No, honey," Nell said. "I'm not. I never did *love* Stellios. Although he was a special, good friend."

"I'm going to miss Stellios," Hannah announced.

"Well, sweetie, I know," Nell said. "But I think you'll like Andy, too. Although he is quite different."

"Well, why do you love Andy instead of Stellios?" Jeremy asked. "Stellios was *nice.*"

Why do these children persist in talking about Stellios, Nell wondered. "It's hard to explain love," she said. "I don't know *why* I love Andy. He's older than Stellios, for one thing, so we have more in common. And we both like the same sorts of things. We read. We like the same sort of music and food and movies.

I love being with Andy. He's nice and he's kind and he's funny, and oh, darlings, I can't explain just why, but I do love him.''

"Are you going to marry him?'' Jeremy asked.

"Oh no,'' Nell said. "I mean, I don't think so, I don't know. It's too early to think about that yet, Jeremy. But we are going to sort of live together. We'll be together a lot. He'll be in the house a lot, and as I said, he'll sleep with me in my bed all night.''

"Like Stellios did,'' Hannah said.

Nell was stunned. "Hannah,'' she said, "Stellios never spent the night with me. How can you say that? You never saw him spend the night with me. You never saw him in my bed.''

"But we saw you kiss him in the living room,'' Hannah said. "And we know what *that* means.''

Nell turned to Jeremy. "Did you think that Stellios was spending the night at our house?'' she asked.

"Sure,'' Jeremy said. "I guess so.''

"But you never saw him there!'' Nell said.

"I thought he just got up and left before we woke up,'' Jeremy said. "And you always go to bed after we're asleep. I just thought he went to bed with you.''

"Oh Lord,'' Nell said, and she sighed.

"Well,'' Hannah announced. "If you didn't go to bed with Stellios, that's too bad. He's a lot of fun to cuddle with.''

Nell looked at her daughter and smiled. "Yes,'' she admitted, remembering. "Stellios is a lot of fun to cuddle with.''

"Maybe if you *had* gone to bed with him you'd be in love with him,'' Hannah said, looking at her mother with exasperation.

Nell wanted to put her head down on the table and weep with frustration. The intricacies and nuances of this delicate conversation seemed beyond her capabilities. At last she said, "Just because you like going to bed with a person doesn't mean you love him.''

Nell thought about trying to find out just what her children thought they meant by "going to bed with someone,'' but she was too tired. She wanted so much to guide her children safely through the perils of sex education, to somehow get them on that sensible and comfortable middle road of knowing that sex was not the sacred and holy act that should be feared, as her mother had taught her, but also that it was not as casual and insignificant as TV seemed to indicate, either. Children knew so much these days. They had sex education in school, and they saw things on

TV and could easily check out books from the library that described the sexual act in clever and whimsical words with accompanying drawings that in Nell's mother's time would have been labeled pornographic. It was hard to know just what they actually did know, Nell thought.

One day in early spring Nell had been fixing dinner and talking with Stellios, who sat at the table drinking a beer. Hannah had come into the kitchen, sat down at the table, scribbled on the telephone message pad. Obviously she was bored and had no one to play with and thought she might be entertained by the adults for a while.

"Mom," Hannah had asked casually, "do you bawl a lot?"

My God, Nell thought: do I ball a lot? She was chopping onions at that moment; at Hannah's question she almost chopped off her finger. She didn't know what to do. Should she scold Hannah? Send her to her room? Sit down with her and have a serious discussion? She didn't dare look at Stellios. She turned a hypocritical face to her daughter.

"Why, darling," she said, smiling sweetly. "I'm not sure just what you mean."

"I mean, do you bawl a lot," Hannah said. "Like on *Little House on the Prairie*. Whenever Laura Ingalls cries, the kids all say, 'There goes Laura, bawling again.' "

Nell felt her eyes go into slits rather like Medusa's as she stared at her darling daughter. "Yes, Hannah," she said evenly. "I do bawl a lot. I think it's a good thing to cry when you feel like it. You've seen me. I bawl at sad TV shows, I bawl when I hurt myself, sometimes even when I'm just tired."

Hannah seemed satisfied with that answer and talked some more before wandering off.

"Wow," Stellios had said when Hannah left the room. "For a moment there I thought she was talking about something else."

"She might have been," Nell said. "I wouldn't put it past her to try something like that just to see if she could get a rise out of me."

"But Hannah's only eight years old," Stellios had said.

"I know," Nell had replied. "But it's amazing what kids know these days."

And it's amazing, Nell thought as she sat at the table on the ferry looking at her children, how little can be explained about love and sex. No matter how explicit the technical details of the sexual act were made, the truth about love and sex remained a mystery. There was no way to explain why you fell in love with someone. Nell talked with Hannah and Jeremy a bit more, but finally ended up with the same vague advice her mother had given her: "Well, you'll just have to wait till you're grown, then you'll see what I mean. You can't help who you fall in love with."

The children grew bored with the subject, and after they finished eating, they wandered around the boat a bit and finally sat down on the hard benches to wait out the end of the trip. They were tired, and the ferry didn't dock until midnight.

By that time Hannah had fallen asleep and was hard to awaken. She didn't want to carry her backpack, but Nell insisted, because she had to carry the enormous old suitcase that held all the children's clothes and toys. She cajoled Hannah into putting on the backpack and following her down the ramp.

"We're in Nantucket. You're here at last!" Nell said, trying to be enthusiastic.

But after all, it was too dark for the children to see anything, and they were so tired. Nell and Andy had agreed that for the children's first night on the island she should probably sleep alone, and so he was at his house. Nell didn't know where Clary was—out drinking with friends, or perhaps asleep in her room at the cottage. But Nell felt an irrational anger at both Clary and Andy because they had left her alone to struggle down the ramp with two sleepy children and a heavy suitcase. She took a taxi to the cottage in spite of the expense. Clary wasn't at the cottage when they arrived, and all the rooms were dark. Nell paid the driver, hauled the suitcase into the house—she couldn't expect the taxi driver to do it; he was so ancient and shriveled he undoubtedly weighed less than the suitcase—and took the children through all the rooms, flipping on the lights, trying to sound cheerful and hearty. But Hannah and Jeremy were exhausted and, Nell realized, so was she. She got the children into bed, kissed them good night, and knew they would fall asleep instantly.

Then she went back through the house, turning off the lights, relaxing. She poured herself a glass of wine. She went into the large back living room and sat down in a chair in the dark. She took a deep sip of wine, then put her head in her hands.

Here she was, alone again, with the weight of her two children pulling on her just as definitely as the suitcase had weighed on her, and she felt she was managing their lives with the same cumbersome sense of solitary struggle. She replayed in her mind her last conversation with Andy. He had been the one who had said, "I imagine that the first night with your children you'll want to spend alone." He had not thought to ask if he could help in any way, help carry the luggage, pick them up at the ferry, and drive them home—and after all, why should he think of such a thing? He didn't even know the children, and he and Nell were only lovers. And Clary, well, Clary, would be glad enough to see Jeremy and Hannah again, but they weren't part of her life, really.

It had been that damn arriving on the ferry bit that had sent Nell into this depression, she decided. It had been that exhausting lugging of the suitcase and the effort of cheering the children on that had tired her—and the sight of so many other people going off the ferry and into the waiting arms of friends or lovers or family. It had seemed to Nell that everyone else on the boat had been met and embraced. One little boy had run down the ramp, calling, "Daddy! Daddy!" and his father, waiting on the wharf, had held out his arms for the little boy to jump into. The father had lifted him up in the air and hugged him in a great squeeze of love. The mother had come more slowly down the ramp, and the father had shifted his son onto one arm so that he could wrap his other arm around his wife and pull her to him in a lingering kiss. Nell had wanted to cover her children's eyes, to turn their heads away from this sight, because she was afraid they would be as hurt by it as she was, by the contrast of this happy, whole family with their own.

"I'm just tired," Nell said aloud to the dark and empty room. She finished her wine, put the glass in the kitchen, then went upstairs to bed. When she was brushing her teeth in the bathroom, she saw a T-shirt of Clary's tossed over the clothes hamper. It was pink and it said LIFE'S A BEACH. Earlier this summer they had laughed over it, saying that the back side of the shirt should read LIFE'S A BITCH. It could be your basic manic-depressive T-shirt, Clary said. Now Nell tried to reassure herself, It's all a matter of attitude. Your life can be as miserable or as happy as you make it.

Sometimes, though, she felt she just did not have the energy to keep at it, to keep trying to turn the sow's ear into a silk purse. Sometimes she wished she had just a little more, a little better, raw material to start with. Finally she fell into bed and was grateful to stop her trudging thoughts.

The next morning, refreshed by her sleep, Nell started the day off cheerfully. She got the children up and dressed and off to camp,

bought lots of groceries at lunch hour, and worked hard in the boutique. She was planning to have Andy over for dinner that evening.

But when she got home, she was confronted with problems:
Jeremy had liked the camp well enough, but Hannah hadn't. Only
two other little girls were in the group, and they were best friends;
they ignored her, and she had had to play alone. Nell said she'd
discuss this with the counselors. Then the children were so clingy;
Nell could understand this, for they were always clingy after
spending a long period of time away from her, but she wanted to
shower and change and prepare a nice meal. And she had gotten
into the marvelous habit in the past two months of having about
thirty minutes of time to herself after the wild days of constantly
talking to people and taking care of customers in the boutique.
Now Hannah and Jeremy followed her from room to room, demanding that she arbitrate arguments, help them decide who got
to choose the television shows, and so on. They had been away
from her for two months. They wanted to be with her every minute now, here in this strange new place. Nell understood this, but
as she walked around the house, she kept bumping into them,
nearly tripping over their feet as they trailed next to her, demanding her attention. Nell unpacked their suitcases to find that
all their clothes were dirty—every single item. Good old Charlotte, Nell thought.

She carried armfuls of clothes down to the laundry room off
the kitchen and started a load of wash. Hannah and Jeremy went
with her, complaining about their stay with Marlow and Charlotte: they had been bored, Charlotte wasn't a good cook, Dad
hadn't spent any time with them, why did they have to go?

Nell fixed herself a drink. She had envisioned a lovely evening,
with all four of them sitting around the dinner table and Jeremy and
Hannah saying the clever and charming things they were capable of
saying while Andy looked on, impressed. But now Nell could see
this vision was not going to make it to reality. She fixed the children
tuna sandwiches and chips and carrots, celery, and green pepper
chunks, and let them eat early, because they were starving after
their day on the beach and would get crabby if they had to wait. If
Andy hadn't been coming for dinner, she would have eaten a tuna
fish sandwich herself and put her feet up and watched television
with the children. But she washed lettuce to make a salad and started
the charcoal for the barbequed chicken, even though just lifting the
bag of charcoal seemed a monumental effort.

When Andy arrived at the cottage, he wanted to sit with a drink and watch the news, as he and Nell had become accustomed to doing. But the cottage had only one TV set, of course, and Hannah and Jeremy were engrossed in a children's show. And so, even though the children and Andy had said hello nicely enough to each other, in only a few moments the room was full of tension, and then resentment, because Nell told the children they could watch TV all evening, but for just this half hour she and Andy were going to watch the news. They could play in their rooms.

Hannah and Jeremy sulked off upstairs. Nell sat glaring at the TV, hating Andy because he wanted to watch the news—which was boring tonight—instead of donating this first half hour of time to getting to know Nell's children. She felt he had slighted her children. While she sat there watching TV and smoldering, the chicken burned on the outdoor grill, and although Andy said not to worry, it didn't matter, he still only picked at it, pushing away the blackened skin with his knife, leaving most of it on his plate. Clearly it was not up to his standards. In defense, Nell chewed away greedily at her share of chicken, pretending it was delicious even though it had gotten tough and tasted dry.

After dinner, she put clothes in the dryer and more clothes in the washing machine. Then, wanting to be cheerful, wanting everyone to be happy, she suggested that they all walk down to Main Street to buy ice cream cones at the Sweet Shop and hear the street musicians play. But Andy said he'd prefer to stay home and read. He hated the crowds of people who gathered on Main Street in the evenings, and he thought the musicians were inferior and tacky—the whole thing degraded Nantucket, in his opinion, and made him angry. So Nell set off alone with her children.

In her mind, she knew that she should not be upset with Andy for not joining them. The local Nantucket paper, the *Inquirer and Mirror*, was full of letters about the musicians who played on the streets at night. The old Nantucketers thought the musicians were trashy and that the hats or violin cases they left open for passersby to throw money into labeled them beggars. They thought the crowds who gathered on the street to listen to the musicians were loitering and obstructing those who wanted to simply walk down the street or into the shops. They were afraid that a crowd mentality might grow and violence might break out. They thought the street musicians made Main Street seem like some street in New York City; it destroyed the sense of peace and serenity that had been Nantucket's ambience for hundreds of years. Nell knew all this. She knew Andy was not alone or wrong in his thinking . . . still, it hurt her that he had not wanted to join her and the children in this, their first walk around town.

But the children loved the Sweet Shop and thought the black musician who sang "Banana Boat Song" was cool, and for a while they, at least, were happy. They sat on a bench, licking their cones and wiping their hands on their shirts. Nell looked up and down the street, which seemed very European tonight, bright with light, flowing with laughter and chatter. She felt that she was the only single adult around. Everyone else was in pairs. Everyone else, it seemed, was in love. She had seen postcards in shops that said, "Nantucket Is for Lovers," and now she had to agree. The street was full of lovers who strolled along, arms wrapped around each other, smiling into each other's eyes. Nell felt bereft. She knew she and Andy would never stroll down a street looking at each other that way. He hated public displays of affection and did not even hold her hand in public. Furthermore, he seemed physically incapable of *strolling;* he always strode along, his slowest walk a sort of lunging gait that Nell nearly had to trot to keep up with. Nell watched the lovers passing by and she yearned after them, wishing that someone loved her as much as those men loved those women—so much that it appeared they could not keep from touching them, pulling them close.

Nell got the children home and made them brush their teeth, then tucked them in bed. She talked to them, or rather listened to them, for a long time, because she knew they needed this sense of closeness, needed to know she was accessible to them in this strange new place. Finally, they went to sleep. She went back downstairs. Andy had spent the evening reading. Nell did some more laundry. She noticed that the dinner dishes still sat on the table. As she carried the laundry back up the stairs, she thought to herself: now cool down, Nell. For she never did the dishes at Andy's house. There was no reason for him to do the dishes here. But tonight they irked her. Tonight she felt like everyone's maid. Tonight, she thought, giving herself a mental kick, tonight you're just looking for trouble.

Finally, she showered and slipped into her pretty black nightgown and went downstairs. The shower had helped. Andy's face when she entered the room helped too. He pulled her to him, kissed her, got her a glass of wine, told her about his book. They talked awhile, and Nell relaxed. He had had a difficult day too, it turned out; complications with his writing, one of his word processors had broken down and had to be shipped off-island, a tax hassle that Andy discussed in detail, incensed. Nell's irritation was soon replaced by the sort of sweet exhaustion that seeps into one's bones after hard work. It was pleasurable to sit grousing companionably with him, knowing that soon they would make each other forget the troubles of the day. It made her almost glad of the troubles. When they went upstairs, Nell checked the children's room to be sure they were soundly sleeping. Then she went to bed with Andy, knowing that soon she would get used to this new routine. It was sweet falling asleep with those she loved all gathered under the same roof.

Elizabeth had warned Nell that the month of August would be very busy in the boutique, but Nell was still surprised by the crowds of people that came into the store each day. It got so that Nell nearly burst into tears if she awoke to find that it was raining, because on rainy days the tourists passed their time in the shops. It was true that business improved. More clothes were sold. But many of the people who came in were only browsing. They would unfold sweaters, hold them up in front of them, then drop them in a pile on the counter and wander aimlessly over to the dresses. They'd take a size 12 dress out, study it a bit, then thoughtlessly shove it back somewhere among size 6's or 8's. The dressing rooms began to look like the space beneath Jeremy's bed from unwanted clothing that had been tried on, then dropped, inside out, onto the floor. Usually the customers were polite, but each day there was at least one person, and often more, who felt insulted by the lack of personal patient attention or by Nell's not having their size in stock. Then the man or woman would take out whatever frustration he or she was feeling at that moment on Nell or Mindy or Kelly, the new part-time girl.

"What kind of shop are you running here?" someone would say.

"Oh well, what can you expect when you've got teenagers running the place," another person said in front of Mindy. "These kids don't care about helping people, they're only passing the time until college starts again." Mindy had been talking to one customer on the phone and writing up a receipt for another when this was said.

More often than not, Nell found she had to spend a few minutes at the end of each day soothing and complimenting Mindy or

Kelly so that they wouldn't quit. She told Elizabeth this during one of their long-distance phone conversations, and the second week in August Elizabeth flew over to check out the situation. She spent two days in the boutique with Nell and took Nell out to lunch the second day at the Water Club. To Nell's surprise, Elizabeth showered Nell with praise: the boutique had never done so well, had never done such a volume of business, had never looked so good so consistently.

"But do you realize," Elizabeth said to Nell, "that you're working yourself to death in there?"

Nell looked at Elizabeth, amazed. She did not think she was working herself to death, but she was working awfully hard. In the past ten days she had invited Andy over to the house only twice, claiming complete exhaustion the other evenings. Then she had fixed some easy dinner for herself and the children and sat around with them, eating with her fingers and watching old TV reruns. On her days off, she had taken the children to the beach. Andy had not joined them, because he didn't like the beaches in August, when they were crowded with tourists. She missed being with Andy, and yet she was just too tired to make the effort that having him around required when the children were there. He was always polite to Hannah and Jeremy, but not charmed or even very interested, and in spite of all her rationality, Nell couldn't help but feel hurt by this.

Now as she sat looking at Elizabeth, she realized how convenient it was for her that the shop was so busy, that she was overworked. Exhaustion from overwork was much easier to deal with than exhaustion from failed hopes. She did not know exactly what it was she had hoped would happen between Andy and her children—but certainly more than this. And she could not help but think of Stellios, who had genuinely liked the children and had enjoyed talking about all sorts of things with them—trucks, cement mixers, astronauts, television shows, *E.T.*, horrible gory accidents, space aliens—sometimes Nell had secretly scorned him for his boyish enthusiasms, but now she saw how his näiveté had permitted him a truer, closer access to the children than Andy's intellectual brilliance would ever permit.

Still, she thought, *she* was having the affair with Andy, not her children. And the two nights during the past ten days that he had been with her had been lovely. He had insisted on bringing dinner both times, and if he had not tried to charm the children or to get to know them, neither had he snubbed them. He had listened to them chatter at the dinner table. He had brought a book to read while Nell played cards with them or let them watch the TV shows they wanted. He had cleaned up the kitchen while Nell put the children to bed. And when he and Nell went to bed—it had been wonderful. Then it seemed to be worth everything. He had turned her onto her stomach and massaged her neck and shoulders and back, her buttocks and legs and arms. "My poor darling," he said. "You're working so hard. I miss you," he said. "It's no fun being without you in the evenings, and it's terrible without you at night." Then he had kissed all the places he had massaged and finally turned her over to kiss her face and shoulders and breasts and belly. Nell had been weak with happiness and love.

Now Elizabeth was saying, "You look awful, you look peaked, Nell. Listen, here's what we'll do. I'll hire Kelly full-time. That should allow you to take a little more time off. Set your own hours. Take the afternoon off now and then and get out to the beach, get some sun. Or leave the shop early some evenings and go out to dinner. Go to parties. Have some fun. If you feel guilty, remember that when you're meeting people at parties, you're advertising the boutique, in a way. People will drop in to see you." She leaned back and scrutinized Nell. "I'm surprised you haven't met any men here."

"Oh but I have, Elizabeth," Nell said. "In fact I met a man in your shop, and I've been sort of going with him ever since. I had seen him on the beach, and he came into the shop to buy a present for his daughter. The next morning I met him on the beach again and had coffee with him, and I've been—seeing—him ever since."

"Well," Elizabeth said. "Good for you, Nell. Who is this character?"

"Character is the right word for him," Nell laughed. The excellent lunch and Elizabeth's kindness and the enormous strawberry daiquiri she was drinking were having a warming effect on her. And now she was having the chance to talk about her lover, which was such a pleasurable thing to do. She wondered how to describe him to Elizabeth, how to capture in words all his intriguing qualities. Smugly, she leaned her arms on the table, leaned forward, and began, "His name is Andy Martindale—"

"Andy Martindale!" Elizabeth said. "Oh, Nell. Jesus Christ."

"Do you know him?" Nell asked.

Elizabeth laughed. "You sold a sweater to Andy Martindale?"

"For his sixteen-year-old daughter," Nell said, defensive.

"Listen, darling," Elizabeth said. "Andy Martindale could buy the whole shop for his daughter if he wanted to. Didn't you know that? No, I can see you didn't. Oh, Nell, you child. Of all the men on the island, you get involved with Andy Martindale. He's wealthy, Nell, and he's also very much *not* for you."

Nell stared at Elizabeth. "Wealthy? I don't understand," she said. "He doesn't act wealthy. He said he used to invent things, things for private planes, and now he's writing a book on twentieth-century technology."

Elizabeth sighed and lit a cigarette. She leaned back in her chair and looked at Nell. "Andy's father," she said, "is dead now. But he invented some damn nut or bolt or screw—I can't remember exactly—that is essential to airplanes. He patented it. It's even called a Martindale. Andy will be wealthy forever on the royalties from that little piece of metal. I suppose he did tinker around with stuff for private planes; Lord knows his family owns enough factories for him to tinker around in. But all that doesn't matter. The money doesn't matter, Nell, I mean. What does matter is that he is a womanizer. No, that's the wrong word. He doesn't chase after women or keep strings of them around. He's really more of a recluse than a cad, I guess. I mean, he is charming and all that, and women fall in love with him, but he is incapable of making any kind of commitment. He'll let a woman make all kinds of concessions in her life, but he'll never make any. Don't look that way, Nell. I know what I'm talking about. One of my closest friends, Rachel Woods, was in love with him about four years ago. She met him in the summer and moved from New York to be near him, because he won't leave this island. She wanted to marry him and she thought he loved her and would eventually marry her. But of course he didn't. Good heavens, the man is a—an *island.* He's content to be by himself. If you want to be with him, you can, if you can make the arrangements. But he's not moving. He'll never chase you. He'll never change his habits for you. Believe me, if he wouldn't change for Rachel, who is one of the most truly beautiful women on this earth and also a terribly classy woman, well, Nell, he'll never change for you. Oh, Nell, don't cry. I'm sorry, I shouldn't have put it that way. Rachel's one of my oldest friends and it was just terrible when she got hurt. As a matter of fact, I don't think she'll ever get over him. She moved back to New York after a few months here—the winter here is grim—and she's going on with her life. But he broke her heart. And he'll break yours if you get involved with him. Oh God, Nell, please don't cry. Shit. Don't tell me you're *in love* with him. Well, now I feel just awful."

"Elizabeth," Nell said, blowing her nose. "Tell me one thing, please. Maybe you don't know the answer. But did Andy ever tell Rachel that he loved her? Did he ever say 'I love you' to Rachel?"

Elizabeth laughed and stubbed her cigarette out in the ashtray. "You are a chump," she said. "Jesus Christ, Nell, you are a natural born sucker. Of course he said 'I love you' to Rachel. Sweetheart, don't be such a little dummy. Do you think saying 'I love-you' means anything to men? Oh, honey, any man will say 'I love you' if he thinks it'll get a woman to lie down and spread her legs."

"Oh, Elizabeth," Nell said. "What a gross, depressing, nasty thing to say."

"Oh, Nell," Elizabeth said, staring Nell in the eye. "How is it you can do such a marvelous job of running the boutique and such a ridiculous job of running your life?"

"You can't help who you fall in love with," Nell said.

"No, that's true," Elizabeth replied. "But you can help who hurts you. You can keep away from fire because your mother told you it's hot, and you can keep away from Andy Martindale because I'm telling you he's poison."

Nell looked at her boss, defeated. She just sat at the table and stared down at the remains of the luncheon, at the white linen, the shining silverware, the rosy daiquiri, still half-full. Nell could not think of any reason that Elizabeth would have to hate her, to want her miserable. But she would rather have it be that her boss despised her enough to tell malicious lies than that she was telling the truth. Nell picked up her daiquiri and downed the rest in one long drink, but even though she was unaccustomed to drinking alcohol at lunch, the cool liquid did absolutely nothing to anesthetize her. It seemed to her that there was no way for her to get up from this moment, from this table, and go forward with her life.

But of course she did get up and move on. She went back to the boutique and worked with Elizabeth for the rest of the afternoon. She drove Elizabeth to the airport at six so that she could catch a plane back to New York.

"Don't look so glum," Elizabeth said. "There are plenty of fish in the sea. Go out to more parties, meet more men! And don't look at me that way. Hating the bearer of bad tidings went out with Cleopatra. You'll thank me someday for saving you a lot of time and emotional agony."

"I suppose," Nell said, though she doubted it.

"Well, dear," Elizabeth went on, kissing the air near Nell's cheek. "It was wonderful seeing you again, and you're doing a fabulous job with the boutique. You are amazing, Nell. Now take care of yourself. Don't work too hard. Remember, we're relying on you." She turned and walked the short distance from the gate to the small waiting plane.

Nell called Andy from the airport to tell him that because of Elizabeth's visit, she was too exhausted to see him that evening. That was fine, Andy said; there was a two-hour documentary on Charles Lindbergh that he wanted to watch on public television. Goddamn you, Elizabeth was right, Nell wanted to shout, but of course she didn't. But his satisfied self-sufficiency only seemed to prove Elizabeth's point. Nell drove home, crying all the way. She managed to be moderately civil to her children, at least to keep from crying in front of them, and they were tired from camp and oblivious of her feelings. After she got them into bed, she took a long hot bath and began crying there.

She had forgotten her theory, it seemed, that some women were naturally lucky in love and some women weren't. She had forgotten it, or thought somehow she had escaped from the wrong side and managed to sneak on over to the side of those lucky lovable ones. But now she felt she had been exposed for a fool, scrambling around thinking she was safe when all the time she was just still on her own home ground, where she would always remain. Alone.

She waited awhile in the living room, hoping Clary would come home so they could talk, but after a while, she realized that if Clary was coming home it wouldn't be early. She went to bed.

The next day did not improve matters. Nell went off to work, trying to be optimistic, trying at least not to be suicidal. She looked up in the middle of the day to see Ilona walk in the door. She had a marvelously handsome man at her side.

"Nell!" Ilona cried. "Surprise! Isn't this fun? Frank and I have come over to spend a few days in the sun, and I said we just had to surprise you. Can we take you out to dinner tonight?"

Ilona had never looked so tall, slim, rich, and stunning in her life. Frank, who was quickly gaining the name "the hunk" in

Nell's private thoughts, gazed at Ilona with adoration in his eyes and couldn't keep his hands off her sumptuously clad body. After just a few moments in their presence, Nell felt as if she were literally growing shorter, older, dowdier, and lonelier. But she had agreed to join them for dinner; she could tell how Ilona wanted Nell around to be witness to her new happiness.

Nell settled her children in front of the TV that night with a pizza and fruit and milk and changed into a fresh dress and diligently put on her makeup. She had called Andy to ask if he could join them, and Andy had accepted. This could be a lovely evening, Nell told herself, but she knew it would not be lovely. She felt strange now, because of Elizabeth's warning. She couldn't decide whether to mention Elizabeth's friend Rachel to Andy or not. She felt miserable and awkward, childish. And she was afraid that if she told Andy all that Elizabeth had said, she would be appearing to ask for some kind of commitment from Andy. It would seem that she was trying to cajole or force something from him that he had not yet been ready to give willingly. She did not want to do that. She had known him for only three months, after all. He had told her he loved her. It should not matter to her that he had once loved a woman named Rachel; it should not matter that he was a fucking *island*. But of course it did matter, so much so that when she looked at herself in the mirror, she saw her face set with lines of worry and sadness. Great, Nell, she thought; he'll really fall in love with you now. You look like some old shrew. She tried to relax the muscles of her face, to smile.

She must have managed to look normal during the course of the evening, because Ilona never nudged her or indicated any concern. And when Nell *saw* Andy, was seated next to him in the car, at the table . . . her body just overruled her mind and went all sappy with love and pleasure. They went to the Dockside for dinner and sat at a table laid with fresh flowers and candles. Nell breathed in deep draughts of the civilized evening air. She liked the crystal, the careful attentions of the waiters and water boys, the murmur and laughter of other people in the room, the way the light gleamed and deepened outside the windows as clouds passed through the sky and night gently fell. The food was excellent. The wine was delicious. Ilona's lover, Frank, was a doctor, and he was an amiable and courteous man. He and Andy got on fine. Everyone seemed so clever.

After dinner, Ilona excused herself to go to the ladies' room and signaled with her eyes that Nell should join her. As they walked down the stairs, Nell wondered just how much to tell Ilona—should she tell her that she loved Andy? She was afraid that if she told her what Elizabeth had said, she'd start to cry.

But Ilona didn't give her a chance to talk about Andy. Ilona was too enraptured with her own luck and happiness in meeting Frank. It seemed to her only natural that everyone should just fall easily and marvelously in love, and Nell knew she would be a spoilsport to bring in her own doubts to darken Ilona's bright joy. Ilona babbled as much of the short and happy history of her relationship with Frank to Nell as she could while they were in the restroom. She was almost divorced, Ilona said: Phillip was being cooperative—he *would* be—she said, frowning for once; he was too damn recessed to care enough to make any kind of trouble. But Phillip didn't matter anymore, she had met Frank, and he was the most wonderful man in the world, and he loved her, and finally, finally, she had found true love!

Nell said she was glad for Ilona. When they went back upstairs to their table to join the men for coffee and dessert, they found that the men had gotten into a discussion about the Boston Red Sox. Nell and Ilona listened for a while, then leaned together to chat between themselves. Nell studied Ilona as she talked. Ilona was clearly flourishing. She had pulled her long blond hair straight back from her face in a chignon adorned by a green silk ribbon. She was wearing huge earrings made from what looked like emeralds and diamonds and a jade green silk dress, a deceptively plain dress with a wide boat neckline that was always falling off one shoulder or another, easily, innocently exposing a gleam of bare skin. Ilona's nails were very long, tapered and painted, and she wore an enormous ring that looked like a flower, with each petal made up of pebble-sized opaque green stones.

"Your ring is fabulous," Nell said. "I've never seen one like it. But I don't recognize the stones. Are they jade?"

"Oh no," Ilona said, casually studying her ring. "They're emeralds."

"*Emeralds,*" Nell breathed. She stared at the ring, quickly calculating that it was worth an amount equal to the mortgage on her house.

"Oh, they're not *good* emeralds," Ilona said. "It's sort of a tacky ring, really. The emeralds aren't good at all. But it is pretty."

"Yes," Nell agreed. "It is."

"Phillip gave it to me for some anniversary," Ilona went on. "I guess that was his way of showing affection. Lord knows he doesn't do it well any other way."

Nell turned slightly away from Ilona to mess around with her coffee, putting the sugar and milk in, stirring and tasting it. Now Frank surreptitiously slid his hand under the table to rest on Ilona's knee, and Nell noticed how Ilona and Frank flashed each other private smiles. She has so much, Nell thought: a husband who loves her with emeralds, great beauty and wealth, and now this handsome doctor who loves her, who *loves* her. Nell felt desolate and jealous. She felt hateful and envious. She looked at Andy and remembered what Elizabeth had told her about Rachel. If only, Nell thought, if only Andy would reach over and put his hand on hers or touch her arm or her knee or even look at her with love. *Please, Andy*, she willed, *if you love me, give me a sign.* She sat like a child, wishing he would make the smallest gesture of love; if he did, she thought all her envy and misery would evaporate. But he talked on with Frank, oblivious to her need. Nell wanted to cry. Stop it, she said to herself. He was not being unkind or rude or slighting her in any way, he was only talking about baseball. He was only *not* touching her the way Frank was touching Ilona.

I hate you, Andy, Nell thought. She stared at her coffee, thinking: only three and a half more weeks till Labor Day. Four days after that she could go back to Arlington. Away from Nantucket, away from this man who drove her so crazy. She would start seeing other men. She would do all the brave cheering-up things she had learned over the years to do to keep going on. She would paint Jeremy's room. She would have a dinner party and invite people she hadn't seen all summer—and she wouldn't invite goddamn cheerful Ilona and her love-sick doctor. She would get involved with the community theater workshop. She had been wanting to do that for a long time. The problem, of course, was finding the money to pay a baby-sitter so she could go out in the evenings to rehearsals. But perhaps, if she fiddled with her budget, and if Elizabeth continued to pay her this salary . . .

She was so immersed in her thoughts that when Andy reached over and put his hand lightly on the back of her neck she jumped and almost screamed.

"Look at her," Andy was saying to Ilona and Frank. At the same time he lightly, teasingly tousled her hair. "I'll bet she's thinking about that shop. Listen, never fall in love with a workaholic."

Nell looked at Andy. He was grinning at her affectionately.

"You look tired," he said. "Are you ready to go? We'd better get you to bed."

Nell felt tears spring to her eyes. She felt like an orphan who had just been given a home, a dog just let in out of the rain. Did you hear that, she wanted to say to Ilona, did you hear what he said—he was talking as if he's in love with me, admitting it in public! Before she could sort out her emotions, the moment had passed and the other three were pushing back their chairs, rising, commenting on the delicious meal.

The two couples said goodbye. Nell and Andy walked back to the cottage. Andy was in a good mood and really seemed to have enjoyed meeting Ilona and Frank.

Nell got up the courage to say, "You know, I liked it when you touched my hair like that in the restaurant."

Andy looked at her. He pulled her to him for a moment and they walked along, side by side, his arm around her. "You did?" he said. "You funny thing. Just wait till we get home, you'll like the way I'll touch you there, too."

And she did. When she came into the bedroom after putting on her black nightgown, he was waiting for her in bed. "You are special to me, you know," he said to her, and pulled her to him. They held each other and kissed and ran their hands over each other's bodies. He removed her nightgown with a slow tenderness that made Nell teary-eyed again. "Oh, Andy," she said over and over. "Oh God, Andy." And he said, "Nell, I love you." He made love to her, and she cried out of happiness the whole time, except for a while when lust overtook sweetness; then she got greedy and grabby and wild. After they were sated, and she lay holding him between her arms and legs, feeling his weight all up and down her body, she cried some more, quietly. "Am I too heavy for you?" he asked, and she said, "Oh no," and would not let him move. She loved holding him like that, feeling such great profound affection for him because he had pleased her so, because she had pleased him so. It seemed to her, as it seemed every time after they made love, that what they had between them was worth everything, meant everything in her life.

Eight

August was a month of splendid days. The sky stayed a calm clear blue, and if the temperature rose to the eighties, one had only to go to the beach or step inside an ice cream parlor or sit at an outside café sipping a Chablis spritzer with ice and lemon to be glad of the heat.

Nell took Elizabeth's advice and worked less. If the day promised to be particularly nice, she kept the children home from camp and went with them to the beach. Sometimes Clary came along. At Andy's suggestion, they drove to find new beaches away from the crowded ones. They went to Dionis, with its high dunes, Surfside or Cisco, where the waves came crashing out of the Gulf Stream, Tom Never's Head, which was too dramatic and dangerous for swimming, where the terns soared screaming out their domain, 'Sconset, which meant a ten-minute drive on a straight road alongside the moors.

The children loved Surfside best because the waves were the perfect height for jumping. They swam, they built elaborate sand castles, and Nell lay tanning on a beach blanket, reading a paperback novel, or talking with Clary about the more ineffable mysteries of men and women and love. One day Nell buried her children in sand and took pictures of them that way, with only their heads showing, their faces bright with smiles.

Clary was a good swimmer and would go far out. When she came back to shore, walking up out of the water, Nell would shake her head in wonder: how effortlessly graceful Clary was. Clary would emerge from the ocean in her scarlet bikini with her taut belly and long thighs glistening and slick from the sea water. She would raise her arms up to press her streaming hair back from her face, a young, beautiful woman, glowing with health, unaware of her glory. She would plop down on the blanket next to Nell and squeeze water from her suit. "God," she would say to Nell, "I've got so much sand in my suit I could lay a pearl."

On the days that Nell worked, she started going out for walks during her lunch hour instead of hiding away up in the boutique's second-floor office. She liked strolling around the town in the afternoon. Nantucket had a holiday feeling about it every day. The people were all so pretty. They wore short flounced skirts, halters, visors, flowered dresses, polka dots and wide stripes, T-shirts the colors of ice cream. Everyone looked tan, and everyone looked in love. Couples lazed along with their hands in each other's back pockets or with their arms linked or around each other's waists. The streets were congested with traffic, not just with the cars and the four-wheel-drive vehicles that people brought over to use on the beaches, but with bikes and mopeds and silly little pedal-carts. Men and women pushed babies in strollers and a variety of cheerful dogs trotted up and down the streets, busy with their own mysterious errands. Flowers bloomed everywhere, and two different groups set up farmer's markets on Main Street, so that Nell could look to her left and see a window full of lacy lingerie and look to her right to see brown-tasseled sweet Nantucket corn, green grapes, watermelon, avocados. On South Beach Street there was a shop that sold nothing but hammocks, and to advertise their goods they had put two hammocks just outside their store. Every time Nell walked past Lyon Hammocks, she would see children or teenagers or even adults lounging in the long hammock, swinging from the chair hammock, and she would think that this was no ordinary street, no ordinary town. It seemed to her such an amiable and goodhearted thing to do, to let passersby have the luxury of being silly in a hammock.

On Sundays or other days that Nell had off, she took Hannah and Jeremy to the museums. They learned all about whales and spermaceti candles and how wealth was accumulated by the sea captains, who built their mansions on the main streets of the town. They saw a ship complete with oars and masts and sailors built entirely of cloves; a dollhouse made of ivory. The museum the children loved best of all was the *Lightship Nantucket,* which had once been anchored on the Nantucket shoals and was now retired, docked permanently in the harbor. Jeremy and Hannah went through the lightship whenever they could, fascinated by the sailor's wooden bunks and the great brass steering wheel, by the engine room, the maps of Nantucket, and the pictures of marine disasters. A long piece of wall, painted with constellations, had been brought up out of the Zodiac room of the sunken ship *Andrea Doria*. The passengers who had been in the cabin of the Zodiac room had drowned when the ship sank, but this much of the ship had been brought up to light. The children touched it lightly, superstitiously, wondering about life and death and the whims of giant forces such as the sea. One day an official of the ship took the time to explain to Nell and the children that lightships were still used on the Nantucket shoals, so that their beacons and foghorns and lights could warn the trading ships of the treacherous shallows. Jeremy could not believe that in this age of technology it was still necessary for human beings to bob about day in and out on lightships to warn other people. Nell watched her son question the official and wondered if it was something in Jeremy's male genes that made him want to believe that modern technology could replace the lightship people. She was rather heartened to know that little human beings and their humble lightships were irreplaceable, and she liked the thought of those men out in the vast ocean, waiting to help others through a storm or fog.

Jeremy and Hannah began to develop a sense of independence. Because Nantucket was small and safe, they were able to roam around the streets by themselves, something they couldn't do in Arlington. Now and then, when Andy and Nell went out to dinner or to a cocktail party, she sent the two children off with some money to eat dinner at the Sweet Shop or at Vincent's restaurant. The first time Nell let them go alone, she had skipped out of the cocktail party and hurried down to the restaurant to peek in the window. She wanted to see if the children were safe, if they were behaving themselves. She was delighted to see Jeremy reading the menu to Hannah, who sat with her thrift-shop pocketbook in her lap like a little lady. When the children looked up to find their mother peering at them through the window, they made disdainful faces at her. Nell left. Later they scolded her for her sneakiness. From then on, she let them go off when they wanted to, and she could tell each time how they grew more sensible, less dependent on her decisions.

Some evenings she and Clary took them to the movies: *The Return of the Jedi, Octopussy, National Lampoon's Vacation.* On Wednesday nights they went to the Coffin School to watch the

slides and hear the lectures presented by Greenpeace; they learned
to tell right whales from killer whales. On rainy days they read
or walked down to the beach in their raincoats, carrying bags of
old bread to throw to the gulls. They watched the adolescent gulls
with shabby gray feathers squawk and bully the white and gray
adult gulls. The young gulls would swoop down, screeching, to
claim any bit of bread. They would proclaim in loud and nasty
cries their dominion. "Gee, those young gulls are mean and selfish," Hannah said. "Like *all* youngsters," Nell replied snidely,
and was rewarded with a chorus of "Oh, Mom," from the children.

They climbed the steps to the tower of the Congregational
Church one afternoon and saw all of Nantucket spread around
them. They browsed in the Seven Seas gift shop, foolishly lusting
after shell necklaces and cranberry-scented candles. The children
bought Turk's head rope bracelets to wear on their wrists, and
their skin glowed brown and smooth against the white knots.
They sat at Brant point, which Jeremy renamed Bug Point because of the tiny long-horned sandfleas that hopped frenetically
up out of the sand, to watch the yachts and ferries and sailboats
coming in and out of the harbor, so close that the people on the
boats would call and wave to those on shore.

One evening Andy took Clary and Nell and the children to a
play put on by the Nantucket Theater Workshop. The play was
Picnic, which Andy remembered as a movie starring Kim Novak
and William Holden. But Nell remembered it more distinctly as
a play: during the second year of her marriage to Marlow, she
had starred in the play, acting Kim Novak's part of Madge. Madge
was a young Kansas girl, falling in love and experiencing passion
for the first time. Nell watched the young actress who played
Madge, a woman with hair almost as red as Nell's, and she remembered what it had been like to be an actress in that play and
what it had been like to be a young woman in the Midwest falling
in love for the first time. The production was a good one, and it
both pleased Nell to watch the play and made her sad. When she
had played Madge, she had still believed she would be a famous
actress. Now here she was, only a saleswoman in a clothing store,
only a working divorced mother, who hadn't acted in even an
amateur performance in years and who might never act again in
her life. All those dreams that didn't come true, Nell thought. All
those dreams that I just let slip away! During the play, Madge

heard the whistle of a train and talked dreamily to her sister about escaping their little town for adventures. But at the end of the play it was clear that the only adventure Madge really wanted was that of being with the man she lusted after. Madge packed her bag and ran off after Hal. Nell sat, silently impressed with Inge for holding tight to what was true.

Out of the corner of her eye she studied Hannah, who had gone through the entire performance displaying a multitude of emotions on her mobile face, hoping that people would see her and be amazed at her sensibilities, imagining, as Nell had at her age, that people were watching her instead of the play. Nell could see how Hannah wanted all the things she had wanted as a girl: fame, success, luxury, a sense of being gloriously above the rest of the human race, a life of magnificent achievement. Nell wondered if Hannah would give up this dream for the love of a man. She imagined Hannah probably would.

The days and nights just flowed by, that August. Nell worked, took care of her children, gossiped with Clary, made love with Andy, did the dishes or laundry all in a dream. Everything was a pleasure. She and the children made a game out of finding a space in the parking lot at the grocery store; they called it the A&P Gamble. She bought models of shrimp boats and schooners and paints for Jeremy and satin cord in crimson and mauve and gold and indigo for Hannah. Hannah would wash and dry the shells she had found on the beach, coat them with several layers of clear nail polish, and glue the satin rope to the shells, making necklaces to take to friends or to send to grandmothers. Kelly and Mindy got slaphappy at the boutique from working so hard, and when Nell entered the store, they would greet her with laughter and chatter, like a pair of drunken squirrels. Clary went out almost every night, and whoever was at home ended up writing endless messages on the chalkboard for her from all the men and women who called for her.

Nell gained weight from banana daiquiris at parties, hot fudge sundaes with the children, and Andy's gourmet meals. She stopped wearing her bikini and wore only her black one-piece suit. Even then she felt like a collection of pillows were stuffed inside the fabric whenever she walked down the long slope of sand to the beach. One evening Clary cut Nell's hair and put a lightener on it, so that again it looked more strawberry blond than auburn. By the end of August, Nell's face was so tanned and freckled and glowing that she didn't need to wear any makeup but a little mascara.

One night, stewing because she was bored with her dresses, she put on a long cotton skirt with an elastic waist. It was violet. She looked at herself in the mirror; the skirt was old and so long that it came to her ankles. She pulled it up just above her breasts and smiled: now it looked like a strapless dress. When she and Andy arrived at the cocktail party, the hostess and several other women made a fuss over Nell's dress—so simple, so sexy, where did she get it, did they sell the dress at Elizabeth's? And Nell was able to smile smugly and say honestly that it really was just an old dress. She enjoyed herself immensely at the party, passing through the various rooms of the house to get herself a drink or greet an acquaintance. She felt unusually young that evening. All the other women there were wearing stylized frocks, clusters of jewels, heavy makeup. Nell felt in contrast fresh and charming, like a real flower in the midst of artificial ones.

But at one point in the evening she saw Andy in the corner of a room talking intimately with a woman who was so gorgeous she made Nell's blood turn cold. She was a blonde in a red dress and diamonds. She kept touching Andy as she talked, in playful ways, in serious ways, now on his arm, now fiddling with his tie, now ever so lightly touching the side of his mouth with one finger. Nell was so stunned that she forgot to listen to the man who was speaking to her. She just stared. Jealousy surged within her. Clearly, Andy and this woman were familiar with each other. Were they old lovers? The woman's dress was skin-tight everywhere, so that it was perfectly clear how flawless her body was. Nell felt her pleasure in her old cotton skirt disappear. She realized how much a camouflage it was, falling full from the elastic band just above her breasts. She could never have worn that tight, revealing dress the blonde wore. Andy and the blonde looked so cozily attracted to each other that they might as well have been wearing neon signs that blinked OLD LOVERS—and they could have run the signs on the electricity of their obvious mutual attraction.

Nell excused herself from the man who was speaking to her and went into another room on the pretext of getting a fresh drink. She was handed an icy Chablis spritzer, and she took it with her into the downstairs bathroom. She stood there a moment, leaning against the closed door. What did you think, dumbo? she asked herself. Did you assume that because Andy never talked about them, he never had any other lovers? Of course he's had other lovers! Nell realized that she had simply put Elizabeth's warnings out of her mind because she could not bear to think of them. She could not bear to think of Rachel Woods, who had been a lover of Andy's—when, how many years ago, what had Elizabeth said? Three years ago? Four? She had not asked Andy about her because she did not think she could stand to hear anything he had to say. Maybe I am just the latest in a long string of lovers, Nell thought. And maybe by love he means something completely different from what I do. Maybe when he says, "I love you," he means only that he likes to take me to bed and cares enough for me that he doesn't want to hurt my feelings. While when I say, "I love you," I mean much more intense, passionate, serious things, I mean I need him and want to live my life with him and am miserable without him and . . .

Nell bit her lip. She could feel tears welling up, and she didn't dare cry because she had come into the bathroom without a purse and if she cried her mascara would streak down her face and her nose would turn red. She knew she had to get herself out of the bathroom, to go back out into the crowd of people and laugh and talk and mingle. She couldn't simply hide in a bathroom all night, indulging in a wild funk of jealousy and misery. She took a sip of her drink and ran her fingers through her hair. She looked at herself in the cabinet mirror above the sink. She knew that earlier in the evening her happiness had made her look so radiant that even her old cotton skirt had been transformed. But now she felt as though a light had gone out within her, and she thought she looked only tired and the clever skirt/dress seemed to her only plain, drab, and silly.

She forced herself out of the bathroom and back into the party. She chatted with people while Andy continued to be monopolized by the blonde. It seemed the evening would never end. Nell felt her self-confidence and all her pleasure in life leaking out of her, as if she were a balloon deflating. She was terrified that Andy would bring the blonde over to meet her; she thought she might burst into tears. At the least she knew she would not be able to carry off the meeting casually; she would not be able to smile smugly and put her hand on Andy's arm with a relaxed and natural possessiveness. Finally, Nell went onto the sun porch and sat down next to some ancient dowager she'd never met before. The old woman had been lonely, had been at the point of nodding off in the middle of the party. She was delighted to have Nell join her, and the two of them engaged in a superficial but enjoyable conversation of the sort initiated on airplane flights, about children and pets and weather. When Andy came to fetch Nell, he was alone, and as they walked through the house and out to the car, Nell noticed the blonde was not in sight.

That night, after they had eaten and Nell had spent some time with Hannah and Jeremy and tucked them in bed, she managed to get up enough courage to ask Andy about the blonde. She tried to be casual about it. She aimed for a light, careless, sophisticated approach. She slipped onto the sofa next to Andy and stretched elaborately—she had put on the black nightgown and peignor—and yawned.

"The party was fun, wasn't it?" she asked. After Andy nodded agreement, she grinned and said, "And you certainly seemed to be enjoying yourself. With the blonde."

Andy smiled. "Jacqueline," he said.

Shit, Nell thought, she *would* be named Jacqueline.

"I guess I did spend a lot of time with her," Andy said, as if he only now were being struck with that fact. "I'm sorry if I left you on your own too long. But you always seem to know people at parties. And I hadn't seen Jacqueline for a long time. We're old friends."

"Old lovers," Nell said lightly, smiling, as if amused by it all.

Andy's smile broadened. "Was it that obvious?" he asked.

"It was that obvious," Nell replied. She leaned back against the arm of the sofa and raised her arms, ran her fingers through her hair, as if she were feeling lazy and at ease, as if she were discussing the weather. "I'll bet you have a lot of old lovers."

Andy looked at her, not smiling now, studying her face. Then he said, "Well yes, I suppose I do. I am an adult, after all. A grown-up, divorced man. It would be rather odd if I didn't have lots of old lovers, don't you think?"

"Oh of course," Nell said, shrugging, smiling what she hoped was a clever little smile, a smile that suggested this conversation didn't mean a thing to her. Her heart was pounding. God, she thought, I'm even capable of *retroactive* jealousy! Stop it, Nell, you dimwit! she yelled at herself within her mind. Listen, don't let this get to you. You have your share of old lovers, too. You're every bit as sophisticated as he is!

Before she could think of anything else to say, Hannah appeared in the doorway. She was wearing her pink-and-white-flowered nightgown and rubbing her eyes. "Mommy," she said weakly, "I had a nightmare. Then I couldn't find you in your bed."

"Oh, darling," Nell said, rising and going over to her daughter. "You're all right. And I wasn't in bed because it's not that late yet." She knelt down. She put her arms around Hannah.

"Oh, Mommy!" Hannah said, her eyes opening wide as Nell approached her. "What a fancy dress you're wearing. Are you going to a party? Are you going to dance?"

"Hannah," Nell said. "This is a nightgown."

Hannah studied the black lace and satin garment that hung so lusciously on Nell's body. Clearly, she was skeptical. "Well, it's not like your other nightgowns," she said. "It's so pretty."

Hannah, I am going to kill you when I get you alone, Nell thought. Or maybe I'll just let you continue to make it clear to Andy just how unglamorous a creature I really am, and then I'll kill myself.

"Let me get you back to bed, darling," Nell said. "You're so sleepy. What was your nightmare about?"

She walked Hannah back up the stairs, took her to the bathroom, tucked her back in bed. All the time she was automatically soothing Hannah, but inside she was seething. When she got back downstairs and entered the living room where Andy sat, she said, almost without knowing she was going to say it, "And of course there was Rachel Woods."

Andy was startled. "What?" he asked.

To her chagrin, Nell began to cry helplessly. "Oh, Andy," she said. "I'm so embarrassed. But a few days ago when Elizabeth O'Leary was here she asked me if I was seeing anyone, and I told her about you. And she told me about you and Rachel Woods. And she told me to watch out, that you played around a lot and that I shouldn't trust you. God, I am so embarrassed." Nell had to get up to go into the kitchen to get a tissue.

"Look," Andy said when she came back. "I don't understand why you're so upset. Just because I had an affair with Rachel Woods a few years ago doesn't mean I'm not trustworthy now. I don't even see how that follows. You know that since I've known you I haven't seen any other woman. And I don't want to. Nell, I love you."

I don't want to be just another affair to you, Nell thought. I want to be the love of your life.

I want to be married to you.

God, Nell thought, how many things there are that I am afraid to say to him.

"Andy," she said, "this is so hard for me to say, but—I'm afraid we might mean different things when we say we love each other. I'm afraid I mean, when I say I love you, all sorts of things. I mean that I care for you and I want to make you happy and I feel jealous and—and I want a future with you. And *you* might just mean that you like to go to bed with me."

"Oh, Nell," Andy said. He stood up and walked over to where she stood in the doorway wiping her face with a tissue. He took her in his arms. He kissed her wet face and then, with a gesture much like a father's, he put his hand on her head and pressed it against his chest and stroked her hair. "Nell, my darling," he said. "Oh, sweetheart, don't be so sad. There's no reason for you to be so sad. I don't understand. You mustn't think things like that. Listen," he said, and he held her away from him so he could see her face. "I love you. I care for you. I want to make you happy. I feel jealous, too. And"—he grinned—"I *also* like to go to bed with you."

Nell smiled back through her tears. Andy pulled her to him and kissed her. They kissed for a long time, until Andy said, "And you look so pretty in this fancy dress, I think I'll take you to a party." Then he picked her up in his arms and carried her up the stairs to the bedroom.

Nell was so pleased by his affection, and then so terrified when he was carrying her up the stairs that he would think she was too heavy and then so overcome with pleasure when they were in bed together, that she could think of little else. But as they lay side by side with each other late at night and she heard Andy fall into his deep and easy sleep, she lay awake, irked by an unpleasant and niggling fact. Andy had not said, "And I want a future with you." Don't borrow trouble, Nell, she told herself. But he had remembered and repeated all her other words so exactly. She was afraid that she was being only realistic to worry about what it was he had so carefully omitted saying.

She had trouble sleeping that night. She drifted in and out of dreams involving Andy and parties and Hannah and clothes. During one dream she saw herself enter a cocktail party in her black satin nightgown. The blonde in the red dress and diamonds turned and looked at her with a smirk, and Andy, standing next to the blonde, said, "Who in the world is that silly woman?" His voice was so clear that Nell awakened, startled, and looked at him, thinking he had actually spoken. But he was sleeping soundly.

She lay awake then, staring at the night sky outside the window. She could sense the gentle rise and fall of Andy's chest as he lay next to her in his deep, contented sleep. He was lying on his side, his long body angled across the bed. He was so tall that he could not lie on this regular bed and get all of himself on it and under the covers. At his house he had a king-size bed, where he and Nell could sleep quite comfortably together. But here he had to bend himself in complicated positions, so that he became all elbows and bony rear and feet and knees, unwittingly waking Nell all night long with pokes as he moved or shifted in his dreams. At the beginning of the night, he would always go into a gentlemanly curl that would leave Nell at least a fourth of the bed. But as soon as he was really asleep, his angular body would loosen and expand, and all through the night Nell would find herself inching over closer and closer to the side of the bed. Often she slept with one arm and leg hanging down the edge of the bed to the floor.

She did not mind this. She liked it. She loved it. It was a wonderful thing to her to awaken in the night, to feel his hairy knees against her back. Sometimes she would carefully place her hand there, on his knees, or his hip, whatever part of him was nudging her. His body was so different from hers, from her children's. There was the difference in size—he was so much longer, wider, and his bones so much heavier. And he was so hairy, where her legs or stomach were smooth; although there was a spot she loved, just at the base of his spine, that was as hairless and silky as a baby's bottom.

It was a good thing to sleep with someone else, Nell thought. It was a good thing to sleep with a man if you were a woman. Sometimes, when she was alone at night, she had trouble going to sleep or staying asleep, because giving herself over to the enormous black space of sleep and dreams and night often required a degree of faith she could not muster. Often, alone at night, she would think that relaxing into sleep took the same kind of courage that jumping out of a spaceship into the empty, inhuman expanse of the dark universe required. She felt like a stranded astronaut, alone, floating, with no human being to pull her back to safety. With Andy next to her in bed she felt safe. His male spirit balanced out her female one. He was there with her. Even on a practical level, it mattered that if there were a fire or a burglar or some other real crisis, he was an adult human being who might smell the smoke or hear the intruder or in some way help Nell in the night. But it was more than that, more than the merely real. It was a spiritual comfort he gave her, a knowledge that even though she sank into the deepest nightmare, she was not alone, she could not fall, reaching out, calling out, to find that her voice and hands reached only cold, uncaring space. His spirit warmed hers just as his body warmed her body.

When the moon was full so that light slanted in through the window, Nell would sometimes lie awake at three or four in the morning and study the slant of Andy's hip and back or, if he was turned toward her, his face. *Body,* she would think, *body of Andy,* you must surely sense the love I have for you, the desire I have to continue to give you pleasure, comfort, and to keep you healthy and safe. You know I need you, body, and I tell you with all my touches and caresses how well I could care for you. Don't you have any powers? Can't you insinuate yourself into this man's rational, cool, careful mind and make him wild with desire for me? Body of Andy, make him love me as much as I love him.

Andy would shift and sigh. Nell would gaze at him, thinking: ten more days, eight more days, and I will leave Nantucket, and he has said nothing about the future. Damn him. Help. Oh God, she would think when she was most upset: are you an Indian-giver? Are you a tease?

She would think she would never fall asleep, but lie awake all night, trapped in her longing, lying still in order not to awaken Andy, but feeling frenzied with need. But at some time before daylight she would fall back into sleep, and when she was awakened by the alarm, she would find that Andy had already risen and gone off for his morning walk. She would be alone in the bed which, in his absence, was wide and cold.

The last Friday night in August, Clary threw a party. She asked Nell if it would be okay if she had a lot of people over for "a sort of end of the summer thing." Nell said sure, as long as the cottage didn't get destroyed. Clary also asked Nell if she would

please come, because she wanted her to get to know some of the
people—some of them, Clary grinned, so she and Nell could laugh
about them later.

So Nell found herself cooking hot dogs—it rained that night,
and they had planned a cookout—in the kitchen oven and refilling
bowls of potato chips and emptying ashtrays. They had set a bar
up on the kitchen table and stocked the refrigerator with beer,
and the guests helped themselves to their drinks. About twenty
people were gathered in the living room, although more came and
went during the course of the evening. Nell set out black plastic
trash sacks, which grew bulky with emptied beer cans. In one
corner of the big living room six or seven people sat on the floor
passing a joint around. Nell felt a momentary rush of conservative
disapproval; she realized she still carried some kind of maternal
residue of feelings for Clary. There was this much difference
between her generation and Clary's: Nell didn't worry about people drinking, but did worry about people smoking pot. Still, she
told herself, Clary was twenty-seven, an adult, and her guests
were all in their twenties and thirties, not much younger than she.
She was not their mother. She decided to say nothing. It was
Clary's party.

Hannah and Jeremy loved the action and the noise. They liked
bringing plates of food to people. Now and then a good-hearted
man or woman would draw the children into a conversation. Nell
would look over from the kitchen to see Hannah or Jeremy holding forth, animated, face glowing, while the strange grown-ups
smiled and listened. She was always occupied too, listening to
Mindy or Kelly chattering on about the boutique, their boyfriends, their winter plans, or getting to know some character
whom Clary brought for her to meet.

During the course of the evening, Nell came to have some
understanding of what this particular group was like. Most of the
men and women were drop-outs, reverse snobs who disdained the
ambitious rat race, had contempt for their contemporaries who
were slaving away as lawyers or medical interns or accountants.
They said *stockbrokers* with a snarl of scorn that reminded Nell
of politicians like Spiro Agnew speaking of "intellectuals"; and
they were not that much different, Nell mused, in their adamant
closed-minded aversion. More than half of the people she met
said they were actors, artists, directors, photographers, dancers.
But if Nell asked them where she could see an exhibit of their

work or what they had acted in recently, they changed the subject. Little by little the truth came out—what they really did was wait tables or work as carpenter's assistants or open scallops. They all told Nell they had moved to Nantucket to "get away from it all," but as the evening went on and Nell watched and listened, she realized it was more than that. These people not only thought they were getting away from being bourgeois, avoiding entrapment in a life of boring money-grubbing. They also thought they were escaping mortality and aging. They thought they were in Never-Never Land; if they weren't tainted by making money, if they weren't enslaved by mortgages or leases, if they never made a commitment to one job or one person, they would stay forever young, carefree, and happy. Jesus, Nell thought after the seventh person told her he had come to Nantucket because he didn't want to be a lawyer, this is sort of creepy.

How different these people were from the ones who attended parties Nell went to. There everyone had been well dressed and rather formal. Here everyone wore jeans, old, faded jeans, and T-shirts or shirts with frayed collars. Three men in their thirties had brought teenagers with them as dates. The women wore little or no makeup and no jewelry and looked as if they'd faint, screaming, if they were touched with a ruffle or satin or silk. No one was married. No one had children. The most attached they got was to have a "lady friend," a "boyfriend." Some of the men were clever, witty, quick with put-down phrases, but for the most part no one had anything especially interesting to say. Yet they were all so smug.

After all the hot dogs had been eaten and people were just drinking, Nell grew bored and yearned to go up to bed, but she didn't want to hurt Clary's feelings. She tried to sneak away on the pretense that she had to get the children to bed, but Clary stopped her at the foot of the stairs. "Come back down when they're in bed," Clary said. "I want you to get to know Harry. You haven't really talked with him yet."

So after Hannah and Jeremy were tucked in bed, Nell went back down to the living room and sat drinking a beer with Harry. Harry, Clary's current lover, her antidote to losing Bob. He was a handsome man, the exact opposite of Bob in every way. He was large and hairy, with long black hair, a black beard, black eyes, black chest hair curling up over the top of his T-shirt. He looked like a pirate. He was by far the most personable of all the people Nell had met that evening. He talked easily, about wind surfing and other island sports. Nell began to smile as she watched and listened. He's all right, she decided. He's intelligent, clever, handsome, kind: he might be all right for Clary! She asked him what he did for a living. He told her he opened scallops and demonstrated how it was done. He showed her the ridge of callus along his hand that had grown from holding the scallops as he dug in with his knife. He told her that opening scallops was the lowest job imaginable: it was cold, smelly, dirty, uncertain work. He seemed quite pleased about this. When Nell finally excused herself and went up to bed, she felt like Alice coming back through the looking glass.

The next morning, a Sunday morning, Nell rose to find Clary already up. She had cleaned up after the party and done most of the dishes. It was raining steadily outside. Hannah and Jeremy were curled up in the living room, eating doughnuts and watching cartoons on TV.

"Wanna talk?" Clary asked.

"Sure," Nell smiled.

They went into the front parlor, a formal room Nell had not yet used. She made a fire to take the dampness out of the air and just for the sake of coziness, and Clary brought in fresh coffee and doughnuts. They sat together in wing chairs, Nell with her legs drawn up under her robe, Clary with her long blue-jeaned legs thrown over the side of the chair, and talked. They discussed the party and the guests at length, but by mutual and unspoken agreement, they saved Harry for last.

"What do you think of him?" Clary asked.

"He's nice," Nell said. "He's really nice. I like him. He's clever."

"He wants me to stay here this winter," Clary said.

"Wow," Nell said. "That sounds serious."

Clary laughed. "Well, it's not," she said. "Not at all. They do something here called 'matching up for the winter.' In the summer, you see, when there are so many tourists and college kids here working summer jobs and so on, everyone sort of hangs loose so they can sleep around with anyone who comes along. But in the winter most of the people go back to the mainland. So the people who remain look around to see which person might be the best to live with during the long, gray, boring months. There's not much going on here in the winter, you know. Only one movie house, which shows one movie a week. Most of the restaurants close. You can't go to the beach, of course. The place really shuts down. About all there is to do for fun is to drink and watch TV. So you look around in the fall for some warm body to get you through the winter—someone to play Scrabble with and go out and buy you cough medicine. That way you don't get lonely, but you don't freak out at responsibility, either."

"Oh, Clary," Nell said. How grim, she was thinking. But she wanted to let Clary make her own decision, so she kept her thoughts to herself. "Does the jewelry store stay open all year?"

"No," Clary said. "I'd have to find another job in order to support myself. That will be hard too, since most restaurants and shops close. There won't be many waitress or salesperson jobs available. Harry said I'll probably have to get a job cleaning houses. That sort of thing is always available."

"Cleaning houses," Nell said, keeping her tone even.

"There's nothing wrong with that," Clary said defensively.

"I didn't say there was," Nell said. "God, I'm always cleaning house. But, Clary—let me at least ask you this. Why would you stay on Nantucket in this temporary arrangement with Harry but not be willing to live in the same sort of temporary arrangement with Bob?"

Clary was quiet for a while. She had pulled a crocheted afghan down from the back of the chair and pulled it over her. She braided the fringe together for a few minutes. "Because I love Bob," she said at last. "I need him. I need him to need me. He is—important to me. If I can't be important to him, then I can't bear to be around him. It hurts too much." Clary leaned forward earnestly, presenting her case to Nell. "Bob *matters*," she said. "Everything about him matters to me. Harry doesn't matter. We are like—we're like *toys* for each other. We know that we won't go very much out of our way for each other or get very involved or care enough to change our lives. Harry is a drifter. He'll never try to buy a house or accomplish anything important in the world. He's not even connected to the world. He doesn't want to be. He doesn't want children. He doesn't want to live real life. He doesn't want to—ha—live 'off-island.' But Bob *is* living real life, and, Nell, *real life is hard*. It's so hard that unless you have some kind of agreement—like marriage—you'll just give up during the rough times." Clary was crying now. "You've got to be *bound*," she said to Nell. "Look at you and me. We were bound for a while by marriage and law and custom and convention, all that crap. And if we hadn't been, well, there were lots of times when we disagreed so much that we would have walked out of each other's lives if we could have. But we didn't have that choice."

"There's always divorce—" Nell began.

"Divorce is a lot of trouble," Clary protested. "Divorce is *trouble*. Almost always more trouble than the work of making up, making the relationship work. Oh, Nell," Clary sobbed. "I want to love, honor, and cherish Bob, I want to take care of him when he's sick and be poor with him if he's poor. All that cornball sappy *shit*. I don't want to live in some attic with Harry or go into a bar and pick up a different guy every night. I want to matter. I want to love. I want to love *Bob*."

Nell didn't know what to say. She could not think of any answer. There was no solution. If you wanted to marry a man who did not want to marry you, there was simply nothing to be done about it. Nell realized she was crying, too. She rose and poked at the logs. The fire flared up. She heard Hannah and Jeremy laughing in the other room. She turned to Clary.

"Clary," she said, "I know. I know. I know exactly what you want and how you feel. Your heart is breaking. I know that. But listen, you are beautiful. You are wonderful. Don't stay on this island with Harry. Go to Boston, find a job that means something to you. You're a biologist as well as a woman. Do some work that you have been trained to do. That's important. You can't give that part of yourself up. And you're bound to meet other men. Someday I'm sure, I *guarantee*, you'll find another man that you'll love as much as you love Bob. You are so lovable and you have so much love to give, you will find someone. Someone who will die to marry you, who will court you, woo you, chase you. Don't feel so hopeless. Bob isn't the only man in the world."

Nell talked on and on, her voice soothing and melodious. It seemed the words just flowed through her, with a rhythm and a meaning that was ancient, with a message that had been passed on from woman to woman for thousands of years, for as long as women had loved men.

It was her lunch hour, and Nell was alone in the cottage. Hannah and Jeremy were at camp, Clary was having lunch with Harry before going off to work, and Andy was at his house, working on his book.

Nantucket was overrun with tourists this last week of August. It was impossible to walk down the sidewalk at a normal pace; the sidewalks were as packed with people as Tokyo at rush hour. Tempers seemed short, especially on the streets, where bikers disdained the stop signs and drivers honked angrily at jaywalkers. Away from the heart of town, people drove their cars at fifty miles an hour through fifteen-mile-an-hour speed zones, as if in some kind of revenge for being thwarted and slowed on Main Street. It became necessary to stand in line everywhere—at the bank, the post office, the grocery store, the pharmacy. The stores couldn't keep stocked in bread and other staples. And it was impossible to get into restaurants without reservations. The less expensive and more informal places where Nell liked to go with Clary and Andy and the children, the Atlantic Café, the Brotherhood, Vincent's, were crammed with people from early in the evening until closing, with lines of waiting people trailing out the doors and down the sidewalks. In order to go to a movie at the Dreamland, it was necessary to get to the theater at six o'clock in order to be in some part of the line that could get tickets when the box office opened at six forty-five; the show began at seven-thirty. The beaches were crowded, even the bike paths were dangerous. But Elizabeth would be happy, Nell thought, for the boutique was a great success.

The quiet of the cottage was balm for Nell now. She walked through it, appreciating the way the late summer light slanted through the windows. With the back part of her mind she noted how much gathering and packing had to be done before they left. The house was littered with the carefree loot of the summer: shells and pebbles from the beach, old bits of dried seaweed and dead whelks on the back steps, handmade paper, batiked fish-shaped pillows, apple-head dolls that Jeremy and Hannah had made at camp, the children's miscellaneous "souvenirs" that they pleaded to keep—napkins and stirring sticks from restaurants, brochures, ads, and tickets from the various museums they had visited, stuffed whales they had bought with their allowance. Half-read books were dropped everywhere, even in the bathroom. Clary and Nell's records were scattered all over the living room, mixed together. Beach towels and swimming suits hung from every possible straight surface, drying, and the rugs and floors were gritty with sand.

How will we ever get this all packed and cleaned? Nell wondered. Clary had decided to look for a good job near Boston rather than remain in Nantucket and her suitcase and backpack sat open and ready on the floor, symbols of life's flux. Each time Nell passed Clary's room and saw the bags through the open door, she was reminded that in just six days they would all be gone from this cottage, this island, this summer life. She roamed through the house, unable to begin the work, unable to change or move a single thing. She wanted time to stop. She wanted the summer to go on and on. She wanted continually to see her children come in the door from camp, all brown and glowing from a day in the sun, proud of whatever craft they had learned that day. She wanted to sit around with Clary every evening, drinking beer, laughing and talking. She wanted to always sit in the dining room, surrounded at last and finally by the people she loved most in the world: Jeremy, Hannah, Clary, Andy. That was heaven. She believed that life held nothing better than that. And then to tuck the children in bed and discuss the day and the news with Andy, and to climb the stairs together, to turn and have Andy right there, his arms reaching around her, pressing her against his body . . .

Tears welled up in Nell's eyes. She leaned against a doorframe, thinking. Would she ever come back to Nantucket? Would she ever have this happiness again? Why couldn't Andy say something to her about the future?

The phone rang, breaking into her thoughts. She answered it in the bedroom so that she could lie down and rest while she talked. It was Ilona, calling from Arlington, and Ilona was so upset that Nell could scarcely understand her.

"Settle down, Ilona," she said. "Ilona, *calm down*. I can't understand a word you're saying."

"I'm pregnant," Ilona said. "I'm pregnant. I have to get an abortion. And Frank—Frank—he's got his answering machine on."

"What?" Nell said. "Ilona, what are you talking about?"

For the next hour Nell talked to Ilona, finally getting a sense of the events that led to this frantic phone call. Seven weeks ago, when Ilona and Frank had first become lovers, they had not used any birth control. Ilona had not thought they would go to bed so quickly after meeting at a party, but Frank was so insistent—so passionate, so ardent, so overcome with love and desire for her—that she had gone to bed with him. They had been at his apartment, where they had gone for a drink. She had told him that she had no means of birth control with her; she did not carry her diaphragm in her purse. And, she said, it was the worst possible day to be without contraception. She knew her cycle well. She was ovulating that day.

Frank had said not to worry, he would take care of it all. When the moment came, he would withdraw. But when they made love, he had worn no protection and he had come inside her, not once, but twice during that night. "I can't help it," he had pleaded. "It's your fault," he had said. "You are too sexy, too beautiful, too irresistible. You drive me crazy, you make me lose my mind."

Ilona had been flattered by his passion. She had been amazed. After living for years with recessed Phillip, this kind of helpless desire came like an answer to her every prayer. Frank's uncontrollable lust for her was real, obvious, gloriously romantic. She held him after they made love, thinking, he loves me. At last, a man who really loves me. I have driven him crazy with desire. He cannot help himself. So what if I get pregnant, she had thought—we'll get married. We'll have a child together. Whatever came of this joyous union when they were both overpowered by mutual desire could only be good.

Frank had showed more desire for her in one evening than Phillip had in all the years of their marriage. He had made love to her three times that night. Surely, Ilona thought, surely this was the Real Thing, this was love.

And they had had such a romantic time together. Nell had seen them, Nell was a witness, Nell knew, Ilona said. Hadn't it been obvious to Nell how much Frank had loved her?

But now she was pregnant. Definitely. She had heard the results of the test from a doctor yesterday. "Congratulations," the doctor had said.

Ilona had called Frank at his office. She had been upset, uncertain of his response. Would he be thrilled? Worried? Angry?

He had been stunned. "It can't be my child," was the first thing he said.

"Frank!" Ilona had cried, hurt. "Of course it is. Remember our first night together?"

After a brief silence, Frank had said, "Do you want me to help you arrange for the abortion?"

The abortion, Ilona had thought. And his voice was so cold. "Frank, can't we discuss this?" she had pleaded.

"I'm sorry, Mrs. Shell, but I've got patients to see now," he had replied. "I'll return your call."

But he hadn't. Ilona had called him again at his office, but the receptionist never put her through, only said, "I'll have the doctor call you. The doctor's busy now." Ilona had called his home all day, all night. The answering machine was always on. She had left countless messages; he had never returned her calls.

Now she didn't know what to do. She couldn't get Frank to talk to her on the phone. She didn't know how to go about arranging an abortion by herself. The thought of killing her own child horrified her, as did the thought of bearing a child who would have no father. What could she do? She needed Nell's help desperately.

Nell talked to Ilona soothingly. She told her she would be okay, it would all be okay. She would be coming back to Arlington in less than a week, Nell said, and then she would help Ilona through it all. She'd help her find a good abortion clinic; she'd go with her to the abortion, keep her in her house while she recovered. She would help her through it all. Ilona would not have to go through it alone. Nell talked and talked to Ilona.

When she finally hung up the phone, Nell lay on her bed, rigid, for a long time. She was late for work. But that didn't matter. She had envied Ilona Frank's love; now she was heartbroken for her. But she could not cry. It seemed her entire body had been turned to stone from the knowledge of how passion betrayed, how men lied, how easily and greedily women believed.

Marlow had had his faults, but mysteriousness had not been one of them. Nell had always known exactly how Marlow felt about every subject man or beast could bring up. If he erred on the side of excess, still, he always let you know where you stood with him. When Nell remembered the summer they first met—which came to her memory strangely devoid of any emotion on her part, as if it had all happened to someone else in another time, on another planet, in a dream—when she remembered that brief wild summer during which they met and married in three months' time, Nell thought that part of the pleasure of it all had been that Marlow had been so *certain*. He had so definitely wanted her. He had had passion enough for two. There had been no room to doubt. Who doubts a hurricane when it's coming straight at you, sweeping you away? Nell had been carried away by her destiny . . . or at least by the heat and velocity of Marlow's desire.

With Steve, with Ben, with Stellios, it had been more or less the same. If they had not courted Nell with the drama and flair that Marlow employed, at least they had made it clear to her that they wanted her. There had been no ambiguity about their intentions. And the two different times since her divorce when Nell thought she was in love with other men had also been clear. Brief, painful, but crystal clear. She had met the men, been overcome with passion, then overcome with pain as they quickly let it be known that she was to be only one of many women in their lives. Even if she had been shoved aside, scorned, at least she had known exactly where she stood. She had stopped seeing those men, because she could not tolerate loving men who did not love her, and her time of mourning had been mercifully short. In both cases it had ended up that out of sight really did prove out of mind.

With Andy, with goddamn Andy, it was different. He told Nell he loved her; he acted as if he loved her. But he never brought up any mention of the future. Two days before Nell and her children and Clary were going back to the mainland, Andy still had not said anything about seeing Nell again. She didn't know how to bring up the subject herself without seeming suppliant. She was terrified that in expressing the desire to see him after this summer, she would give away her deeper hopes—that they might be on the way to being truly connected with one another.

The night before, she had called Katy Anderson in Arlington to tell her when she and the children would be arriving home. It was not imperative for Katy to know this at all; it was more that Nell felt a sudden need to get back in touch with those she cared for who lived in Arlington. To make her old life, her Arlington life, seem real. She had been away from it for three months. She had been living a dream for three months on Nantucket, working, playing, sleeping with a man she loved. In three days she would be back in Arlington and all of *this* would be the dream.

She did not want to leave Nantucket. She did not want to leave Andy. She did not want the summer to end. She desperately did not want this summer to end. But of course it would end, and life would go on. She called Katy to remind herself that there were people in Arlington she loved, who loved her, too; she had friends.

Katy's voice had been warm. "We can't wait to see you, Nell," she said. "And wait till you see me. This baby's due any day now, you know. I look like I've got an entire basketball and net inside me . . . what's that?"

Her voice trailed off, and Nell could tell her attention had turned away from the phone. When she came back on, she was laughing. "John said to tell you I look like I've got an entire *fieldhouse* inside me. Thanks a *lot.*" She addressed the latter remark to John, then spoke to Nell again. "Anyway, I bet you look gorgeous, all brown and healthy. How're things going with that Andy person? Your postcards have been cryptic."

Before Nell could answer, Katy's attention disappeared from the phone again. "No, darling," she was saying to John. "I can do that. Honey, don't bother. You've had a long day. Sit down. That's one thing I can still do."

She spoke into the phone again. "Sorry, Nell. I just wanted to stop John before he stacked the dishwasher. He's been doing *everything* for me, in addition to keeping his practice up. He's more exhausted by my pregnancy than I am. Now, what were you saying?"

Nell tried to sound enthusiastic about Andy, but it was hard work. She had to summon up her old acting talents. Faced with the marital bliss of the Andersons, faced with Katy's unwitting security, faced with Katy's *life*—she had a man who was doing *everything* for her—Nell's joy in Andy's halfhearted love failed. As did her feeling of security about having friends back in Arlington. Katy and John loved her—but they loved each other a million times, universes, more. Nell had hung up the phone feeling more bereft than before she had called.

It was two days after Labor Day; two days before they left Nantucket. Camp was over for the children. Nell had given them money and told them to walk to town to buy doughnuts and souvenirs and to take as long as they could doing it. She had to do some laundry and housecleaning and packing; she would take them to the beach in the afternoon. The jewelry store had closed for the season, so Clary was home too. She was also cleaning and packing, up in her bedroom and in the upstairs bathroom. Nell was working in the kitchen, tossing stuff from the refrigerator and cupboards into a giant black trash sack. She found two old plastic bags with the heel ends of bread molding inside the cupboard, popsicles stuck to ice cube trays, cans of tuna that had been opened and half eaten and covered with tin foil and placed in the refrigerator to get shoved to the back, where the fish turned brown and dry. How had the place gotten so disgusting in just three months?

Nell and Clary had agreed that they worked better to music. They had stacked the stereo with records, alternating Clary's favorites with Nell's, although they both liked the same music. In fact they owned several of the same records, which made it possible for them to hear both sides of the Police album or *Flashdance* without having to flip the record over. They had turned the stereo volume as high as it would go so they could hear it all through the house as they went about their chores.

Nell was wearing jean shorts and a white T-shirt and was barefoot. She had on no makeup and her hair was tied back with a scarf. But in her mind she was in concert, onstage, wearing a mini dress dripping with sequins, with spangles braided into her hair; she had a microphone in her hand and was bellowing out a song about the pain of love while thousands in the audience cheered and clapped and went mad with desire at the sight and sound of her. *That* would make her happy, Nell thought; *that* would be the right way to live a life. She shouldn't have tried to be an actress, she should have tried to be a rock singer. God, how wonderful it must be to be a rock singer, she thought, to be able to really scream out your passion that way.

"I really want you tonight!" she yelled along with the record, and turned to drop some withered lemons into the trash. As she turned, she caught sight of something new in the kitchen; startled, she screamed and jumped. Then realized it was Andy. She had not heard him come in because of the music.

"Andy!" she said, smiling. God, she wondered, how long had he been standing there?

"Sorry to scare you," he said. "But the music . . ."

"I know," Nell said. "Want some coffee?" She wiped her hands on her jeans.

"No thanks. But I'd like to go for a walk with you."

"Oh, Andy," Nell sighed. "I don't think I can right now. I've got to get all this cleaned up. . . .''

"Well, I don't really want to go for a walk," Andy said. "I mean I would like to *talk* to you. But I don't know how we can talk with that—noise—going on."

Nell was shaken. He wants to *talk*, she thought. Her heart pounded in her throat. Oh God, she thought, why does he want to talk when I look so especially grubby? Why couldn't he want to talk at night, after dinner, when we're alone and my hair's combed and my eyelashes are curled? This is not how I've imagined our romantic conversation would be. Still, she did not want to lose this opportunity. He had come to *talk*. She was elated.

"Oh, Andy," she said. "Well, umm, well. Why don't we go sit in the front living room? We can shut the door. I don't want to turn off the stereo because Clary's upstairs cleaning and she likes to listen to the music; it sort of gives her energy."

"I would think it would give her a headache more than energy," Andy said. He followed Nell into the front parlor. "Awful stuff they're turning out these days," he went on. "It all sounds like a bunch of chimpanzees have been turned loose."

"Do you really think so?" Nell said. "You don't like rock and roll?" She shut the door behind him and crossed the room to stand by a window.

Andy leaned against the opposite wall. "Not much of it," he said. "It's all amplified. It requires no talent. It's just noise and cheap sentiment. Mostly noise."

"Oh I don't know," Nell said. "I think a lot of it is marvelous. The new synthesizers—some of the music is quite complex."

"Complex!" Andy said. "Nell, listen to that music that's playing now—if you can call it music. It's not much more than a drumbeat. We can feel it coming through the walls. We might as well be primitives hitting animal skins and shaking gourds. And that woman isn't singing; she's got no voice at all. She's *screaming*. I'm surprised you like that music, Nell. It's so juvenile."

"Well, at least it's definite!" Nell snapped. "At least it's clear. At least it's not ambiguous!" She glared at Andy. It seemed that without planning it, they had stumbled onto a different, more intimate topic.

Andy glared back at Nell. Then he crossed the room and took her in his arms. "Yes, that's true," he said. "It's not ambiguous. That's one of the advantages—and disadvantages—of being juvenile. You can see everything in absolutes. There are no complications, no gray areas. Everything is clearly right or wrong.'' He spoke into her hair. ''But when you get older, it gets more complicated, doesn't it? Decisions, I mean.'' Before Nell could respond, he said, ''Nell, I've been thinking a lot about how we can continue to see each other. You know I want that. I think you want that. But you've got to be in Arlington; your home is there. You work there. The children go to school there. And I have to be here. I'm going to miss you. Nell, I love you. You know that.''

''I know that,'' Nell said. ''And I love you.'' She was glad he was holding her pressed against him so that he could not see her face. She was smiling, wild with hope.

He gently pushed her away from him then and walked around the room. ''But there's this problem,'' he said. ''I hate leaving Nantucket. Especially now. I mean, after all the tourists go it's as if I have 'my' island back again. I really don't like going onto the mainland. I hate the traffic, the people, the filth, the noise. I don't suppose I've been off Nantucket but nine times in nine years. What I'm saying is that I'm going to have to ask you to be the one to travel here to see me. That's a lot to ask, I know. But I'd be glad to help you financially. And you might enjoy coming here occasionally in the fall and winter. It's pleasant here then, in a different way. You could come the weekends that Marlow and Charlotte have the children. I'd pamper you. Cook you gourmet meals. You could have a vacation from real life every time you came. You could fly over on Friday nights and back on Sunday nights; we'd have two days and two nights together. I'd be glad to pay for your plane tickets; I'd insist on doing that. I want to keep seeing you. I just selfishly want to see you here, as much as possible.''

Nell sank onto the sofa, stunned. She looked at the floor and dug her fingernails into the palms of her hand, and the sharp pain distracted her and kept her from crying. She was shattered by the difference between what she hoped he would say to her and what he was in reality saying.

''I'm upsetting you, I can see,'' he said. He came over and sat down on the sofa near her, but not touching her. ''Is it because I'm asking you to come here to be with me?''

What shall I say? Nell thought. All the voices of her past warned her: be cool! Play hard to get! Don't be clingy! He won't want you unless he has to work for you. Don't make it too easy for him.

"No," Nell said. "It's not that. It's just that—Andy, there's such a difference between what I want to talk about with you and what you want to talk about with me. I want to talk about the—the future and you want to talk about *seeing* each other."

"But I am talking about the future," Andy said, bewildered.

"Seeing each other?" Nell asked. "Andy, we've been practically *living* with each other for three months now. Are we going to go back to *seeing* each other? Andy, the future I want to talk about is—is a long-range future. I mean, our *lives*. I mean, don't you ever think about the two of us sharing our lives?"

Andy had been looking at Nell intently; now his eyes dropped to the floor. "Nell," he said, "I've lived alone for a long time now. I've gotten to like it a lot. I don't have any idea how good I would be at really living with someone else. And after all, we've known each other for only three months. Don't you think it's a little early to talk about the distant future?"

I hate myself for being a fool, Nell thought. I hate myself for being the beggar here, and I hate you, Andy, for rejecting me. Yet how subtly this is all being done, she thought. None of the crucial words was being spoken. At least there was that. Maybe that's all the grace you gain by growing older. She had a lump in her throat and was afraid to speak, afraid that any movement on her part at all would start tears cascading from her eyes, would make her voice quaver, would start an avalanche of emotion. She did not want to fall apart in front of him.

"Yes," she managed to say. "I suppose it is a little early to talk about the distant future."

Andy looked at Nell, pulled her into his arms, held her against him. "Oh, Nell," he said. "I do love you. Believe me, I love you. I want you in my life. I can't promise more than that, and I'm sorry. I don't know what's going to happen. I don't know how much I can change. I've been a terrible recluse for a long time. But I want to keep seeing you. I love you, Nell."

He held her against him, kissing her face and hair. Nell couldn't stop herself from crying then.

"Please," he said. "Please say you'll come see me. Let's make some plans. And I'll call you often. And I'll try to come to Arlington sometime. I want to see your house, meet your friends. Nell, don't cry."

"Oh, Andy," Nell said. She was completely confused. She felt like a starving beast whose owner is throwing him crumbs instead of the whole and satisfying meal. And yet, she thought, Andy was right. They had been together for only three months. If he was erring by his slowness, she was erring equally by her impetuosity.

"Oh, Andy," she said again. "I love you. I love you so." Say you need me, she was thinking. Say something more, anything more, I need to hear more from you.

"Oh, Nell. My sweet Nell," Andy said.

That's not it, Nell thought.

"Mommy! We're home!"

Hannah and Jeremy came through the front door, their voices and movements coming loud and clear even through the rock music. They passed by the closed front parlor door and went thundering into the back living room. "Mommy?" they yelled. "Where are you?"

Reluctantly, Nell released herself from Andy's arms. "The children are back," she sighed. "Can we talk about this later?"

"Sure," he said. "Look, let me take you all out to dinner tonight. And I'll dig out some airplane schedules. We'll make some plans."

"I really can't plan much until I talk to Marlow," Nell said. "We usually have had the children alternate weekends, but I don't know what he'll want to do this year."

"Well, but that's great," Andy said. He smiled. "We'll be able to be with each other every other weekend. Who could ask for more?"

I could, you stupid goddamn fool, Nell thought. Then she thought, no, Nell, it's you who are the stupid goddamn fool. She opened the door to go out into the hall.

"Nell," Andy said. "Nell. I love you."

"Mommy!" Jeremy said, running up to her. "Look what we bought!"

Nell turned to her children, both angry at their interruption and grateful for their presence. She knew they would keep her from saying more, asking for more. "Let me see what you got," she said, her voice normal.

Andy came to her side and surveyed the children's loot with Nell. "I'm going to take you all out to dinner tonight," he said. "So think of your favorite place."

"Vincent's!" Hannah yelled.

"Henry's!" Jeremy yelled.

Andy laughed. "Well, you two decide and I'll pick you all up at six. Be sure to tell Clary she's invited, too."

He left then. Nell told Jeremy and Hannah to put their purchases in the room and to get ready to go to the beach. She walked back through the house, and she was numb. From the stereo, a male rock singer sobbed raggedly about a love that was so deep, so true that it was eternal from the first instant they kissed. Jesus Christ, Nell thought, I'm going to have to stop listening to this sentimental slop. It's doing me no good. When I get off this island, she decided, I won't listen to this kind of music ever again. I'll just listen to Beethoven, Mozart, Erik Satie. Maybe that will calm me down. Maybe then I'll learn to be cool as crystal inside, *restrained*.

But she was afraid that for her, restraint would always come as an imposed curbing, like the reins biting into the mouth of a galloping horse, rather than like the inner integrity of a pure block of ice that stood alone, cold to the core, disdainful of heat.

For one last time Nell, Jeremy, Hannah, and Clary spread their beach towels on the sand. Today they had driven out to Surfside. Tomorrow Clary would take the children to Jetties Beach to spend the morning while Nell did the last-minute packing and cleaning. This was the last time they would all four be here together.

The waves were rolling in. The children dropped their T-shirts on the sand and raced for the water. They joined a crowd of people who jumped and dove with the incoming waves.

"Come on, Mom!" they yelled back at Nell. "Come *on*, Clary!"

"Let me get hot first," Nell yelled back. She stretched out on her stomach, watching them. She yearned for a little peace so she could think about her conversation with Andy that morning. She wanted to replay it in her mind, word by word. She wanted to replay it for her innermost self, then to lie as still and receptive as a seismograph, to discover exactly the reaction their discussion had caused within her. Was she damaged? How badly? Was she broken or merely fractured? What did it all mean? What could be read into it? She put her head on her arms and envisioned herself and Andy in the front parlor, heard him speak his first few words.

"Mommy!" Hannah stood directly above her, dripping water on her. *"You promised."*

Nell looked up at her daughter. At this moment, she thought, I could as easily kill you as swim with you. Then her own needs faded in the face of Hannah's beauty. My daughter, Nell thought. And I did promise.

"All right," she said. "I'll go with you. But then you and Jeremy have to let me rest. Deal?"

"Deal," Hannah said in a rush. "Oh goody, Mommy, you're going to love it today!"

Nell could not resist Hannah's exuberance. Here, at least, she thought, was one human being on earth who got genuinely excited by Nell's presence. Hannah pulled her mother into the water. It was cold, but not painful. Together they walked out deeper.

"Where's Jeremy?" Nell asked. Hannah pointed to her brother, who was far out, turned away from shore, watching for the giant waves. They had been told there was some rhythm to the waves, that every sixth or seventh wave was the big wave that would billow in to lift and carry them on its back. The other waves were too flat, good only for little jumps. Nell and Hannah walked out until the water reached Hannah's shoulders. After a few minutes, Nell's stomach stopped contracting at the chill and she felt comfortable in the water. She could feel against her feet the sharp points of shells and pebbles mixed in with the sand. Here the water was opaque, a thick moving turquoise. The safe white edge of foam ran several yards back up on shore. She held her daughter's hand tightly, waiting to lift her child from the crash of the wave.

The first few waves were silly, easy; she and Hannah just jumped lightly, playing a little game. Then they saw the giant wave approach. Nell knew from past experience it was better to stay this far out, where the wave might overwhelm them but throw them into the relative softness of water. If they raced back to shore now, the wave's force would hurl them headlong into the sand. This had happened to Nell more than once, and her children had scrapes on their legs and arms from being in too close to shore when a giant wave came. It took courage, though, to make a stand here, watching the swollen water, a sail full of sea, heading for them. Just before it hit, she turned and lifted Hannah up. Hannah pushed off the sand with both feet. They rose of their own accord, and then came that fabulous sensation of being lifted up even more, so that they soared for a moment on the water's curved back. Hannah screamed with glee.

Their feet touched the sand again, the ocean flattened around them. Nell turned back and searched the water for her son. Where was Jeremy? She saw him, surfacing from the water, far out with some teenagers and adults. He had gone out this far before, she knew that; she had seen him. She had to let him trust his own judgment, his own abilities to judge and swim. Still, it was hard to watch him, hard to let him make his own decisions in this way. Nell's eyes burned from the salt in the water.

Clary came wading out toward them, smiling, her slim body slipping into the sea like a knife. "Great waves!" she called. She stationed herself a few feet from Nell and Hannah. The next few waves were small again, and Hannah and Nell and Clary jumped lightly, as if they were skipping rope. Then, "Look!" Clary called, and pointed. Once more a giant wave came rolling toward them, turning in the sunlight so that the water seemed a solid thing, a whale's back, perhaps. Nell squeezed Hannah's hand tightly. They looked at each other, giggling with fear, then back to the glistening wave, which had swept up and over past Jeremy so that Nell could not see him and which now approached her and her daughter like a great blue tongue that would overwhelm them and pull them down into the belly of the monstrous sea. They held hands, gauged the wave, jumped—and were lifted up, lifted free, carried, dropped. It was surprising how gently the wave set them back down each time.

Nell stayed out with Hannah for a long time, until her eyes were stinging from the salt. Hannah didn't seem to mind the sea water, and although she came in to play on the sand, to run on the teasing edge of surf, she wouldn't stop to rest. Nell threw herself onto her towel, wiped her eyes, caught her breath. She saw that Clary had gone further out and was with Jeremy now. Hannah was on the sand; both children were safe for a while. She could close her eyes.

The sun beat down on her back, warming her through and through. She stretched, felt her limbs relax. She meant to think over the events of the morning. Instead, she fell asleep.

She slept only a few minutes. When she awoke, things were all as they had been. Hannah was making a sand castle. Clary and Jeremy bobbed out in the ocean. The lifeguards in their orange trunks sat on their high chairs or strolled the beach, life preservers and whistles in hand. People laughed nearby. The sun was high and still; it seemed it would never move, it would never be dark again, nor would summer ever end. Nell sat up, ran a comb through her salty hair, put more lotion on her face. She watched her children play against the endless blue of water and sky.

In only a matter of hours we will be gone from Nantucket, Nell thought. We will be gone, and then this summer will be gone from our lives except in memory. Fall will come, then winter. I will grow older. I will once more sleep alone through long cold winter nights. Oh God, she thought, why can't Andy want me as I want him? Why can't he see that life is short and happiness is rare and each day can be a treasure . . . or a waste? We could be so happy together. Why can't he see that, want that, why can't he trust the lesson of this summer we've shared enough to commit himself to more seasons? I will miss him so, his body, his voice, his presence. I want to *live with him*. He wants to *see* me.

Oh, I am like a child whining after a toy, Nell thought. I am like an animal hungering for food just out of its reach. I am a fool.

Out in the ocean, Clary waved at Nell. Nell waved back. Now *think,* Nell said to herself: what if Clary had confided that she was upset because a man she had known for three months had not wanted to marry her? Nell would have advised Clary to have more patience. Three months, she would have said to Clary, three months is no time at all!

He has said he loves you, Nell, she told herself. Be happy with that, stop pushing for more. If it's good, it will last.

Although, said another voice from inside Nell, look at Clary: she loved a man for sixteen months, the man loves her, and yet he does not want to marry her. . . .

Nell suddenly rose to her feet. She was restless with emotion, with a scramble of confusing thoughts. She could settle nothing sitting here, she thought. She could do nothing. She could only go on with life. Nothing would be resolved no matter how hard she thought, and if she continued to sit on her towel thinking in circles like this, she'd end up crying and embarrassing herself in public, alarming the children.

She decided to take a walk down the beach. She asked Hannah if she wanted to join her, but her daughter was too intent on building her sand castle. Clary and Jeremy were indefatigable, *still* out in the water. Nell waved at them and began to stroll down the beach. The movement felt good. She walked for a long way, so that when she turned and began to walk back, her children were only specks in the distance, small dots in the space of water and sand.

Surfside, Nell thought: Surfside, Cisco, Dionis, 'Sconset, the Jetties. This island of sibilant beaches is charmed. It is beautiful and magic. No wonder she was so miserable to be leaving here, Nell thought; she had been so happy. She didn't think she had ever been this happy for so long a time in all her life. That is something, she thought, that is quite a lot: three months of love and happiness.

She walked, looking at the ocean and beach, and smiled, thinking of this summer, this happiness. She had had days and days on Nantucket when life laid pleasure at her feet like the sea casting up shells onto the shore, with a careless, prodigal gesture. She had had sun, warmth, the singing sea, love, her children's laughter, friends, Andy's kisses, again and again and again. The days had not been eternal, but they had seemed that way, and for a while she had lived as if summer were the only season. For a while she had lived, here on Nantucket, with her life as harmonious and glittering as music and she had been as happy as music in the midst of being played. She had had that much.

And, she thought, nearing her family, though it was all ending now, she had the memory of this time. And her children had learned to ride the waves.

She was about a good city block away from her blanket when she saw the lifeguard in his orange trunks grab his surfboard and race to the water. At the same time, people began to rise from the sand and walk to the water's edge; those in the water started coming out, then turning to stand and stare. Nell searched the shoreline for her children, but she was too far away to make them out in all the motion and glare. She began to run.

As she ran, she scanned the water over and over again, back and forth, searching: she thought she could see the red of Hannah's suit and the shine of Clary's blond hair—but where was Jeremy? It *can't* be Jeremy, she thought, but she ran faster, knowing that people were looking at her, not caring, until she reached the water's edge and Clary came up to her and grabbed her by the shoulders so that, just like that, in one brutal flash, Nell's fear became a certainty.

"Jeremy," Nell breathed.

Clary had the wide-eyed look and monotonal voice of a pan-icked person trying to stay calm. "I think the undertow carried him out," Clary said. "The lifeguard's gone after him. It hap-pened so fast, Nell."

"Where is he?" Nell asked.

"We can't see him," Clary said. "He's too far away."

Nell pushed Clary out of the way so that she could see the water. Another lifeguard was on his way out, paddling the surf-board over the waves. Nell could see nothing—how could they know where her child was, one small child in all that expanse of water? Then, far out, she saw a brown sheen, a lump, the top of Jeremy's head, bobbing up for a fraction of a second, before the water washed over it.

"There he is!" Nell yelled, and started into the water.

"Nell, you can't swim that far!" Clary said, grabbing Nell by the shoulders and restraining her at the sand's edge. "You wouldn't be any help out there. Stay here. They'll get him."

"Mommy!" Hannah cried, wading up to her mother from the waves. "Jeremy's out there!"

Nell looked down at her daughter. She put her hands on Han-nah's wet head, wet shoulders, goosepimpled arms.

"You stay here with me," Nell said. "Don't go away. Stay out of the water now."

"Will they get Jeremy? Is he going to drown?" Hannah asked. She was shivering and crying.

"I don't know," Nell said. "I don't know." Her body had gone cold.

"They'll get him," Clary said to Hannah. "He'll be okay, honey."

Oh God, Nell thought, this can't be happening. *Dear God*, she prayed, *save Jeremy. Let them save Jeremy, please, God.*

The lifeguards, who had streaked out into the ocean with amaz-ing speed, were now slowly padding in circles, searching. They appeared so calm, so aimlessly drifting. Goddamn them, Nell thought, what were they doing?

"FIND JEREMY!" Nell yelled at them, her fists clenched, and as if in response to her demand, one of the men reached into the ocean and dragged a body up onto his board. Together the two guards brought the boards and the boy in to shore.

They came in a few feet from where Nell stood and rolled

Jeremy off the board onto the sand. She had thought that Jeremy would be choking, crying, scared, and so the sight of her son when they brought him in came like a kick in the stomach. She couldn't breathe. She reached out for her son, but Clary held her back.

Jeremy's entire body was grayish-blue and limp. His eyes were closed, and he was not breathing. He looked cold, lifeless, unreal. When they rolled him onto his back, his head lolled loosely to one side. The blond lifeguard knelt behind Jeremy and pushed his shoulders up, then, dissatisfied, flipped the boy over and pushed hard on his back. Finally, a gush of water and vomit came from her little boy's mouth, spread over the sand, and sank.

"Jeremy," Nell said. She wanted to take her son in her arms, to warm him, cradle him, talk to him; only then would she know he was all right, but Clary still held her back by the shoulders.

"Leave them alone," Clary said. "Let the lifeguards do their work, Nell. They know what to do."

A crowd had gathered around them and everyone was shouting. People were racing up the hill to the phones to call an ambulance, and the gulls still dipped and called overhead and the sun still shone down keenly with that seaside brightness that made the moments seem eternal.

"He's not breathing," a guard said to the other, and flipped Jeremy over and began to apply CPR. For a few minutes he breathed into the boy's mouth, then pushed on his chest.

"Nothing," he muttered. "Fuck." Then he bent over Jeremy again.

Nell felt the hairs on her arms rise, the skin of all her body go icy cold. Hannah stood in front of her, sobbing helplessly. Nell gripped her daughter's arms.

"No fucking heartbeat!" The guard's voice rose angrily. Or was he afraid? He slapped Jeremy's face, pinched his arms, then rubbed his knuckles fiercely across the boy's sternum. In response, Jeremy's face constricted.

"Good," the guard said. "We've got a chance." He bent back over her boy.

"Please," Nell said. "God, please. Oh please, God, please, please, please." She was not aware that she spoke out loud. All her will was intent on Jeremy. All of her life and its meaning was forced now into one true, absolute need—that Jeremy live.

Ambulance attendants arrived carrying a stretcher. They headed up the long path of sand to the ambulance, the lifeguard walking beside them, still breathing into Jeremy's mouth. They went at a crawl, and there was a slope from the beach up to the parking lot that seemed to stretch upward with nightmarish cruelty. The hot sand sucked at their feet. It seemed they would never reach the ambulance.

Someone came up to Nell and said, "We'll drive your daughter and your friend to the hospital."

Nell nodded. At the top of the hill, an attendant took her arm.

"You can ride with us. In the cab."

"Can't I be with my son?" she asked.

"He'll need too many people around him. You'd only be in the way," the man said gently. "You'll be able to see him, there's a window," he added, then handed Nell up into the cab.

Nell turned to look back at her son. They had put a black rubber mask over his face.

"What are they doing?" she pleaded, nearly hysterical.

"That's an ambu bag," the driver said. "It's oxygen. It's better than a person breathing for him." Then he turned on the siren and began to drive.

Nell watched through the little window as people in the back bent over her son. They looked as if they were fighting back there in the careening ambulance, for they were shouting and moving with such haste that Nell had to dig her fingernails into her hands to keep from screaming. Someone rubbed Jeremy's arms and hands and legs. Someone put hot packs under his armpits and at his groin. Someone covered him with a blanket.

Nell watched, cold with fear. She knew she was helpless, at the mercy of those people who were gathered around her son, at the mercy of fate. She could only pray, and so she prayed, silently, as they drove to the hospital.

At last the driver slammed them all to a halt and raced out to open the doors at the back. Nell jumped out and raced to the group of people around her son. Inside the emergency room, Jeremy was put on a rolling cart and wheeled into a room where a doctor waited.

"Start an intravenous," the man said to a nurse, and then it seemed to Nell that everyone in the room went mad, that they were all mauling her son. She saw someone savagely jab his arm with a needle and someone else rip his swimming trunks away, exposing his small genitals. Nell sobbed.

"Hook him up to the cardiac monitor," the doctor said, and then came the moment when the screen of the monitor came on and even Nell could understand from the wavering green line that her son's heartbeat was weak and irregular.

"Please!" she cried out. "Save him!"

"Get her out of here," the doctor snapped.

A nurse came up to Nell and put her hand on her arm and gently pushed her back.

"No, *please,*" Nell said, sobbing. "Please. Please. Don't let him die."

The nurse put her hands on Nell's arms just as Clary had done and gripped her firmly. "They can work on him better if we're out of the way," she said.

"Please don't let him die," Nell said.

The others ignored her; they continued to work on Jeremy's body. The cardiac monitor beeped and the green line jumped along more evenly.

"There," the nurse said. "There. We've got a heartbeat. We've got a heartbeat. Now let's get out of here and let them work."

She half pushed, half pulled Nell from the room and placed her in a chair in the hall, then sat down next to her. "He's got a good chance," she said. "He's young, he looks healthy, we've got a good doctor, the best doctor, he's got a good chance."

"Just a chance?" Nell asked. "Isn't he going to live?"

"I don't know," the nurse said. "I don't know. But we've got a good heartbeat."

"He's so young," Nell cried.

"That's good," the nurse said, her voice soothing. "That's good. That helps. Little kids survive better than old folks. Their heartbeat and temperature go down fast, and that maintains life better. Remember that kid who was under water for half an hour last year? Half an hour, and he lived. It was on TV. They'll warm your son up—what's his name?"

"Jeremy," Nell said.

"They'll warm Jeremy up. Things will start functioning. They're giving him an electrolyte solution because of the sodium in his system from the ocean, they're doing what they can. He's young. That's a big help."

"Could you please go see?" Nell asked. "Could you please go check to see how he is?"

"Sure," the nurse said, and left Nell's side. She came back and said, "They're working on him. They've got a heartbeat. He's not dead."

"But is he alive?" Nell asked.

"He's critical," the nurse said. "I'm telling you the truth. He's still critical. But we've got a heartbeat."

Clary and Hannah came up to Nell, accompanied by a strange woman. They were all in their swimsuits and looked out of place in the technological formality of the hospital.

"How is he?" Clary asked.

"We don't know," Nell replied. "Oh God, Clary."

"I don't want Jeremy to die," Hannah wailed.

Nell looked at her daughter, whose face had collapsed in grief. "Oh, Hannah honey," she said. "I don't want him to die either." She reached out and pulled her daughter to her, pulled her onto her lap. Hannah wrapped her arms around her mother and cried into her chest. Nell bent her head and sobbed into her daughter's wet hair.

"Well, shit," Clary said. "Isn't there anything we can *do?*"

"They're doing all they can," the nurse said. "Drowning's not easy."

"I'll pray for him," the strange woman said, and sat down in a chair across from Nell and bent her head.

"You pray too, Hannah," Nell said.

"I am, Mommy," Hannah replied.

Nell leaned her head onto her daughter's and prayed. Her praying was more a form of memory, a holding in her mind of the liveliness of her son. She saw him in his blue blazer, dressed for the school concert, somberly holding his violin to his chin; she saw him sprawled on the floor of his room in jeans and T-shirt, playing a fantasy game with plastic characters and bits of wire and plastic; she saw him asleep in bed, the way he liked to sleep, with the blanket not tucked in at the bottom of the bed but rather wrapped around his feet and legs, cocoon-style, dumb Ginger the dog stretched out blissfully at his side. "Good night, guys," Nell would say. Once Jeremy had described to Nell an ache in his throat and chest which, after they discussed it for a while, turned out not to be a physical ailment, but rather to be a kind of melancholy, a wistful longing for things he had had as a child and longed to have as an adult.

Let him live, God, Nell prayed. You have got to let him live. Just let him live. You know I'll give up anything, I'll trade anything—excepting Hannah—for his life. I'll give up Andy, I'll give up love, *I'll give up anything. Just let him live.*

The nurse stood by them, then went away. She came back and said, "They're working on him." Then she stayed by their side silently, respecting their silence.

"We've been waiting for *thirty minutes!*" Clary suddenly yelled.

"They're doing what they can. It takes time," the nurse said. "Can I get you a cup of coffee?"

"Coffee," Clary said. "Christ." She looked away, annoyed.

The nurse left them. She was gone for what seemed a very long time, longer than she had stayed away before. Nell felt panic rise inside her.

"He's alive," the nurse said when she returned. "He is alive. Things are going well. Things are still critical, but they're going well."

"Can we see him?" Nell asked.

"Not yet," the nurse answered. "They're still working on him."

"I don't understand," Clary said. "Either he's alive or he's not."

"Well, it's not that simple," the nurse said calmly. "He's got a lot of salt in his system. Salt upsets the electrolytes. And water in his system. It's a major trauma to the body. His fluid and electrolytes are out of whack. But he's got a good strong heartbeat now." She turned to Nell. "Can I get you a cup of coffee?" she asked. "You must be cold."

"No," Nell said. "Thank you."

"Is Jeremy going to live?" Hannah asked Nell.

"I think so," Nell said. "I think so. You heard what the nurse said."

"They've pulled him out, I think," the nurse said, looking at Hannah. "Your brother has a steady heartbeat now. He's responding. Honey, would you like some hot chocolate?"

"Yes," Hannah said, looking guilty. "I'm sorry, Momma, but I'm cold."

"Have some hot chocolate, sweetie," Nell said. "It's all right."

The nurse went away, came back, handed Hannah a plastic cup of hot chocolate.

"Are you vacationing here?" she asked Nell.

"Working here this summer," Nell replied. Feeling was beginning to return. "I run Elizabeth's. A boutique on Orange Street. I'm sorry—I can't talk about this until I know he's okay." Tears flooded her eyes.

"He's going to be okay," the nurse said. "The doctor's really good, and he's got a strong heartbeat now. Listen, do you want to call your husband?"

"I'm divorced," Nell said. "Jeremy's father is in the Midwest now. I wouldn't know how to reach him. I don't need to reach him now—unless—"

"No," the nurse said. "He's not going to die. We've got him out."

"Please," Nell said. "Could you please ask if I could see him?"

"Okay," the nurse said.

As she turned back to the room, another nurse came out. She was smiling. "He's awake," she said. "Conscious, and he wants his mommy."

"Oh, thank God," Nell said, and nearly threw Hannah off her lap in her efforts to get up from the chair and into the room. She found Jeremy lying flat on his back on the table, covered with a blanket, his body stabbed with IVs and strapped with monitoring equipment. Blood dripped down his arms at various spots. His skin was pale but no longer blue, and his eyes were open, and he was alive, awake, and all there.

"Mommy," he said, and tears rolled down his face. He was trembling.

"Oh God, Jeremy," Nell said, and bent over to hug him. "God, you're alive."

"He's a good strong boy," the doctor behind her said. "He's got a powerful heart. He's as healthy as a horse."

Nell half lay on the table, enveloping as much of her son's body in her arms as she could. "Oh, Jeremy," she said, sobbing.

"Mommy," Jeremy replied. After a moment he said, "I'm scared."

Nell pulled back so he could see her face, but still kept her arms around him. "You're okay," she said. "You're okay now. You had a close call, but you're all right. I promise."

"You've got a good heart," the doctor said from behind Nell. "You've got a good heart, son. You're going to be fine."

"I almost drowned," Jeremy said. "It was awful, Mommy. I couldn't do anything. I fought to get up to the air, but I couldn't."

"It was the undertow," Nell said. She could feel Jeremy trembling harder now. "Sssh, it's okay," she said. "You're all right. You almost drowned, but the lifeguards rescued you, and the doctors saved you; you're okay."

Then Hannah and Clary were at her side. Hannah burst into tears at the sight of Jeremy tied and bloody. "Oh, Jeremy, I didn't want you to die!" she wailed, and grabbed one of his hands in hers and kissed it.

"Oh, duh," Jeremy said, embarrassed, but he did not pull his hand away.

"Well, you made two lifeguards proud of themselves," Clary said, taking Jeremy's other hand.

"*Two* lifeguards?" Jeremy asked.

"Yeah," Clary said. "It was really neat. You were the star of the show today for sure, Jeremy. Everyone on the beach was watching."

The *star* of the *show,* Nell thought, looking across the table in wonder at Clary. Jeremy had almost died—how could she talk about it so lightly? But looking back at Jeremy, she saw that his face was relaxing, and she could feel with her hands and arms how he was taking deeper breaths now, how the fear was fading.

"*Two lifeguards,*" Jeremy said, almost smiling.

"Yeah, and you should have seen yourself when they brought you in," Hannah said. "Ugh, you looked so *gross.* Like an old fish!"

"Hannah!" Nell said, but Jeremy was smiling, obviously thrilled now to know what he had caused to happen in the world. He wanted to hear everything. Now that he was safe, his drowning was being turned into a drama—a good story to tell everyone.

Nell moved back from the table a little and let Hannah and Clary gleefully describe the entire event to Jeremy in colorful detail. The doctor came up to Nell and told her that in most cases they sent patients over to the Hyannis hospital, but because Jeremy's heartbeat was so good and he was so alert, they could keep him here for the night.

"But I thought you said he was okay!" Nell said. "Look at him—"

"It's necessary to keep him at least overnight," the doctor said. "He's got lots of water in him, high sodium in his system. We need to keep an eye on him, be sure he's oxygenated sufficiently before we send him home. He's okay, but we don't want to take any chances. You can stay with him. We'll set up a cot for you in Intensive Care."

"Intensive Care," Nell said.

"It's only for the best precaution," the doctor said. "Don't worry. He'll be fine."

"Oh thank you," Nell said. "I haven't thanked you. How can I thank you?"

The doctor smiled. "Well, you know," he said, "it's a pretty nice feeling when you pull them through."

Then he turned away and gruffly began to give orders. They wheeled Jeremy into the elevator and up to the Intensive Care Unit. The nurse led Nell to a chair and asked her to fill out some forms. This turn toward financial and administrative details gave Nell a sense of certainty that Jeremy was all right. She looked down at the clipboard and began to shake. She was suddenly exhausted. She did not have the energy to write her name. And she was cold—she was still wearing her swimsuit. She felt foolish now, barefoot and half-naked in front of all these people, although it wouldn't have mattered if she had been totally naked this past hour—nothing had mattered but that Jeremy live. And he was alive, and now she was cold and tired, and she shook so hard her teeth chattered.

The nurse who had stayed with them came up to Nell and put a sweater on her, lifting her arms to put them in the sweater as easily as if Nell were a child.

"Drink this," she said to Nell, handing her a cup of coffee. "You'll be okay," she said. "It's delayed reaction. Nerves and fear and relief. You're getting it all at once. You'll calm down in a minute. Don't worry. You guys have good luck. You've got a good strong boy."

The nurse went on talking, and Nell, trying to fight off a whirling sense of dizziness, stared at the woman's name tag. She had seen it before, all the time she had been in the hospital, but only now could she read it. CHERYL CABOT, R.N. was inscribed into the ivory scrimshaw pin. The letters grew darker, then lighter, as

Nell watched, and for a few moments the best Nell could do was to keep the letters in focus and hold on to the sound of the nurse's soothing voice. Finally the dark whirling receded, and Nell's eyesight and hand steadied. She took deep breaths. "Thank you," she said. "I'm okay now." She turned to the hospital forms.

The rest of the day moved in fits and starts. The woman who had driven Clary and Hannah to the hospital drove them to the cottage to get their clothes. Clary drove Nell's car back and brought her warm clothing. Nell stayed with Jeremy, talking to him, listening to him, until evening came. At last she was so calm and assured of his aliveness that she admitted to herself that she was getting restless. The subject of his accident and rescue was not a source of entertainment to her as it was to Jeremy. She was glad when Clary and Hannah came back to visit Jeremy; she let them indulge in repeating the gory details of the day. She went out into the hall.

It was six o'clock in the evening. They had gone to Surfside at ten; had been there for about two hours before Jeremy's accident. It had been a long day. Nell was tired, and she leaned against the wall and wondered about calling Andy. She hadn't called him right away because she simply hadn't thought of it, and later, when the crisis passed, she hadn't called because she felt irrationally angry at Andy, because she had been alone to hope for her son's life. Not completely alone—Hannah and Clary and the doctors and nurses who had really saved his life had been there, but there had been no other parent to hope for him in the way a parent hopes. Now she felt the loneliness of her life, and a mean anger at Andy because of it, and a perverse desire not to let him know what had happened. After all, what would he care? For it was true that he was so strangely unlike other people where the matter of children was concerned. He had never been much interested in his own daughter, and although he was polite to Jeremy and Hannah, after all this time he had not become fond of them. Then, too, Nell was aware of how overdramatic she often appeared emotionally, compared to Andy, and what could be more dramatic than a near-fatal drowning? She could almost predict how he would grow cool and aloof in proportion to her need for warmth and affection.

But finally she called him and explained what had happened. He expressed shock and said he wanted to come to the hospital to see her and Jeremy. When he arrived, he looked genuinely affected, his dark eyes serious, and he embraced Nell tightly, pulling her against him with a strong, real tenderness. Nell's defenses broke and she felt washed through with love and need.

The nurses had Hannah and Clary leave Jeremy's side so that Nell and Andy could go in. Jeremy was propped against pillows now, wearing a hospital gown; his color was healthy, his mood ebullient.

"Hi, Andy!" he said when Nell and Andy walked in. "Guess what! I drowned. I almost *died*. I was *blue*. Hannah said I looked like an old fish. It took two lifeguards to get me out. And Mom rode here with me in an ambulance and I didn't even know it. I was *unconscious*."

"But you're okay now," Andy said. He lounged up against Jeremy's bed and leaned against it, but he did not touch the boy.

"I'm fine. I'm great. But I get to stay here overnight so they can be sure I'm okay. I've got too much salt in my system."

"Well, look," Andy said. "I'm glad you're okay. It must have been pretty scary. Uh—here. This is for you."

Andy reached into his pocket and took out a fifty-dollar bill and stuck it in Jeremy's hand.

Jeremy, ungraciously, looked puzzled to the point of skepticism.

"What is it?" he asked.

"It's, uh, money," Andy replied.

"I know. It's a lot of money," Jeremy said. "But why are you giving it to me?"

"Well, because you had an accident," Andy said, and now he looked as puzzled as Jeremy. "I mean, people give people presents in the hospital. And I couldn't think what you would want, so—" He stopped and shrugged his shoulders.

"Mom?" Jeremy asked, looking at Nell.

"Of course you can take the present," Nell said, trying to turn Andy's awkward gesture into the kindness he meant it to be. Tears had come to her eyes: it was a stupid and clumsy way to show affection, and yet it was something, it was more than she had hoped for. "Thank you, Andy," she said. "It's not necessary, you know, but it's awfully nice of you."

"Yeah, when I get home I can buy the robot I've been wanting," Jeremy said. "Thanks a lot!"

They stood there a while longer talking to Jeremy, or rather listening to Jeremy describe the accident in complete detail. Andy listened, nodding his head and saying, "Wow" at the appropriate moments. Nell just stood like a cow with sun on its back, watching her son breathe, listening to him talk, knowing he was all right, and soaking in the extra warmth of the knowledge of Andy's endearingly well-meant gift.

Finally everyone but Nell had to leave. Clary promised to take care of Hannah overnight and to call the steamship authority to change their boat reservation. Nell slept all night on a cot near her son, awakening each time a nurse came in to check Jeremy. Early in the morning, another nurse came in to draw blood from Jeremy's arm, and soon after that breakfast was served to both Jeremy and Nell. By then Nell was so tired she was grumpy, and she drank her coffee slowly, trying to plan the next few days.

The doctor kept Jeremy in the hospital for another day, although he put him on the medical-surgical floor. The pediatric ward had only three beds and no other children, and when Nell came back in the afternoon from changing clothes at the cottage, she found Jeremy boldly cruising the halls in a wheelchair while Hannah trailed at his side begging for a turn. Clary, who had come to watch Jeremy while Nell went home for a while, was lounging on Jeremy's bed, reading *Glamour*. Nell stood watching it all, marveling at the fact that only twenty-four hours before, her son and this hospital had been fighting for his life. Yesterday had been one of those days when time stopped for a while, and, as if time and light were the same thing, illuminated life with a vivid motionless clarity. Now time was going on again, reckless and meaningless, and Jeremy was alive and Nell's life was organized once more in its meaning and in its order. Her children raced up to her, giggling. Hannah was now seated precariously on Jeremy's lap in one wheelchair.

"Settle down, you two!" Nell reminded them. "This is a hospital."

They wheeled away from her, whispering now, leaving her to watch them in their exuberance. Nell leaned against the wall and thought that she had learned something this summer, had remembered something—that we all need to be admired, we all need to be loved, we need to eat and drink and be warm and laugh and achieve, but that what we need most in the world, above all our other needs, is for our children to live.

Nine

APPARENTLY, the fleas had been bad that summer. At least that was what Donna, the college girl who had lived in Nell's house and taken care of the animals, said. The cats and especially the dog were miserable. Donna had sprayed them, had checked to be sure they wore flea collars, but still the fleas had come. Nell had called her friend the vet the day she came home and had been advised to get an insecticide bomb for the house: everyone who owned animals was having the same problem, she reassured Nell. Nell sighed: bombing the house meant that they would all have to keep out of it for several hours. They had only just gotten back into it, and school had started. She didn't know when she'd be able to bomb the house. So the animals continued to scratch.

"Breakfast!" Nell screamed at the top of her voice. It was the third time she had called her children this morning. If they didn't hurry, they would all be late. "Come *on!"*

Jeremy came down the stairs, his face sullen.

"Honey, what's wrong?" Nell asked.

"You know," he said.

"Oh, go eat your breakfast," she told him. He was still sulking because she had told him he could not have guinea pigs. A child at school was giving them away free, with a cage and food. That should tell you something, Nell had said to Jeremy the night before when they had discussed the matter. If she's so desperate to get rid of them that she'll give away a cage, they must be troublesome or something.

"Guinea pigs are not troublesome!" Jeremy had stormed. "They are interesting and beautiful!"

"No," Nell had said. "We have enough animals."

"Medusa sleeps with you and Fred sleeps with Hannah," Jeremy had pointed out.

"But you can have Ginger to sleep with you," Nell had said. "Ginger always slept with you when you were little."

"Ginger farts," Jeremy had said, glaring.

Nell had sighed. It was true. Now that their German shepherd was approaching her first decade, she did seem to be having more intestinal gas. Nell couldn't blame Jeremy. She didn't want Ginger sleeping in her bedroom, either. The occasional smell was unbelievable. Yet they all loved the dog.

Now Ginger sat beneath the kitchen table, scratching and digging and snurfling at her fleas. It was a disgusting and unsanitary sound, not the sort of thing one wanted to hear at breakfast.

"Come on, Ginger, let's go outside, honey," Nell said, and put the dog out. "It's a beautiful fall day," she called to her children. She stood for a moment, taking in the flawless blue sky, the leaves just beginning to be tinged with red, the sweet crisp air. The old yellow baby dress Fred had worn still hung from the shrub, she noticed. She'd have to be sure to get that down today when she came home from work. And Jeremy could get the shovel out and pick up the dead squirrel Medusa had laid on the back steps. She went back inside.

Back to real life, she thought, looking at her kitchen with despair. The first few days home Nell had been almost euphoric, driven by Jeremy's accident to vow that from now on she would live each day fully, treasuring each moment, being the perfect mother to her children. But after all, not all moments were as sweet as others, and some moments were absolutely grueling. The college girl had taken care of the animals, but had not done anything to clean the house— and Nell couldn't blame her, that hadn't been part of the deal. She had simply camped out in the house. And she had done her part: the animals were alive and not any more neurotic than usual. But the bathrooms were scummy, the stove was grimy, the entire house was dusty, and the kitchen floor was coated with several layers of oily filth. Nell had already mopped the floor, but that had done little good. She was going to have to scrub it with a brush, on her hands and knees. They had been home only ten days, and in that time Nell had gotten the children ready for school, unpacked, done some basic cleaning when she got home from work—but she still had so much left to do.

Hannah came into the kitchen. She was walking like a hunchback so she could scratch her legs as she walked. Oh Lord, Hannah thought. She had been planning to attack the kitchen floor when she got home from work, but now she'd have to go see what else she could do about Hannah's room.

"There are still fleas in my bed," Hannah told her mother.

"I know," Nell said. "I'll see what I can do." Ginger had apparently slept on Hannah's bed all summer. They had come home to find Hannah's bed speckled with fleas. "Oh, *gross,*" Hannah had cried. "Damn old Ginger!"

Nell had reassured Hannah. She had run all the bedding through the hot water cycle with strong detergent. She had vacuumed and sprayed Hannah's room. She had scrubbed the baseboards and walls and windowsills and closet. Now she would have to see what else she could do.

"Please eat your breakfast," she said, sipping her coffee and buttoning the cuffs of Hannah's shirt in an absentminded routine.

"I don't see why I can't have a guinea pig," Jeremy said.

"Mom, didn't you hear me?" Hannah said. "There are still fleas in my room!"

"Oh, *good!*" Nell shrieked. "That's wonderful. That's just wonderful. More pets for the house. Sure you can have the guinea pigs, Jeremy. Why not? And let's name the fleas. Let's not kill them, for heaven's sake, let's make them little bonnets! Why don't you go out and see if you can resuscitate the dead squirrel? It can live in here with us too!"

Jeremy and Hannah looked at each other. They sighed. They bent their heads and began eating their breakfast.

Nell stormed through the house, collecting her purse, the children's lunch money, her car keys, noticing as she passed the hall mirror that her tan had already faded a great deal. Just like the sweeter memories of the summer.

"Mom, do you know where my sneakers are?" Jeremy said.

"I told you, you left them in the bathroom last night when you took your bath."

"I looked. They're not there."

"Oh Jesus," Nell said. "We're going to be late." She streaked up the stairs. "*Here they are!*" she yelled. "They're under the goddamn *towel.* You dropped your towel on top of them after your bath. How in the world can you expect me to think you can take care of guinea pigs when you can't even keep track of your own sneakers? I have to follow you around, telling you to hang up your towel, brush your teeth, I have to find your sneakers for you. You are too irresponsible for guinea pigs. Do you have your violin?"

Finally they were all out of the house and on the way to their destinations. Nell drove to work in a funk, hating herself for haranguing Jeremy so awfully. Two weeks ago her son had nearly died, and already she was breaking her promise to herself to treat him like the precious child he was. He would grow up to tell his wife that his mother was an old nag, she thought. But if she didn't nag him, he'd vague out and never get anything done. Although, she reminded herself, he was in the top groups in all his school work and was making excellent grades. And his teacher said he was doing beautifully on the violin. And this year he had started coordinating his clothes by himself, actually wearing blues with blues and browns with browns. Maybe there was hope, she thought. Probably he would turn into an organized human being after all, even if *she* had to come apart at the seams helping him get there.

After the mess of the house, the calm of the boutique seemed like heaven. Nell opened the shop and slowly began the day. She didn't expect many customers in this early, and at least it would never be as rushed and crowded as the boutique on Nantucket had been. Nell practically felt she was resting when she came into this airy store; she was never plagued with the needs of children or the hair of animals here. She moved around the shop, dusting, straightening, being sure that the clothes were hung on the correct racks. The UPS man wouldn't be in for another hour. She didn't expect it to be a busy day. She let her thoughts wander. Like a nurse checking for the vital signs of a patient, she checked the vital signs of her life.

First of all, her children were alive and well and happy; that was most important. Nell had written long thank-you letters to the lifeguards, doctor, and nurses at Nantucket hospital. She had sent the nurse a large box of expensive chocolates and asked her to share them with everyone at the hospital. She had written a long letter of gratitude to all those concerned, which was published in the Nantucket *Inquirer and Mirror*. Now she was more than ready for another discussion with Andy about the goodness and evil of nature and of human beings.

Andy had called several times in the past ten days, and he had been charming and pleasant; she would fly down to see him the weekend after next, when the children went to stay with Marlow.

He had said he loved her, but he had not seemed to miss her desperately, he did not seem to ache for her, as she ached for him, and Nell felt a certainty growing within her, like an ugly bitter weed, that she would end this relationship soon because she could not bear to be wanted in such a lukewarm way. She could not take the insecurity, the ambiguity. She would rather face the hard long flat road of loneliness than the roller coaster of hope and loss.

At least that was what she told herself, but still she waited each night, hoping Andy would call. And she had made plane reservations for the next weekend.

But she was determined not to make Andy all-important in her life. She was determined to somehow forge ahead on her own. Three nights ago she had gone to a meeting of a local community theater. An announcement in the paper stated that this was the theater group's fourth year and that they were holding auditions for the play they would put on in November, *Charley's Aunt*. That was one of Nell's favorite plays, and she thought perhaps she could get some part in it, and she was encouraged by the fact that the group seemed relatively new. She knew no one who belonged to the theater group, but she summoned all her courage, hired a baby-sitter for the children, and went. It would be fun to act again, she thought. She remembered the way her heart always whipped about inside her just before she went onstage. Even a bit part, she had thought . . .

But they had not cast her for even a bit part. The theater group had been surprisingly close-knit. She was a newcomer, an outsider, and as soon as she entered the church hall where the meeting was held, she realized this. She felt very much like a kindergarten child entering a new school in the middle of the year. She almost walked right out again. But she auditioned and then forced herself to stay for the chatter that took place after auditions.

During that time, the director, an enormous young woman with equally enormous energy, approached Nell and asked her if she would be interested in working with the theater in any other way. They especially needed help with costumes for this play, the woman said. It was a period piece; they needed someone who might be willing to sew. Nell had told the woman she would let her know, and after talking with her for a while, had fled the building. Driving home in the dark, she had cried. I used to be an almost professional actress, she thought, and at the least I used to be *good*. No one's ever heard of me, and I can't get a part in even a small community production—all my childhood dreams have come to nothing.

But today, as she moved around the boutique, she thought perhaps she would take on the job of helping with costumes. It would not be so different from what she did every day of her life—fitting, sewing, cutting, working with materials, arranging fabric on bodies. It would be pleasant and she would get to know people and eventually she could become part of the group, perhaps, eventually she might be given parts. That was the way those things worked, she knew that. It would be a pleasure to be around the theater again, even if from behind the scenes. She called Susan, the director, and told her she would help with costumes. Susan was delighted and gave her the name of the woman in charge of costuming, and Nell said she would get in touch with her that night after work.

Nell hung up, cheered. *Charley's Aunt* was Victorian; the costumes would require lace and satin and ribbons, long dresses, top hats and morning coats. It would be fun to work with fancy elaborate clothes. And the play was so funny that rehearsals, she knew from past experience, would be amusing, sometimes hilarious. This play would allow the cast to enjoy each other; they would be involved in entertainment rather than serious drama that strained to get across some heavy message. Nell could vaguely remember a line about "Brazil, where the nuts come from . . ." She grinned to herself and looked up to see Charlotte coming in the door of the boutique.

Charlotte was looking rather strange these days. She was letting her short spiky hair grow out a bit, or at least she had decided not to dye it again, and so the hair near her scalp was brown but the ends were all orange. She didn't look quite sane. On the other hand, she was pretty enough so that she didn't look frightening either.

"Hi, Nell," Charlotte said. "Listen, can we go to lunch today? I want to talk to you."

Nell stared. She had not gone out to lunch with Charlotte or done anything *alone* with Charlotte since Marlow had announced he was going to marry her. She and Charlotte were polite to each other, even amicable, because of Hannah and Jeremy. But Nell had no desire to become intimate with this woman again. They had managed to coexist peacefully, a pair of countries that shared Marlow as their common boundary, for five years that Marlow and Charlotte had been married.

"Charlotte," Nell began. She intended to say something definite but not unkind, perhaps simply: I stopped having lunch with you years ago.

But Charlotte interrupted her. She leaned on the jewelry counter toward Nell, looking as imploring and pathetic as one of Dickens's orphans. "Nell," she said. *"Please."*

So at lunch Nell found herself seated in a ferny café facing Charlotte over quiche lorraine and a glass of wine. Charlotte made small talk about the summer while they ordered, twisted her napkin until it looked like a piece of origami, and alternatively avoided meeting Nell's eyes and leaned forward, catching Nell in staring contests.

Finally Nell said, "Charlotte, what is this all about? What's up?"

Charlotte took a sip of wine, paused for dramatic effect—as if the entire morning already hadn't been a giant build-up—and announced, "I'm leaving Marlow."

"You're leaving Marlow?" Nell echoed, astounded.

"Divorcing him," Charlotte said.

Nell's first thoughts were for her children. Because the adults had been pleasant to each other, Hannah and Jeremy had had a relatively smooth transition from living with Mommy and Daddy and having Charlotte as a friend to living alone with Mommy and visiting Daddy, who had married Charlotte. If it has been confusing for them, at least they had known Charlotte, were accustomed to her, understood her quirks, even liked her. Now Marlow would be going out with other women—he would, Nell knew, sooner or later marry again, because he was a man who liked being married. This meant that Hannah and Jeremy would have to get used to yet another stepmother.

Nell's second thoughts were for herself. Damn, she thought. If Charlotte leaves Marlow, that means I won't be able to get over to Nantucket very often. Marlow loved his children, but in an abstracted way; he wasn't very good at the basics of feeding and entertaining, not when they were still so young. If Charlotte left him, he soon would be involved in a series of new affairs—he would be far too busy with all that to want to give his weekends over to playing Chutes and Ladders with his kids.

Nell pulled her thoughts away from herself and focused again on Charlotte, who by now had taken out a cigarette and was smoking it in a long black holder. The cigarette holder gave her

a very dramatic, 1920s effect. Where on earth did she find it?
Nell wondered. She must have stolen it from some props department, she decided, and Nell thought to herself, in spite of herself,
what a really marvelous creature Charlotte was. She was unique,
a jazzy, crazy, and not unkind stick-figure of a girl.

"I can tell you're surprised," Charlotte said.

Nell laughed. "Well of course I am," she said. "Shouldn't I
be? I had no idea you and Marlow weren't happy together. Shall
I ask why you're leaving him, or do you want to keep that to
yourself?"

To Nell's dismay, Charlotte began to cry. She did it, however,
with great style, arching her head disdainfully at her own display,
inhaling deeply on her cigarette, letting the tears just run down
her face to plop on her blouse. Nell watched, entranced, because
Charlotte's nose didn't run: how does she manage *that?* Clever
Charlotte, she thought, admiring her.

"Oh, Nell," Charlotte said, in a dramatically defeated voice,
"I envy you so much."

"What?" Nell said. The shock of this statement made her
smile, the way she had sometimes smiled as a child when she
heard that a person had died.

"You have so much," Charlotte went on. "You have all the
things I want."

Nell stared at Charlotte, silent. She couldn't imagine what in
the world the girl would say next.

"I mean you have *children,*" Charlotte went on. "Jeremy and
Hannah. They are so beautiful, so clever. Oh, Nell, I want children
more than anything in the world. I want to have a kitchen like yours,
with children's drawings on the refrigerator and sunny little toys on
the floor and those sweet dimpled hands holding mine."

"Jeremy and Hannah don't have sweet dimpled hands anymore," Nell said.

"Oh, you know what I mean. I mean, if I had children, they'd
have sweet dimpled hands when they were little. Oh, Nell, I want
to have a baby."

"And Marlow doesn't," Nell said.

"Marlow's a sneaky old Scrooge," Charlotte said. "All I had
to do was to mention to him that I was thinking I wanted to have
children, and do you know what he did?"

"I can't imagine," Nell said.

"He started using *condoms,*" Charlotte announced. "Now I

can't even have a *mistake*. He hardly makes love to me anymore, he's so terrified I might get pregnant. I've been trying for about a year now to sort of, oh, you know, overwhelm him with lust, get him when he's wanting it and when I don't have my diaphragm in. But he's always so careful now with those damn condoms. And *now* he says he's going to get a vasectomy. Nell, he's made the appointment.''

Nell could only laugh. "Oh, Charlotte," she said. "What can I say? You know as well as I do that Marlow isn't interested in fatherhood.''

''Yes, but he's interested in me, or he used to be, and he knows it would make me happy to have kids, so he ought to let me have kids so I'll be happy.''

''Well, they'd be his kids, too,'' Nell said, sobering up. "And he already has some of those to ignore. Two separate generations of them.''

''Yeah, it's too bad Clary has to come grubbing around right now. Part of this is her fault,'' Charlotte said.

''Part of what is Clary's fault?'' Nell asked.

''Well, if she weren't hanging around Boston now, bugging Marlow to help her find a job, making him feel he's still responsible for her, he might be more interested in having more children. Don't you see what I mean? Clary's twenty-seven, after all; she ought to be on her own instead of whining around after her daddy, expecting him to spend his time fixing the world up for her.''

''Charlotte,'' Nell said firmly, ''I don't think Clary ever 'whines around' after anyone.''

''Well, you know what I mean,'' Charlotte said, and inhaled deeply and defensively on her cigarette.

What you mean, Nell thought, is that you don't want Clary to exist. There had been times in her own life when she hadn't wanted Clary to exist. She understood Charlotte perfectly. Charlotte was only three years older than Clary: living proof that Marlow was an *old* father, had done his share of furthering mankind, deserved a rest from raising kids. Marlow had been a father for twenty-seven years, and although he still looked young and was capable of producing more children forever, he really did deserve a break, especially since he didn't like children all that much in the first place.

''Listen,'' Nell said. ''Don't dislike Clary because she's Marlow's daughter. She is a very good person. Even if Marlow didn't have Clary—even if he didn't have Hannah and Jeremy—he still wouldn't want to start a family now, not at his age. Charlotte, Marlow's *fifty*."

"I know that!" Charlotte said. "Don't you think I know that? I'm his *wife*, you know!" She glared angrily at Nell, then her tears started up all over again. "Oh, Nell, how did you manage it?" she asked. "How did you manage to get such a neat life? Two beautiful children and your freedom, too?"

"Well," Nell said dryly, "I guess I have you to thank for at least some of that—the 'freedom' part." Charlotte doesn't have the first idea about my life, she thought, listening in gentle amazement as Charlotte carried on about her. Charlotte is determined to envy me, she thought. She always did envy me, but God knows why. "Look," Nell said. "You shouldn't want my life. Charlotte, you don't understand. I'm all *alone* in life. I've got to work hard to raise the children, but they'll leave me in a few years for their own lives. I want them to do that. But I am really *alone*."

"Oh, everybody is *alone*," Charlotte intoned with dramatic gloom.

"Charlotte, damnit, this is not some existential play we're talking about!" Nell snapped. "This isn't some theater of the absurd. This is real life. When I say I'm alone, I mean when I'm sick in the night I get up and fix my own Seven-Up and when I'm lonely in the night I've got only the cat to hug. I am financially and emotionally and physically my sole support. Tonight I will have no one to discuss the evening news with and no one to rub my back and no one to kiss, and if I have a nightmare, I will have no one to turn to in the dark. That's what I mean by *alone*."

"You have lovers," Charlotte said.

"Sometimes," Nell replied. "Sometimes I do. For the most part I don't. I certainly don't have any kind of security. Charlotte, no one has *chosen* me, chosen me above all others. Jesus, don't you see that? Marlow has chosen you."

The two women looked at each other, deadlocked in their battle to be the most deserving of pity.

"Well," Charlotte said at last, stubbing out her cigarette in the ashtray, "Marlow might have chosen me, but only part of me. He doesn't want all of me, and he certainly doesn't want me pregnant. I figure if I get divorced right away, I'm thirty, I still have plenty of time to find a new husband and start a family. Right?"

"Oh, Charlotte, thirty is *young*," Nell said. "Of course you'll have time to marry again and have lots of children. I'm sorry you and Marlow can't work things out. I hope you get what you want.'' She caught Charlotte's glance. ''Charlotte, I *mean* that,'' she said.

Nell walked back to work by herself, thinking about Charlotte and her announcement, about divorce and babies and the complications of modern life. Clary had known Marlow when he was married to her mother and Nell and Charlotte, and there would undoubtedly be more to come. Hannah and Jeremy had seen their mother with Marlow, then in a way, with Steve and Ben and Stellios and now Andy—and undoubtedly, Nell sighed, there would be more to come, because she had no real hopes that she and Andy would ever marry. Parents used to have lots of children, Nell thought; now children have lots of parents. How will we help our children believe in the reality and values of enduring love? she wondered. Oh dear, she wondered, how will we help ourselves believe? How will we help ourselves?

The third weekend in September, Clary and Nell took the bus and ferry together to spend the weekend on Nantucket. Clary stayed with Harry; Nell stayed with Andy. For Nell, it was like going to heaven. She arrived at midnight, and Andy met them, dropped Clary off at Harry's house, then took Nell home to his house and bed. Saturday morning Nell woke early with him, took a long, invigorating walk on the empty beach, then showered while Andy fixed them an enormous breakfast of cheese omelets, sausage and bacon, wheat toast with wild beach-plum jelly. They ate and ate and drank pots of black coffee—then went back to bed. They stayed in bed, making love and dozing and talking, until evening, when they decided they were hungry again. They walked to the Brotherhood and ate, walked home to watch an old mystery movie on television, and went back to bed at midnight. It was a perfect, lazy, luxurious day; it was, as Nell told Andy, ''pig heaven.''

Sunday morning they walked again and ate another marvelous breakfast of pancakes and maple syrup, then spent the afternoon reading *The New York Times* and the *Boston Globe*. In the afternoon they made love. Then, so incredibly soon, it was time for Nell to leave.

Nell met Clary at the wharf, and they boarded the ferry together. They bought beer and sandwiches and sat at a red table, idly talking and looking out at the sea. Clary had had a good weekend too.

In fact Clary had had a good month: she was staying with Marlow and Charlotte while looking for an apartment, and last week she'd met two women who shared an apartment in Cambridge and were looking for a third woman to join them. The apartment was spacious, each woman had her own room, the location and rent were good, and the women seemed tolerable, even people Clary would like knowing. She was up about that; she was up about the possibilities of getting a good job. Through Marlow, she'd interviewed for several staff positions at colleges, and she already had an offer for an industrial position. She had partied all weekend on Nantucket. She had had fun seeing Harry but was not heartbroken to leave him. And at a party on Saturday night, she'd met a fabulous man who was planning to come to Boston soon and would give her a call. She was wired; she was skied; she babbled on and on to Nell, full of plans and gossip.

Nell watched Clary as she rattled on, only half listening to her. She was glad Clary was happy, truly, but she was also puzzled and envious. Was it really so easy, Nell wondered. Had Clary actually put Bob out of her mind and moved on, moved away from that source of love and pain? She envied Clary her lightheartedness.

The beer Nell drank gave her a headache. She rose, told Clary she needed to walk on the deck to see if the fresh air would help. I am getting old, Nell thought. I am getting old and cranky. It hurts to come and go from Andy in such a brief period of time. It jars me. Change is hard on me. I'm like some old horse.

She walked on the deck, passing other tourists, who stood in their sweaters and jackets watching as the ferry surged through the waves. Goddamnit, Nell thought crabbily, why do people smile and laugh on ferries? It suddenly seemed to her such a heartbreakingly foolish enterprise, all this passing back and forth over the water from one piece of land to another. Why do we do it? Why do we travel? Nell wondered. She plopped down on a plastic chair near the rails and stared at the darkening waves. Why do people go to Nantucket? she wondered. What do they find there? Quaint streets, seagulls, beaches—but all that can be found on the mainland. No, there's something special about going to an island, and part of it is the voyage itself. Time must pass. Boats and people must pass over water, an unconcerned element. Andy seemed far away to Nell now, because water was coming between them, and water was different from land, water was a fluid, heartless element that would not be held or stayed. That would not be trusted in any way. Like life. Like luck. Like love?

All this beauty, Nell thought; you have to be strong, you have to be intact, to survive all this beauty and the gift of it and the loss. So much flash was involved: sunlight on water, people's laughter in the air. That flash, like scarlet leaves in autumn or skyrockets on the Fourth of July, provoked a fierce longing, a need for that beauty to stay.

Clary joined Nell on deck. "Are you okay?" she asked.

"I'm okay," Nell said. "Just tired."

"God, I know what you mean," Clary said. "I'm going to have to wash my hair when I get home. I've got another job interview tomorrow, and—"

Nell let Clary talk on, but she didn't really listen. What Clary means when she says she's tired and what I mean are two different things, she thought. Clary could go to Nantucket, Nell decided, because she was still young, still optimistic, in spite of her cynicism. Clary could still find the energy to make the trip and bear the transitions. Clary was still intact enough to handle all the greetings and partings. But Nell thought she almost could not stand it anymore—the emotion of coming and going, of saying goodbye. Because Nantucket was an island and was approached or left by water, the arrivals and departures were always so much more dramatic, as if archetypal scenes stretching back to ancient times were being repeated whenever land came into view or faded.

Nell looked away from the water. She put her arms on the back of the chair in front of her and rested her head on her arms. She did not know how much longer she could continue to make this voyage. She had already had so many people enter and leave her life that the actual physical event, especially in such overwhelming beauty, stunned her: hurt her. Clary was still young enough to feel only the adventure. But Nell could not resist feeling the resounding metaphor.

"Bad headache, huh," Clary asked.

"Yes," Nell said. It was true. Her head did hurt. So did her stomach. But she was past tears. Where am I in life? she wondered. Will I always be traveling to find love?

"Want some aspirin?" Clary asked.

"Do you have any?"

"Yeah," Clary replied. She went off and returned with a cup of water and two aspirin.

"Thanks," Nell said. She took the aspirin, drank the water. "I'm sorry I'm such a bore tonight, Clary," she said. "I'm just so tired." She put her head on her arms again.

Clary put her hand on Nell's back for a while. When the ferry got to Hyannis, Nell went below, to avoid watching the boat approach the land.

Ilona did not have to have an abortion. A week before her appointment at the clinic, she had a miscarriage. It was a scary, bloody, messy event that landed her in the hospital for a few days, and in the midst of it all she called Phillip and asked him to come see her. He came, and before the day was over, they had made up, canceled their divorce, and made plans for a long second honeymoon in the Bahamas as soon as she was well enough to travel. As soon as the hospital would release her, Phillip brought her home and put her in bed with a nurse-housekeeper to look after her. Thursday night Phillip had his regular squash game and steam night, so Ilona called Nell and asked her to come over.

"I'm bored," Ilona said. So Nell came, bringing Hannah and Jeremy. They were installed downstairs in the den with a TV and with whatever delicacies the housekeeper could tempt them, and Nell was upstairs with Ilona, in her bedroom.

In fact, on her bed. Ilona's bedroom was not very much smaller than Nell's entire house. It had a fireplace at one end and French doors at the other, opening onto a private balcony. It had a cream brocade chaise longue with a deep brown bearskin rug thrown over it and bearskin rugs on the floor.

"I love walking on fur, don't you?" Ilona asked Nell.

"I suppose," Nell replied. "I've never walked on fur before." She was in Ilona's bedroom for the first time and was rather daunted by its size and opulence. "That is, unless you count cat and dog fur," she added.

"Oh, Nell, you're so funny," Ilona said. "You always cheer me up."

Nell had started off by sitting in one of the wing chairs by the window. But the housekeeper had brought them dinner on trays, and the distance between the chair and the bed was so great and made Nell feel so ridiculously formal that finally she carried her tray over to Ilona's bed. Ilona sat resting against pillows and the headboard with her tray on her lap, and Nell sat on the other side of the bed at the opposite end, a pillow cushioning her against the footboard, her tray on her lap. The housekeeper had fixed them lasagna and brought them huge helpings of it with garlic bread and Chianti.

"Well, you certainly have managed to land on your feet," Nell said to Ilona when they finished eating.

"Yeah, I suppose," Ilona said. "I guess. Although I'm certainly not sure I'm doing the right thing. I wish I were courageous like you, Nell. Then I'd have more fun."

Nell was scraping the rim of her plate with her fork, trying to get every tiny bit of the lasagna. "Courageous," she said. "More fun. What do you mean?"

Ilona played with her bread. (There's one difference between us, Nell thought, watching her: I eat my bread and wish for more, and she just sits there tearing her bread into unappetizing little pieces and stays skinny.) "Oh well," Ilona said. "If I had the courage to live alone, then I'd have more fun. That's what I mean. I mean, it's so wonderful falling in love, isn't it? That part is really the highlight of life, don't you think? The falling in love? You know—when you first meet a man and then you begin to wonder if he likes you and then you get all shivery and sick at your stomach when he asks you out. You know, I've had more thrills from having a strange new man just touch my elbow than from *hours* in bed with Phillip. Oh, Nell, I don't want to give that up."

"Well then, don't," Nell said.

"Could you take my tray?" Ilona asked. "Thanks," she said as Nell rose to put her tray and Ilona's on the table between the two wing chairs. Ilona stretched. "I'll tell you a secret," she said. "I've almost stopped bleeding. I feel fine. Actually, I feel great. But I'm going to stay in this bed and milk this situation for all it's worth. At least this way I get Phillip to pay some attention to me. Oh look," she said, interrupting herself, reaching to her neck to part her negligee. She brought out a necklace that had been lying against her chest, a gold chain with an enormous gold and diamond heart. "Corny, isn't it?" she grinned. "He gave it to me when I got home from the hospital—a coming-home gift, he said." She let it fall back against her skin. "It's the only way he can express his love," she sighed.

"Jesus Christ!" Nell exploded. "Ilona, sometimes you really do make me angry!"

"I do?" Ilona said, surprised.

"Yes, you do." Nell had gotten up to put the trays on the table and now she shoved her hands into her sweater pockets and walked around Ilona's bed as she talked. "You sit there in diamonds and gold, with a housekeeper bringing you your food, and snivel about not having fun! I think having diamonds and gold and a housekeeper might be a lot of *fun,* but I've never had the chance to find out. You whine that Phillip doesn't show you enough affection—my God, Ilona! Here he's treating you like a queen, like a precious damsel in distress, after you went out and got knocked up by another man! You think it's more thrilling to be single and keep falling in love—well, why don't you do it? And listen—don't start that 'courageous' bit again. I'm not single because I'm courageous. I'm single because I have no fucking choice! Here you are, with all your security and luxury, expecting *me* to give you sympathy! Well, I won't. I just fucking won't!" Nell stopped talking, but her anger was still with her. She stood poised by Ilona's bed, her eyes wide, her mouth pressed in a line, her fists clenched. She was shaking.

"Oh no you don't," Ilona said, her voice low. To Nell's amazement, Ilona began to yell. "No you don't get away with that! Don't you try that pitiful single mother routine on me, Nell!" Ilona pushed back her covers and rose to her knees to face Nell.

"I *am* a pitiful single mother!" Nell said. She nearly sobbed it.

"You could have married Ben Hedges!" Ilona said. "Don't forget, I know all about that. You could have married Ben and have had plenty of diamonds and gold. Why, you could probably marry old Ben right now; he's still single, I hear. But you won't will you? You wouldn't *dream* of it, would you? Nell, *what do you think you want?*"

"I know *exactly* what I want," Nell said. "I want to be married to a man I love. I want to go to sleep next to him and wake up next to him. I want to bring him chicken soup when he's sick and listen to him complain about his troubles and care for him and have him care for me. I want to be married to a man I love. I truly, truly do, Ilona!" Now Nell was crying.

"But you wouldn't marry Ben," Ilona said.

"No. I didn't love him. He was—boring."

"All right. He was a lawyer and he had money and he was kind, but he was boring, so you wouldn't marry him. And you wouldn't marry Steve, and I bet you wouldn't marry Stellios either."

"Well, Ilona," Nell said. "Stellios and Steve—you know them. They're—"

"They're what?" Ilona asked. "Go on. Be a snob. They're poor and they're laboring class and they ride motorcycles over dirt mounds, so even if they're adorable and love you and are kind to your children, you wouldn't dream of spending your life waking up next to them. Right?"

"Right," Nell said. "But, Ilona, come on, you wouldn't either."

"I think I would," Ilona said. "I like to think I would. I like to think that if I found a man who made me feel—a man who loved me *passionately,* I'd marry him in a minute, even if he were a pauper."

"Ilona, you've had *passion.* You got all the passion you'll ever need from Frank," Nell said. "And look where it got you."

"I know where it got me," Ilona yelled. "It got me right back here in my diamonds and gold with the world's shortest fuck one night a week—if Phillip's not too tired!"

The bedroom door opened. The nurse-housekeeper slinked in on her rubber-soled shoes. "Is something the matter, ma'am?" she asked, looking from Ilona to Nell, who were facing each other like a pair of prizefighters, fists clenched to strike, Ilona kneeling on her bed in all her frothy lace, Nell standing by the side of the bed, her blue-jeaned legs spread slightly in a boxer's stance.

"Everything's fine, Hilda," Ilona said in a calm voice, haughtily lowering her eyelids over her huge eyes.

The housekeeper paused a moment, puzzled, unsure of her duty just now, then turned and left the room, closing the door behind her. Nell and Ilona collapsed on Ilona's bed, laughing. "Oh *God,"* Ilona said. "I feel like a little kid who's just been reprimanded by the headmaster!"

"Are you all right, Ilona?" Nell asked. "I mean, did you just hurt yourself right now?"

"Heavens no, Nell," Ilona said. "I don't think yelling and laughing can do much more harm to my poor old uterus." But she crawled back under the covers all the same. As she smoothed out the sheet and blankets around her, her face grew more solemn. "I wish Frank hadn't been such a shit," she said. "He was such a yummy lover. He could go on and on." She looked at Nell. "He never called me again after he found out I was pregnant. Can you believe that?"

"No," Nell said. "That's awful, Ilona. That's horrible."

"He's a *shit,*" Ilona said. "The shit of the ages."

"Yes," Nell said. "He is."

The two women sat together a moment, contemplating Frank's shittiness. Then Ilona looked up at Nell and said, "And I suppose you want to marry Andy."

"Yeah, I do," Nell said. "Yeah, I sure do."

"Well, what do you think?"

"I think it's not going to happen. There are too many complications. No, that's not true. I think it's not going to happen because he doesn't want to get married to me. Oh, Ilona, when I was a girl I thought I knew how it was going to be. I thought I'd meet some man and it would be true love forever. I always thought those tales about lovers who didn't get things worked out were *tragedies.* I thought they were about unusual people. I thought ordinary people just fell in love and got married. And here it turns out that we're all muddling around in love, making mistakes, never finding the right person, getting our hearts broken, discovering that love brings us more pain and misery than joy or peace. God. Here we are falling in love with people who won't marry us."

"Or," Ilona said, "marrying people who don't know how to love."

They looked at each other in silence. Their eyes dropped, and for a moment Nell and Ilona each silently reflected on their individual miseries. "Well," Ilona brightened, "I guess Phillip and I will be going to the Bahamas next week. Do you have any gorgeous outfits for me at the boutique?" And they began to talk about clothes.

For the entire month of October, Nell did not see or hear from Marlow. She did manage to get in touch with Charlotte, who had moved in with a woman friend. "I keep calling his number," Nell told Charlotte, "trying to find out if he wants to have the kids for a weekend, but he never answers. He's never home. Where do you think he is?"

"He's out screwing every woman he can get his hands on," Charlotte said. "I've seen him on campus. He looks exhausted."

"Oh dear," Nell said. "Do you think he's having a breakdown over the divorce?"

"Are you kidding?" Charlotte said. "I think he's having the time of his life. I certainly am. Gotta go, I've got a date."

So Nell had no free weekend for taking a trip to Nantucket to see Andy. In the back of her mind lurked a secret hope that he would miss her enough to fly over to Boston to stay with her. But he remained content with an occasional phone call or letter. "I miss you," he would say. "I can't wait to see you again." Then why are you waiting?, Nell would want to yell, but wouldn't. Oh, I don't *love* him, she told herself. He's just another man. Why do I think I love him? What is love anyway? She'd get in the bathtub with a Tab or a brandy and cry.

All month Nell tried to keep herself busy so she would not spend her time missing Andy. She worked, took care of the children, helped them with their school work and music practice, washed the windows and put down the storms, cleaned the garage, got Fred's baby dress out of the tree, and did other necessary tasks to get the house ready for winter. She did what was requested of her by the community theater, although she remained disappointed by her new foray into another world. Loretta, the woman in charge of costumes, relegated the solitary busywork to Nell, and Nell spent much more of her time bent over her sewing machine, making lace-trimmed bonnets, or driving around to various college campuses to beg and borrow top hats and morning coats, than she did in actual contact with the actors. Still, she kept at it. She attended rehearsals once or twice a week, whenever Loretta asked her to come, bringing the costumes she had finished, leaving with her arms full of fitted material, and people were beginning to recognize her, to say hello. In about five years, she thought wryly, someone in the cast or production crew would ask her to join them for a drink.

Halloween came, and Nell and her children carved pumpkins and roasted the seeds. Jeremy dressed as a monster, Hannah as what she called a "wealthy lady," but in something that looked to Nell's eye more like the outfit of a lady of the night—the dress was so short and the heels so high and Hannah's face so covered with lipstick and rouge. Every night after Halloween, Nell sneaked into the children's room and stole some of their candy. She tried to believe that the tiny little bars of Snickers and Hershey's had so few calories they didn't really count.

One night a week Clary and Nell went out to dinner together; Clary had moved into an apartment in Cambridge with two other women and was reasonably happy, and she was dating both Harry and another man off and on.

Ilona sent Nell postcards from Eleuthera.

Nell's skirts got tight around the waist because she spent so much of October eating consolation doughnuts or Doritos.

One morning while she was working in the boutique, rearranging the sweaters in red and green and white combinations, Steve walked in the door. Just walked in, as large as life. She had not seen him for five years. She was kneeling down behind a glass case and she saw him from his boots up: work boots scuffed; jeans tight; plaid flannel shirt and camel-colored vest bulging with muscles; wonderful blue-eyed face. He looked older than he had when she last saw him. He was a little stockier, but the lines crinkling around his eyes made him look only kinder, not any less handsome. Just looking at him made Nell feel as warm as if she were wearing all the wool sweaters in the case. She felt her face flush. I look older too, she thought.

"Steve," she said.

"Hey," he grinned. "I heard you were working here and thought I'd drop in. Pretty fancy place, huh. You must be doing all right."

"Yes, I am, I guess," Nell said. She rose, bracing herself on the edge of the counter. "How are you?"

Steve leaned on the counter, smiling his wonderful smile. He has the whitest teeth, Nell thought.

"Well I'm all right too, I guess," he said. "You know I got married?"

"No, I didn't know, Steve! Why, congratulations!" Nell smiled, but to her amazement a little green devil of jealousy jumped in her stomach. Where did *that* come from? she wondered, surprised at herself.

"Yeah well, I just got divorced," he said, looking hangdog.

"Oh, Steve. That's too bad. I'm sorry to hear that," Nell said.

"Are you really?" he asked.

"Why, of course I am!" Nell replied, not sure how she felt at all.

"How sorry?" he asked, grinning again, leaning toward her.

His arm touched hers on the glass countertop. She looked down at their hands: hers, long, slender-fingered, ringless, almost bony, the nails perfectly curved for once and painted a pale pink, her small wrist cuffed in beige lace; and his, huge, thick-fingered, long, hairy, swollen with veins and muscle, the nails smooth but stained from outdoor work. He still had his silver ID bracelet, and it glinted from the light now just as it had glinted five years ago on Katy and John Anderson's patio.

Lust, Nell thought, I am feeling pure animal lust for this man. I might as well be a goddamn cat. I might as well be some kind of animal. She was having trouble getting her breath and felt her breasts rising and falling like some gothic heroine's. If I were a man, I'd have an erection right now, she thought.

Yeah, and what do you think about loving Andy *now,* a voice said inside her.

Nell cleared her throat. "Steve," she said.

"Nell," he answered. "Wanna go out tonight?"

"Steve," she started again. "Listen. I'm kind of—involved with somebody."

"Oh yeah?" Steve said. "Well. What do you know? That's too bad. I mean too bad for me. Good for you—I hope. You happy?"

Nell looked at him. "That's a good question," she replied. "Love and happiness do not necessarily go hand in hand, do they?"

"Are you all right?" he asked then, looking genuinely concerned.

His concern made her nearly want to weep. Made her want to come around the counter, throw herself in his arms, and wail, Oh, Steve, take care of me! I am so tired of taking care of myself! But she caught herself: she thought, Steve would take me bowling. He would take me to bars where everyone sits watching a football game on TV. We'd watch reruns of *Little House.* There was no enduring joy to be had with Steve, only brief pleasure. And brief pleasure was not to be sneezed at—but neither was it what she needed just now.

"I'm all right," she said. "It's good to see you again. Maybe in a while we can go out, but for now, well, as I said, I'm involved."

Steve looked at her, shook his head. "If you ever need a friend, give me a call," he said. "Or if you ever want to go riding."

"What?" Nell asked.

"Horses," he said. "If you ever want to go riding horses again some day."

"All right," Nell said. "I'll remember the offer. And Steve—it is good to see you again."

"Kiss me?" he asked, leaning forward.

"I don't think I'd better," Nell said. But at the same time she leaned forward, too, and kissed him gently on the mouth. She drew back first. They looked at each other, then Steve left.

Well, Nell thought, wow. It *had* been good to see Steve again. It had been good to know that in spite of her obsession with Andy, her body could still respond to another man. And it was a real comfort to know that if she and Andy stopped seeing each other, Steve would be there as a friend, if nothing else.

She went back to rearranging the sweaters, her mind circling in on itself, tangled with desires and questions and suppositions. It always seemed to her that if she could only recreate any past conversation with Andy to herself in a clear enough form, it would give her some kind of guidelines to follow. But everything was muddled, and it only seemed clear that she wanted more than he could give and that perhaps she wanted to give more than he wished to receive.

She was grateful when a customer came into the boutique. It was a professor named Cora Donne; she was a biologist who taught at a local university and who, because of her successful work in biology, was always being asked by feminist groups and high school and college groups to talk about the role of women in the world. Cora was comfortabe enough teaching, where she wore old turtlenecks and cotton wrap-arounds or jumpers, often covered by lab coats. But she was always at a loss as to what to wear when giving her speeches. She was told she was a role model to the women who heard her, that she represented to them the ultimate woman; she was a *successful woman.* How could she look the part?

The first time Nell had ever met Cora, the professor had emerged from a changing room wearing a pink silk dress with ruffles at the neck and cuffs, the sort of thing a young girl or a very sophisticated woman with the right hairdo could get away with. But Cora, though not actually dumpy, was a large, plump woman with straight, short, sensible hair. She wore no makeup. She had stood in front of Nell, frustration vibrating from her, her face pale and plain above the shocking pink ruffles, and said, "Excuse me, but do you think I look *feminine* but *successful?*" Nell had wanted to burst out laughing, but knew that would be unkind.

"Well, what kind of success is it you want to express?" she asked.

This led them into a discussion—a sort of confession on Cora's part—and Nell found a beige tweed suit for her and a rose and beige and cream scarf to go at the neck to be held with a brooch and matching earrings. Both women were delighted with Cora when Nell was through with her: she looked intelligent and elegant, but not, as Cora feared, unfeminine. At Nell's suggestion, she had gone out at the age of forty-five to have her ears pierced, because her clip-on earrings pinched her, distracting her from her work. She was always taking off her earrings, or taking one off and going through the day with just one on, giving her a slightly mad appearance. She had not thought to have her ears pierced because her mother, who was now dead, had told her that only gypsies and whores had their ears pierced. Nell convinced Cora this was no longer the case, and Cora discovered that the right earrings gave just the perfect touch to her otherwise unadorned face. They made her look feminine without being overdone.

Now Cora always came into the boutique for her clothes. Nell had assumed that after a while Cora would pick up some fashion sense for herself, but after three years Cora still picked out the wrong things. She was always preoccupied with her professional concerns. It was too late now for her to begin to pay attention to fashion articles or advertisements or to learn a sense of style. She had come to rely on Nell's help, and Nell was always delighted to help her. In a way, Nell felt almost maternal toward Cora, even though Cora was older and larger than she. Nell liked fixing up the amiable, serious woman, liked knowing that Cora's life would be just a little easier because of Nell's ministrations.

Today Cora was in a state: she was to be presented with an award at an evening ceremony with a reception afterward. Nell took Cora by the arm, and together they faced the challenge.

Around Thanksgiving, Nell kept running across a new medical finding in all the magazines she read—a medical finding that was of particular interest to her and filled her with new hope and determination. It had been proven statistically that single men died younger than any other group of people, younger than either married men or single women or married women. She wanted to clip this item from a magazine and mail it to Andy, but she knew he would know its sender. And it was not, unfortunately, the sort of thing that would be printed in his technological magazines. Still, it gave her hope, this fact; it made her feel right about her emotional convictions. The family *was* the best way to live—it was proven statistically. Regardless of the problems, and there were always problems, people still lived better, longer, more comfortably, with fewer illnesses and heart conditions and suicides, if they lived in a married state. So her longings to live with Andy were not foolish; they were part of the natural order.

Her new insight gave her the courage not to fall apart over their Thanksgiving plans. She invited Andy to Arlington for Thanksgiving. He accepted. She was wild with delight at the prospect of showing him her home, such as it was, of having him with her in her own world. As they talked about their plans on the phone one evening, discussing the movies and museums they would see, what he liked to eat and what he could bring, the conversation naturally wandered into the bedroom.

"It will be wonderful sleeping with you again," Nell said. "I mean really sleeping. I've missed sleeping with you through the night."

"And I've missed you," Andy said. "My bed's been lonely without you."

Nell went warm at his words. I love him, she thought, I love him so. "Well, I've had Medusa in bed with me, but I'll kick her out for you."

"Medusa?"

"My cat."

There was a long pause. Then Andy said, "Nell, oh God. I forgot. You have cats. Nell, I'm allergic to cats. I'm allergic to dogs. I'm seriously allergic to animals. That's why I don't ride horses or keep a pet. My eyes swell up until I can't see, and I have trouble breathing. It's the fur and the dander."

Nell went into a silent frenzy. Even as she heard Andy talk, she heard Ginger in the other room, drinking out of the toilet bowl, a disgusting habit they couldn't break her of and so had learned to live with. It had gotten so they almost didn't see the fine hairs that Ginger occasionally left on the seat. She could put the animals in a kennel, she thought, while Andy visited. But how could she ever get all the hair out of the house? It seemed an impossible task.

"Look," Andy said. "I don't want this to be a problem. I'd

forgotten about your animals. Now I remember how much they mean to you. You talked about them all summer.''

"I can put them in a kennel," Nell began.

"No, that's crazy," Andy said. "I don't want you to have to do that. I'm sorry, Nell, it's always been a problem with me, this damn allergy of mine. I wish I could do something about it, but I can't. It's a real disability on my part. But look. Let's have Thanksgiving at my house. You come here.''

"The children—" Nell began.

"Oh, bring Jeremy and Hannah, of course," Andy said. "I've got plenty of room in the house. I'll fix all three of you a feast you won't forget!''

He seemed quite pleased with the thought of having them come for Thanksgiving, and Nell pushed away a niggling little devil of discontent that stabbed at her innards, sniveling: *this isn't fair!* What isn't fair? she demanded of herself, that Andy doesn't come here and die of allergic reaction? Be sensible, Nell! Shut up, you damn demon! Then she had to push away not only that demon, but also the image of the card Clary had sent her for Halloween. It was a Hallmark Snoopy card. The question was: Why do ghouls like to hang around with demons? The answer was: Because demons are a ghoul's best friend! Snoopy had been lying on his doghouse cracking up, but Clary and Nell had both agreed that there was some truth to his pun. Often, it seemed that those unwanted fiends of doubt and suspicion that raised their nasty heads to irritate them with petty questions were actually sources of real and necessary truth.

Still, she took the children to Andy's for Thanksgiving. The week before the trip, she was manic with excitement. It had been over seven weeks since they had been together, and she was wild with desire just to *see* the man, to watch him walk and hear him speak. She spent hours deciding which clothes to wear, as if the perfect clothes might make him at long last declare his undying love. She bought jigsaw puzzles for Jeremy and Hannah to take along. She thought: we have been in love with each other for six months—almost seven months. That seemed to her an auspicious number.

But two days before the trip, her Toyota broke down and had to be taken away to a garage for repairs. She cursed and fretted for a while, then decided just to take the children to Hyannis on the bus. On their day of departure, Nell woke up with a sinus headache and congestion in her ears, eyes, and nose. With the skin beneath her eyes all puffy and her eyelids swollen and sore, she had a fat and stupid look, she thought, and almost decided not to go. But then she summoned up her courage once again: if he really loves me, he'll love me with swollen eyes, she told herself. She filled herself with as many decongestants as she could and was glad they were traveling on the bus, since she was too spacy from the pills to drive.

The Wednesday afternoon bus from Boston to Hyannis was packed. Nell sat next to Hannah and sent Jeremy apologetic and inspirational smiles as he sat sending her exasperated glares; the man seated next to him in the bus was enormous and took up all of his seat and most of Jeremy's. Furthermore, Nell could tell, even from across the aisle, the man smelled of garlic and sweat and something like old socks.

The day was gray and gloomy, a real November day, and the ferry crossed over turbulent waters. Jeremy said the waves were "wicked good," but Nell noticed that he stayed inside, looking at them from the safety of a window rather than leaning dangerously over a rail on the upper deck as he would have done before his accident. Hannah was frightened and kept wanting to sit on Nell's lap to be reassured. Nell held her daughter and tried to be kind, but the rolling motion of the boat had combined with the decongestant to make her nauseated. Several times she felt bile rise to her throat. Great, she thought. I'm going to arrive to see my lover with swollen eyes, green skin, and bad breath.

Andy met them at the ferry and drove them to his house. The children were hyper from the trip and chattered all the way. Andy listened. Nell kept stealing sideways glances at Andy; it had been so long since she had seen him that he seemed a little strange to her. His thick black hair was cut differently, she thought. But she still went weak all over with desire for him, and the evening with the children stretched before them interminably.

They managed some stolen kisses behind the kitchen door while the children watched television, and they cooked dinner together. But the TV was upstairs, and the children felt spooked in the large empty house and came downstairs to hang around the adults for comfort. Then Jeremy and Hannah didn't like the dinner; Andy's hot chili was too spicy for them. Nell found some cheese in the refrigerator and made cheese sandwiches, took them back upstairs to eat in front of the TV, and threatened them with death and worse if they didn't give her some time alone with Andy. At last she got them settled down in the double bed in the guest bedroom, where they teased and tickled each other endlessly before falling asleep. *Finally*, Nell and Andy were alone and able to go into his bedroom, to renew their love in privacy and peace.

Thanksgiving Day brought rain. Nell awakened to the giggling of the children in the next bedroom and the louder, more steady noise of rain battering against the windows and walls of the house. Oh Lord, she thought. What would the children do all day? They could work their jigsaw puzzles on the floor—there were plenty of bare floors in the house. They could read the books they had brought. They could watch TV—once Andy was awake. Unfortunately, the only TV in the house was in Andy's bedroom. He had arranged his large house in a peculiar way that suited his bachelor way of life: the kitchen downstairs was furnished and used, but the front rooms were empty. The long, spacious master bedroom that spread across the back of the house, with windows looking out over the ocean, was furnished luxuriously. His bed and stereo and huge TV and VCR equipment were all in this room. The guest bedroom held simply a double bed and a chest of drawers.

The only other furnished room in the house, besides the kitchen, was the upstairs study, which contained his desk and filing cabinets and a solitary reading chair set before a fireplace. Near it was a low table covered with technical journals and books. The room was crowded with bookcases and elaborate audio-visual equipment, including a word processor and other computers Nell didn't understand. It was a serious working room, off-limits to children.

Oh Lord, Nell thought. *If* it stopped raining, they could all go for a walk. The museums were closed, though, and so were all of the shops, though some might open on Friday. What a mistake, she thought, to bring the children here. Back in Arlington they would have friends to play with on a rainy day, or at least some toys. Nell suddenly realized that in the deep recesses of her mind she had been hoping that Andy might surprise the children with some kind of gift or toy to show his pleasure at seeing them again, to help them through a holiday in an adult world. But she scolded herself for these thoughts: he knows nothing about children, she thought. They are *my* children and I am responsible for their happiness.

She slipped out of bed, trying not to awaken Andy, who had told her earlier that he never took his early morning walks when it rained. She quickly dressed and went into the children's bedroom.

"Let's go for a walk by the ocean," she said.

"In the rain?" they asked, amazed.

"Oh, yes," she said, rationalizing it as she went along. "It's so *exciting* to walk in the rain. So *dramatic*. It'll make you think of wild things: mysteries and witches and crazed whales and winds that whirl children away to never-never lands."

So she had cajoled them out of the house, hoping to use up some of their energy on the walk. But the sea was not dramatic; rather, it was at its dullest. It just lay there, its waves poking sullenly into shore in choppy little slate-colored slaps, while the rain streaked down on water and sand, making everything sodden and gray. Before long, Nell and the children were soaked and chilled to the bone. Nell had thought she was on the easy side of her cold; but as she walked on the soggy beach she felt her sinuses fill. There was no way to romanticize this day. It was the sort of day best spent by the side of a fire with a good book; but children could never spend an entire day's time that way.

Still, they did their best. Nell got them back to Andy's house, where they showered and changed. She took some aspirin and decongestant, then fixed the children breakfast. Afterward, she sent them upstairs to do their puzzles while she and Andy lingered over coffee. Andy built a fire in his upstairs study and brought in a chair from his bedroom. He let Nell have the big leather chair and he took the smaller one. For a while they sat talking while the children lay by the fire, reading. While Andy fixed Thanksgiving dinner, Nell found a deck of cards and played countless games of Go Fish and Old Maid and War with the children. She taught them solitaire. She told them they were wonderful, polite, intelligent children and she would kill them if they didn't mind their manners at the Thanksgiving dinner that Andy was working so hard on.

The dinner went nicely enough, even though the children made faces at the oyster dressing and only toyed with the yams. They sat up politely, didn't spill their milk, ate carefully, chewed with their mouths closed, and did not interrupt Nell and Andy's conversation. In turn, Nell tried to get the children to talk about their own interests, and the meal passed pleasantly enough.

But when the meal was over, it was only five in the evening. They had eaten early; Andy thought they could have a late snack before bed. Nell sent the children upstairs to watch television while she and Andy cleaned up the kitchen. Night was falling. It was dark outside and still raining. She and Andy had so much to talk about; all the little details of the events of the past weeks. Nell was happy in the kitchen with Andy, cozy with a tummy full of delicious food and wine, content to be involved with the man she loved in the intimate task of cleaning up after Thanksgiving dinner. *The first holiday we have all spent together,* she was thinking, when suddenly the staccato sound of slamming doors came from upstairs.

"What on earth is that?" Andy asked.

They both listened. After a minute, Nell was able to decipher the unmistakable sounds of children chasing each other—their footsteps resounded through the large house like jackhammer jolts, and the slamming of doors and wild screeches indicated that they were playing.

"Tag," Nell said. "Or some kind of game. You know, it's hard for kids shut up inside all day like this. I don't think they can hurt anything, running through the empty rooms. Do you mind?"

"No," Andy said. "No, it's all right. I can understand. They need to work off their energy."

But Nell could tell, as the doors continued to slam and the children's voices mounted in pitch, that Andy's shoulders and neck and jaw were growing increasingly taut with tension. She loved him so; she loved her children so. She didn't know what to do. If she had had her own way about how she was to spend her time, she would have gone to bed with Andy right then, because she was hungry for him after all their weeks apart. But how could she ignore her children? And she didn't want her children to irritate him; yet she didn't want him to be oblivious to her children's needs. She sipped some more wine, hoping it would tamp down her mounting tension. She went upstairs to halt the children in the middle of their wild game.

"But we're playing spook house, Mom!" Hannah said. "It's so perfect here, so spooky."

"Yeah, Mom, come on," Jeremy said. "Let us play just a little more. We'll be quieter."

Nell relented. And the children tried to be quieter. They took off their shoes when they ran—but that meant sliding in their socks across the wooden floors to crash into the walls with thumps and squeals of hysterical giggles. They hid from each other in silence, so that for a few moments Andy and Nell were able to sit in Andy's study in front of the fire, talking, only to be sent nearly straight up out of their chairs when one child found the other with bloodcurdling screams of glee and terror. It was like trying to relax in a madhouse. Finally Nell stopped the game altogether and marshaled the children into Andy's bedroom to watch TV.

That night, when the children were at last asleep again and she and Andy were lying in each other's arms after making love, Nell said, "I know it's hard with the children here, but I hope you understand. They're without friends or toys. They're trying their best."

"I understand," Andy said. "They're good kids. I know that. I hope I'm not acting too irritable," he went on. "I hope I'm not acting like some surly old grouch."

"Oh no," Nell said, touched, delighted by his concern. "No, Andy," she said. "You're being wonderful." Perhaps, she thought, in her old railroad train way of rushing into optimistic inferences, perhaps this means he *cares* what my children think of him. She reached up to run her hands through his hair. How I love him, she thought. How I wish we could all live together. She was just about to say: if we were in a house where they had their own rooms and toys, it would be different.

But Andy continued to speak. "It's just that I have never been able to deal with children very well," he said. "I wasn't very good with my own daughter during the few years I lived with her. And to tell you the truth, I just can't find children interesting. I'm lucky I've been able to arrange my life so that I don't have to live with any. It wouldn't be good for the children or for me."

Nell was immediately suffocated with despair. An invisible weight sank right down on her chest and throat and she was speechless, fighting for breath. He was not trying to tell her anything through innuendo, she realized; he was only stating facts. He was a man who was blunt about everything. He was not saying that he specifically could not deal with Hannah and Jeremy. He was talking about children in general. And his life in general.

And he had no specific thoughts on the subject of living with Nell and her children. Such thoughts had not even entered his mind. Obviously, his plan for his life was to remain solitary.

I don't want to plead with him, Nell thought. I don't want to demean myself. I don't want to say: Andy, what are the rules of our relationship? Do we have any future? I want him to initiate the discussion; I don't want to have to drag it out of him.

But she also did not want to lie there all night long dwelling on the fact that he had not thought about a future with her, that he was content to let things go on as they were, seeing each other occasionally, nothing more.

She didn't know what to do.

"I love you," he said to her before falling asleep.

"I love *you*," she replied. But she was not content. She lay awake late into the night, her stomach twisted into a knot, her thoughts twisted, too.

She had been trying to hide the truth from herself, but Andy had set it before her with what he said about children and with what he continued not to say about the future. She could ignore it no longer. She had hoped for a long time to marry him. Clearly, he did not entertain similar thoughts. She was ready to change everything in her life to be with him, for she needed and wanted him more than she had ever needed and wanted anything in her life. But for him, their relationship was not so serious. He did not miss her terribly when they were apart; he did not include her in his thoughts of the future. When he told her he loved her, he really didn't mean much by it at all. They meant two completely different things by their love. Nell did not think she could live with the difference.

She did not think she could go on like this, loving him so strongly yet never really *with* him, always coming and going, touching only to be left, warming up only to be hit by the cold, arriving only to leave. She had found the one place in her life where she wanted to *stay*, and she knew she would rather turn her back on it and never see Andy again than to live her life in a teasing, tortuous routine where the joy of joining was always overshadowed by the knowledge of the sure and imminent pain of separation.

Nell looked at her watch at one point in the night: it was almost three-thirty. She was exhausted, and at last, some time after that, she managed to fall asleep.

But in the early morning she was awakened by Andy. He was shoving her sideways. She scooted closer to the side of the bed, thinking he needed more room, and almost fell out of bed. But the bed was king-size; he couldn't have needed more room. She was mystified. She lay on her side, quiet, and heard the sound of

Andy breathing in a deep sleep. Perhaps he had had a nightmare, she thought. After a long while, she managed to fall asleep again.

But around dawn, Andy shoved her again. She awakened because he had reached out to put his hand on her shoulder and rock her back and forth roughly. She was stunned. She turned over on her side to face him, but he was once more asleep. She lay on her pillow, looking at what she could see of his face in the dim light, and began to cry. What more do I need to know? she thought. How much clearer can a message be? Andy does not want me in his life, she thought. In the deepest recesses of his mind and soul, he does not want me, and so when he sleeps, he tries to push me away from him, out of his life. What other conclusion could she reach? Why else would he shove her away so?

She could see from the streetlight's gleam on the window that it was still raining. Rain streaked down the window. Nell raised her arm and looked at her watch. It was five-thirty. If she hurried, she could wake the children and get them up and dressed and packed in time to make the six-thirty ferry. They could be home by one, in time for them to have friends over. Tonight she could take them to a movie. They had done well in school, worked hard, made good grades, practiced their piano and violin faithfully. Nell felt they deserved a little fun on their school holiday. She could tell by looking out the window at the overcast sky that today would be like yesterday: chilly, gloomy, wet. If they stayed, Nell would spend the day trying to keep her children entertained, trying to keep them from irritating Andy, remembering his words of the night before and her decision. There was no reason to stay. She had to forge ahead with her life.

She looked at Andy sleeping beside her. He was beautiful. She truly loved his long rangy body and his handsome doggy face. There was no good reason for it, but she loved this man and she was certain that she would never again in her life love another man as much. Only with him had she known real joy and days of consistent contentment. She would have given years of her life, she would have given almost anything to be able to live with him, for when she was with him, she was at peace . . . until this night she had just passed in despair. Oh, she would have given anything to live with him, to stay with him—anything except her children's happiness.

And he had not asked, would not ask, her to stay with him. Through this long night he had twice literally shoved her away.

Nell rose, slipping out of bed quietly. She had brought few things, and it did not take her long to dress and pack. She tiptoed down the hall to wake the children.

"Sssh," she said to them as they sat up, rubbing their eyes, confused with sleep. "Ssh. Be as quiet as you can. It's going to rain all day today and so we're going to go back to Arlington. Get up now, sweeties. You can sleep on the ferry and the bus. And you can invite friends over this afternoon."

She supervised them as they dressed and packed their few belongings in their backpacks. Downstairs, she poured them glasses of apple juice to drink while she called a cab. She kept hushing the children, wanting to leave the house without waking Andy.

They succeeded. They slipped out of the house as silently as ghosts and ran through streaming rain into the waiting taxi. On the way to the ferry, Nell frantically searched her purse and the children's packs: she could not find their return tickets for the ferry. The taxi got them to the boat in time; Nell paid the driver and hurried into the office to buy new tickets. They rushed onto the boat just before it pulled up the ramp and away from shore. For a while then they all stood inside, staring out the window at the gloomy sea, at the steady rain, at the lightless day. The world outside the boat was as colorless and cold as old ashes.

Nell gave the children her only large bill—a ten-dollar bill— and told them to go buy themselves breakfast. She sat on one of the benches, leaning her head against the window, staring at nothing much at all. She felt dead. She had had little sleep, and now the rocking of the ferry as it passed over the stormy waters made her feel slightly sick. She was too exhausted to think anymore, and her cold had come back full force.

The children came back from eating and curled up in chairs near her. They all snoozed on and off during the rocking voyage. Nell drifted in and out of sleep, stupefied by misery. Just before the boat landed, she decided to buy herself a cup of coffee. But when she asked the children for the change from the ten-dollar bill she had given them for breakfast, they gave her only a one-dollar bill and a quarter.

"My God," she said, nearly crying. "What on earth did you two eat for breakfast?" She hadn't counted on paying for a taxi back to the ferry or on buying more boat tickets. She hadn't brought enough cash. She decided she couldn't buy coffee; she needed all the remaining money to pay for a taxi from the ferry to the bus depot. It was raining too hard for them to walk.

It was pouring rain in Hyannis too, and they had to stand in the rain looking for a taxi for what seemed hours. At last they found one and got to the bus depot to find they could board a bus to Boston in only twenty minutes. The Hyannis bus depot was one of the grimmer spots on earth, Nell decided. It had public toilets, but it cost money to even get in the door. The children both needed to use them, so Nell fished out her last bits of change from the bottom of her purse. She had been embarrassed to give the taxi driver only a ten-cent tip, but now she was glad to have the change. There was no coffee machine or snack machine in the depot, but Nell had no money left anyway. She was glad the children had eaten on the boat. But while she stood with her children in the depot, which smelled of old cigarettes and damp hair, her stomach growled. It was after ten, and she was hungry. She was tired. She was sad. She had a cold. Her sleepless night had left her stunned, so that she couldn't think sensibly about herself and Andy, but though thoughts were no longer coming through to her with any force, feelings were. She felt teary and heartbroken and stupid.

Getting onto the bus was a major project today, because so many people were traveling on this holiday weekend and fewer buses were running. Strangers in wet woolen coats shoved and bumped against Nell and Hannah and Jeremy, trying to get in front to be assured of a place on the bus. Tickets did not mean a seat; it was first come, first served. Nell hated it, hated having to elbow her way along, clasping the hand of each child, dragging them with her. A man hit her in the back with his suitcase, and a woman walking beside them carried a cigarette in her hand. Her arm dropped to her side so that the burning end was right at Hannah's eye level. If Nell hadn't kept pulling Hannah close to her, the woman would have burned Hannah's face. Stupid old bitch, Nell thought crossly. The world suddenly seemed full of stupid, mean, hopeless, nasty people.

Nell gave the driver her tickets and marshaled her children onto the bus. Jeremy and Hannah were tired and cranky and fussed over who got to sit next to Mom on the trip. Since Hannah had received that honor on the way down, it was logically Jeremy's turn now. But Nell felt it would be better for her son, who was after all bigger and older, to sit next to some grimy stranger, than Hannah, who was so tired she was practically vibrating with tears. Nell had to decide: she made Jeremy sit alone and was rewarded with a look of pure anger from him. She collapsed in her seat next to Hannah and watched to see which nasty stranger would take the seat next to Jeremy.

Each new passenger that passed by their row of seats carried his own particular smell: gasoline, dirty feet, cheap perfume, garlic, dead fish. Who *rides* this bus? Nell thought. She felt as though they had all climbed into the Twilight Zone.

Then a lovely girl about college age wearing a peacoat and carrying a bag of books came down the aisle and smiled at Jeremy.

"May I sit here?" she asked.

Jeremy's face lit up and he smiled. "Sure," he said, and scrunched up next to the window so the girl could have her seat and most of his. Hannah, seated by the window next to Nell, watched all this taking place and her eyes narrowed in envy. Hannah loved being around college girls, loved just looking at them.

"Would you like a doughnut?" the girl asked Jeremy, and pulled out of her bag a big fat sugar-covered doughnut.

"Sure! Thanks!" Jeremy said.

Nell watched in childish amazement as her son took the plump sugary doughnut from the girl. Her own stomach growled and rumbled and threatened to revolt: she had been up five hours without any food or liquid. Beside her, Hannah too had noticed the doughnut.

"Mom," she whispered. "Jeremy got a doughnut!"

Jeremy looked over at his mother and sister, grinning triumphantly. Nell and Hannah could only glare back.

The girl followed Jeremy's look across the aisle and saw Nell and Hannah. She turned to speak to Jeremy.

"That's my mother and sister," Jeremy admitted grudgingly. "We just got here on the boat from Nantucket and we're going back to Arlington."

"Oh," said the girl. She turned and leaned forward to talk to Hannah. "Would you like a doughnut?" she asked.

"Oh yes, please!" Hannah said.

The girl took another sugary powdery doughnut from her bag and handed it across the aisle to Hannah.

"Thank you!" Hannah said.

Nell looked at her daughter's doughnut. Her mouth watered.

Her stomach turned. The bus started up and began rolling down the road, rocking its passengers gently side to side in a lumbering sort of rhythm. The movement of the bus and the mingled smells made Nell's empty stomach even more demanding.

Nell lost all her dignity. "You had breakfast on the boat," she whispered to Hannah under her breath, between clenched teeth. "I gave you *all my money* for breakfast on the boat. I didn't even get a coffee."

Hannah looked at her mother, assessing the seriousness of her implied demand. Nell squinched up her eyes at her daughter, trying to send desperate pleas and threats by ESP. After an eternal moment, Hannah reluctantly pulled her doughnut in half and handed half to her mother. Then she leaned forward, around her mother, to talk to the college girl, who was, Nell discovered, watching them.

"Mom didn't have breakfast," she said. "She's hungry, and she gets sick when she's hungry."

"Oh, I'm so sorry. I don't have any more doughnuts," the girl said. "My friends gave me a bag when they brought me down to the bus, and I ate two of them. I'm really sorry," she said to Nell earnestly.

To Nell's terrible chagrin, this girl's kindness made tears spring into her eyes and streak down her face. "That's all right," she said. "You're so nice to give the children doughnuts. It's so nice of you."

The girl looked slightly uncomfortable at the extremity of Nell's gratitude. "Oh it's nothing, really," she said. "It's just doughnuts. I have to watch my weight, you know."

"Well, thank you very much," Nell said. Then she felt compelled to add, "Please don't mind my crying. I always cry when I'm tired." She forced a huge false smile on her face.

The girl smiled back, a gentle puzzled smile. She reached into her bag and took a textbook and began to read. Nell crammed the entire doughnut half in her mouth and chewed. There, she thought, that would hold her until she reached home. She leaned her head back against the bus seat. She would take a long hot bath when she got home. She would make a pot of coffee and drink it thickened with milk and sugar. She'd put on her elephant robe. She'd let the children invite friends over to play. She'd spend the afternoon and evening in bed, trying to recover from her cold, trying to recover from love.

Ten

THE phone was ringing when Nell and the children arrived home. They had taken the subway from the bus terminal, then walked the five blocks from the stop. It was pouring here in Arlington, too. Nell could hear the phone ringing as she unlocked the door of her house. The sound irritated her. Everything irritated her. She was exhausted and soaked and starving and miserable. She hoped the phone would stop ringing before she got inside the house.

But the phone kept ringing. Nell told the children to run upstairs and change their clothes. She turned up the thermostat to 67; to hell with the gas bill. Then she trudged in to answer the phone.

"Nell!" Andy said. "What are you doing? Why are you back in Arlington? What's the matter?"

Nell leaned against the wall. She had no energy left. Andy's voice seemed to be coming to her from so far away, from the moon, from a former life. "I have such a bad cold," she said. "And it was raining again. I thought it best to come home."

"But you should have awakened me," Andy said. "You didn't have to sneak out like that."

"Andy," Nell said, "I just got in the house this minute. I'm sick and I'm cold. Let me take a hot bath and call you back."

"All right," Andy said. "Call me back as soon as you can. I'll be waiting."

Nell went to the bathroom, ran a tub of hot water, stripped off her clothes, and sank into the steamy warmth. The children called to her through the door: Jeremy was going over to Bobbie's, Cathy was coming over to play with Hannah. Good, Nell thought; Cathy was one of Hannah's quieter friends. The two girls would spend the afternoon playing with dolls.

Nell lay in the bath until she was warmed to the bone. Then she dragged herself out, dried off, and slipped into the comfort of her old familiar gray robe. She globbed her hair up off her neck with pins and cleaned her face. She saw her reflection in the bathroom mirror. Well, she thought, I'm no movie star, but I'm not exactly a dog, either. She took more aspirin, then went down to the kitchen. She fixed herself hot chocolate instead of coffee, and scrambled eggs and a childish treat: cinnamon toast. She made three pieces just exactly the way she liked it, thick with butter and sugar, heavily speckled with cinnamon, toasted under the oven broiler until the sugar and cinnamon were crunchy on top and soft in the middle. She put out granola bars, apples, peanuts, crackers spread with cheese for Hannah and Jeremy, in case they got hungry while she slept. Then she carried her tray of food up to the bedroom.

The house was growing cozy with the heat from the furnace, and from behind Hannah's bedroom door came the sound of the two little girls playing, whispering, laughing, clues that happiness could exist in the world. Nell sat in bed like a patient, eating her toast and eggs, drinking the hot chocolate, warming up. She felt better, but she did not feel sharp-minded and alert. She longed for rest, oblivion. She slipped down into the covers and fell asleep.

When she woke up, it was dark. She was disconcerted. For a moment she didn't know where she was or what had happened in the past few hours. Her room was completely dark, though the hall light was on and she could hear sounds coming from the rest of the house. She rose and stumbled downstairs, trying to shake off the fog of sleep and decongestant. Her mind and body were all rubbery. She found the children in the living room in front of the TV. They had brought in the plates of crackers and fruit she had prepared.

"What time is it?" she asked.

"Sssh," Hannah said. "Oh, this is so sad."

Nell looked at the TV. Someone was dying again on *Little House*. That meant it was somewhere between five and six o'clock at night.

"Are you kids okay?" she said. "I'm sorry I fell asleep. I have such a bad cold."

"Yeah," Jeremy said vaguely, engrossed in the TV show but knowing he had to make some reply to his mother.

Nell wandered into the kitchen. She poured herself a large glass of orange juice and just sat at the kitchen table for a while, still stupefied. Then she took a deep breath and dialed Andy's number.

"That must have been some bath," Andy said when he heard her voice.

"I'm sorry, Andy," she said. "I have such a terrible cold. I must have some kind of flu. I fell asleep right after my bath. I couldn't help it."

"You should have stayed here and let me take care of you," Andy said.

Nell was quiet a moment. I don't really have the energy for this, she thought. But in a way her cold was a help; it muted her feelings, it made everything numb. "Well," she said, plunging in. "I don't think so, Andy. I don't think you actually wanted me there at all."

"What're you talking about?" Andy said. "How can you say that?"

"Well, for one thing," Nell said, "you kept trying to shove me out of bed all night. Face it, Andy, in your deepest subconscious you don't want me in your life. You don't even want me in your bed."

"Nell," Andy said. "What has gotten into you? I wasn't trying to shove you out of bed."

"Andy—" Nell began.

"Nell!" Andy said, his voice harder now. "Nell, I was not shoving you. I was shaking you. I had to shake you all through the night. I was trying to get you to change positions. You were snoring."

"I was what?" Nell asked, indignant.

"You were snoring," Andy said.

"I don't snore," Nell told him.

"You do snore," Andy said. "You snored last night. You snored terribly. You woke me up two or three or four times. You sounded like a chain saw. It must be your cold."

This is absolutely the worst thing that anyone has ever said to me, Nell thought. She was mortified. She had tried so hard to be beautiful for Andy, she had even aimed for a little glamour with her black lace nightgown. And there she had been, lying next to him, snoring away like a chain saw.

"I didn't hear myself snore," she said petulantly.

"Of course not, you were asleep!" he said. "Once or twice I sort of rocked you and you turned over and got in a different position and stopped snoring. I tried to do it as gently as possible so I wouldn't wake you up. But I guess I did wake you up and you didn't know what was going on. Is that why you left? Are you angry?"

"Oh, Andy," Nell said. "I don't know what I am. I don't think I should talk about anything now. I'm all confused, and mostly I just feel tired and sick."

"But, Nell," Andy began.

"Look," Nell said. "It was hard being there with the children in the rain. They were bored and had nothing to do. The trip was difficult. Our whole—relationship, oh God, I hate that word—is just too difficult, I think."

"You *are* tired," Andy said. "Nell, don't think that way. You are tired, and you're sick. Listen, go to bed. Get some rest. Get well. Call me when you feel better and we'll talk about all of this."

"All right," Nell said.

"Nell, I love you," Andy said.

Nell was quiet for a while. I don't want to say this to him anymore, she thought, because I don't want to feel it. It hurts too much to feel it. But she said, in a voice that held no strength, "I love you too."

She hung up the phone. The kitchen was a mess of dirty dishes and pans. She spent the evening sitting on the sofa with the children, watching Thanksgiving specials and cartoons. Finally, they all went to bed.

"You won't mind if I snore, will you, Medusa," Nell said to the cat as she crawled back under her covers. She felt so cold that she was wearing socks and a sweater over her robe. The cat looked at her with slanted eyes, indicating neither affection nor dislike, and Nell turned off the light and fell into bland and dreamless, snoring sleep.

Nell slept almost all Saturday and Sunday. The sun came out over the weekend, so the children played outside during the day. They were good, understanding how sick she was, and made their own lunches. At night Nell staggered down the stairs to heat up soup or canned ravioli for them and to clean up the kitchen from the mess they had made at lunch. Her cold was so bad that she could not taste anything, so she ate very little but drank great amounts of juice. By Monday she felt well enough to go to work.

As she walked the three blocks to the boutique from the subway

stop, she noticed how all of Cambridge, just like the rest of the
world, was gearing up now for Christmas. *Christmas.* It seemed
to Nell the dreariest of all holidays for a single parent, because it
was supposed to mean so much. It was so important to be *happy*
then, and all the commercials on TV showing beautiful people
drinking champagne under the mistletoe only emphasized her own
lonely state. She enjoyed playing Santa Claus for the children;
she loved their excitement and pleasure at opening presents, at
finding what was left under the tree. But with all the childishness
left inside her, she always felt so sorry for herself, stuck there
among the glitter and wrapping paper with so little given to *her:*
books and a small check from her parents, perhaps a consolation
present of perfume or fancy chocolates from a thoughtful woman
friend, dime-store treasures of heart-shaped soaps from Hannah
and Jeremy. Almost always some friend, trying to be kind, gave
Nell a fruitcake. Nell hated fruitcake, and the thought that she
would go through yet another Christmas with only books, cheap
soap, and a *fruitcake* made her want to cry.

If she was still seeing Andy, she thought, he would certainly
give her some kind of present. It would be a present just to be
with a man she loved at Christmas. But she did not think she
would still be seeing him. She was certain that she would break
off with him. Yet she thought about him constantly as she worked
through the day.

And that night, after the children were in bed, when she finally
crawled into her own bed, exhausted from work and the bleakness
of November and decongestant, Andy called.

"How are you feeling?" he asked.

"Better," Nell said. "A lot better, I guess. But tired."

"Too tired to talk?"

"No, I guess not. Although I'm probably not going to be Miss
Merry Sunshine," Nell said.

"Look," Andy said. "Nell, you really left me hanging, just
leaving me that way. You—"

"Andy," Nell interrupted. "I feel like you are *always* leaving
me hanging."

"I am? How?" Andy asked. He sounded genuinely puzzled.
"I don't mean to," he went on. "I always tell you I love you. I
call you a lot. What more would you like for me to do?"

Oh shit, Nell thought, this is so demeaning. "Andy," she said.
"Oh, Andy." She was silent for a moment. Then she swallowed

her pride. "Andy, I guess it's that you and I mean different things when we say we love each other. I haven't said 'I love you' to anyone except the children for years. It means so much to me. Part of what it means is—is that I want to live my life with you. I want to plan a future with you. I want to know what's going to happen between us. If I didn't love you, I could just go on day by day, without a commitment. But because I do love you—"

They were both quiet for a while. Then Andy said, "No one can plan the future, Nell. You and I should both know that. We've both been married and divorced. We both know that there are no guarantees. There is no way to promise that anything will last. Can't you just enjoy what we have now? It's so good between us. And I do love you. I'm not going to wake up some day and not love you just because we haven't made some kind of formal commitment to each other."

"But don't you miss me?" Nell asked. "You seemed to like living with me this summer. You seemed happy. Wouldn't you like us to live together, to be together more?"

"Of course I would. That would be nice. But it's not possible, is it? I don't want to leave Nantucket, and you can't leave Arlington. You've got your job there and your house and your children."

Nell was quiet. I could leave here if you'd ask me to come, she thought. If we were married. "I could give up a lot to be with you," she said. "Oh, Andy, I miss you so much. It hurts me to be without you. Don't you feel that at all?"

"Well, I guess a little," Andy said. "I love being with you. But I can't say it *hurts* me when you're not here. I'm so used to living alone, you see. I like living alone."

Well, Nell thought, I've known from the start he was painfully honest.

"Well, it hurts me," Nell said. "It hurts me a lot not to be with you. It hurts me a lot not to know how long we'll be together. I want to plan. I want to trust. I want to have—Andy, I want to have a permanent relationship with you."

"But we don't know that what we have is temporary," Andy said. "No one is saying it's temporary."

"And no one is saying it's permanent," Nell said.

"But wouldn't it be worse not to have it at all?" Andy asked. "Wouldn't you be hurt more if we didn't see each other at all? I don't understand your reasoning."

"It's not just *reasoning,*" Nell said. "It's—feeling. And I guess

I'll have to decide whether or not it will hurt more to have you sometimes than to have you not at all.''

"Oh, Nell," Andy said. "I hope you make the right decision. I love you."

Nell wanted to throw the phone across the room and hit the wall. She wanted to throw the phone across the ocean and hit Andy in the head. She was frustrated: *I hope you make the right decision.* What a pompous thing that was for him to say! He was giving her no help at all. He was not giving her an inch. He was not going to commit himself. He would always expect her to continue with things as they were.

"Anyway, it's early to talk about the future, don't you think?" Andy said. "We really haven't known each other that long."

"I suppose," Nell said. "I suppose. Look, Andy. I'm tired. These cold pills have wiped me out. Can we talk more another day?"

He said of course, and Nell hung up the phone.

Over the next two weeks they did talk to each other again, several times, but although the words varied slightly from time to time, the messages remained the same. Nell felt she was pushing for a commitment, and was demeaned to be doing it, and Andy did not respond in any way that helped. What it finally came down to was the sad truth that she really did love and need him more than he loved and needed her. She would have to decide if she could live with that.

Thanksgiving weekend, the community theater had put on their first performance of *Charley's Aunt,* but because she was in Nantucket, and then sick, Nell was unable to attend. But they put on their final series of performances the first weekend in December, and Nell took the children to the play one night and went by herself the last night, because she had been invited to the cast party.

It took all her courage to attend the party, and to stay there, because she was such an outsider. The party was held at the director's home, and everyone else seemed to have been there before. Nell sat in a chair in a corner, sipping her champagne, watching all the others, who were extravagantly pleased with their play's success. They talked to each other in an insider's code, using lines from this play and others in their conversation and laughing hysterically at things that made no sense to Nell. Nell hadn't felt so miserable and wallflowerish since she was twelve.

At least thirty-five people crowded the room, all ages, actors and crew and friends and spouses, and although the costume designer had taken a few minutes at the beginning of the party to thank Nell for her help, after that no one had spoken to her very much at all. Nell felt like a fool. She felt her face sinking into lines of defeat, so that she had to work to look cheerful.

She had vowed to herself before the party that she would stay for two hours no matter what, to give herself time to get to know people, that she would not be a coward and run away. But after an hour, she knew she couldn't last. She didn't blame these people, they were not being mean to her; they just had their own firmly set group, their own history, and they did not know her, and they did not need her. She would never try to work with them again. God, Nell thought, sitting there, how many dreams do I have to watch die? She thought she was being resilient, even valiant, to let go her dream of acting and settle for just working as part of the crew of a community theater company. But now she was seeing even that pathetic little hope fade in the laughter and smoke of this party. She knew she had to get out of the house and to her car before she burst into tears.

"Hi," someone said at her elbow. "How're ya doing? I don't think we've met. I'm Chris Hubbard. I did the lighting. You're costumes, right?"

Nell looked at Chris Hubbard. He was a hairy little guy with pock-marked skin and slicked-back hair; he had a sort of hoody allure about him. He was not the sort of man she would ordinarily be interested in—and as she studied his face, she felt even more despair, because this guy was only about thirty years old. I never want to meet another younger man in my life, Nell thought. Then she said to herself: now look, he's only being polite. You can at least be civil back. At least he's *talking* to you.

"I'm Nell St. John," she said. "Yes, I helped with the costumes. The play went well, don't you think?"

They talked about the play for a while, and Chris told her about other productions they had put on and told her about some of the actors. He turned out to be articulate and clever and educated, which was a relief to Nell. But as they talked, he let his eyes wander slowly over her body, his gaze resting on her bosom, then returning to her face. He seemed just the type of man who would say, "So, Nell, you want to fuck?"

Instead, he said, "So, Nell, you want to go out sometime?"

Nell looked at him. He was not as physically attractive as Steve or Stellios, but he was more intelligent, more on her intellectual level. He was not attractive, but on the other hand he was not repulsive. Through him she might get to know others in the theater company and be given an acting part. And if she were really going to break off with Andy, this Chris Hubbard character with his gangster face would at least be a human being she could spend time with.

"Maybe," she said. If only you were forty instead of thirty, she thought. "Yes," she said, smiling. "All right. Sure."

They spent the next hour talking. When he told her he worked in a bookstore, he grew even more attractive to Nell. I don't have to love every man I date, Nell thought. I may not even want to sleep with this guy. He might turn out to be a *friend,* and that would be great. When she dropped the news on him that she had two children who were ten and eight, he took it in his stride. When she told him she had to leave the party because of the baby-sitter, he took her phone number and suggested they get together after the holidays. He suggested a concert in Cambridge. Nell's spirits improved even more: a *concert,* she thought. A concert, not a Clint Eastwood movie or a bike rally, but a concert.

But when she got into her Toyota and began the drive home, her spirits plummeted again. She was so tired of men, so tired of the futile little dance of meeting and mating and running away. And she was so tired of *young* men, because that always meant to her a brief and doomed relationship. And she was so damn tired of *herself* for wanting, always *wanting* more than a brief and doomed relationship. She cried all the way home. It seemed she was crying a lot these days.

Nell had invited Clary to spend Christmas with them and Clary had eagerly accepted, but ten days before Christmas, Clary called Nell at the boutique.

"Can we have dinner tonight?" Clary asked. "I need to talk to you."

"Sure," Nell said. "Come on over. I don't know what we're having, but there'll be enough for—"

"No, no," Clary said. "I mean let's go out for dinner. Let's get fancy. My treat."

"What's happened?" Nell snapped, alerted by Clary's tone of voice. She could *hear* Clary grinning ear to ear.

"Come out to dinner with me and I'll tell you," Clary said.

"All right," Nell said. "I can't wait."

She got the children's favorite sitter to come and put on some glittery earrings and met Clary at seven at the Blue Parrot. Clary was already seated at a table, drinking—drinking, Nell realized, champagne. A bucket rested in a stand next to the table, and as Nell slid into her seat, Clary began to pour Nell's glass.

"*What*," Nell said.

"I'm getting married," Clary smiled.

"To whom?" Nell said.

"Nell!" Clary said. "Who do you think? You think I'd marry just *anyone*? Jesus, Nell! Bob, of course."

"Oh, Clary," Nell said. "Oh, Clary, wow. Well, I'll certainly drink to that!" She toasted Clary, sipped her champagne, then said, "Now tell me everything."

"It was wonderful," Clary said. "It was romantic. I had just gotten home from work and was standing in the kitchen talking to my roomies about whether to fix a stew or just do TV dinners, and the doorbell rang, and Mary went to open it and came back and said, 'Clary, it's for you.' So I walked into the living room, and there Bob was. I thought he was out in Michigan! I nearly fell over just to see him. And Nell, oh God, Nell, you know how he loves to wear those T-shirts with messages? Well, he was wearing jeans and a tweed sportscoat and sneakers—he looked weird, but good—and a red T-shirt. He took off his sportscoat and I saw that the T-shirt said, in white letters, MARRY CHRISTMAS. MARRY ME. I just stood there. I couldn't think of a thing to say."

"I have to admit that's original," Nell said. "I've heard of being proposed to on a billboard, but never on a T-shirt."

"Oh, Nell," Clary said. "Isn't it wonderful?"

"It is," Nell said. "It really is."

Clary was so happy, so high, that she needed to tell Nell every word that was said that evening, every gesture that was made; she relived it in the telling and glowed while she talked. The waiter approached them four times before they finally collected their wits enough to look at a menu and order. By that time they had finished off the bottle of champagne, and Nell, feeling magnanimous—and this was an occasion!—ordered another bottle, her treat.

Clary was quitting her job, giving up the apartment, moving to Michigan with Bob within the week, as soon as she could get everything done. She'd move into Bob's apartment with him and they would live like paupers, saving money for furniture and eventually a house. Clary was sure she could find some kind of job at the university.

"But you know," Clary said over soup. "Now that it's finally all settled, Nell, I'm *scared*. I'm really scared. I didn't think I would be. I almost wished I weren't getting married. It's so scary. It's so definite. Do you know what? It means I won't be able to date anymore!"

"That's true," Nell grinned. "That's definitely one of the things getting married means."

"How do I know I'm not making a mistake?" Clary asked.

Nell smiled. "No one ever knows that for sure, Clary. You're flying on faith on this one."

"Well, you know," Clary said, growing serious. "That's kind of hard to do. Flying on faith, I mean. Trusting Bob, I mean. I mean, after the music stopped last night and after all the kissing and so on, after we made love, well, he fell asleep, and I lay there thinking. I thought about our whole relationship, from the time we first met. And I kept stumbling over that horrible time when he betrayed me on his birthday. His thirtieth birthday. When I made him that cake and he went out and slept with teenagers. That was only a year ago, Nell. If he could do that to me then, how can I trust him never to do that to me again?" Suddenly Clary began to cry. "Oh, Nell, I'm so scared. I don't want him to break my heart. I don't want him to betray me after we're married."

Nell was quiet. She couldn't think what the right thing would be to say. "Don't be scared, Clary," she began. "He won't break your heart. He—"

"Nell!" Clary said. "How can you say that? How can you sit there and say that? God, haven't you ever had a man betray you? Haven't you ever once had a man break your heart?"

Nell looked at Clary, shocked. Clary seemed in dead earnest. Nell could not believe it. She wanted to say flippantly, Well, Clary, there was your father, for starters. But even though she realized that she and Clary were becoming progressively drunk, she knew this was a time for telling truths, and she did not want to lie. Marlow might have hurt her pride, but he didn't break her heart.

"Clary," she began, "my heart's been broken so many times it looks like a road map."

"Really?" Clary said, leaning forward so that her long blond hair nearly dragged in her soup. Her dark eyes, always impressive, were now almost terrifying with their dark demands. "Has your heart really been broken so many times it looks like a road map?"

Nell leaned back in her chair, as if to ease out of the circle of Clary's drunken intensity. "Let me think about that a minute," she said. "You know, it's broken right now, Clary. Andy isn't nearly as serious about me as I am about him. I don't think we're going to last much longer. I—"

"But in the past!" Clary interrupted. "Nobody's broken your heart in the past. You've always done the heartbreaking."

"Oh no," Nell said. "Oh no, Clary, that's not quite true. I just haven't talked to you much about the times my heart was broken. After I was divorced from Marlow, I met a man who I thought I was really in love with. I had this sort of belief—anyway, a really dumb, naïve belief, I can see now—that NOW, AT LAST, after Marlow, I'd find true love, the real thing. I had just broken off with Steve, who was a nice lover, but—well, you know all about him. And I had dated Ben and broken off with him. My hopes were beginning to fade.

"Then at a party I met this man named Quinn. That was his last name; he went by his last name. He was a professor of English. He was handsome, charming, God, was he charming. He said things so beautifully; he knew just how to compliment. He was so clever, so understanding, so flattering. I just fell in love with him like falling down the stairs. He had a problem, though: he drank. I didn't realize it at the first party we went to. It took me a while to catch on to his alcoholism, because he never slurred his words or got nasty. If anything, he got wittier and more clever. Then, *boom*, he'd be over the edge, driving without knowing what lane he was in, kissing me while calling me by other women's names, staggering, blanking out. It worried me, this drinking of his, but I was hooked on him."

Nell stopped. "Hooked on him," she repeated, sipping her champagne. "I only knew the man a month. From start to finish, a month."

"What happened?" Clary asked.

"He dropped me," Nell said. "Just like that. I met him at the party, he took me home, we went out to dinner the next night, he came over the third night and we went to bed together and it was heaven. We spent every night for two weeks together, and he called me on the phone during the day . . . he said he was going to write a poem about me. Ha.''

"And he dropped you?''

"Flat,'' Nell said. "I don't know why. One night we were making passionate love and the next day I didn't get a phone call from him. He didn't show up at my house that night. I called his home; there was no answer. I was out of my mind. I finally got his secretary at the university the next day. I left my name and number. He didn't call back. I, oh God, Clary, I even wrote him a letter asking him what had happened. He never replied. I just simply never heard from him again. I was wild. I was heartbroken. Believe me, I was really heartbroken.''

"Maybe he died,'' Clary said with drunken optimism.

"No,'' Nell said. "He didn't die. And he didn't get put away in a clinic to dry out or anything like that. He just simply dropped me.''

The waiter brought them their salad, and Nell dug into it and ate two buttered rolls, realizing that she wasn't far from drunkenness, hoping the food would soak up some of the champagne.

Clary was eating too, but she managed to say, "Oh, men. They're such fools, aren't they? Sometimes I think they're an inferior breed. It's like they've got something *missing*. Like they can't make that crucial *connection*.''

"Well,'' Nell said, "you don't have to worry about *men* anymore. You've got the man you love ready to make that crucial connection with you. Oh, Clary, I'm so happy for you.''

"Yes, but you didn't answer my question,'' Clary said accusingly. Seeing Nell's confusion, she said, "How can I be sure Bob won't betray me again?''

At that moment their main dishes arrived, and Nell was grateful. She needed the time that the changing of plates and tasting of their food gave her. She had a feeling that her answer would carry more weight for Clary than it should: perhaps Clary, having seen Nell marry and divorce Marlow, having gained some idea of what these past five years had been like for Nell, thought that Nell had some bit of wisdom, or at least experience, that would make her sage and perceptive to the point of clairvoyance. It was obvious that Clary was not going to be satisfied with easy answers, and now was not the time for Nell to be cynical. It was not even the time to be truthful; Nell could not say, "Clary, no one really knows that she won't be betrayed by her lover. It's always a matter of trust." Clary wasn't going to get a wedding shower or an engagement ring or any of those ritualistic presents of optimism. Nell felt, in her champagne wisdom, that she had changed in responsibility to Clary. She was no longer stepmother; she was fairy godmother, who was about magically to present Clary with a gift of hope, hope which would determine the way Clary stepped into her marriage. But how to do it right? What were the right words to say?

"Clary," she said, "do you remember the Christmas you were fifteen?"

"No," Clary said. "Not really. I'd have to think about it."

"Well, I'm talking about that whole hassle we had with the money I sent you. Remember, I sent you a fifty-dollar bill in a Christmas card with a letter suggesting you spend some of it on a present for Marlow, because I knew you never had any money to buy Christmas presents for Marlow and me, and Marlow, in spite of the fact that he often forgot all sorts of holidays, always felt miffed because you never sent him a present. I thought I'd be this wonderful human being and bring us all closer together by sending you fifty dollars without Marlow knowing it, and you could get him a present and he'd be thrilled and everyone would live happily ever after. But Christmas came and went and you not only did not send Marlow a present, you didn't even send us a card. So I wrote you a snotty letter saying that I was deeply disappointed that you wouldn't spend even five dollars of the fifty I sent you to send your father a present. And that you would take the money and not even write me a thank-you note. God, I really was furious at you."

"Oh yeah," Clary grinned. "I remember that letter. It really was pretty heavy-duty. You were trying to make me feel about one inch high."

"I slaved over that letter," Nell said. "I was so mad at you. *Then* I got a phone call from your mother, and was *she* mad. She said you were crying, heartbroken, because I had hurt your feelings—and that you had never received that fifty dollars."

"It's true," Clary said. "I didn't."

"I know," Nell said. "It must have gotten lost in the mail. Or been found by someone else. Who knows? We'll never know.

But your mother was so furious with me for hurting your feelings, and she said a lot of terrible things to me over the phone."

"Yeah, I remember that too," Clary said. "I remember standing there in the kitchen, watching Mom go red with indignation. I had let her read your letter. Then she called you, and she got madder and madder. She got carried away. I felt so bad for you. She didn't mean all those names she called you. She was just upset."

"Your mother told me that you hated me even before my snotty letter," Nell said. She put her fork down and went still with the bleakness of that particular memory. "Your mother told me that you hated me and thought I was a vain, stupid, snot-nosed old witch. She said that you had never respected me at all before, but now you certainly would have nothing but disdain for me."

"Oh God," Clary said, laughing helplessly and looking miserable at the same time. "Oh God, I remember. Oh, Nell, I *never* said any of that stuff. I never told Mother I hated you. Well, maybe I did once after that snotty letter. But I never called you a vain, stupid, snot-nosed old witch. *Never.*"

"She said you had nightmares about coming to stay with Marlow because of me. She said—"

"Nell, I never said any of that—" Clary exclaimed.

"—that when I was coming down the stairs on opening night, in *The Little Foxes*, I tripped and fell all the way down the stairs and looked like a complete clumsy fool—"

"Oh, Nell," Clary said, biting her lip, for Nell *had* fallen down the stairs on opening night in *The Little Foxes*.

"She said when I took you swimming in the ocean in Maine that summer, I had nearly drowned and came staggering out of the water with the top part of my swimsuit hanging off me so that my breasts showed and it embarrassed you so much you didn't want to be around me ever again because I was such a klutz—"

"Oh, Nell," Clary said, leaning back, for it was true that Nell had been hit by a wave that summer and nearly drowned and staggered out of the ocean with her suit half off her.

"She said that she knew that I had applied to an acting school in California and that *that* meant I was willing to leave Marlow, so that my marriage was not very good, and that I had furthermore been rejected, so that meant my acting was not very good."

"Oh shit," Clary said.

"And I knew that you couldn't have known any of that unless

you had gotten into my desk and looked through my papers and letters and diary," Nell said. "Not even Marlow knew I had applied to that school. I was twenty-six that year; I thought I still had a chance to act in movies, onstage. I never told *anyone* I was rejected. And she said that I kept photographs of old lovers, so she knew I wasn't happy with Marlow."

"I did go through your desk," Clary said.

"I know," Nell said. "And you told your mother every single thing."

Two fat tears rolled down Clary's face. "What a little shit I was."

"Not really any shittier than I," Nell said. She sighed and leaned back from the table, remembering. "That letter I wrote you about the fifty dollars was pretty spiteful. I had just been hoping something like that would come along, to prove you were really a terrible child. I didn't want Marlow to love you. I wanted him to love only me."

"Well, you were successful at that."

"No, Clary, you know that's not true. Marlow's always loved you as much as he could ever love a child." Nell and Clary sat in silence for a while. Then Nell laughed. "The funny thing is that Marlow never knew that any of that happened. He was out of town when your mother called me. I did apologize to your mother and to you for the letter. Then I spent several days weeping and gnashing my teeth and wondering what to do. I couldn't believe you'd gotten into my desk."

"But you didn't tell Marlow on me," Clary said.

"And you didn't tell him about my snotty letter," Nell said. "We never mentioned it again. You came that summer to stay with us, and we both acted as if it had never happened."

"That was the summer we took golf and tennis lessons in New Hampshire," Clary said.

"And you were sixteen and trying to act eighteen so you could go out with that yummy tennis coach."

"And you persuaded Marlow to let me go," Clary said. "He was a hunk. What was his name? Chip, Chuck, something like that. But Nell, I never looked in your desk again. I never read your diary again."

"I'm sure you didn't. I hid it," Nell grinned.

"I haven't thought about this stuff for a *long* time," Clary said.

"I don't really enjoy thinking about it, you know. It was so awful, it still makes me sort of sick to think about it."

"Yeah," Nell said. "It was terrible. But it did happen a long time ago. And it never happened again."

"Oh, Nell," Clary said, and just sat there considering the implications. After a while she said, "You're so fucking pretty and so fucking smart and so fucking nice: why aren't you married?"

Nell laughed. "Maybe," she said, "maybe *marriage* isn't the prize we were brought up to believe it is. Maybe we get rewarded with something else for being wise and good."

"What?" Clary said. "What? What could be a better reward than getting to live your life with the man you love?"

Nell looked at Clary. She was feeling strangely numb from all the champagne. "I don't know," she said. "I'll have to think about that."

Nell was dehydrated that night from too much champagne. She woke up at four in the morning and went down to the kitchen in her elephant robe to drink as much water as she could hold. It was the middle of December, and the furnace hummed. She did not turn on any lights, but moved through the rooms of her house with the easy navigation of familiarity. The kitchen was dark; the windows framed a silvery outdoors. She sat drinking water, watching the trees in her yard, which were bare, and a shrub by the house tapping against a window pane. Tap-tap-tap. She could see the long arms, narrow wrists, elongated, multiplied fingers of trees gesturing eloquently in the winter wind. The movements were repetitive and definite. It looked as if the trees were trying to send a signal through some kind of code.

Nell drank a lot of water, went to the bathroom, came back to sit in the dark kitchen and drink more water. Medusa and Fred and Ginger gradually all padded quietly in to join her. They chose places in various corners of the kitchen, made themselves comfortable, then fell asleep. Nell sensed them more than she saw them. She could hear their breathing—Ginger was snorfling with a cold—she could feel their living presence. Outside, the trees tapped and motioned.

Nell liked the kitchen dark like this. She realized she liked her house dark like this, liked the world dark like this. As she sat in her kitchen drinking water, she could not see the school menu Scotch-taped on the refrigerator or the children's pictures displayed on the cupboard doors; could not see the animal fur under the table and in the corners; could not see hanging on the kitchen door the calendar full of necessary dates (choir practice, skating lessons, piano lessons, birthday parties—all for the children). She could not see the mess of the house around her; could not see the back porch steps, which still had not been fixed; could not see the cold of the December air. Her house and the yard outside were familiar to her, and she was safe here, yet not everything was exposed. Her house and the world itself held a bit of mystery now. She had a deep sense of contentment in being in a place that was safe yet not completely discovered, a refuge not without considerable possibilities. Here in the dark she knew the world still held undiscovered pleasures for her; she sensed how the entire world lurked with opportunity.

Lights gleamed in little splashes off the faucet and the stove and from the streetlight onto the road. But in the dark there was no mirror, not even a bit of shiny metal, to reflect Nell's body and face. She was not being seen. She was only sitting there, warm, drinking water. She could have been beautiful or ugly. She could have been any age. She was there, awake, because her body, with its complicated network of checks and balances, had awakened her to the need for water. It seemed to Nell in the silence that she could actually feel the cool liquid floating down into her stomach and then somehow into her circulatory system, cleansing her blood, bringing all those chemical and electrical systems back to normal. She was glad her body worked so well.

She thought of an exercise she had seen on a Jane Fonda videotape. It was necessary to lie on the floor, raise one's legs and bottom and back into the air, balance on one's shoulders with hands and arms flat on the floor, and slowly bring the legs, held together, down over the head so that the feet touched the floor. Nell got down on the floor and tried it. She could do it, though her legs quivered. She lay there, holding this pose for a while. She had been told this was good for flexibility of the spine and that flexibility of the spine was crucial for a youthful appearance. Medusa came padding over to her and looked down at Nell's face, so close to Nell that the cat's whiskers tickled Nell's cheek. Medusa's eyes were wide; the black pupils fully expanded in the dark room. She purred.

Clary's getting married, Nell thought, her bottom in the air and her legs quivering down over her head. And I'm not. But if it had to be one or the other of us, I'm genuinely glad it's Clary, Nell thought: she's young.

Nell had been thinking of her diaries since the dinner with Clary. After that awful telephone call from Clary's mother, Nell had written less and less in her diary, afraid someone else would find and read them. Afraid Marlow would find and read them. For as her marriage had gone along, month by month, year by year, Nell had begun to wish she weren't married after all. She had begun to long to be free. It was not that she wished to have affairs. It was more that she simply wished to be free. *To have freedom,* if that was possible. To be as free as one could be in this world. Then, "having a husband" meant nothing to her, or meant an encumbrance.

Nell straightened her legs, rolled up to a sitting position, and took a deep breath. She was pleased that she could do that exercise. She stood up and drank more water. The wind whispered around the corner of the house. The trees tapped. *I am alive,* Nell thought, smiling, *and I am free. Nothing, and no one, is between me and the world.*

At times when she was younger, in her twenties, she had been terrified to walk through a dark house. She especially had hated walking up the stairs, thinking that something, someone, was following her. But now as she went through her darkened house and up the stairs to her bedroom, she felt nothing but contentment. If something was following her—a ghost, a poltergeist, a spirit, a dog or cat—that was only natural. She had finally come to realize that mute, inhuman things were just part of her life, that there was more in the world than she had known, that she could walk through the dark alone.

Eleven

It had been a perfectly beautiful Christmas.

Nell sat alone on Christmas night, curled up in her elephant robe on the living room sofa. The glittering debris of crumpled wrapping paper and cat-clawed ribbons littered the room, but Nell could ignore all that by keeping the room dark. The only light came in rhythmic sparks from the tiny multicolored bulbs that blinked from the Christmas tree and their reflection in all the windows of the room. It had snowed, and everything was silent now. Nell sat alone and felt as though she were in some cozy machine gliding through space, her voyage lighted by the fleet, brief flashes of stars.

She was sipping Baileys Irish Cream liqueur, a present from Cora Donne, the biology professor for whom Nell helped choose clothes at the boutique. This drink warmed Nell doubly. It was delicious, and it made her happy to know that she had helped Cora so much that the woman had wanted to express her gratitude in this way. Nell was not, then, completely without her little influences on the world, and this was as satisfying to her thoughts as the creamy liqueur was to her tongue.

It had been a good day, much different in tone from the previous day. Then Nell had worked frantically at the boutique, helping last-minute shoppers, and had come home exhausted to shepherd her children through Christmas Eve alone. Her parents had established certain rituals in their home, which made all the Christmas Eves of Nell's childhood memory blend into one lovely time; Nell wanted to do the same for her children. She had served them a traditional Christmas Eve meal of vegetable soup and corn bread, then listened to records of carols by the fire, sipping eggnog and eating the cookies they had decorated last week. They had hung stockings, and Jeremy read Luke 2:1–20 from the Bible, and Hannah read "T'was the Night before Christmas." Nell let the children open one present each on Christmas Eve, so that they wouldn't die of suspense before the twenty-fifth, and the children had taken their new presents and gone to bed fairly early, hoping that would make the morning come faster.

Nell had done the dishes and cleaned up the kitchen. When she was certain the children were asleep, she became Santa Claus, setting up the goodies for the children to find the next morning. Usually she enjoyed this part of the evening, but this Christmas she had had to assemble a doll crib for Hannah and it had required almost more strength and mechanical ability than she possessed. She had been stumped, trying to get Part B into Slot B. When she finally did manage to get it in, it was only by breaking a fingernail off just below the quick. That hurt a lot. She had cursed softly, and tears had come to her eyes, and she had thought to herself, oh, why wasn't some *man* there to help her? Then she had remembered that the man who by rights should have been there was Marlow, and he was never any good at that sort of thing and never interested in it anyway.

This year Marlow had completely forgotten the children's Christmas again. He had gone off to some island for his vacation, to enjoy his once-again single state, and in that state he had forgotten the children. He had forgotten Clary as well as Hannah and Jeremy; and they were all used to it by now. The children almost didn't think of their father at Christmas. Nell wished she could let it go, the memory—the false memory. Marlow had never been good at Christmas, and she was truly happier without him.

Still, Nell had been lonely on Christmas Eve, and lonely for her children's sake. Sometimes it seemed to her that she just could not stretch enough to accommodate all her children's needs and desires. It was a matter of energy, of joy. When she was happy, she expanded, so that an overflowing ease was in her mothering; when she was happy, there was more than enough of her to go around. But when she was sad, she felt her soul and energies become shriveled and stingy, so that it was hard work to be cheerful or creative or kind. And this Christmas Eve, she was sad, because she was not with Andy.

Andy had not wanted to come to Arlington for Christmas for all the usual reasons: the allergy to animals, the noise and chaos of the season in the city. It had been agreed between them that

Nell would try to go to Nantucket for New Year's Eve. They would exchange Christmas presents then. He had not thought to send anything to the children. Nell had gotten angry enough to think of him as an old Scrooge, to think she just would not see him ever again, when he had confused her by calling late on Christmas Eve to tell her he loved her and missed her. The sound of his voice had been sorcery. She had been enthralled. She had not known if she was happy or sad when she finally went to sleep.

Christmas morning had been a delight, with the children nutty with joy over their presents. Nell had sat, sipping creamy coffee, listening to the carols that Jeremy insisted be played full blast, watching the children open their presents. Her parents had called from Iowa for a long Christmas Day conversation. The children had opened package after package—from Nell's parents, from Nell, from Clary, from their friends. And Nell had fared well, too. She and Clary had not always exchanged Christmas presents, and Nell had not thought they would this year, because Clary had taken off for Michigan with Bob. But the day she left, Clary had stopped by with presents for the children and a big box for Nell.

"Don't open it till Christmas," she had instructed, and Nell had been glad to have that big red-foil-wrapped box sitting under the tree, waiting for *her*.

Inside the box, Nell discovered on Christmas morning, was a beautiful pair of white figure skates, just her size. It was a real extravagance of thought and expense on Clary's part, and Nell was stunned. She took the skates out of the box and turned them around in her hands, looking at them, feeling the supple leather, the sharp bright blades.

"Oh, Mom, skates. Neat!" the kids said, then turned back to their own presents, not impressed. To them skates were just skates.

But to Nell this present meant all sorts of things. She had skated a lot as a child, but had not been out on the ice for years. She and Clary had talked about skating this summer, and Nell had confessed that she doubted if she'd ever skate again. What if I fell and broke an ankle or an arm? Who would take care of the children? she had said. Although I hate thinking that I'll never skate again, she had told Clary. I used to love it so much, that feeling of effortless motion, that easy sweep and glide.

Now here were these skates from Clary, with a card saying, "Merry Christmas, Nell—now go on and glide."

Nell had nearly cried, she was so touched by Clary's thoughtfulness. She had put the skates back in the box and set it among her other presents—the soaps from the children (shell-shaped this year, to remind her of Nantucket), the perfume and check from her parents, the foil-wrapped liqueur from Cora Donne, the fruit-cake from a neighbor. The skates were the nicest present she had received in years; Nell knew she could not resist using them. They seemed to have an almost symbolic power.

In the afternoon, she and the children had gone to the Ander-sons' for Christmas dinner. It had been hard to drag the children away from their loot, but once at John and Katy's, they had been mesmerized by Teddy, the Andersons' two-month-old baby, and when the infant had finally fallen asleep, Jeremy and Hannah had occupied themselves by playing with the multitude of baby toys Teddy had received, toys they could remember playing with themselves when they were tiny. While Teddy slept, everyone else exchanged presents, then ate an enormous Christmas dinner. It was a lovely evening, so sweetened by the Andersons' friend-ship that when Nell and her children left to go to their own home, Nell felt only a slight twinge of envy and despair to see Katy and John standing there in the doorway, arms wrapped around each other in good company, two adults loving each other, while Nell led her children through the snow to her cold car.

Back at home, they had put on the Christmas tree lights again and lit a fire and sat around in the living room feeling fat and smug. The children's favorite baby-sitter dropped by, all fresh and glowing, to exchange gifts with the children. Then Ilona and Phillip had made a surprise visit. They gave Hannah a beautiful porcelain doll with antique clothing; Nell shuddered to think how much the doll cost and what Hannah would do to it when she played with it. They gave Jeremy an enormous Capsela set. They gave Nell a cashmere sweater.

"Oh," Nell had cried, "this is too much. I didn't intend to exchange presents, Ilona, you knew that, we agreed on that."

"Oh, Nell," Ilona said, "be quiet. We wanted to do this. God knows we can afford it. It's a real pleasure for us—don't take the pleasure away by grunching around in some kind of unnecessary guilt!"

Nell had stared at Ilona over the wrapping-covered boxes. She knew that Ilona would never appreciate the realities of her own single life, knew that Ilona believed Nell liked wallowing—grunch-ing around—in misery; and that thought made her irritated enough to accept the presents. They had brought champagne, too, and so they finished off the evening sipping champagne by the fire. Even Hannah and Jeremy were allowed small amounts of champagne in the good crystal glasses; it made a perfect finish to the day.

Now everyone was gone, and the children, exhausted from pleasure, had gone to bed. Christmas was officially over. The long school holiday stretched in front of them, when Nell would leave Jeremy and Hannah with their sitter during the day and get the boutique ready for the New Year sale. And the new year would come.

How time slipped away, Nell thought, and not wanting to fall into one of her grunching around moods, she rose and put the new Elton John record—a present from the Andersons—on her stereo. Katy had wanted Nell to listen to "I'm Still Standing," an upbeat song about surviving love. Nell thought the song would be great to exercise to, but the song she got hooked on this evening was "I Guess That's Why They Call It the Blues," a song about being separated from a lover. Nell played it over and over again until she could sing along with the record. After a while, she began to cry. She put her head in her lap and sobbed. "Oh God, you dirty bastard," she whispered into the Christmas night. "You really are going to let me live my life all alone, aren't you?" The record finished playing and the stereo switched off automatically. Nell sat alone crying until she had to wander off into the kitchen to get tissues for her nose.

She knew that she would never love another man as she loved Andy. She never had before, she never would again. Whatever caused love, brought love, was a mystery and an unreachable thing. This much had happened to her—she had fallen truly in love with Andy—and that was beyond her control. Her only point of control in it all was in the choice to continue seeing him, knowing he would never say to her the words she wanted to hear—"I need to be with you, Nell. I choose you. Marry me"— or to stop seeing him because that knowledge hurt too much. She wanted to make the decision, needed to make it, needed the clean finality, the clarity it would bring to her life. But she did not know how to decide.

A beam of light crossed her living room windows, like a searchlight in the night. Nell went to her window and looked out, puzzled. A car had come into her driveway and parked; she saw a man getting out, his arms laden with presents. For one moment her heart leaped as hard and high as if she had been kicked. Then she realized that the man was a little too short to be Andy. She went to the door. It was Stellios.

"Merry Christmas," he said. "Can I come in?"

"Of course, Stellios," Nell said. She smiled and opened the door wide. "Come in. Merry Christmas."

Stellios stomped the snow off his work boots, and shoving the presents under one arm, brushed snow off his shoulders and took off his wool cap. His dark hair fell tousled around his face.

"I've been thinking all day about whether or not to come over and see all of you," he said. "And now I suppose it's too late and the kids are in bed."

"Well, the kids are in bed," Nell said. "And asleep. Wiped out, you know, from the excitement. But come in anyway. I'm drinking some yummy new stuff—let me give you some. Stellios, you shouldn't have brought presents, really."

They went into the living room as they talked and sat down side by side on the sofa. "I know, but I wanted to," Stellios said. "I like giving gifts, especially to children. I bought Hannah a pretty doll. And Jeremy a book. Ripley's *Believe It or Not*. Lots of neat facts in there. And this is for you."

"Oh, Stellios, thank you," Nell said, taking the present. It was a beautifully bound copy of *A Country Diary of an Edwardian Lady*. Nell could tell how carefully Stellios had thought about these presents, these books, how he meant to show her he appreciated her as an intelligent, literate woman. She doubted if he ever read anything more demanding than the comics in the evening paper.

So this was a sweet and generous thing, this gift-giving of his, and as Nell poured Stellios a glass of creamy liqueur, she wished she could love him. He was a kind man; it shouldn't matter that he didn't read. He was certainly handsome enough. And he was not dumb. He had learned from experience, if not from books. When his fiancée had left him, dumped him, he had not grown bitter and hard like many people would, he had not come to hate all women, to want to hurt them in return for the hurt one woman had given him. No, he had learned compassion. He had learned gentleness or, more probably, had learned how to flow with the natural gentleness inside him. He was in so many ways a lovely man, and Nell wished right then more than anything in the world that she loved him. He made her feel so special; he had chosen to be with *her* this evening. She had met his relatives, his friends, his crowd; she knew that there were any number of women younger and more fun than she was that he could be with now. It was puzzling to her that Stellios would choose to be with her at all when he could be with someone whose stomach was taut, who would like his jokes, and who would not accidentally use words he didn't quite understand. It was puzzling to her—but it was also flattering. It was irresistibly flattering.

"How was your Christmas?" Nell asked. She turned to face him on the sofa, and as she did, she realized how she must look in her old elephant robe, with her face smudged from crying, and her hair, well, heaven knew what her hair looked like, she hadn't brushed it in hours.

"It was wonderful," Stellios said. "A feast. My aunts cooked for days. We had a huge party, many guests, wonderful food."

Nell studied Stellios as he talked. He had sharp, slightly slanted eyes and cheekbones that gave him a lean, exotic look, softened by a mouth as full and sensual as if painted by Renoir. He was wearing a thick, intricately knit wool sweater over a turtleneck.

"Beautiful sweater," she said. "It looks new. And handmade. A Christmas present?"

"Yes," Stellios said, looking down at the sweater.

"From your aunt?"

Stellios grinned sheepishly. "No," he admitted. He shrugged. "Just a woman," he said. "A friend."

Nell laughed. "Some friend," she said. "Some *friend* to go to the trouble of knitting you that beautiful sweater."

"Well." Stellios grinned again, embarrassed. "I guess she kind of likes me."

"I guess she kind of does," Nell said. "Stellios, why aren't you with her, the sweater-knitter, now? I mean, poor thing, she went to all that work. I bet she expected to be with you tonight?"

"Yes, well," Stellios said. "I suppose. But I was with her last night. And most of today. I didn't think she'd do anything like this. I mean, I told you about her in the spring, Nell. She's a very nice girl. But . . . I think she's a little boring. My family likes her more than I do. I don't want to disappoint my family, but—I can't be in love with her no matter how I try. And I think she loves me. I don't want to sound arrogant, but I think she does. It is so *difficult* when someone likes you more than you like them. It's sort of embarrassing. You begin to feel—*pity*—for the person." Stellios was silent for a moment, and Nell could almost see an idea blooming in his head, like a flower unfolding on time-lapse film. "God," he said. "I hope that's not the way you feel about me. I mean, we broke off and now here I am, with gifts for you . . ."

Well, Nell thought, it's all in the spirit of Christmas. . . . "Oh no, Stellios," she said, for she had her own idea blossoming within her at the sight and sound and smell of this handsome, gentle-hearted man. "I have a present for you, too. Wait a moment. I'll go get it."

Nell slipped from the sofa and went up to her bedroom. She lit a candle there and smoothed the bed and turned back the sheets. She washed and creamed her face and put on light touches of makeup. She brushed her hair so that it flowed down around her face and shoulders. Then she took off her elephant robe and put on the black lace negligee she had worn for no man other than Andy. Stellios had never seen her in an outfit so romantic. She put on perfume and brushed her hair once more. She checked—both children were sound asleep. She went back down the stairs.

"Merry Christmas," she said to Stellios as she entered the living room. She was rewarded by the look on his face.

"Nell," he said, staring at her, and she could tell that he thought she was beautiful. "Nell," he said again, and his voice broke.

He started to rise, but Nell crossed the room and pushed him back down on the sofa, placing both her hands on his shoulders. Then, keeping her hands on his shoulders and her eyes meeting his, she slowly knelt before him on the floor, her body between his blue-jeaned legs. She slowly brought her hands down from his shoulders to his chest, then to his stomach, until she came to his belt. She undid his belt and leaned forward, her hair and the lace of her gown sliding silkily over his legs. Stellios was a beautiful man, and Nell was not alone now; for a while she would not think about Andy. This Christmas night she would not think about loneliness or about the meaning of love. There were, after all, other things than love in the world—there was kindness and pleasure and the luxury of affectionate flesh.

Four days after Christmas, Nell piled her children into the old Toyota and drove off to a mammoth indoor shopping mall on the outskirts of Boston. It was a clear day, but bitterly cold, too cold for Jeremy and Hannah to play outside for long and yet they needed to get out of the house for a while. They had been good this past week, entertaining themselves with their Christmas toys while Nell worked at the boutique. Today was her day off and she was feeling cheerful. She was going to treat them all: she would buy a delicious junk-food lunch for the children at the mall and let them ride the escalators as much as they wanted while she scouted around to find some good sales. She was thinking of spending her parents' Christmas check on some knockout dress to wear on New Year's Eve at Andy's.

Elizabeth O'Leary thought shopping malls were tacky, but Nell knew that what Elizabeth really disliked about them was the competition. Who wanted to face the acidly cold winter air to get to boutiques when one could enter a vast, warm, brightly lighted world like this shopping mall? On certain days the Muzak that blared from all corners irritated Nell, but today she smiled when she heard it and let it carry her along down the wide aisles of the mall with a steady stream of fellow shoppers.

The shops were still flamboyant with Christmas decorations. A ten-foot-tall Frosty the Snowman bobbed an electric smile from a toy store; the shop opposite him was luscious with a display of red, white and green evening gowns for women. The main part of the mall was full of tables, tents, and stalls from special-interest groups who had come to display their wares during this busy holiday season. Blue-haired ladies from a local church offered hand-knitted mittens and caps, hand-decorated candles, and hand-sewn aprons at their charity bazaar set up at one end of the mall. Turning a corner, Nell saw a rock-and-gem display taking up the middle of the L of the mall.

"Here," she said to Jeremy and Hannah, giving them each a dollar. "You may buy yourselves any kind of pretty rock you can afford, but be sure you look all of them over carefully first so you get just what you want."

Happily unaware that they were being bribed, the children ran off with their money to inspect the tables and cases glittering with semiprecious stones and metals. Nell went back to the shop that sold evening gowns and spent a long quiet time considering whether to indulge herself. Andy had not said what they would be doing on New Year's Eve. She didn't know if they'd go out to a restaurant for dinner, or to a party, or whether they'd simply stay at home together to see the new year in. She held a full-length red silk dress up against her and studied her reflection in the mirror. The dress was dazzling, with a rhinestone buckle at the waist and a plunging neckline. She didn't dare try it on or she'd buy it, and it wasn't practical, and since she didn't know what they would be doing . . . She put the dress back on the rack with only a slight tang of regret. It was luxury enough to be thinking this way: to be thinking of the *two* of them, to be planning which dress to wear with the man she loved.

"Hey, Mom," Jeremy said, coming up to her as she left the shop. "We've been looking all over for you. We want to go ride the escalators."

"All right," Nell said. "Look, meet me at noon at the little pizza shop. Okay? We'll go there for lunch. And *be careful.* Don't lean over the sides too far!"

"Oh, Mom!" Jeremy said. "Come on, Hannah." And they were off.

It took Nell a few moments to stop worrying about her children. Since the accident, she had had to check a desire to follow them everywhere, crying out, *"Be careful!"* every step of the way. But the presence of other kids their age wandering through the mall reassured her, and finally she turned her mind to other thoughts. She drifted in and out of stores for an hour, checking to see what was on sale, buying warm tights, which Hannah desperately needed, and new socks for Jeremy—she had resisted giving them to him as a Christmas present.

She met Jeremy and Hannah at the pizza shop, and they had lunch while showing Nell the treasures they had bought at the rock exhibit. The noise level was rising in the mall now and Nell was getting a slight headache from it, but the children were still energetic and the thought of going back out into the freezing cold of the outside or back to the littered mess of her house gave Nell new strength. She agreed to tag along with the children down to the end of the mall they hadn't yet seen.

People streamed past the three of them, young women pushing crying babies in strollers, older women wearing their wool coats buttoned up in spite of the warmth of the mall, teenagers with green hair and safety pins in their ears. Nell was smiling to herself, thinking how endlessly amusing people were, when Jeremy yelled, "Wicko! Hey, Mom, look!" and took off from her side. He was headed toward a gigantic exhibit of computer technology that was gathered in the middle of the main section of the mall under a vast metallic banner that read:

COMPUTERMANIA!
COMPUTERMAGIC!
COME SEE THE COMPUTER FOR YOU!

Children of all ages were grouped around tables set up with computer games, while in less frantic sections of the exhibition, grown-ups more cautiously touched keyboards and control sticks. A child-size robot with blinking lights, wearing a Santa Claus cap, rotated through the tables and booths, bleeping when he got close to any solid object, his round head whirling this way and that as he announced in an electrified monotone, "Hello. I am Roger, the Roaming Robot. Want to be my friend?"

"Hey, Mom, look. There's Andy," Hannah said.

"Oh," Nell laughed. "Sweetheart, I don't think so. Andy never leaves Nantucket."

"Mo-om, *look!*" Hannah insisted.

Nell looked in the direction Hannah was pointing. And Hannah was right: there he was. He was wearing a tan corduroy sports jacket with leather elbow patches and a pair of baggy brown slacks; he was sitting on the edge of a table watching intently as a man seated at a keyboard made a graph revolve with three-dimensional reality on the screen in front of them. From time to time the man turned to say something to Andy or to take directions from him.

Nell plunged forward, making her way through the crowd, the display tables, the giant wastebaskets overflowing with green and black computer print-outs. She walked so fast, so intently, that she nearly collided with Roger the Roaming Robot, who slammed to a halt and bleeped at her. Finally, she was at Andy's side.

"Hello, Andy," she said. Her heart was pounding so hard and so much adrenaline pulsed through her that she wouldn't have been surprised if she had short-circuited every computer in the area.

Andy turned slowly away from the computer screen. When he saw Nell, he broke into a big grin. "Nell!" he said. "What are you doing here?"

"I think the question is what are *you* doing here? Off Nantucket?" Nell asked.

"Well, I flew over for the day to come to this exhibit," Andy said. "I read an ad for it in the *Globe* and knew there were some things I wanted to see here."

"But, Andy," Nell asked. "Why didn't you call me to tell me

you'd be here? On the mainland. Why didn't you come to see me, too?''

Andy looked genuinely puzzled. "Well," he said, shrugging his narrow shoulders, "I guess I just didn't think of it."

Nell drew on all the resources and tricks she had ever learned as an actress. Andy in his bumbling honesty had hurt her so much that she needed to burst into tears—and she was not going to let herself do that. She would not cry now. Her hair was down today, falling slightly over one eye, one cheek, and with a gesture she knew to be graceful, she raised the back of her hand to sweep her hair away from her face.

"You left Nantucket to come to the Boston area and you just didn't think of me," she said. "God, Andy, don't you know what an insult that is?"

"Is it?" Andy asked earnestly. "I didn't mean for it to be."

Nell could feel the computer salesman looking up at them from where he sat, hands poised on the keyboard. She looked down at the man, an older fellow in a brown suit. "Perhaps you can help," she said icily. "My lover here seems to have more in common with robots than with human beings. Perhaps you could explain to him that people who say they love each other usually want to see each other. He's been my lover for almost eight months now, and the one day he leaves his precious Nantucket island to come to Boston, he *just doesn't think of seeing me.* Don't you think that's a little odd?"

The man grinned. "Well, lady, *I* wouldn't forget to come see you, that's for sure," he said.

"Did you hear that, Andy?" Nell said. "Did you hear what he said? *He* wouldn't forget to come see me."

"Nell," Andy said, flustered. "You don't understand. This was strictly business. Work. Important to me." He leaned forward and tried to put his hands on Nell's shoulders, but she drew back. "There's a software program I've been designing for months now, and I think this company's already done it. I wanted to check the competition, don't you see."

The man at the computer keyboard hit a button, and the screen above him went blank. He looked up at Andy. "You're a turkey, mister," he said.

"You're worse than a turkey," Nell said to Andy. "You're— you're a *casual user,*" she announced, recalling the computer term in a flash of brilliance.

Andy looked surprised, then disgruntled. "Hell, Nell," he said.
"Let's go somewhere private where we can sit down and talk."
He took Nell's hand and led her to where some wooden benches
circled a bed of indoor trees and plants. As they walked, Nell
desperately tried to use those few seconds to plan some kind of
rational speech, but she was shaking all over, and that seemed to
have affected her brain. Andy's hand on hers felt as it always had
when any part of his body touched hers—it felt *right,* absolutely
right. There was something about this man that made her want to
wrap herself around him.

And yet some wild voice in her mind was screaming such a
vast number of insulting things about Andy and about what kind
of sucker Nell was for loving him that she couldn't think straight.
She could sense that Hannah was following them at a distance;
she could sense that other people in the mall were staring at her.
She knew that her anger and her fierce determination to control
her shaking were making her have the kind of blazing good looks
that had often served her well onstage. She was brave now because she was truly furious.

"Nell," Andy said, turning to her. "Here, sit down."

"I don't want to sit down," Nell said, yanking her hand away
from him, glaring at him.

"Well," Andy said. He shoved his hands into his pants pockets so that his jacket bunched up around his arms a little. He
always had such an endearingly unaware charm. "I hate to see
you so upset," he said. "I don't understand."

"Okay," Nell said. "Let me see if I can make it clear to you.
You say you love me. Yet you never come to see me. I always
have to make the trip to see you. You've told me that you hate
leaving Nantucket. I've accepted that. Yet here you are—oh *shit,*
Andy!" Nell said, losing her logical pace. "How can you *not* see
how insulting it is to me that you won't make the trip to see *me,*
but you will make the trip to see a fucking *computer!* You should
have planned to see me, too. If you didn't want to come to my
house because of your allergies to my animals, you should have
called and asked me to meet you here for lunch or dinner. If you
were making the trip anyway, you should have booked a room in
a hotel so we could spend some time together. You should have—
oh *God!*"

Andy stood there looking worried and sorry, but most of all,
perplexed. At last Nell couldn't take it anymore. "You are not

that dumb!'' she yelled, so loud that from behind her Hannah whispered, ''Mo-om.''

Andy blinked. Nell wanted to burst into tears. She wanted to jump on him, kick him in the crotch, scratch his eyes out. She wanted him to take her in his arms and kiss her for the rest of her life. She wanted to burst into tears and to blither and whine, to plead, ''Oh, Andy, I love you so much, I want you so much, I'd do anything in the world for you, why can't you love me the way I love you?''

But she would not let herself do any of those things. She held herself in control so fiercely that she thought she might explode; she held still for one long moment, thinking: *Nell, are you sure about this? You'll never see him again, Nell. Is that what you want? Don't be rash, Nell.* She stood there in the mall, quaking and glaring at Andy, thinking that she was going to end it now, and she was going to do it with some kind of pride.

''Well,'' Andy said slowly, obviously trying to figure something out. ''I can still do all those things, Nell. I mean I can still make a hotel reservation. And I'd like to take you out to dinner. You know how I get, my mind just goes along on one track, but, Nell, I never meant to hurt you, to make you so upset. Look, let's get out of here and go someplace where we can be alone.''

Nell shook her head. ''Oh, Andy,'' she said. ''You are such—'' She stopped, feeling tears shimmering in her eyes. She had used up all her sassy cleverness with the term *casual user* and now she was just in despair. She held her hands up in front of her in a hopeless gesture, hopeless of finding the word that would express exactly what Andy was.

''A dumb fart,'' Hannah prompted from behind her, her voice calm.

Nell turned to look at her daughter. Hannah grinned. Nell grinned back. She turned back to Andy.

''You are such a *dumb fart,''* she said. And now she really was triumphant. The tears had vanished. ''You'll never meet another woman who could love you as much as I did, as well as I could have,'' she said. ''Oh, Andy, you really blew it.''

Andy reached out to grab her shoulders, but Nell stepped back. ''Nell,'' he said. ''Why are you talking this way? It's not over for us.''

''Oh yes, yes it is,'' Nell said.

"Because I came to see computers instead of seeing you? Just because of that? That's crazy," Andy protested.

"No, *you're* crazy," Nell said. "You're crazy not to have loved me better. *You're crazy to have let me get away.*" She knew that exits pulled more punch if they were done unexpectedly, and she knew a good exit line when she said it. So she tossed her head and turned around and took Hannah's hand. "Come on, honey," she said, and stalked off, majestic in her determination.

"Nell," Andy said. He came a few steps after her. She could feel his presence. "Nell," he repeated. "Don't go off like this."

Nell did not turn around. *If he wants me, he'll pursue me,* she thought. In her mind she envisioned him running after her down the length of the mall. In her mind she heard him say at last, "I don't want to lose you, Nell—marry me!"

But that was only in her mind. In reality, she felt the invisible bond between her and Andy stretching as she walked, until it snapped and broke in two.

"He's standing back by the computers, Mom," Hannah said.

"I know," Nell said, her head held high.

"How do you know?" Hannah nagged. "You don't have eyes in the back of your head."

"Sometimes I do," Nell replied. "Sometimes I really do."

She strode down the mall, full of energy, purpose, and determination, a madwoman among all the lazy strolling holiday shoppers. Her mind was wild with words and images. At the last moment, before she came to the door leading out to the icy parking lot, she heard someone running toward her. She could feel the crowds of people parting as someone pushed through to her. There was one last nearly ecstatic moment when Nell felt Andy rushing to her, finally desperate with need, and then Nell heard her son yelling, "Hey, *Mom!* Wait a minute. Where are you going? How come you didn't come get me?" And she turned to find that her pursuer had been her son. Andy was nowhere to be seen.

No one spoke while they ran through the freezing air and crammed themselves into the cold Toyota. They sat, teeth chattering, waiting for the engine to warm the little car. Hannah was in the front seat, buckled in with a safety belt so that she could only turn halfway around to see Jeremy.

"Mom broke up with Andy," Hannah said to her brother. "She was wicked good."

"Andy? Andy was there? I didn't see him," Jeremy protested. "Hey, Mom, why did you break up with Andy?"

"It's a long story," Nell said. "I guess you could say I broke up with him because he cares more for computers than for me."

"Boy, is he stupid," Jeremy said loyally.

"Mom called him a dumb fart," Hannah said gleefully.

"She did?" Jeremy grinned. "Mom, did you really say that right to him?"

"I did," Nell said, grinning back. "I really did. I said, 'Andy, you are a dumb fart.' "

"Wow!" Jeremy said, laughing. "I bet no one's ever called him *that* before."

Hannah and Jeremy got into one of their contagious laughing fits then, saying "dumb fart" whenever they needed inspiration for a fresh burst of laughter. Nell drove home smiling. Her children were right, she knew: without them she might have told Andy he was an insensitive egotist or a selfish fool or any number of other things that he had undoubtedly been called by other women. She doubted very much that anyone had called him a dumb fart before. It was such a nice, short, definite, disgusting phrase. Nell was pleased with herself for using it. She was very pleased with herself for breaking up with Andy. She would have hated herself if she had weakened.

At home, she distributed the new underwear to her children and told them to put it away before playing. They ran off, eager to call friends, start games, watch TV. Nell went into the kitchen and fixed herself a celebratory glass of white wine. She stood very still for a moment, holding the wine in her mouth, then letting it slide down inside her, and she waited for a similar cold tang of grief to join the taste of wine. But there was no grief now. She had no tears. She realized that only when she had felt hope had there been sorrow. Now she had neither. Andy was truly gone from her life, and she felt her life expand with his absence, the way a stage expands with light and sound once the heavy curtain has been raised.

New Year's Eve, even the cats were sick. Fred and Medusa were disgusting, slinking around the house with watery mucus streaming out of their eyes, staining their fur. Fred even had laryngitis; when he opened his mouth to meow, he could only squeak. It would have been a funny sight if it weren't so pathetic and if the children hadn't been feeling as bad as he did. Hannah and Jeremy were both sick too. They both had a fever, runny nose, congested head, upset stomach, aching arms and ankles, sore throat, the works. Nell had called the doctor, who had said nothing could be done but to wait it out—it was yet another new flu bug. A very contagious flu bug. Nell was so tired and achy tonight that she was afraid she had caught it, too.

For two days now she had been the soul of patience and sympathy, carrying trays with aspirin and ginger ale and chicken broth to her children, rubbing their backs, coddling and cuddling them. But now she was exhausted, and when they crabbed because the orange liquid medicine she gave them tasted so foul, she heard herself snap, "Shut up, damnit, and take this stuff or I'll kill you."

God, what a nasty-mouthed mean old mother I am, Nell thought, carrying the sticky spoon back down to the kitchen. But she knew instinctively that her bad temper came as a sign of relief—the children were over the worst part. They were sick, but not dangerously sick anymore. They would be tired and cranky for the next few days, but they were going to get well. They were not going to die. And that was really the only thing that mattered.

Thank God, Nell thought, for her children. They drove her crazy, but they saved her life. When she looked at them, she thought, I have done this much in the world, I have made these children and kept them safe and healthy and taught them to be good, and that is a wonderful thing.

Someday, Nell thought, these children will leave me. They'll go off to college, to work, to marry. I'll be really alone then. I'll manage—I'll even enjoy it. I'll be able to travel, to have more freedom. We'll learn to live without each other. But for now—for now, thank heavens, they were still little children who had to live with her, who needed her love, and who gave love back so naturally.

Nell poured herself a huge glass of orange juice and carried it upstairs with a handful of chewable Vitamin C. If she could help it, she was going to stay well. She peeked into the children's bedrooms—both Hannah and Jeremy had drifted off into sleep already, carried away on waves of the decongestant medicine. It was nine-thirty. Nell left all the doors open so she could hear the children if they called her. At least they were old enough now to call her if they needed her; she no longer had to spend the night on the floor wrapped in a blanket, only half sleeping, trying through the night to monitor the breathing of a sick child.

Now Nell crawled into her own bed. The sheets were gritty with crumbs from sandwiches. She didn't care, she was too tired to care. She didn't even particularly care that when the new year came she would probably be asleep instead of celebrating its arrival. She would be sleeping truly alone tonight—she had shut Fred and Medusa in the kitchen for once. Her tolerance for her animals had ended earlier in the day, when Fred had butted his sickly head against her stomach, leaving a long trail of greenish eye-slime on her sweatshirt. Nell didn't want to awaken to the sound of either cat throwing up or sneezing. She didn't want to feel *any* material rubbing off a cat and onto her during the night. The cats would get well too, she knew, but until then, she didn't want to sleep with them.

It had looked like such a promising New Year's Eve. Nell had been up for it in every way. She had been invited to a huge party at Ilona's and had asked Stellios to go with her. She had found a silver sequined tube top at a secondhand shop which looked great with an old long black velvet skirt. She had planned to greet the new year looking as gorgeous as she could, dancing the night away in Stellios's arms, drinking Ilona and Phillip's first-class champagne, putting into practice Ilona's new philosophy of "saying yes to life!"

"I don't believe I've ever said no to life," Nell had said to Ilona when her friend exploded with her newly found catchword and religion. "I mean, after all, here I am," Nell had said.

"Oh, don't be so *literal*," Ilona had cajoled. "Don't be so stuffy. You know what I mean. I mean, grab life by the balls and run with it!"

"What?" Nell had asked, aghast. "Ilona, aren't you mixing your metaphors?"

But Ilona was in too good a mood to be sensible. She had come into the boutique to buy a special dress for the party she and Phillip were giving New Year's Eve—a party with a live band and a champagne fountain and catered breakfast at dawn. Ilona looked through dresses, trying to get Nell to share her excitement. She kept saying things like, "You've got to grab your joy where you find it! You can't always wait for it to come to you, you have to create it! You've got to start saying *yes* to life!"

The season has scrambled your brain, Nell thought, but she was

glad that Ilona was so cheerful. And Nell *had* been looking forward
to the big party. But Cora Donne had invited Nell to a New Year's
Day brunch, and Nell wanted to go there even more than to Ilona's.
She knew who Ilona's crowd would be, but Cora's guests would be
all new faces to Nell, new people, mostly professors from the university where Cora taught. Cora had hinted to Nell that there
would be quite a few single men at her party who would be
delighted to meet Nell. They'll probably be stodgy old intellectuals, Nell thought cynically, but she was still excited about going.
She was gladly missing Ilona's party so that she could go to sleep
early and fight off the flu. She wanted to be fresh and bright-eyed
for the new day.

The new day. The new year. Nell stretched out all over her
bed, loving the soft warmth, and smiled at the thought of tomorrow. She felt so clean about it all. She felt so fresh.

For the past two days she had worried about her scene with
Andy in the same way the dog worried her leather bone, poking
at the thought of it over and over again, twisting it around, wondering if it had been the right thing to do. She had half thought,
half wished that Andy would, in a mad flare of desperate passion,
rush to Arlington, pound on her door, take her in his arms and,
eyes swollen with allergies, declare eternal love for her.

At the least, she had thought he would call her. But he hadn't.
Last night, as Nell sat by the fire listening to the music with her
flu-sedated children, she had felt all her sorrow turn into a numb
exhaustion much like apathy and all her love for Andy become
disdain, an emotion too weakened by the memory of love to be real
contempt. She supposed that finally what she felt for him was pity.
He had said he loved her, but either he was lying, in which case he
was a creep, or he was telling the truth but could do so little to
show his love. In that case he was a limited man. Oh, he *was* a
limited man. He did not know his daughter's size or favorite color,
he had found no charm in her children, he was even allergic to
animals! She thought of how his enormous, sparsely furnished house
spread around him like a protective bubble around a person allergic
to the world. She thought of him making his careful, precise, repetitive movements in that house as he worked with his computers
or made his meticulous gourmet meals. He did not have to deal with
the real world because of his family's money; he would never have
to get messy or dirty. If they had married and lived together, it
would have ended in disaster, Nell could see that now. He would

not be able to bear the fuss and bother of her life, the children, animals, friends, drama, action—and she would have been driven, sooner or later, to screaming at him: "For God's sake, stop *organizing* the food and just *cook* it!"

Nell thought that perhaps she had fallen in love with Andy in much the same way she had fallen in love with severe black suits when she was seventeen and punk hairstyles when she was thirty-five—all yearnings for what was inappropriate for her, for what was basically *wrong*, for what would never work. She knew she had made the right choice in breaking off with Andy. She felt like some small country that had declared its independence from some dictatorial nation. Perhaps she'd no longer get shipments of sugar from that country—but she could learn to do without sugar. In her new freedom, she'd learn to love honey.

She had been only slightly melancholy last night. The cats had snoozed, drugged by the heat, on the hearth; the dog had gnawed on a new rubber bone; the children had read books, Christmas gifts, and littered the floor with used tissues. They drank hot chocolate. Hannah had asked, "Do you miss Andy, Mommy? Are you sad?"

Nell decided to be honest. They had seen a lot this summer. She didn't want to pretend that nothing of importance had happened. "I'm a little sad," she said. "Not *broken-hearted*, but a little sad. You know, I had kind of wanted to *marry* Andy."

"Why?" Jeremy asked, surprised.

Nell had to be so careful here. She needed to explain to them in terms they would understand just how she had felt about Andy without at the same time inadvertently insulting Marlow or making light of the marriage she had had with him. She thought a moment. Finally, she said, "Well, you know, there are very few people in the world that you like enough to live with. And if you meet someone you like that much and love that much, then it's as if you've found a home. And that's nice. That feels good. But if the other person doesn't want to live with you, then it's sad. But then you go off and make your own home somewhere else."

"You have a home with us," Jeremy said.

Nell looked at her son. "Yes," she said. "I do. You children are my home, and I love you and I like you and it's wonderful living with you. But you know someday you'll go away—to college, to get jobs, to marry and live with a husband or wife. Then you'll have new homes, your own homes."

"Then what will you do, Mommy?" Hannah asked, alarmed.

"You can come live with me and my wife," Jeremy offered.

Nell smiled. "Thanks, Jeremy," she said. "But no, I won't come live with you; you'll have grown-up lives. But don't worry. I'll have my own home by then. I'm making my own home now."

"Daddy's divorcing Charlotte," Hannah said. "So he's leaving his home."

"Yes." Nell smiled. "That's true. Well, your daddy's a sort of wanderer. He likes the travel, the adventure; he doesn't need a home. Some people don't."

"Maybe Andy's a wanderer too," Hannah said.

"Or a hermit," Jeremy said.

"Well, whatever he is," Nell said, "he's out of our lives now, and I'll be blue for a while, but don't worry. Just bear with me while I get over it—like you're getting over the flu."

"Mom," Hannah said. "I've got an idea! When *I* get married, I'll throw *you* the bouquet! Then you'll get married and we'll all have homes."

Nell looked at Hannah, who had a red nose and watery eyes. My sophisticated, optimistic children, she thought. "That's a great idea, Hannah," she said. "That's thoughtful of you. But, sweetie, don't worry. Even if I never get married again—and I'm pretty certain I won't—I'll still be happy. I'll make my own home. I really can do that. I *am* doing that."

And it was true. Here she was, on New Year's Eve, in her own house, her own bed, her own room. It hadn't always been this way. There had been years when Marlow had possessed this room too, had thrown his clothes down on the floor for her to pick up and wash, had scattered his papers around the room and claimed his share of the bed. When the children were small, they had also possessed this room, by right of necessity; there had been soiled diapers, sticky bottles of orange juice, stuffed animals, half-gnawed crackers everywhere.

The room was pretty much all hers now. From time to time one of the children left a shoe or a book, but they were old enough to keep their belongings in their own rooms, and this bedroom was now Nell's own private place. Only her clothes hung in the closet or were scattered over the back of the chair, only the magazines and books she was interested in took up the extra space in the bed, and recently she had driven a nail into the wall and hung her ice skates there, as if they were some kind of symbol or trophy or good luck charm.

She had gone skating three times since Christmas, and each time had been better than before. The first time out she had made Jeremy hold one hand and Hannah the other as she went out onto the ice—but suddenly, to her surprise, it all came back. She was wobbly in the beginning, but by the end of the two hours she was impressing her children with her speed and spins. It all came back to her. They played rock music at the rink she went to—the same sort of music she exercised to—and as she skimmed across the glistening white ice, she had been at once lost and found in the matching of music and movement. She liked skating along alone, at her own speed, folding into a spin whenever she felt like it, racing past her children, coming up behind them, passing them with a laugh, skating backward and making faces at them. She liked the occasional admiring glance she saw tossed her way by men who skated past. She liked the way her red fuzzy scarf flipped when she turned, the way her hands, encased in red fuzzy mittens, darted gracefully along with her, like giant cardinals. She knew she looked pretty, skating along in her blue jeans and sweater and red hat, scarf, and mittens; she knew she was a cheerful sight. She liked all that, being pretty and being seen.

But more, she liked the feeling of gliding on ice, the way her legs worked for her, how reliable her body was, after all. She liked the way she could disappear from the outer world into a world of her own, so that she became simply muscles and limbs that were taut and cooperative; she loved speeding, spinning, dancing on cold ice as if the music she heard became the movements she made. For a while on the ice, she was in a state of grace; she felt as if she were the very definition of grace. There was no time in her life when she was happier or more herself than when skating in her own glistening, private world. She would slice the ice with her blades, hear the responsive shushhh . . . she would glide.

Nell was using her parents' check to buy membership into the skating club so that she could use the rink twice a week. She had decided it was good therapy for her—physical and mental therapy. It had been a very long time since she had skated in her youth, but those times were with her somehow, there in the very strength of her ankles, there in the tension of her legs. Just so, she knew, all the years of her life were somehow with her now in the form of strength and agility; she could not remember them all, did not want to remember some of them, but she was what she was because of them. Now she was going to take skating lessons. She was going to improve herself. She was not going to stop or rest. And the ice skates hung on her bedroom wall, a testament to her determination.

She didn't feel like skating tonight, though. She was tired, and she could feel an ominous tickle in the back of her throat. She could almost sense cold germs thriving and multiplying in the air around her. She didn't want to get sick—she had too much to do. She drank the rest of her orange juice in one long swallow, then slid down beneath her blankets. She wanted to be well tomorrow.

Yet she felt the need for some small sense of occasion, some slight celebration. She had had to phone Ilona to tell her she was too sick to come to her party. She had canceled her date with Stellios, who had been very disappointed. He had wanted to bring champagne to her house that night so that the two of them could welcome the new year together. But she had told him no, she was too sick, too groggy for champagne or company. She had promised to see him as soon as she was well.

In fact she was glad she had the flu. She was glad to be spending this New Year's Eve by herself. It was honest this way. She did not want to gaze soulfully into Stellios's eyes and pretend they were facing the new year together. She wanted to do exactly what she was doing: to greet this coming year surrounded only by those things that were genuinely hers—her animals, her children, her house, her memories.

"Should auld acquaintance be forgot and never brought to mind," Nell sang softly to herself. She grinned while she sang thinking, what a goofy thing to do, singing to herself in bed! "We'll drink a cup of kindness yet for auld lang syne," she sang.

Her song floated out into the night air and disappeared. She reached out her arm and switched off the light. She snuggled down into bed, content. Nell turned onto her side, closed her eyes, and fell asleep, alone.